Intrigued by the mystery of the story, the way the main characters fight devastating odds throughout the story makes it an excellent read. The plot takes you down the twisted and gripping path of danger and death, horror and dreams. Finely knitted events take you to places in your imagination and back again.

James Sapsford

THE RED CURSE

AUSTIN MACAULEY PUBLISHERS™

LONDON * CAMBRIDGE * NEW YORK * SHARJAH

A CIP catalogue record for this title is available from the British Library.

ISBN 9781398469938 (Paperback)
ISBN 9781398469945 (ePub e-book)

www.austinmacauley.com

First Published 2023
Austin Macauley Publishers Ltd®
1 Canada Square
Canary Wharf
London
E14 5AA

Table of Contents

Chapter 1
The Timeline

For the love of Mike, how many poxy times do you want me to tell you the same fucking story of what happened to me and my mates? I've already gone over this five fucking times with that idiot copper who just walked out of here. I suppose this is the old good cop, bad cop scenario, is it? My god, what's happening to me? I can't believe this, that dick out there wants to charge me for murder, so what's your plan? This ain't real, for fuck's sake, someone wake me up. I suppose, your next idea will be to try and string me up. I've heard of police setups before. How long before my execution then? Have I time to speak to a solicitor then? Jesus, this is nuts.

Right, so you want me to go over the events once again? What can I tell you that's different from before? What the fuck do you want me to say? Why have you given me these sheets of paper? Oh no, you don't, no bloody way. Do you honestly expect me to write all this shit down? No bloody way. Tell you what, why don't you stick it where the sun doesn't shine?

I don't believe you want me to go over this again and again; look, all I want to do is have a sleep; you've had me locked up in this police station for a solid thirty-eight hours straight. I'm shattered, just let me kip, an hour, can't you give me that? I'm so sick to death of all this shit. Have you got that tape recorder working now? You need to sort it out as I'm not going to go through this again.

For fuck's sake, events took place about a month ago; okay, these events would change my life; now I'm going to tell you lot what took place for the sixth and fucking last time.

I need the world to know what actually took place; now you lot need to sort this shit out; you either charge me or lock me away in an insane asylum, but these events actually took place.

My brain's running around like a headless chicken. All you lot keep going on about is, tell us what happened, tell us what happened; nobody is listening to me, right.

It was around February 30, on a Thursday evening, or was it a Friday? Anyway, it was roughly around a month ago, as I've already said, I can't really remember the exact day, a lot has happened since then. I remember grabbing my jacket off the back of a seat; it was around five or six o'clock in the evening; my working day was done, a long boring seminar on the supernatural.

My boss thought it would help creative skills, five hours of listening to speakers who had no bloody idea on how to present a lecture in the first place; it was shit. Well, it was crap for me, others enjoyed it mind, but I'm afraid it's not my cup of tea.

I was moving towards the exit as I was stopped by one of the lecturers. "Well, that was enjoyable. How was it for you, Peter?" he asked.

"Oh yeah, it was excellent, Mr Harris."

"Well, glad you enjoyed it, see you next year," he says as he walked off.

"Not if I can help it," I mumbled under my breath.

The daylight hours were seriously starting to fade fast; the wind had started to pick up; it was really growing stronger with every minute. As I approached and entered the car park, the wind was howling through each of the car park levels, churning up leaves with gusts of wind from one end to the other, talk about fighting the bloody thing. After a struggle, I had managed to get to my car. My car was, well, it was my pride of joy, my little Capri gear.

Sixteen years old but she was my baby. Jumping inside, I started the engine and drove towards the exit; a good six-hour drive was waiting for me. As I approached and got nearer to the exit barrier, the heavens opened. With a massive thunder crash, the rain fell down; it was the start of a predicted storm earlier in the week.

Driving off at a steady pace and with my windscreen wipers on maximum, I struggled to see; naturally, concentration was bloody difficult. Slowly, I made my way through the traffic and out of town. After an hour of driving, I began to feel pretty tired so I decided to call it a day. I then paused for a few moments as I recollected my visits to a motel from years back; now I was sure that it must be close by.

Great memories came into my thoughts; I remember proposing to Tracy on one of our visits there, a place I used to frequent from years ago; my wife loved it there, but I do remember having a few worries as well due to the fact the girlfriend liked it as well. I can't really remember for sure which one I last took there, but it must've been the wife, yeah, must've been. Anyway, after another hours driving, I managed to finally find the motel.

I drove up to the motel's car park. Up went the handbrake, out of the car I got! After locking up, I approached the front entrance to the motel; everything seemed to be as I remembered it; nothing to what I could remember had altered, but that was soon to change for the worst.

I entered the building; a short little hallway was awaiting as I quickly passed through it; the reception desk stood way back in the hallway towards my left-hand side; the hallway was in total darkness. I thought to myself, had there been a power cut because of the storm. I received an almighty shiver down my spine, like someone had walked over my grave. I hated getting them. I was feeling reasonably chilly. Now some time back, I was told that I had a sixth sense towards being able to recognise danger; it was that feeling I felt, something was almost certainly. Over and over again, I kept thinking to myself that this don't feel right, this don't feel right, but I just couldn't put my finger on it.

I walked up to the reception desk, there was no one around, not a single soul was visible. I looked up and down the hall in the hope of trying to see someone. I got the shock of my life when an old gent then strolled out from behind a blackened curtain that was hanging at the rear of the reception area; his arm waved the curtain around and behind himself as he passed through it; he then approached the desk. Now this old guy looked, well, I couldn't put my finger on it, but he just seemed out of sync with time.

His appearance was such that he gave me the impression that he had someone else dress him; someone for that matter who had no idea as to what some sort of fashion sense was, extremely odd. Now across and opposite the reception area was the bar, large pots of overgrown flowers obscured the bar view. Now not five minutes ago, I could've sworn I hadn't seen or heard anyone, but now, there must have been a good twenty to thirty customers; everyone seemed jovial, laughing and joking whilst drinking their drinks and puffing on some type of cigarette. Now I couldn't for the life of me work out how I had managed to miss this amount of people, especially as I was only a few feet away from them as I stood at reception.

The dress code was completely out the window as each one of them was dressed out of time; some were dressed in the old Victorian style, top hat and tails, white frilly shirts, you know, all the trimmings; some other blokes were wearing Edwardian style; there was even one of them who was wearing a wig. Amongst the crowd, there were different types of First World War soldier uniforms, but thankfully, I couldn't see any weapons. You even had a couple of Roman centurions; they even had swords down by their sides; now they really did look impressive. I must have been seriously tired as the sudden realisation that this was some sort of fancy dress party hit me like a rocket up the aris. None of them acknowledged my presence as I was now clearly visible to all; they never uttered a single phrase towards my direction; they just one at a time bowed their heads; this was quickly followed up with them swiping their arms across their bellies. I dismissed it. Walking back to the reception desk, I said, "Well, must be a fancy dress. I should've brought a few bits with me." I gave a little giggle in a feeble attempt to crack the ice with him; he just stood there glaring at me; around his left eye, his cheek held on to a monocle with a tatty piece of worn string attached to it; a stupid flat rounded hat with a tassel lay over to its right-hand side; he also hadn't shaved for weeks; his collection was gaunt, to say the least. I thought to myself, well, that's unprofessional for a start.

Amongst all of his faults, you could clearly see that his waistcoat was half done up, two sizes too small, and his trousers, oh my god, they were only tied up with a piece of string; it was unbelievable.

It then crossed my mind that maybe he too was dressing up for this fancy dress shindig, just like the ones at the bar I had just recently witnessed. Anyway, he removed his monocle and rested his long arms whilst leaning slightly forward on the counter, guess, he must've been around eighty years old, I thought. If it wasn't the fancy dress do he was dressed for, then he had to be an eccentric old fruit bat.

With this installed in my brain, I politely stated, "So how's thing going, busy?"

The old boy just looked deadpan and replied, "Evening." As blunt as you would like. "Not exactly." The old boy wasn't that quick with his reactions either.

"Can I have a room for the night, please, that's if one's available?" The old guy turned around and removed a key from the key cabinet.

"No, there's only number five, one's already been taken out already."

The old man had just cracked a joke just then. I'm sure he did. This guy has humour, after all, well, he must have dressed the way he was. Within seconds, he had passed over the room key and the register over for me to sign.

I placed the key in my trouser pocket and signed the register once all our business was done. He came out from behind his desk, and slowly, he started to clamber up this old creaky staircase whilst clutching an old-style gas lamp. He paused after he had managed the first three steps. Turning towards me, he bluntly said, "So, you is the Peter?" I immediately stepped backwards, looked at him in a strange and surprised manner and hesitantly I responded by saying, "Yeah, yeah, I am. Tell me, have we met before? Is there a problem?" The old boy just turned around; as he did, he gave me a slight smile, as if he knew something.

This wasn't funny in the slightest, I was seriously getting spooked out, as I watched him close. He placed his gas lamp higher than his head; the corridor was long, dark and bloody eerie; the wind could be heard brushing against the windows with the trees outside. We then turned to our left, this led us down another corridor, but this one was bloody narrow. I thought to myself, *Surely, there're no rooms this far down.*

We walked for a further fifty paces, and without any warning, the old boy stopped dead in his tracks. I had to stop rather sharpish before I knocked him flying to the floor. I presumed we were outside my room. Now I don't know what it was but I was feeling very strange and uneasy; it felt like I was in a horror movie. As I was glancing around, I thought to myself that any moment now Dracula is going to bite into my neck and have his supper.

Without hesitation, I thanked him and steadily opened the door; the door creaked as it slowly opened. I walked inside and immediately closed the door on him as he just stood there gaping and stealing; it was as if he was trying to read my thoughts. That eerie feeling once again grew down my spine, a tingle that made my entire body shake.

I walked across to a table and placed my room key on it. I then went into the bathroom and gave my face a quick once over. As I was splashing the last of the water onto my face, I gradually looked up and into the mirror that stood in front to where I was standing. At that moment, I could have sworn blind that I witnessed some sort of a reddish shape; it was only there for that split second. I rubbed my eyes and looked again, there was nothing there. I dismissed it out of hand, thinking that I just needed to get my head down.

I shudder as I felt as though I was being observed by something within the walls, but again, I took this as tiredness. Now I moved towards the chair by the window and plopped my wiry bum on it. I was completely knackered, to say the least.

I looked out of the window and gazed at the wind moving through the trees. Now the funny thing was, the fact that I didn't recall anything from within this motel, it was just the outside that was clear in my head, but I knew that I had stayed here years ago, but nothing seemed to be what I expected my memory to serve.

Pulling myself together, I took a moment to scan around the room, yet again, to my astonishment, I once more witnessed that everything wasn't right for this time period; everything just seemed out of sync, the furniture, the four-poster bed, even the decorating was dated; it all felt like I was living in the 1800s, come to think about it, even the register that I had signed earlier in the evening, but I just took that in my stride and ignored it as a bad memory lapse. In hindsight, coming back to this place was looking as one big mistake, but naturally, I didn't know that at the time.

It was now close to 8 pm, and my stomach alarm was buzzing, I was getting hungry. Grabbing my keys, I left the room and walked downstairs to the lounge area in the hope I would be able to grab a bite to eat, even a sandwich would've done at that point. I was also dying to have a beer, maybe two or three perhaps.

Entering the dining area, I moved to a table and sat down. I waited for the waitress to attend me as it was the general custom. I waited. I then waited some more; half an hour had passed and still no service. By now, I was bloody starving. "Hello!" I shouted in the hope I would grab someone's attention, but it was dead quiet. Looking and listening, it became apparent that there was no one here; I was alone.

The old boy I had spoken to earlier had simply vanished. *Fuck this*, I thought. Standing up from my seat, I decided to have a snoop around to see if I could find someone; after ten minutes of searching, I gave up.

I thought to myself, Sod this, I'm gonna grab a beer. That was exactly what I did, over to the bar I went as I thought if I get caught they could put it on my bill come morning, but to my amazement, the bar was completely bare, no beer, no spirits; the bar was absolutely bone dry, empty. In place of the beverages lay thick dust. I once more gazed around and felt very uneasy at this point. The motel felt abandoned, but not two hours ago, I had witnessed a good thirty people drinking in this very spot.

Concern for my safety now really kicked in. I approached the windows that looked over onto the grass verge, a beautiful-looking church stood opposite the grounds; it was a stunning-looking building I thought. As I observed the building, to my utter dismay, everywhere went into total darkness, and I mean darkness; it was absolutely pitch black outside.

I attempted to open the window closest to me to see if I could hear something or someone, but the window was secured with screws. I then examined the other windows, they too were fixed with screws. I stood there transfixed. Had there been a power cut? Where was everyone? What the fuck is going on around here? It was clear to me that I needed answers to these questions that were storming in my brain.

I became fearful for the first time, for out of the darkness way off in the distance, I noticed something moving. I had to rub my eyes as I just couldn't believe what my vision was showing me, for across the way side over the long grass, there seemed to be a small mass of what I can only describe as an illuminated reddish transparent mist; it seemed to be drifting in towards the motel. Then it dawned on me, it's not just heading to the motel, it was coming in my direction, but there had been disparate damage, the trees weren't moving, so how the hell was this mirage shifting itself, it just didn't compute. In my amazement, I repeated to myself, *How the hell was this thing moving?*

Not a whisper of breeze could I see; the trees showed no sign as far as I could see.

I stepped back quickly and stumbled over a chair and table, knocking them flying across the room. Now I was mortified, I just watched this thing. To my horror, the mist just floated then as if it had consciousness; it sharply changed its direction. I watched with full disbelief and amazement as it moved to its right, then its left, then another right.

My thoughts then turned as it dawned on me that this thing was scanning the area; it was actually bloody scanning, but scanning for what? It was then to my horror that it once more changed its direction then paused for a few moments, then began to float towards my location; it stopped within 15 feet from where I was standing. *Thank god*, I thought. The clock on the mantelpiece then died; its ticking just stopped working as before I was able to clearly hear it.

Freezing temperatures filled the room; it was as if I was in the presence of a ghost, or an entity; my breath was visible in the air as my carbon dioxide was clear to see. I was horrified, the mist rose up into the air as it moved ever so closer, then paused once more and again it hovered; it was now only two feet off from the window. I blurted out, "What the fuck are you!" Instantly, the mist transported itself into my area, drifting high on the ceiling just above my head.

Gradually, the mist began to solidify; its molecules were changing its form; it then unbelievably materialised into the old guy I had met earlier. Not knowing what to do, I just stood there frozen in time. It felt like an eternity, like a gun fighter in the old wild west, two persons in a quick draw situation. Once the image was in its solid form, I said, "What are you?" I for some strange unfathomable reason felt calmer; it was as if I felt safe being in its presence; my voice pacified.

The mist uttered in a slow muttering but peaceful voice, "YOU, you is the PETER." Now I had heard that phrase from the old guy earlier on, my fear struck at me like a full on vengeful attack.

I yelled out, "What the hell are you? How the hell do you know my name? What are you?"

The trembling once more began increasing within myself as it raised its ugly head.

The mist spoke again, but this time, there was a change to its voice, a hurried broken English; it was as if it didn't have a lot of time. "YOU, you, time is short, you me now. Time is short, come with or cease to be."

Holding its hands outstretched and with a beckoning manner waved for me to approach it. I stepped back with alarm. Confused and hesitant, I felt myself moving towards this thing, but for some strange reason, I knew that whatever it was, it wasn't here to do me harm, for if it was, I'd be dead already.

After a few moments had passed, I slowly placed my hand very uneasily onto its hand; my emotions were all over the place; one minute, I was in fear of my life, the next, I was calm. What was going on? As soon as our hands collided, in that split moment, there was a blinding red flash of light; we were gone.

Unbeknown to me at that time, as we disappeared, another deep red mass of power erupted into the now desolate space that we had just occupied; it lasted for about a second then instantly it disappeared.

I was totally out of my comfort zone as to where this so-called mist was taking me. I had yet to find out. As if the second hand on a timepiece had flicked over, I found myself alone, standing in a puddle of rainwater to the side of a muddy country path. Nothing but fields lay around; a few trees wavered in the breeze from a distance; the only thing that was visible was an old abandoned church, a broken rusty iron gate swinging on it rusty hinges. The church was surrounded by a dry brick wall about four to five feet in height; it must have been a lovely building when it was last used.

I thought, you could imagine horse-drawn carriages galloping up the country lane to this place a hundred years ago.

It must have been around midday as the sun was above my head and beaming its hot rays upon my uncovered head; it was a boiling day and extremely humid; the breeze had dropped sharply away. Looking around the grounds, I walked through the gate onto the church grounds.

Graves were scattered all around as you would expect to see from a graveyard. The red mist was nowhere to be seen.

This mist had time travel and telepathic capability, this was totally clear to me, for as if by magic it had forced into my mind information that was immediately bloody important to my survival. I had to meet up with another five men I didn't know anything about, maybe it would give more information later, who knows, I certainly didn't at the time! I only knew that I had been taken out from my timeline; thank god, I was still in England, well, that's what I was praying for. I had no idea really as to when or even where for that matter this five would show up, all I knew at that moment was that I was near the coast. Thank god, I thought as being in England was confirmed for near to me an old traffic road sign stood around ten feet away.

I was here to meet a bloke called Alan Stoppage. Now who was this guy to me, well, he was my first port of call so to speak; there was no explanation whatsoever, no idea as to why, or when, or for that matter, where, but this meet up must be seriously important; it had to be, otherwise why all this.

As I approached the church, I could hear something, but I just couldn't make out what it was, so slowly, I crept towards the church wall; the faint murmur was still whispering.

I listened intently to try and understand what this murmuring was saying. I then made sense of it, it was saying just one single word, 'forward', over and over like a scratched record.

I was really convinced that once I turned this corner. I'd see whatever it was. Gently, I peer around the corner's edge, and to my amazement, there was still no one in sight.

I was still unaware as to what was making this noise. I paused for a few moments to process my thinking, I was convinced that I had heard something. I carried on walking.

Circling the building twice, I came across a large oak door and gave the door a yank, then a pull; it was locked as tight as a drum. I gave the building one more tour to give myself peace of mind that there was no one around, and soon, I had returned to the oak door, but to my alarm, the door was now ajar. I stepped back a foot in amazement. Now not five minutes earlier that door was closed and locked, I was really starting to doubt myself at that moment, was it shut or is my mind playing tricks with me.

I was startled to say the least for a moment. Slowly, I pushed open the door, it creaked with age as it opened, you know, as it does in the old horror movies. Peering inside with just my head slipping through the door and framework, I saw absolutely nothing, totally deserted and desolate; no one had used this place for at least fifty years; deep dust lay everywhere. Carrying on trying to scan the place, I noticed in the far right corner a door that again was ajar.

Once I got closer, the realisation hit me in the face like a cricket ball, it was an entrance. I took a wild guess as to where this would lead me and was right, it led me down to the crypt.

Looking down at all the dust and the debris that lay around, I could see footprints as clear as day.

I knew then I wasn't alone. Grabbing hold of a chunk of wood nearby, I slowly but surely crept through the crypt. "Here goes nothing." I fearfully gulped and gently trotted. I could see a couple of large tombs; it was bloody chilly and damp; the daylight from upstairs gave me enough light to see but only just.

This search was taking me far too long for my own liking so I decided to return and leave the crypt. Once again, I could hear this mumbling sound saying the word forward, but I was alone, my ears must be playing tricks on me. I'm imagining again I thought. I spun around to leave, and instantly and without any kind of sign, a foot away from my face stood a young man, similar in age to myself; we both jumped backwards startled, confused. "Jesus!" I cried out. Now you can imagine, our hearts were beating like a wild bull; we were extremely startled, then he spoke for the first time.

"Where am I?" he cried out.

"Don't you know?" I muttered.

"I ain't got a clue, one minute I'm getting ready to hit the sack from a nightshift, this red mist appears from nowhere, called my name, offered an outstretched hand, next minute, I'm here. By the way, where is here anyway?"

"You're five miles from the coast of Scarborough to be precise. Other than that, I have no idea as to anything else. I've only been here a short while myself, so I guess your name's Alan then?"

"Yeah, how did you know that?" answered Alan.

Responding to him, I stated, "Well, you're who I've been sent here to find. By the way, my name's Peter; now you and I have got a hell of a lot to talk about, in the meantime, may I suggest we get the fuck out of this crypt, it's giving me the willies."

"Yeah, too right, I feel that way too," replied Alan.

As Alan was in the motion of turning himself around as if by magic, a deep crack suddenly materialised just in front of him; blistering heat and lava came trickling from within; the crack enlarged, clouds of simmering ash came pouring into the atmosphere. It for all intense purposes seemed to be a volcano on the verge of an eruption, from out of the ground. Then from out of the now enlarged crack, as fast as a microsecond came a pair of red shadowy-like strands; with tremendous speed, they rushed forward and grabbed at Alan's feet. I shouted to him to get clear, but it was too late. Before Alan could react, he had been flung backwards whilst landing heavily on his back; the dust scattered all around as dust clouds rose a few feet from the ground; the shadowy thing was desperately trying to pull Alan into the hole; he immediately cried out for help, as he struggled to break free.

I wasted no time as I dropped down, clutching his hands; a tug of war then ensued between me and this hideous thing, as Alan continued to fight for freedom and break free from this monstrosity.

The grip on my trainers, I could feel them slowly slipping away. I knew I was on the verge of losing this fight.

It felt like an eternity as I struggled to free him from this thing's clutches; at the last moment before Alan's feet were to drop into the hole, the thing suddenly released its grasp; the hole and the shadowy thing instantly vanished in less than a millisecond. I fell backwards. Alan just lay there trembling, visibly shaken by the dramatic event. I moved forward to him, and placing my hand on his shoulder, I asked if he was okay. Alan shortly replied, "Yeah, I'm okay, thanks, Pete. What the fuck was that?" My expression was one of sheer disbelief.

"I've no idea, mate, but we were bloody lucky. I nearly lost ya then. I've got a great idea, Alan, why don't we get the fuck out of here before whatever that was comes back and has a second bite of the cherry?"

"You can say that again," answered Alan; we then together took flight and hurriedly clambered out of the crypt pretty sharpish.

Soon we were out of that ghostly place; we entered the church and sat down on a pew. I explained all that I knew of the situation so far.

Ten minutes had passed, and we had finished passing information to each other; at that moment, I felt something from beneath my feet. I asked Alan, "Can you feel that?"

He instantly responded, "Yeah, what the fuck is it?" There were shimmering vibrations from under the ground; the vibrations gradually increased in strength as then the rest of the area, the floor began to then rumble and shake with greater ferocity; it dawned on me as to what was beginning to happen; the two of us looked at each other as I blurted out my thoughts to him, "It's a bloody earthquake!" Without pausing, I grabbed Alan by his arm and stated with great authority, "Move!"

We scrambled towards the doorway, the stained-glass windows started to blow out one by one, dodging boulders and masonry rubble fell around us from the ceiling and upper sections of the walls. We ran as fast as our feet could carry us, dodging everything as we struggled in the fight to stay alive; we got to the doorway as it started to close. Alan and I grabbed the door before it slammed shut on us; it took a great effort as if the door decided that it wouldn't let us out; we had an almighty fight on our hands, and slowly, we were winning, for a good five minutes had gone past.

We managed to squeeze through as it closed shut. Finally, we had managed to get out of the crumbling church. After we had removed ourselves from the danger, we turned around; it was a horrific sight to behold, the beautiful building was ripping itself apart. After three to four minutes, it had caved in on itself, and then as the last lump of masonry fell, a massive vortex appeared from above, hanging over the church, like a great vacuum cleaner; the remains of the church building were sucked into it, and as fast as this vortex had appeared, it vanished.

We looked in total disbelief as the grounds then repaired itself; we also realised it was only the building that was devastated for the graveyard headstones were untouched; there wasn't an earthquake, after all. Something was focussing on us two. I turned to Alan and said, "This doesn't make sense, why would this thing try to kill us when all it's done so far is help?"

Alan then replied with a chilling statement, "Maybe it was something else, Pete?" We looked at each other bewildered and in dismay.

There was no trace that a building had ever existed.

Everything was back to normality; a hideous laughter echoed in the air around us. As it grew in strength, we could hear it intermittently between laughter and screeching yell of 'DIE, DIE'. As suddenly as it came, it was gone.

The air was clean, no humidity as before; it became apparent that there was no sound coming from anywhere; it was as if we were deaf. The only way we knew that we weren't was when Alan shouted out, "What the fuck's going on, Pete!" It was at that moment I had a strange queasy feeling of sickness; my head began throbbing. I fell to one knee, but seconds later, I was back to normal and stood. "You okay?" Alan asked.

I had been receiving more information telepathically by the mist. I grabbed Alan's arm. "You were right, there is something else, there's an entity out there somewhere; it's trying to destroy us before we do something to it in the future. Why can't this bloody thing give us the whole picture instead of giving me bits and pieces."

Alan inquired, "So what's the next step then? Any ideas as to what we do now?"

"I guess we're walking, Al, that's unless you know where we can borrow some transport."

Alan remarked, "Oh yeah."

I then continued about my car. "We could do with my Capri about now, mate. God, I loved that car." Looking at each other, we started the long stroll towards Scarborough, a lovely five-mile trek. God knows what awaited us there.

It was around 2 pm in the afternoon; we finally had a change of scenery; our first sighting of life, or so we thought, was an old public house; it stood proudly against the backdrop of the countryside that lay all around.

Decent-sized car park too but no cars in it. As we got closer, we noticed that all the windows and doors were boarded up, so it was blatantly clear that this pub was out of business. Across the road on the opposite side of the pub was a layby; we could see a lovely green car, very similar to my Capri. As we got nearer, I could see the number plate, PE6 TAT, this was actually my Capri. Without pausing for a thought, I instantly jumped into the car; gazing around, my coffee cup was still in its compartment, and my CD was still playing and prized dice were still hanging from the window screen rear-view mirror. "Alan, come on, jump in, this is my car." I was like a ten-year-old kid opening my first Christmas present. Excited wasn't the word, I was elated, to say the least. Alan looked at me as he got into the car. "Jesus, Pete, what's going on?"

I answered with, "Who cares? It's my car." I then gave out a chuckle whilst I jumped up and down in the driver's seat; childish, I know, but what the heck. I drove off; now that we had transport and my first contact, all we needed to do now was collect the other four, but as usual, we had no idea as to where, when or how this was supposed to happen.

Keeping the speed down, we cruised through a little secluded village around a mile and a half from our objective. Once again, I received this sickening feeling along with a blistering headache. "You okay, Pete?" Alan asked as he could see that I was in a bit of discomfort.

"Yeah, I'm okay. I've just got some more information." I then went completely silent and gazed towards the road.

Chapter 2
Death Is Calling

It dawned on me that what I was receiving from the mist was a clear telepathic link for want of a better word. "We're going to meet up with our third member soon, mate. He's going to be waiting for us just about now." We were nearing a corner shop that was just coming into view. Alan and I could see three blokes pushing another one around, and what's more, they didn't look to be very friendly towards him; this guy was in big trouble.

I gathered up speed and headed straight towards them. As I got closer, I performed an emergency stop and half mounted the kerb. "Come on, Al." Alan, to give him his due, without hesitation leapt out from the car. He then followed me.

We immediately jumped onto the gang to aid and assist this guy for I knew he was the one we had come to join up with; we fought for around five minutes. Now these guys were bloody tough nuts. I was soon tussling around on the floor like a wrestler. Thinking about it now, it must have looked pretty funny if there were passers-by looking on.

Alan managed to catch one of the other guys with a right upper cut. This caused the bloke to leave the floor as it sent him flying and straight through the shop window; glass flew everywhere as this bloke landing inside the shop.

Now this stranger for now was no jerk when it came to getting his hands dirty as he was pretty decent with fighting for as twisted his body, he produced a thunderous karate kick to this bloke's head knocking him out instantly; the guy spun in the air as he then hit the deck hard. Alan then delivered two karate chops and a swift kick into this bloke's face. After a few moments, the gang once recovered from their injuries, stepped backwards a few feet.

The tall one was about to blurt out something, but at that specific moment, time froze all around them; they were like statues. I was mesmerised by what I was witnessing. I then stated, "Jesus, look at 'em."

Andy spoke next. "Do you think they can still breathe?"

"Who the fuck really cares?" As I said that, we moved over to our new friend.

Alan then with surprise stated, "Pete, I've never trained in martial arts, ever, how the hell did I do that?" We just gazed at each other.

Andy had sustained a few minor cuts and bruises to his face, a few drops of blood were on his arm. I had received a small cut to my lip, but these were only minor injuries. "How're you feeling, are you okay, Andy?" I asked.

"Yeah, I'm fine. I'm a bit battered and bruised, but, hang on a minute, have we met somewhere before, you just called me by name!"

I responded to his question with, "Let's just say you have a lot to catch up on. Now this ugly brute is Alan. My name's Peter." I was replying whilst pointing to each of us in turn. As I proceeded to gaze at these three still frozen in time statues, the atmosphere started to grow seriously cold around us all; we started to shiver like crazy; above their heads around eight feet away, a red discolouration began to form. The red mist began to grow in mass; we three stepped back with fear gripping our faces, but this was not the mist that we had already met; it was soon to become clear that this was the thing that entered the motel just after I was removed. This colour was a strong, deep blood red; it resembled congealed blood. Gradually, the mist materialised into a solid mass. Roughly a few feet across and a depth of around a metre wide, the three of us stood totally still; we were terrified; it was then at that moment that the old boy that was in the motel appeared behind us. "God," I gasped, as I witnessed his materialisation. "We're in the shit now," I stated. At that moment, the strange deep red thing evaporated and zapped up the three solid statues. We turned towards our friendly old boy; I guess it was easier for it to communicate.

"Scarborough must you go, meet others, meet others, time short." Again, the old boy stated that time was short. As I was pondering on its final words, the old boy disappeared as before with a blinding flash of brilliant light that engulfed us all.

"Come on, lads, jump in the car!" I cried.

Andy then asked, "What the fuck was that? What the fuck's going on here? Where the fuck are we going?" Andy was a complete mess as his continual outbursts were.

Alan laughed as he said, "Swears a lot, Pete, doesn't he?" That brought on a laugh from all three of us as Andy slowly started to relax a bit more.

I looked at Andy and stated, "Scarborough, where else?"

The three of us jumped into the car, and I drove off. Whilst driving I explained the situation to Andy, "Right, I'm just going to be brief with this, Andy. For some unknown reason as yet, we've all been moved out of our time, well, timeline thing, and placed here; we've all come into contact with this mist. I've now come to call him the old boy from now on, just sounds right. Anyway getting back to it, now this old boy is somehow connected with me; it's created some sort of telepathic link. Now I don't know why it's chosen me, but there it is.

"At some point, something has happened in the future, and for whatever reason, we're all involved in it, so we've been put into the past of this so-called timeline; it's a brain meltdown, I know, so please don't ponder on it, just do what Alan and I have done and just accept it, cos I'm telling you if you spend too much time thinking about it, you'll go completely nuts. Now apparently, there were six of us when whatever happened, well, happened.

"I'm also now aware that this, oh by the way, Alan, that old boy, it's an entity."

"An entity?" Alan stated with wonderful curiosity.

I continued, "Yeah, now it's become two, two separate strengths, parts of the same thing. On one side is the old boy, we all know by now that it's here to help and assist us, the other wants us dead."

Andy must have been really having difficulties accepting what was happening as he stupidly asked, "Which one wants us dead again?"

Alan without a care blatantly remarked, "For god's sake, the dark red one, you bloody doughnut!"

"Okay, Alan, chill, mate, can't you see he's struggling with all this?"

Andy looked on out the car window as Alan then replied to me, "Well, he better switch on his fucking brain cells that's all I can say, Pete; otherwise, he's going to be dead quicker than I can piss."

"Okay, Alan, okay now, you listening, Andy? Firstly, we had the church where Alan and I met, it tried to kill Alan then."

"Don't remind me, Pete," answered Alan.

"Second, we were helped with my car's miraculous appearance; now these three goons showed up and tried to take care of you."

Andy then came to life and responded, "Yeah, did you see how fast that blood red thing pissed off, well, vanished, when the other one showed up?"

Alan spoke next, "Mist, it's more like a poxy curse to me; it's probably seeking its revenge."

I then jokingly stated, "You mean the red curse, don't ya?" We laughed at the funny moment, so far there hasn't been much for us to laugh about.

We reached Scarborough within a further thirty minutes, not much was happening; we drove along on the front of the shoreline. Okay, there were a few people walking their dogs along the shoreline; shops were trading, pubs still had their usual drunks strolling around outside there.

I just kept driving around turning down streets not knowing where exactly I was driving to, left, then right, left and right again; we were getting dizzy at this point as we just drove around in circles. the telepathic link came on me once more, the same sickness feeling and the headache. I pulled over and stopped the car whilst holding the side of my head. "What's up?" Andy asked.

Alan replied to him stating, "He's okay, it's just this telepathic link he gets each time the old boy contacts him; it communicates with him that way; he goes like that, pretty normal now."

"Cheers, Alan."

"Sorry I didn't mean that way," replied Alan.

As I looked across the street, there was something shimmering above a dimly lit lamppost; it was a good eight to ten feet high above it; whatever it was, it was bloody gigantic, a shapeless mass of some description, but for the life of me, I just couldn't work out what this thing was; it then darted at terrific speed like Superman rushing to save Louis Lane and disappeared into a darkened out alleyway. I thought, what the fuck was that, then decided to investigate so I got out of the car. Switching the engine off, I grabbed the keys.

"Well, what you two up to then, you two coming or what?" I asked.

Alan then responded, "Where're we going?" Now neither of them had seen this shadowy shape, which to me was amazing for its sheer size should've been enough for them to see it.

Naturally, I then stated, "Well, what're you doing, coming or waiting here?" With that, the pair of them gazed at each other, shrugging their shoulders they too got out of the car and followed me into the bleak alleyway.

Now this alleyway was completely black, the only light that was possible were two very dim streetlights that were able to give us some sort of visibility from the street. Slowly, we carried on taking terrific care with the noise issue as we didn't want to alert whatever we were to bump into. Gradually, the further we walked, the darker it became. Alan then produced a mobile from his trouser pocket.

He flicked on his torch app. "That's better," I said. As we reached the end of this alleyway, in front of us stood a doorway; strange I thought as this was the only door we had seen; the door wasn't locked. The three of us looked at one another for a second as I gradually pushed the creaking door open; there in front of us lay a long corridor. I walked in slowly.

Quickly followed by my brave mates, it was after some forty feet or so when we then stumbled upon steps. Andy yelled out, "For fuck's sake!"

Alan then whispered his reply to Andy's outburst, "Will you shut the fuck up? Why don't you buy a foghorn then you can let the fucking street know we're here, for fuck's sake, Andy, wake up."

You could see that Alan wasn't really letting Andy get away with much, but then again, you could see where Alan was coming from.

We began our trek up these steps up, and as we climbed higher and higher, Andy said, "We go on much further, mate, I'm going to need oxygen; it's never ending." Up and up, we walked; as Andy had said, the steps seemed endless. Another three flights we managed as Andy finally stopped and sat down. "I've had it, lads, I need a breather." He then positioned his bum on one of the steps.

"Sorry, but enough is enough." Alan without moaning sat down alongside of him. I then placed my hands on to my knees and took a few deep breaths.

I stood up straight and gazed on to see if there was any ending to this climb, and to my utter dismay and belief, a door just appeared in front of my very eyes. "Oh my fucking god!" I shrieked. Andy and Alan both reacted sharply, for they managed to see this door suddenly appear from the wall. I then said to them, "You ready?"

Andy responded with utter and justifiable concerns, "You're not going in there, Pete, please tell me you're not."

"No, I'm not, Andy, we are." I without a thought gradually open the door. Inside was a plain looking room; it was so bright inside for we all had to shield our eyes; this was simply because we had spent an eternity in relative darkness.

As we entered the single room, there stood an old-fashioned-type desk; it must've been four hundred years old; it was immaculate. As we got closer to the desk, a marvellous-looking coloured haze of light glistened on the desk top; with a flicker from it appeared this; it was some sort of mechanical piece of equipment as it was still pulsating a pure but dull light; it was still hazing as I touched it.

God knows what it was for, well, we certainly didn't at the time.

Andy exclaimed, "What the hell is that!" We looked at each other in bewilderment.

I responded, "Well, it has to be what we need; let's get the fuck out of here, grab it, Andy."

Alan then stated, "Yeah, that's a good idea, Pete, let's get the hell out of here before something else shows up."

It was a matter of seconds as then we could hear this low-pitched laughter that was coming from somewhere in the room, the laugh of a mad psychotic person. Gradually, the pitch grew louder and louder, and at that moment, the walls began to glow red and blistered; the laughter reverted to a hideous voice screaming through the room, continually repeating over and over again with one simple single word, DIE, DIE, DIE. Streaks of flames were now surging through and up the walls, thunderous bursts of flame engulfing the entire ceiling; it was unreal how quickly this fire was spreading; there were eruptions through every new cracks every few seconds; it was horrendous to witness it.

Eruptions of heat were now becoming far too extreme for our safety.

Andy grabbed the device from the desk top as we started our hurried trek back down the stairs; the fire then decided to follow us; it was a race between it and us as the fire moved; it felt like it had a consciousness for it moved as if it had a purpose.

Here came our first major question, which one would reach the doorway first, the fire or us. Running as fast as we could, the fire just kept gaining ground.

With extreme effort, we eventually got out of the room and were virtually falling down the stairs. Rushing along through the corridor, we finally got to the door; this time it was locked tight shut.

Struggling to get the door open, panic ensued. Andy began to whack the door as Alan was trying to kick it open; fire was almost upon us; we were virtually witnessing our own execution when at the last moment before the flames licked our bodies, a massive shield of ice appeared from out of the blue.

The old boy had saved our lives again. I gave the door a massive final kick, and luckily, the lock broke from its fixings and fell to the floor; the three of us then got the door open and jumped out onto the street. It was great timing for the ice cracked and broke from the heat as the flames engulfed the doorway with a terrific blast; the laughter re-emerged, screaming DIE, DIE.

It was once more that this hideously loud laugh was echoing in our eardrums, and seconds later, it was gone. "That was too close," I said; sweat dripped off our faces from the heat. "You still got that device, Andy?" I asked.

"Yeah, it's safe and sound, Pete, now can we get the fuck out of here now, please?"

We left the area without any one of us speaking to one another for we all knew what had just taken place; my thoughts reverted to the old boy, was it watching our every move, did it know our situation from this telepathic link; it then dawned on me that it was a two-way link.

Once in the car, we tried to work out what this device actually was, a device that nearly cost our lives. Passing it to each other, none of us had a clue as to what this thing was; none of us had never seen anything remotely like it. I took the gadget from Andy and put it in the glove compartment; time was moving on, but none of us were tired, hungry or thirsty for that matter, again, this was down to the old boy, it had in some way altered us. I was partially telepathic, Alan and Andy both were bloody good in karate.

I drove off, and as I did, I thought to myself that I needed a break, so I made for the beach; soon I had managed to park the car in a parking layby, up went the handbrake, grabbing my keys I said, "Come on, lads, let's grab some fresh air." Before we had even stepped out of the car, the old boy had transported us more; the sun shone brightly; as we found ourselves sitting on the beach roughly twenty feet from the sea, the waves were crashing onto the beach as we just sat there collecting some decent sun and trying to forget our recent adventures.

The old boy had read my mind for that was exactly where I wanted to go; it even provided us with three ice creams that miraculously just appeared within our hands. Alan remarked, "Fucking hell, glad I wasn't picking my nose." Andy then cracked.

"Could've been worse, mate, you might have been wiping your bum." The lads had finally accepted the time travel issue.

Alan, Andy and myself just looked at each other, shrugged our shoulders and enjoyed the gift. "This ain't that bad, you know, this time travel shit," Andy stated as he engulfed the ice cream, that made us grin.

I stood up and said, "I'm just going to have a little stroll, stretch my legs so to speak, see ya in a bit."

"You sure that's a good idea, Pete, you know you're splitting our forces," stated Andy.

"I will be fine, got my angel looking after me, remember? See ya in a bit."

I strolled along the beach near the waterline and listened to the sea as it rushed its way onto the beach; the tide was well on its way. I had literally forgotten time as I sat down to watch the waves; my mind drifted away in my thoughts! I then realised the distance I had walked from my mates, I must have walked for at least two miles. Shit.

I better start making tracks back, guess they're wondering where I am. I turned and started to walk back; the tide was still in, but this time, I didn't allow my thoughts to take over, I was completely focussed on the task in hand.

After a few feet, I noticed that the sand had a strange motion to it; it also felt a little mushy, not firm as it usually was. I continued walking, and shortly, I then realised that my steps were beginning to get tough whilst lifting my feet with each step; within seconds, my feet had disappeared into the sand. "Oh hell!" I cried.

I knew what was going on, the sands structure had been altered; instead of the firm sand on a beach, it was now changed into a mire, a quick sand mire. I was in serious trouble; it was within a few more seconds later that I had slipped down into the sand up to my kneecaps.

I looked around to see if I could see my mates, but no, this part of it was empty. To my horror, there weren't even seagulls in view. I realised soon enough that struggling made you sink faster so I stopped moving.

I just stood there slowly being dragged to my death when suddenly I noticed that within ten feet of my position and around twenty odd feet in the air, the air began to shimmer; the deep blood red mist that we'd come to nickname the red curse was appearing; within a brilliant deep red blast of light, it showed itself. I had to turn my eyes away from the light.

I heard that voice that I had heard before; by this time, the quicksand was waist deep; the red curse then with a cruel evil tone said, "Alone you die, the Peter, dies the Peter." What an evil voice!

Now panic started to set in, was it right, was this my time? I was about to start yelling for help even though there was no one around. My friendly old boy once again revealed itself, but this time, the red curse didn't move an inch, instead it just grew slightly larger. It then began to move over towards my old boy, both entities started to try and outdo the other in mass; neither of them was attacking; they were, well, it seemed as if they were trying to psych each other out. As they focussed on one another, from out of view I could hear Alan and Andy shouting as they were moving towards me. "Pete, Pete!" Alan called out. I twisted around as much as I could to see Alan and Andy running towards me.

I shouted, "Hurry, I'm sinking fast."

Alan and Andy got to me. "You okay, mate?" asked Andy. I looked at him, then I looked at the quicksand that was now up to my chest, it was at this moment that Alan was shaking my shoulders.

"You okay, Pete?"

I had been dreaming the whole thing, all this time for I had fallen asleep once I had sat down listening to the waves crashing onto the beach. Thank god, I honestly thought my time was up then, poxy bloody dreams they should be universally banned.

I stood up. "Come on, let's get back to the car. As we walked, I gave the old boy a quick message telepathically, *Please no more dreams, no more dreams.*

As we were walking back to the car, I explained to the lads the nightmare I had just woken from. "I'm just going to give you the short version. I was caught in quicksand, the red curse came, the old boy showed up, they faced off against each other then you two came over, the quicksand nearly sucked me down, thought I was dead.

Alan responded with, "Jesus, no wonder you looked as white as a ghost when I woke ya."

After around ten minutes, we were finally back to the car. "Where now?" asked Andy.

"The castle," I answered.

"What you mean a real castle or something else?" asked Andy.

"It's a real castle, well, what's left of it, anyway; it's in ruins now, but there's a labyrinth beneath it."

"So where is this castle then?" Alan asked.

"It's not far, around a ten-minute drive from here. I've just received some new info."

"Oh great," Andy stated.

Alan then remarked, "That sick headache feeling's finally gone then, mate?"

"Yeah, thank god, you know Al, I didn't even notice it."

Andy then remarked, "Well, is that it then? What was the rest of the information?"

"That's it, I'm afraid. I just know we need to go there," I answered.

Alan muttered under his breath, "Oh yippee." As we drove, I then gave a little lecture on the castle.

"Did you know that the English King John was here in around 1210? He was responsible for some of the building work around then. Henry II, he too did some work as well; there's a lot of history here, then you had the Romans, but that was before the castle was built; they had some sort of wooden structure then, 1645, during the civil war, parliament forces took the castle from the Royalist."

Andy then stated, "How much more of this, Pete, sorry, but I hate history, hated it ever since it was drummed into me at school. I didn't mean to come across as rude."

I then responded to him by saying, "It's okay, mate, it's okay. I'm gonna shut up, just thought you might be interested as we're getting closer to it."

"Sorry, mate, but I had history poured down my throat years back by a mad history teacher, hate the subject now, did not mean to offend you," Andy replied.

I then came back with, "You're okay, Andy, don't worry about it, but I'll tell you something, this old boy certainly knows its history."

Alan then mentioned, "This old boy is certainly passing on some really decent information to you, Pete, shame it can't give the full version to us as to why it wants us to go to this castle."

I then responded with, "Wish I had an answer for you, Alan, it just gives me scraps of information from time to time, well, you know that."

We drove out of the town and shortly arrived at the castle; it was an impressive sight; right on the edge of the cliffs, the castle naturally had four sides, three were facing the sea whilst the fourth was our way in; it was a damn shame that the place was in ruins, history had not been particularly nice to this structure.

We parked up and entered the grounds. Across the way was King John's chambers, the Roman signal station that I quickly mentioned whilst we were in the car, the keep, that stood proud. I loved it, shame the others weren't so keen. "Right, let's not waste time, I'm gonna go over there," said Andy.

"Oh, no you don't, Andy, we're not separating any more, no bloody way; we stay together," I replied. Andy gave an acknowledgment.

"Let's start over at the king's chamber." I pointed to it, and off we moved. The king chamber lay about 150 to 200 metres from the keep. Across the way was a group of around ten men; they gave the impression as if they were all foreigners, as there were a few with cameras; it soon became apparent and completely obvious that they were Chinese tourists; the Chinese were roughly 300 metres over near the medieval chapel; a few locals were strolling around the king's hall with their dogs. Shortly, we entered King John's chambers; it was aptly named as it was King John who was responsible for having the place built in and around 1210, can't be a hundred percent, but close enough. We came up to an information board that showed the layout; there were three floors, and a spiral stairwell gave access to each level. "I fancy the basement," stated Alan. Andy and I looked at each other.

"Okay, let's go," I replied. Andy led the way as we moved down the stairs. Looking around, it gave the impression of calm and tranquillity, yeah, right. After a few moments, we were down in the basement; the first thing we noticed was the prison pit.

Andy popped up with a stupid statement, "Wow, that's deep."

Alan answered, "What did you expect, it's a prison pit, the idea is to stop people from escaping, you dick."

Andy then back fired, "I know that, I'm not stupid. I was just saying, sod being down there." Alan then grabbed Andy's shoulders and pretended to throw him into it. "Fucking knock it off, stop it, it ain't funny!" Andy shouted whilst shrugging him off. Alan and I found the funny side to it, but Andy, I'm afraid, didn't. Stepping away from the pit, we carried on with our tour investigation, and gathering pace, we then proceeded up to the next level which was the level we had entered the building through; there was nothing to write home about, meaning no signs, no significance to us being here. I came out of the building followed by the lads. Now across the way over in the direction of where we had seen the Chinese party, I noticed something was seriously wrong with them; we witnessed them as one by one they began to cough, and I don't mean a single cough, more like choking, clutching their throats, each one in turn fell to the ground as if the Black Death had paid a visit to the castle grounds. I pushed out my arms to prevent my mates from rushing over to them. Andy muttered, "Pete, we've got to help 'em."

"No," I responded, "no, we ain't, Andy, just wait a bit, I know what's coming next."

Alan then replied instantly, "What's coming next?" I pointed towards the Chinese, and by this time, they had stopped choking and laid as stiff as boards on the ground. As we watched them, a deep reddish mass of some kind crept over there lifeless bodies; it was like what I can only describe as a thick glue substance. As we continued looking on, this glue engulfed them, swallowed them; this was a new thing as I knew the curse was behind this; it was horrific.

Slowly, I started to move away from the area quickly followed by the other two; we had now managed to get to the king's hall; we had originally passed it on the way to the chamber. After a few short moments, we turned and looked back at those poor sods who were covered in that stuff. Slowly, one by one in the reverse sequence as to when they fell, they struggled to their feet; the glue slowly began to slip and slide off them; they were not alive anymore for what we saw was horrific, their skin was gone, they were nothing but skeletons, clothed in soldier's uniforms. I mean uniforms from different time periods from history; these types of soldier uniforms must have fought here over the centuries, a reasonable assumption I thought. We gasped as we watched; firstly, their stood two First World War soldiers, dating back to 1914–18, seconds later, followed by another eight Roman legionnaires from two thousand years ago.

I mean they were dressed exactly from head to toe, that included all of their military equipment and hardware.

Well, from their periods in time, it was like watching something from the old classic film called *Jason and the Argonauts*; it was amazing to see but scary too. "Oh shit," I yelled, "let's get the hell out of here!"

Now I like a bet from time to time but three against ten, no, not good. I looked around to see where we could go, there was always the car I thought. I was just on the verge of saying something else when all of a sudden I heard a voice from behind us. "What the hell are those dicks doing?" I twisted around; there stood two guys, twins to be precise.

"Oh great, it's a re-enactment," stated one of the twins.

I bluntly responded, "I'm afraid, there is little more than that, mate, look, sorry, don't mean to be rude, but we haven't got a lot of time for a chat. Andy, Alan, let's go." We started to move away from the two strangers. As I made my point, I received a verbal shock by the same guy.

"Are you Peter by any chance?"

Shocked by the comment, I replied, "Yeah, I am."

"Oh great, here you go." The brothers handed me a note.

"What's this?" I asked.

"It's a note," he answered.

I bluntly replied, "Well, I can see that, who gave it to you?" Without reading it and without thinking, I put the note into my pocket.

The brother then responded with, "Well, before we came in here, we were eating some chips down by the harbour and saw an old boy trip over so we went to help the poor sod; he then asked us if we were going up to the castle.

"I told him we were after we had eaten; he then asked us to give a bloke called Peter that note I just gave you; he gave us twenty quid for our troubles, but naturally, if we didn't meet, we could keep the cash, trusting old boy he was; he then went on his way."

"He didn't have a monocle by any chance, did he?" I asked.

"Well, yeah, he did, how did you know that?" he asked.

I replied, "Sheer guess work, mate, just a guess."

Alan piped up stating the obvious, "Erm, excuse me for butting in here, but I thought I would just remind you all, two of 'em have guns." He pointed over to the soldiers.

"Really, I had no idea," I answered sarcastically. Reacting quickly, I shouted, "Cover, lads!" As my words rang out, the two First World War soldiers opened fire, bullets ripped through the air; it was at that very moment we all cowered in fear, but to our amazement, the bullets somehow missed us. I looked at the wall that we were up against, the bullets did not even hit the wall. Now they were either blanks or the old boy is doing us proud once more I thought. Standing up followed by the others, the other brother who hadn't said a lot then mentioned something of interest to us all.

"Look, we've only just come away from the medieval chapel over there, and there are weapons in there."

I faced him and answered, "What are we waiting here for then!" We all raced at top speed to arm ourselves, the soldiers didn't, as they didn't seem to be in any type of rush to get towards us; they moved terribly slowly, more like controlled toys. Within a few minutes, we had reached and entered the chapel.

All around us lay medieval weaponry from double-edged swords to maces, shields to heavy chain mall. Tony, shouted, "Grab what you can!" None of us really needed to be told twice; we all went for the blades apart from Andy who grabbed a ball and chain. Hurriedly, we left the building to face our foe.

Standing outside, we were dumbstruck as the soldiers were lined up in a straight line; it was as if they were on parade as they all stood to attention.

They were waiting for the order to attack; we lined up in front of them.

The sun was beating down heavily; the curse once again shimmered through the air as it once again showed its ugly form; with its hideous voice, it cried,

"You the Peter, DIE, DIE!" It then hovered over the heads of its soldiers, and with a blast of demonic breath, it screamed; the soldiers then began their advance; swords swinging through the air, they advanced yelling out stupid grunts and moaning loudly, the same boring word we had heard time and time again, Die; it seemed that this was the only word it and/or they knew. Each one of us took on at least two soldiers; dancing in and out as not to make a clear target, we sliced and thrusted our swords; the soldiers started to force our numbers back. Crying out, one of the brothers shouted, "They're too strong, let's get back to the prison pit."

"The prison pit," I shouted back, "you wanna trap us in a hole?"

"No, not us, them!" the brother shouted back.

Alan then joined in. "Worth a go, Pete, we can't keep this up much longer."

With reluctance, I then agreed, "Okay, lads, back off, get to the king's chamber."

We broke away and moved hurriedly to the king's chamber whilst the soldiers sped up; we fought a fighting retreat; it was touch and go, but we all managed to get back safely; throwing whatever we could between us and them, we got down into the basement.

We then each in turn positioned ourselves around the prison pit; as the soldiers came down the spiral stairwell, we did all that we could to make sure they fell into the pit; fighting as one unit, we were slowly managing to force each of them to lose balance; it was getting easier as time moved forward as their numbers gradually dropped away. As each of them fell, you just witnessed them walking around in a circle at the bottom of this deep pit; they were like zombies, After a strong five minutes had passed, we finally got the last soldier to fall; we had achieved our objective; it was not long before each one of us were on our knees with exhaustion. We looked around at each other and started to grin; our grins got bigger as we realised what we had managed to accomplish. I grunted, "I need a beer." Everyone joined in with agreement.

Andy then spoke with importance. "Why did their ammunition not work, I wonder. Their swords were real enough."

"Yeah, they were bloody strong too," remarked Alan. I then realised the truth.

"For god's sake, it's got to be a bloody test; it has to be; this fucking thing is testing us. Every time it puts something in our way, it's bloody testing us."

"What do we do with these cretins?" asked Andy.

"Nothing," I answered, "They're not going anywhere. Let's get some fresh air." The group of us went out of the building and into the fresh air. If I said we sat down on the grass, that would be an understatement, for we virtually dropped to the floor exhausted, how many people have sword fights these days, our arms were heavy and worn out. I turned to the brothers who were sitting together. "So, introductions then, I'm Pete, this is Andy, and this guy is Alan."

One brother then replied, "Well, I'm Tony, and this is my younger brother James."

I then happily said, "Well, it's nice to meet you two, welcome to the party, tell, so what's your story."

"Our story, what do you mean, our story?" Tony asked confused.

"Well, for one, how did you get here? Did the old boy have something to do with it?"

"The old boy, sorry, but I ain't got a clue what you're talking about, mate. Tony and me are locals, we were on our way here for something to do; we just saw you three having some sort of issue, as we were over by the keep," Tony replied.

James then mentioned, "What's this about an old boy?" Andy, Alan and myself looked at each other in dismay.

I then said, "What, don't you remember the note?"

James responded with, "Note, what note you talking about, Pete?" The old boy had erased their short-term memories so I thought this was a good time to end it. "Oh right, well, in that case thanks for the help."

"Don't worry about it, probably a misunderstanding," replied James.

Tony then said, "No worries, just give us a shout if you need us again, we'll be over by the king's chambers." Both Tony and James got up to walk away.

"Hang on, can you take these weapons with ya?" I asked.

"Yeah, sure thing." Tony then proceeded to gather up the weapons as his brother joined in; taking the swords, they then left us behind.

"Well, we certainly put the cart before the horse that time," remarked Alan. I looked at him and shrugged my shoulders, well, it was a pretty good bit of timing. I assumed that our lads were here to collect, guess not. We remained seated for a while, after the short break.

A few minutes had passed as I then said, "Right, come on then, let's give this keep a looking at." Otherwise locally known as the great tower, now this building had lost part of its side due to maybe the Second World War, probably hit by a bomb, or it could've been attacked during the civil war, who knows, we walked inside, the three of us separated but only by a short distance.

Andy walked out of view, he called out, "Lads, come here!" We did as commanded; there in front of us was a solid iron grilled gate, rusty as hell, a padlock and chain lay across the gate and its post.

Alan remarked instantly, "Well, that's out of bounds then." He rattled the chain. At that moment, the chain broke away and dropped to the floor. "You have got to be kidding, what now" asked Andy, Looking at each other, Alan then spouted out, "Right, here's the million dollar question, is it our friendly old boy doing this magic trick or the poxy curse thing?"

"Wish I had an answer, mate, but I don't, we going in?" I asked, we gazed at each other.

"To be honest, Pete, I don't really want to. I guess Alan feels the same, but then, we're here for a reason, so let's just get it over with."

"Well, that was a mouthful, Andy, come on then, who is going in their first?"

"Well, it's your party," Andy stated; they then both smiled and waved me forward. After a few moments, we realised pretty quickly that we had entered the notorious dungeons.

The scene was bleak, dark and damp, but as before the mobile phone came out once more, this gave us ample light as the torch lit up our immediate area. "Keep together, lads, don't want to have to call out a search party." This was made crystal clear to all concerned.

Prison cells were on both sides of us; in the middle was a stone-floored passageway; we continued to follow it. After roughly eight to ten minutes, I got a sharp reminder from Alan. "Shit, Peter, the note."

"Oh hell, I had totally forgotten about the paper in my pocket." Asking Andy for some light, I removed the note from my pocket and opened it; to my amazement, it was blank, totally blank. I frowned in frustration then said, "It's a blank piece of note paper." I waved it about then handed it over to the others who in turns inspected it.

"What was the idea of a note if there's nothing written on the bloody thing?" said Alan, then it dawned on me.

I blurted out, "I know, Jesus, it's so simple. I was astounded by the way the old boy was working." I turned to Alan and Andy. "Look, we three had in some way shape or form come in contact with the old boy before it zapped us here, yeah?"

"Yeah, carry on," answered Alan.

"Well, don't you see, Tony and James have meet have just meet him, this was just a ruse for us to meet up with those two; it was ingenious how it was joining us together; it's brilliant, all they saw was an old man; it makes perfect sense now. They have no idea as to what's going on."

Andy then asked, "What do we do now then?"

I looked at him and stated, "We go back and find them before the curse does, come on." We turned and left the dungeons.

We were now on the hunt to find our new friends; we headed to where they said they would be, the king's chamber. Hurriedly, we reached the building and entered calling out for Tony and James; there was no sign of them; we then went back down the spiral staircase; they were not there either. "Shit, where are they!" I shouted.

Alan then made a startling discovery. "Erm, Pete, the soldiers aren't in the pit."

"What're you talking about, course they are." I looked for myself. Alan was spot on, the pit was empty, Now somehow, the soldier had freed themselves from the confines of their prison; it was more plausible that the curse had had a hand in it. "Ha, hell, come on, lads, let's hope we're not too late," I stated as I moved away and back up the stairwell; we scurried out of the building. Across to the king's hall, we finally caught a glimpse of Tony and James; they were nearing the inner bailey of which was situated near the great tower. "Tony!" I cried, immediately Tony raised his hand as he noticed us and the twins then began to walk across in our direction. After a few minutes had passed, I said, "Where did those soldiers go to?"

James then replied, "What do you mean, they're still down in the pit."

"Sorry to be the bringer of bad news," said Andy, "but they ain't."

"Crap," announced Tony, "where are they then?" We looked around in the hope of not seeing these things anymore whilst staying together I spoke to the twins.

"Right, Tony, James, you remember when I had mentioned the old boy earlier."

"Yeah, what about it?" answered Tony. I then began to explain further.

"Well, this ain't gonna be easy for you two to accept, but it's the truth. Andy, Alan and myself at different times have been placed in this timeline, this is our past; by an entity we've come to know as the old boy, you came into contact with it when you first met him when he gave you that twenty quid and a note, well, the note was blank, it was its way of getting you two to join us; it also uses that image when it communicates with us; you see, there's also an evil entity out there that wants us all dead, hence the skeleton soldiers."

"Bullshit," said James.

Andy then backed me up. "He's telling you the truth here, mate, so ears open, shut your mouth and listen to him. The information may well save your life one day so pay attention."

"Look, I know this sounds like bullshit but we're being manipulated in time; somehow the old boy knows what's in store for us all; we don't know anything else apart from this that the evil thing is putting obstacles in our way, trying to trick us or kill."

Tony then showed some brains by stating, "Obstacles, you mean the skeleton soldiers." I acknowledged his remark.

"Okay, okay, let's say we believe you, what happens next?" asked James.

"Sorry, James, if you want answers, I ain't got any, the only thing I have got is a two-way telepathic link, but I only get snippets of information, nothing substantial."

Chapter 3
The Skeleton Soldiers

Andy at that time was just casually looking around as then he saw the skeletons once more. "Lads, lads, look." He pointed to the Roman signal station; to our utter dismay, the skeleton soldiers were moving as awkwardly as a three-year-old, talk about being unsteady on your feet; it was ridiculous, but saying that, they were heading straight towards us and armed to the teeth.

We didn't have a great deal of time to organise anything; now the twins Tony and James had returned the weapons earlier, yeah, I know it was my fault that they did, in hindsight, one big bloody mistake.

I turned to Andy and Tony. "Can you lads get over there and grab whatever you can? We'll try to occupy them till you get back."

Tony said, "You sure you want to do that?"

"No," I replied, "but if you have a better suggestion, then please tell me now." With that, Tony and Andy ran off circling.

It was then we began to play hide and seek with these monstrosities, moving from pillar to post as we knew they weren't that fast. But it wasn't long before some of us started to get out of puff as Alan then yelled out, "For fuck's sake, Pete, behind us."

I twisted around; we were now in a seriously extreme position as we could see a further group of ten skeleton soldiers approaching from the great tower that was behind us; they were identical to the first batch.

Just as I was running out of ideas, Tony and Andy returned with as much weaponry as they could carry; we all took a sword plus a ball and chain; the fight for our very souls had begun; it was twenty against five, outnumbered four to one; if there was a miracle out there, we needed it now.

As the fight developed, we found ourselves suffering with complete and total confusion as each of us just kept swinging our swords with both hands; now

Tony was showing some really interesting moves for it was clear that he was no stranger to sword play; on the other hand, his brother James was having some issues as he was seriously struggling. I rushed over to him and grabbed his attention. "Here!" I yelled, then handed him the ball and chain.

Without a pause, he then dropped his sword to the ground, grabbed the ball and chain and started; it was like he was possessed; now some of these skeleton soldiers were bashing their shields and swords; it was unreal for each time one of us managed to decapitate or remove at least one limb, like an arm or a leg, James had actually taken the head off two skeletons, but even that proved useless, for within micro seconds, they were being rebuilt before our very eyes.

They were indestructible; it was as if by magic that they could reassemble themselves; we were in a no win situation; panic was rife. "Back off, back off!" I shouted to everyone in the hope we could retreat to another position that we would be able to defend, try and create further plans. As we started to withdraw, Andy lost his balance; as his footing slipped away from him, within seconds he had hit the floor with a tremendous slump to the ground; immediately, he began screaming in agony; he had twisted or broken something. As he was grabbing his ankle and with a loud cry he called out for help. "Pete, for god's sake, help me." I looked across.

Andy was in serious trouble; I hacked my way across to him. Alan had seen what was unfolding as he too moved across to assist. I dropped my sword and grabbed Andy from under his armpits; slowly I got him up off the ground, without hesitation, I then threw him onto my shoulder and gave him a fireman's carry out of the battlefield. Alan quickly whilst covering our retreat did the same; each one of us had scratches or cuts of some description, some small amounts of blood were also visible, but no one was badly wounded, well, at the time, that's what I had thought.

I still had Andy over my shoulder when Alan moved towards me, and in a calm voice he asked, "Pete, put him down, mate."

"Yeah, I will in a minute. I'm gonna lower you now, Andy." Andy made no sound, no movement. I lowered him to the ground, not known to any of us apart from Alan, whilst I was carrying him back and out of danger, Andy had received a thrown dagger blade that had deeply embedded itself into his back.

Andy was dead. I yelled out, "You bastards!"

We all stood looking down at Andy's corpse, our first casualty of war so to speak; death in this place was real enough as we mourned over our fallen comrade, the skeleton soldiers were still on the war path, and we hadn't much time.

I didn't give a shit at that particular moment as I knelt down besides Andy's lifeless body and held his shoulder; all I could do was look at him.

I was devastated by his loss. Alan came beside me in a terrific hurry as he shouted, "Pete, for god's sake, mate, come on unless you want to be laying there beside him, get your fucking arse up and move." He grabbed me from under my armpit and forced me onto my feet; no one was showing any signs of remorse for the loss of Andy as we just did not have the time.

We were in a life-or-death situation, and I for one had no idea how the hell we were getting out of it.

For one, we knew we couldn't kill these things. "Let's get to the car, Alan." Alan didn't question me at all as he immediately acknowledged and nodded in agreement.

Tony and his twin James also followed off at speed; the loss of Andy had also hurt Alan as well as myself, but naturally, there was not as much feeling with the other two as they had just come on the scene.

Hurriedly, we moved going around buildings trying to flank these ugly sons of bitches. As we were nearing the entry barrier, roughly about two hundred metres away from the car, now, on top of everything we had just had to go through, we came upon the curse once more; the ground started to shudder and break as if an earthquake was starting, but this earthquake only covered a six foot section of the ground; cracks then started to appear within the concrete. Seconds later, arose the red hideous thing in the natural form of a mist; it began hovering around ten feet off the ground.

Tony cried out, "What in the name of Christ is that?" Tony moved backwards a few feet as the scene was a little hard to swallow.

I then stated, "Gentlemen, I give you the red curse."

Tony then continued whilst still in a nervous state. "So this is the poxy thing that's been trying to wipe us out?"

I responded with, "And it won't stop till we're all as dead tone and that's a fact."

"Well, what the hell are we going to do now?" asked Tony.

I looked at Alan. "Any thoughts?" Before Alan could even mutter a word, the old boy then appeared like a genie from a lamp; it slowly materialised and faced its foe. they stood tot to toe; the curse then tried altering its position as it veered from one side to the next; it was doing its utmost to get nearer to us; the old boy then with excellent speed and precision copied every move its enemy took. I then lost it as I became totally out of order. "Where the fuck have you been?"

I unleashed my emotion towards the old boy, as I approached it. Alan pulled me back. "Pete, no." I stood there fuming; the skeleton soldiers had just reached the exit of the castle; the group of us stood there like brainless idiots; we had the curse in front, skeletons behind, we then got a shock as without any warning the two entities opened fire on each other; thunderbolts of some type of alien energy force were exploding at fantastic speed.

Both of them had some kind of force field surrounding them, as they were pounding one another with the same weaponry as the battle grew more intense; the skeletons came closer, our great old boy raised its arm, from out of its fingers, it produced a massive flash of some sort of energy; it directly released this power against the skeletons, seconds passed, this formidable energy now fully engulfing them, they were completely trapped within another force field. As we watched these dramatic event unfold, it was clear to see that it was gradually decreasing in size; the skeletons were now being slowly crushed. After a good three to four minutes of watching this, the skeletons were virtually crushed bone; the energy field then zapped from existence.

There was nothing left of them, just an empty space remained; it had only taken the old boy less than fifteen seconds to obliterate those things; frustration was building in my head so I shouted at the mist, "What now!" At that moment, all of us, Alan, Tony, James and myself instantly evaporated, transported into the car; we sat there looking at each other for a few seconds processing the transportation. Tony and James were both shaken up due to the strange sensation they were feeling because of it. Tony then inquired, "So you two do this sort of thing on a regular basis, do ya?"

Alan then remarked, "Frequently, mate, don't worry about, you'll get used to it."

James then asked, "Don't take this the wrong way, guys, but do you think we could get the hell out of here?"

Laughing out loud, I started the engine; we drove away from the castle grounds like bats from hell. As we were still driving away from the castle, to another unknown destination, Tony asked as we had already driven for thirty minutes, "Can you pull over at some point, mate? I'm having a few problems digesting all this."

"You okay?" I asked.

"Well, no, feel like I'm gonna throw up."

"Has to be the transporting thing, I'm also having trouble taking this all in." It was then that he started to retch; as he placed his hands over his mouth, I then thought, *No, you bloody don't, not in my bloody car.* Now I wasn't thinking of this poor sods feeling like shit, my only concern was that I just didn't want sick over my seats. Within seconds, I had stopped.

Instantly, Tony got out of the car; he then immediately fell to his knees.

Thank God, I stopped when I did for as soon as he had got out, he was throwing up.

James got out and went straight to him. Alan then remarked, "Jesus, Pete, he won't have any stomach lining if he carries on like this." We both then looked out of the window as Tony finally stopped; after throwing out a few spits out of his mouth, Tony then raised himself off his knees.

James asked, "You feeling better, mate?"

Tony replied with, "Yeah, I'm okay. Jesus, I hope I don't get that again." As they both jumped back in the car, Tony asked me, "Can we have a little chat before we get going, Pete?"

I then responded with, "Yeah, I think it's probably a good idea, mate, be nice to know each other a little."

I twisted around in my seat to face Tony and James. "Right then, introduction already done, who is going to start the ball rolling?"

James stated, "Best if you do, Pete."

"Right, okay, now where do I start? Well, to put things in a nutshell, I will give you two the breakdown. Now everything started a couple of days back. I was in a motel taking a break on my own, then the friendly old boy showed up; next minute, I was removed from there, had no idea as to where I was, or what was happening, by the way, we call it the old boy as it's just easier for us, and it's also the reason as to why we're here.

"Basically, it's responsible for the situations we seem to get into. Since my first time warp, I have had a telepathic link with it, somehow it transmits information to me. Now I don't know why it's just me, but there it is; recently I've come to learn that it's a two-way link that we have. Now comes the evil thing we call the red curse.

"Now that's a different story entirely so now at some point in the future we four plus Andy witnessed or helped or didn't do something; god, it does your nut in thinking about it, but I have no ideas as to what yet, both of these things are mixing up the timeline; we don't know where or when all this happens; all we can do is go with the flow, but this red curse is going out of its way in trying to kill us before whatever took place takes place, so then I met Alan. We had our first encounter with the curse who then tried to snuff us the pair of us out, then we came across Andy, one decent bloke. I'm gonna miss him, then you two guys show up, the rest you know."

James then made a startling statement. "Look, I don't understand this, now if what you're telling us is the truth and we're all in this, then why has Andy been killed? It don't make sense, if we're like all of us are there to whatever, then why is he dead?"

Alan responded, "Well, these two entities have altered all of our timelines; it's like we're in an alternative reality, in other words, what took place, hasn't happened yet, so therefore, the curse is getting rid of each of us before we finally do what we did."

I then said, "Well done, Alan, couldn't have said it better, mate, well done." It was then that I remembered. "Hang on a minute." I reached in the glove compartment and took out the device that we had found a while back and simply forgot about. "Well, we were sent this, any ideas as to what this bloody thing may be?" I then passed the device over to James.

He, without a moment's pause, immediately recognised it. "Oh my god, it's—"

I interrupted him. "It's a what?"

"Well, it's a trans mobility isolating drive," said James.

"Sorry, say again, it's a what?" I answered.

"Trans what?" Alan calmly said; the two of us were completely in the dark, no idea what James was talking about.

"Yeah, I read about these devices on the computer and science magazines I've got at home; it's only been public knowledge since its disclosure last month, how the hell have you two got your hands on one?"

I responded by saying, "It miraculously appeared on a desk top when we were—"

James interrupted as he got back onto the magazine article. "There's a whole page about it; it's the latest invention of, what's his bloody name now, oh yeah, Professor War-pen if memory serves."

Alan then jumped in with, "Right, okay, it's a trans warp thingy we get that, but what the fuck does it do?"

In a calm voice, James then shut the pair of us up with, "Well, before I start which one of you knows anything about time travel—"

"Time travel, what like *Star Trek* you mean?" Alan was getting really interested at this point.

"Yeah," stated James.

Alan and I looked at each other and together stated, "Well, nothing."

"Well then, I'm not going to waste my time boring you with explaining what it does, apart from stating it's an important piece of equipment if you're planning on escaping to Jupiter say, it's only the greatest invention in history; it's going to put us humans on a different plain; it's for time travel."

"TIME TRAVEL!" I exclaimed.

Alan then opened his gob. "Well, that explains a lot, cheers, James." We allowed us a quick giggle to ease the tension.

It then dawned on me. "Hang on, can you lot see the connection here?"

"What connection, Pete?" asked Alan.

"Look, this professor War-pen has created this time warp thingy, the curse and the old boy can also travel through time. Don't you see, Jesus, it's all starting to fall into place now; he has made time travel work, but in doing so, somethings happened, now we've got these two entities. James, have you any idea where this professor lives?"

James responded, "Well, no, the magazine won't give out confidential information like that. It's against the law, he could take the magazine to court."

I replied with, "Well, that's a shame, but we're certainly getting closer though."

"Great piece of luck we meeting up then, ain't it, Pete?" stated James.

"Don't kid yourself, James, it was not luck that brought us together, that old boy knows exactly what it's doing, it doesn't make mistakes or takes chances. You were made to join up with us because like it or not you were with me in what's now our future, but right now, all we need do is find this professor before the curse kills him."

45

Remarking in an excited state, Alan said, "Well, what are we waiting for, let's go."

"Where to? You got some information that I don't have then, Al?" I asked.

"Yeah, I see your point, okay, I got a little ahead of myself then, sorry."

"Well, let's hope the old boy puts us in touch with him soon. Can I have it back, James?" I asked as I pointed to the device.

With great regret, James passed the device back to me, back into the glovebox it went. "Right then, James, tell us about yourself."

"Oh right, yeah, well, you know my name. I've lived in Scarborough for most of my life along with Tony.

"I've always had a thing about science fiction even during my school days, that's why I got so excited when I saw that device. I'm just fascinated with technology. I got an honours degree in computer science! I love taking computers and such apart then putting them back together again can be a little tricky but it's what I do, schematics, you name it, I do it."

"So, you're a computer whiz kid?" I said.

"Well, I wouldn't say that exactly, more like a technician. I just love it."

"Right, so you're our technical guru, so that's why you've been chosen to join our little party, you're probably going to be responsible for putting that device into operation at some point. Tony, what's your speciality," I asked.

Tony answered with, "In my spare time, I travel across to York, they do re-enactments of the English civil war from 1640s, right up to 1645 and the Battle of Naseby."

"Oh right, so that's why your first thoughts were that those skeletons were doing a re-enactment; it also explains you're proficient with the swords and such earlier."

Tony continued with, "Well, yeah, I guess, rather have had a submachine gun, but yeah, I'm okay with a sword."

"Right then, so to recap our skills, I drive and have a telepathic link with this entity. Alan's a black belt in karate. James is a computer genius and Tony's a weapons expert, how the hell can we fail?" Without a second passing by from the last word spoken, there came a blinding flash of light from within the car; it was so bright we all had to cover our eyes. As the light gradually decreased with its ferocity, the old boy once appeared yet again; this time, it sat between Tony and his twin brother James. "Son of a bitch!" I yelled.

46

Tony and James reacted with total surprise and shock as they jumped from their seats as this entity suddenly materialised in between them; it was then that as soon as my eyes had seen him, I wanted to tear his head off for not preventing the death of Andy, our dead teammate.

Alan held my arm and said, "Cool it, Pete, let's see what it has to say first." The old boy started to communicate with all of us, again not in a fluent manner.

"York must go, York must find, York you go."

Tony piped up, "Why York? York is a bloody big place, where in York?"

The old boy immediately faced me, glared straight into my eyes and simply repeated itself with four words, no explanations, nothing, it just said, "The York, Peter, York."

It disappeared as fast as it had appeared. Alan stated, "Well, that was useful I must say, you never know, Pete, it may surprise us yet again and it's gonna send you some more information as we go."

I then muttered, "It's possible, highly unlikely, but possible."

"How far is York from here then, Pete, any idea? asked Alan."

"It's roughly an hour's drive, mate, it's roughly about forty odd miles from here."

Alan then replied, "Well, I guess we're off to jolly old York then," Tony muttered.

I once again started the engine and we set off; after a while, it was clear that everyone including me had not said a dicky bird, so without another word from my brain, I started a joke to break the solitary mode that everyone seemed to have. "Okay, you boring bunch, let's see if you have heard this one, how do you sink an Irish submarine?"

Tony was the first to jump out with an answer. "You knock on the door." James thought that was pretty hilarious as he broke into laughter.

Alan gave him a strange puzzling look as if to say it wasn't that funny.

Alan took his turn. "Right then, get this one then, a bloke lives on the thirteenth floor in a block of flats, he gets in the lift, goes to the basement, gets in his car, drives to a nightclub, meets a woman, drives back to his place, they get in the lift, go to the tenth floor then walk the rest, why didn't they take the lift straight to the thirteenth floor?" Now that was a puzzle; we spent ages pondering over it.

The faces we pulled as we all tried to work out the answer, now that in itself was funny. James got the answer after thinking for five minutes. "He was a midget."

"Oh, you clever clog," ranted Alan.

Tony then stated, "I don't get it."

Alan faced him and said, "Well, it's pretty simple, he could not reach past the tenth button."

"I still don't get it," replied Tony, that was it, wasn't it, the rest of us nearly cried laughing.

Tony was a complete dick when it came to humour. I think he had left his humour at home.

The tears faded as the laughter slowly passed away and stopped. I then received a message by the telepathic link. "You okay?" asked Tony.

"Yes, mate, I'm okay. I always get like this, it's the side effect from the link; it'll pass in a minute. Look, has anyone heard of the Cold War bunker based in York." No one said a word, so it was blatantly obvious to me that no one had; as the silence continued, I stated, "Well, that's going to be our next stop, lads, that's our destination; it's basically a subterranean building built in 1961 in case of a nuclear war; now apparently, there are around thirty of them scattered around England, but this is the only one that still has all the operational machinery left inside; it's been closed for around the last eight, nine years, but apparently, we won't have a problem getting inside."

Tony then asked in a concerning manner, "We're not gonna be transported again, are we, that last one made me feel like shit."

James responded with, "Oh, shut up, you tart."

Alan and I chuckled. "So, I suppose this old boy's just gonna open the front door for us, yeah?" remarked Tony.

I then fired back with, "You got it in one, Tony, well done, five points." The atmosphere was finally starting to improve.

"We there yet?" asked Alan. James looked at him as he referred to an old film that he had once watched.

"You've been watching too much of Shrek, mate."

I responded, "Please, please don't get me wound up with stupid verbal quotes, please. We're gonna be there soon." After a few minutes had passed, the other two cottoned on to the Shrek movie, so one by one, each one of the three asked the same stupid phrase, 'We there yet?', the phrase was slowly drilling into my nut causing a headache. "Seriously, lads." They then shut up with their so-called humour. "Anyone fancy a coffee, I'm paying?"

"Where we getting them then?" asked James.

I came back with, "We've a garage coming up, we can grab a latte there."

"Make mine a mocha," said Alan.

James then followed up with, "Yeah, mocha sounds good." Shortly, I pulled into the service forecourt.

Alan and myself got out of the car and walked inside the garage shop; it was reasonably busy, not fully chock-a-block, but nevertheless the staff seemed reasonably chilled and relaxed; we went to the cashier and asked for four coffees and shortly returned to the car to have a relaxing ten-minute break.

My thoughts took me back as I recalled events that Andy and I had had, events such as when we met and how the curse tried to take him out, the fight that we had to save Alan; it was nice to think back and reminisce.

I really did miss that git. I gave myself a little smirk, then from out of the blue like someone had just thrown a thunderbolt to clear my brain cells, it dawned on me that I was told that I had to meet five blokes during my journey, now I thought and how stupid my thoughts are with these guys, well, I just assumed that these guys were with me when we do what we did in the coming future.

But now with the death of Andy, everything needs a rethink. I mean this as to mean that these guys I'm with now may not be the ones with me at the end, so the future as been so muddled now. I soon felt a dig in my ribs, it was Alan trying to grab my attention. "Hoy, you okay?"

I replied with, "Yeah, I was just thinking."

"Anything we should know?" asked Tony.

"Na, nothing important," I answered.

I said that as I did not want to cause discomfort to them; it was so stupid of me to just assume that nothing could or would happen to these guys. James popped up and then asked, "Where's this place we're going to again?"

Alan then stated, "You need a memory booster, it's the Cold War bunker in York. It's basically a nuclear fallout shelter."

"Don't you ever forget stuff, Mr Smartarse?" moaned James.

James just gave him a stare; with that, I started the car engine and we carried on with our journey; after a further twenty minutes, we finally got to our destination; slowly, we drove and parked up.

I got as close as I could to the front entrance to the bunker; it really looked a daunting place from the outside; an eight feet silver metal spiked top fence encircled a grassy mound and beyond that was this large mound or earth grass covered; behind the gate of which was padlocked, we could see two flights of steps with a little landing in between them; at the top of the stairs stood a massive solid green iron door.

Well, from here, it looks like iron but it was green anyway, rusting around its hinges. We got out of the car and looked around; it was clear that no one had been around here for some time; in view that's exactly what I was expecting, seeming this place hadn't seen action for close on ten years.

We approached the gate, and as we did, the padlock that was supported by a thick solid chain snapped and fell to the floor. I leaned forward and collected the items. "Well, then, gentlemen" – I paused and with a deep intake of breath – "let's go in." I opened the gate and entered, quickly followed by Alan, then James and following up from the rear came a nervous Tony. With great confidence, we climbed the steps. I approached the iron door, the door started to open as if it was on automatic unlock, but we all knew it was the old boy doing its bit for us. With that thought, I felt pretty confident, and into the cold bunker we went and it lived up to its name, it was freezing. The door closed behind with a sudden whack, but then what do you really expect? Our entity somehow turned the generators on which was on the lower level. Lights, one by one flickered on, a floor plan was the first thing that stood out, it was fastened onto a near wall. "Right, lads, as it stands at the moment, none of us have a clue why we're here or for that matter, what we're looking for either, so eyes open and keep your wits on full alert. If you see anything, open your mouth and we will all be there as soon as possible, everyone okay with that?" I asked. Each one of us nodded in turn. "I guess we better stay in pairs, just to be safe, Alan, you're with me. Tony, James, you stay together, right, let's break up and for god's sake, be careful, we don't want another one of us leaving the team."

Nice and easy, we separated from each other and headed in different areas. Tony and James took a stairwell that lay across the corridor just up a few feet from where they were; they then followed it down. Alan and myself walked straight ahead. "Thank god, we had the lights switched on, Pete," Alan muttered.

"Too true, mate," I eagerly replied. After a few moments, our first room was the sleeping quarters, well, one of them anyway; nothing going on there I thought. After a few moments of observation, we entered the control area, this must have been the nerve centre to this place, large computers from back in the sixties.

It was prehistoric to the technology of today; today you could store tons of information just on a USB stick, back then you needed an entire room. The room was full of buttons and reel to reel gadgetry. Gradually as we moved on, I was starting to feel rather unsettled in my head, an uneasy feeling of sickness quickly followed by dizziness. I held my arm out and laid it against the wall. "Pete, what's up?" Alan asked in a concerning manner.

"I'm okay, mate, just came over dizzy for a moment; it's passing now, god, gives you the willies, don't like feeling dizzy at the best of times, not nice," I answered. After twenty minutes had passed by, I received my second surprise, we had got as far as the recreation hall when as if by magic my legs gradually started to grew weak. I reached out to Alan who was nearby. I called his name, "Alan." At that moment, the dizziness returned. "Shit," I exclaimed, "this ain't good, mate, get me to a chair, will ya, god, I feel shit." Alan responded in a worrying manner. Once I was seated, I stated, "What the bloody hell's going on with me, Alan, first dizziness, feeling sick, now weak as a youngster, hell with this." I stayed where I was until all the symptoms had faded enough for me to continue; after some deep breaths and a few sighs, my ability to carry on was coming back; my legs felt much stronger, well, that's how they felt at that moment. "I'm feeling much better now, Alan, let's get moving." I stood up onto my feet and like a hammer blow straight across my head, I hit the ground. I was out cold, totally unconscious.

"Holy shit, Peter!" shouted Alan.

Alan then managed to place me in a more comfortable position as I flopped like a bag of spuds, resting my head up as to make sure I could breathe. He said, "Got to get the others, take it easy, mate. I'm gonna get help." He then rushed off in the hope of finding Tony and James. Meanwhile, Tony and James were having a few problems of their own for a few moments earlier Tony had walked into a doorframe for he too had had a dizzy spell; he had received a nasty gash above his right eye, must have been at least an inch long and reasonably deep, a stitches job but we had no way of getting medical assistance.

Tony immediately collapsed to the floor; he was dazed but not knocked out. James was covered in his brother's blood as he was trying to stop the bleeding. James then had a great idea for he tore open his own shirt and managed to rip some of the cloth to act as a temporary bandage.

As he continued to help his brother, Alan finally found them, for he came rushing into the room. "Peter has collapsed, help." He then noticed Tony and James covered in blood. "What the fuck's happened to you too?"

James explained, "Tony had a dizziness spell, smashed into that poxy doorframe over there, mate." James then realised what Alan had just said about Peter. "Peter's what?" he exclaimed. He then addressed his brother, "Can you walk, Tony?"

Tony replied, "Course I can, here give me a hand, will ya?" Both James and Alan assisted him to his feet as they moved off. Meanwhile back with me, my mind began to wander into the imagination, or was it an out of body experience that you sometimes hear about? I didn't know what was happening so I just went with the flow, well, I didn't have much choice really.

I was back in 1941, but I was not in York anymore, it was Liverpool for there was a plaque on the building walls that my eyes were deliberately drawn to.

I could see a building, it was the cold bunker in York, but it was not where I had just come from, now it was being opened by some serious-looking soldier from the British Army; it was difficult to work out this bloke's rank; this guy was probably a general, well, someone in high authority, yeah, it must have been, otherwise why wear a military uniform in the first place? It was like watching a TV movie but without the sound turned on, strange dream this I thought. I witnessed a group of at least twelve men and six women in civilian dress enter with this military bloke.

The general made a speech in the middle of this large entrance hall; he then saluted the staff and left the building leaving this eighteen strong team to get on with whatever they were there to do. Another bloke then came out of a side room whilst carrying a clipboard, whilst talking he was pointing as if he was instructing them where to go; this guy was around thirty years old; he stood tall and upright, a very thin guy, virtually no muscle on his body whatsoever; his complexion wasn't great either; he looked ill to be perfectly frank; he had full facial beard and moustache, round-framed spectacles, with a red stripy tie and a decent three-piece suit, I thought.

After a few moments, each person in turn moved away from the clipboard man and was taken to their stations of work by another guy, or some were going into the dining area; my eyes kept trying to look around the area, but for some strange unforeseen reason, my focus kept going back to this guy in the suit. I glared at him for, well, it felt like a lifetime, then and within a nano second, the man's face zoomed in on me, it was as if he knew I was there! At that very moment, I was crashing my way through time, again like the flick of a switch, but this time, I was now back in York, England, in 1961.

I was witnessing a twenty years' zap into this man's future. I was back in the Cold War bunker as when it had originally opened, but still in my past.

Chapter 4
The Dover Event

There guiding his team was this guy again; money must have been seriously tight back then as this guy was still wearing the exact outfit he wore from all those years ago; his facial hair was now a deep grey; he was by now at least fifty years old, yet again there was no sound, just a silent movie screen. There across the way was a room I hadn't seen before.

Be it twenty years in the past or was it with my present timeline with the lads, anyway it was a laboratory, a great white door, great big words reading 'Keep Out' in bold black writing.

Inside the lab, I could see people walking around in white suits, as I looked on, I could plainly see a commotion within the lab, people rushing about like there was no tomorrow, some were trying to get out of the lab. At that instant, there was a massive blast from within one of the lab quarantine sections; all I was then witnessing was this guy's face from the time zooming in and out at me, just like before.

Zooming in at me, he was trying to say something, was he addressing me, I hadn't a clue.

At that moment, I felt Alan's hand shaking my shoulders, as he was crying out, "Pete, Pete!"

"Alan, is that you?" At that specific moment, I was blind, couldn't see a fucking thing. I was extremely dazed, but thankfully, over the next few minutes my eye sight gradually came back slowly, and a few seconds later, I was coming to my senses.

"You okay?" Alan asked.

"Give me some time, mate, I'm still feeling a little groggy."

James then brought us all up to speed as to the reason why we were feeling the way we were. "Eh, guys, it's carbon monoxide poisoning."

"You what? what you going on about, James?" asked Alan.

"Look, how long has this place been closed down for, ten years, yeah, it's been airtight, no oxygen in or out, the air is dead, no air means no oxygen, we've only been breathing oxygen that the old boy gave us when we entered. Remember, the door closed once we were inside, it's carbon monoxide, it can be fatal, we've got to get these guys out into the fresh air, Alan, especially Peter, he has been struck the worst." Alan grabbed me by the arm and helped me to my feet. James then stated, "We've got to get him out, otherwise we're all gonna be in a hell of a lot of danger."

Alan then stated a good fact, "Well, the old boy wouldn't try to kill us now, would it?"

"No," replied Tony as he was still clutching the blood-soaked cloth, "but the curse would." With that, Alan and James glared at each other for a second or two. Alan put my arm over his shoulder. James did the same with my other arm; we then struggled on our way up to the front door; the old boy then opened it as if it knew our predicament; we managed to get outside and out of the gate.

We were nearing the car, and as we did, I then received a bloody strong chest pain; it was the beginning of a heart attack brought on by the poisoning.

I grabbed my chest and fell to the floor once more. Alan wasn't expecting this as I showed no real signs that I was in trouble; he was caught off guard.

I landed hard on the deck, to all intents and purposes, I was clinically dead; my thoughts were still processing though, as my brain still had enough oxygen to keep me going.

The guys just stood over me helpless, none of these lads had any type of medical training whatsoever, so they were helpless in assisting me with any medical attention; all they could do was watch me as my life began to dwindle away, but as this continued, every moment I had left was focussed on that guy in the suit, the one whose face kept zooming in at me was in my head, over and over zooming in and out. Who was this bloke? What's the connection? My oxygen was fading away fast, and so was I. After a few moments, it was all over. I lay there still, for all intents and purposes, I was clinically and medically dead.

Within seconds of my passing, the old boy began to seep out of the ground in vapour form; it solidified around ten feet from where I lay; the guys watched and stepped backwards in disbelief. Slowly, the old boy engulfed my now dead corpse with the same type of force field it used to destroy the skeletons. After a few more moments had elapsed, there was a strange humming sound coming from within this field, slowly the humming grew strong, louder it became, each volume increases produced a colour change from it; soon it was hard to bear as the lads clutched their ears and fell on their knees; the colours of the spectrum passed through the force field, then it vanished; the humming slowly dropped to a simmer, then it too passed away.

I was still lifeless, then without warning the surge of life engulfed my body; I started to breathe at long last.

I then bent forward as if I was doing sit ups, fully alert and energised. I stood up onto my feet, stretched out my arms, gave a yawn and looked around. I could plainly see the look of total disbelief on my mates' faces, but all that mattered was that I was alive and well. I looked around again, my mates were still just glaring at me. "God, Tony, what happened to you?" I gasped, as I saw the blood.

Tony still in a state of shock replied, "Me, what about you, you were dead a minute ago, Pete, now you're talking to me as if nothing had happened."

"Well, in my defence, I don't know what the fuck happened now, do I? I was dead, remember, but I ain't now, so let's get you patched up. Alan, can you go to the boot of the car, I've got a first aid kit in there." Alan too just gazed at me.

"I don't understand any of this, Pete, what on this fucking planet is going on?"

"Look, lads," I said, "whatever has happened, has happened, let's just accept the fact; time as we know it has taken a few days off; the old boy can transport us at any time, we now know it has the power over life and death.

"Alan's a pro in martial arts, I'm telepathic, Tony, well, he seems to be an excellent swordsman, James is our mechanical god, now this is just the start, remember that, so just take what happens with a pinch of salt. I'm sure everything will come clear as, well, excuse the pun, time reveals itself."

"Well, that's easy for you to say, Pete, but we just watched you die and then come back to life."

Alan then said whilst still in shock, "Pete, look, we need time for our brain cells to process stuff like this."

I responded with, "Okay, okay, look, take as much time as you need to process everything, but while you're thinking about it all, I need that first aid box." I threw my car keys over to him.

I had never felt better in my entire life. I felt invulnerable, like I was Superman reborn. I walked over to Tony, and slowly, I removed the now blood-soaked cloth away from his face and placed my fingers around the cut to examine the wound, right, let's have a look at this; as I did so, I could feel a sensation running through my fingers, something was taking place within me as I could plainly see a glowing film of mist leaving my fingers. I was astounded by what I was witnessing but had no idea what was happening.

I couldn't explain it, but the wound on Tony's face was closing in on itself, somehow I had the ability to heal, it was miraculous to say the least; within a few minutes, the cut had completely healed itself.

I turned my hand around and looked at it confounded and confused. Alan came over with the first aid kit and stood there gobsmacked. "What the fuck!" Alan bellowed.

Tony then replied to him, "Pete touched the cut and it healed up. Now if we were in the sixteen hundreds, they would have burnt him as a witch on a stake for what he had just done."

James muttered in astonishment, "It's a miracle, oh my god, if it is a miracle."

I then added, "It's a wonderful old boy miracle. I think we better get the hell out of here, don't you lot?"

Alan threw the car keys back to me and we were soon speeding off down the road wondering what the hell was going to take place from here on in.

As we drove, I asked James, "This Professor War-pen."

"Yeah, what about him?"

"Well, do you have any idea what he actually looks like because I have a strong feeling that I have seen him in my thoughts when I was incapacitated. I kept on seeing these images as if it was on video but without any sound; this bloke's face towards the end of each video kept on enlarging and coming straight up to the camera so to speak; it kept facing me, it was as if he knew I was watching him; he had glasses and a full beard and moustache, thin build, but hang on a second, saying all that the maths don't make sense."

"What do you mean?" James asked.

I responded with, "Well, I first saw this bloke in 1941, he was around thirty years old at the time, then I saw him again in 1961, but if he was born in 1911 that would make him over a 100 years old by now, when did you read about him in that article again, James?"

"Last month if I remember."

"Right, last month," I replied whilst processing my thoughts and calculating. "Oh shit," I blurted out, my brain went into an overdrive with thoughts as the realisation poured out of me. "I have it." I nearly pinched myself for not realising this earlier, how slow do you have to think?

I then continued to speak to the lads, "He has a bloody son then, a son who is carrying on his work. I bet you any money War-pen died in 61, that must have been the start of the explosion I saw, that's what killed him. I'm sure that was what I saw; he has a bloody son."

The realisation was overwhelming. "And his son has now taken over his profession, he has followed in his dad's footsteps. I bet my bottom dollar I'm right."

"Certainly possible," responded James.

Alan then asked a very different kind of question, "I don't want to tip the apple cart, Pete, but something's really bugging me since you were miraculously brought back to life, it just won't let go."

"Okay, Al, what is it?" I asked.

Alan took a few minutes then said, "Why are you alive?"

I looked astounded with what Alan had just said. James also said, "What the fuck, explain that, will ya."

"Look, sorry, but Pete's alive yet Andy's dead, why, that's my question." We all fell silent. I then received a message from the old boy.

"Well, Alan, I can now finally answer that question, the old boy's just this second given me the understanding behind it, to be honest with ya, it's been playing on my mind as well. Andy's body was physically damaged when he received that knife in his back, my body wasn't, that's the sole and only reason as to why and how the old boy got me back."

Alan then said, "Sorry, Pete, I just needed answers, that's all. I had to get it off my chest. I didn't mean to upset anyone."

I again replied to Alan, "It's all right, Al, it's fine, no worries." By now, we were around thirty miles out of York.

As I finished my sentence, I received a feeling in my head; now this feeling even though I knew it was from the old boy, but it was different somehow; it then became clear that it was a warning.

I knew something was wrong, something was about to occur. "Something's on its way, lads."

"What, the old boy's sending you a warning, Pete?" asked James.

"Yeah, it's warning me of something, but I don't know what." I pulled off the road and into a layby that was just ahead of us. I then stepped out of the car, the others followed; we were all on edge, understandably under the circumstances.

We kept searching the area in the hope we would see something; deep down, we were praying that we did not, then from behind some trees, we could see the red curse slowly forming into its solid mass, but it was still transparent. As it hovered and approached, the lads were understandably on edge, they started to jitter about; the curse was now a hundred metres off; it then split itself into three equal parts. "Oh great, this is new!" I called out. "Stay close, boys." As I raised my voice, within moments we were surrounded, the curse then began to spin itself around our position, faster and faster; the pace was becoming incredible.

It was twisting itself on all three sides, encircling all of us as its speed increased; it soon dawned on me as to why it was performing this way, it was attempting to create a tornado. Suddenly, we were all scooped up and flung through time yet again, but now we were thrown a lot further back than ever before, it was 1645, we were near Naseby in Northamptonshire on 14 June; it was in the early hours of the morning shortly before battle would commence between the Roundheads and the Royalist; it was to be a major battle between the two sides, during the English civil war.

And we were now stuck right dead in the middle of two armies, god, did we get some looks from the soldiers on both sides.

Tony was transfixed by what he was seeing, mesmerised by the uniforms and weaponry of the time.

He mentioned the fact that he was into re-enactments. I cried out, "Let's get the fuck off this battlefield!" We took flight running as fast as our legs would carry us; shortly, we had arrived in the trees with a great view of the coming battle.

"That's if you were a historian," James blurted out whilst catching his breath. "What now?"

"I guess we're gonna find out pretty soon." At that moment, there was cannon fire from the Roundhead position, the battle had started.

It was then that Alan noticed. "Where's Tony?" We all looked around. I then caught sight of Tony, he hadn't run when we did as he was still mesmerised by the whole scenario.

I had no choice in the matter, my position was very clear to me as to what I needed to do, I had to try and save him; after all, it was the only good deed left for me to do for him as I blamed myself for his brother's death.

My pace grew as I moved away; running faster, I picked up my pace as I began to run back towards Tony. I shouted, "You two stay there!" By this time, I was running flat out; explosions were erupting all over the place as cannon fire destroyed whatever the cannon balls hit. Craters formed, men dying and or dead, horses and men being blasted out of existence, it was carnage.

I had made it across the ground to where Tony was and shouted at him as I was desperately trying to avoid any projectiles that were traveling in my direction. "What the fuck do you think you're doing?" Tony turned and looked at me with a smile of absolute joy on his face.

"This is awesome, Pete, look at it."

I grabbed him by the arm and shouted at him again, "Come on, you fucking twit, do you want to die out here, think about your brother, now move your fucking arse." I then grabbed him by his arm.

Tony shrugged my arm away as he then looked and said with great surprise to me, "You go, Pete, this is wonderful here, I'm staying." I looked at him like he was completely insane.

I then remarked, "Tony."

Tony immediately looked directly at me with total disdain; he replied, "What?" With that, I produced a stunning right hook to his jaw. Tony fell like a ton of bricks to the ground. I had completely knocked him out.

Without wasting a moment, I grabbed him by his upper arms, threw him onto my shoulder and managed a fireman's carry; hurriedly, I moved back to Alan and James as fast as I was able to. The cannon fire was bloody impressive, but we just didn't have the time to watch and appreciate its glory.

A good five minutes had elapsed as to when I got back. I threw Tony onto the ground as James went up to him. Alan asked me, "You okay?"

I responded, "Yeah, I'm fine, mate, it's that fucking dickhead. Al, he only wanted to stay out there."

Alan looked gobsmacked and replied, "Well, no wonder you hit him, nice punch by the way." James meanwhile was bringing Tony back to life as he heard what I said to Alan; he wasn't impressed with his brother in the slightest.

As Tony recovered, James then gave his brother a lecture as he said to him, "What were you fucking thinking, wanting to stay out there, you lost your fucking brains, Tone? It's a fucking battlefield for fuck's sake; men are dying out there, and you wanted to stay and watch."

Tony looked at his brother and answered, "Sorry, bro, I just lost it." Tony then looked across at me and shouted, "Pete, sorry okay!" As the battle raged on, we watched from the safety of the trees. It was then that I noticed something out of the corner of my eye, turning around to get a better view, I gasped.

"Not again, for god's sake." I then pointed across as the lads looked in the direction to where I was pointing.

James said, "Oh my god."

Alan cried, "Holy shit!"

Then Tony made a lovely phrase. "Those motherfuckers, don't they ever fucking stay dead?" It would have been hilariously funny at another time, but this was not one of those times.

The skeleton soldiers now numbering twenty strong were marching towards our location; they were wearing the uniform of Roundheads; again they were all adorned with all the accompaniments and weaponry; now the only weapons that they were carrying were swords.

We hadn't even had a flick knife, we had nothing whatsoever, but as quickly as we had been taken out of time, weapons miraculously appeared within our grasps, swords and the old favourite, the ball and chain; the ball and chain was mine; the old boy was doing its part in giving us a fighting chance by levelling the playing field. Tony and Alan stepped forward. "Okay, you lot, fall back. Alan and I will do what we can."

Alan then passed his sword over to Tony and said, "I won't be needing that, you take it." Tony then took the sword. Within a second, we had started our second engagement of our own. Alan had skills none of us knew for his martial arts was fantastic. Bruce Lee must have trained him. Tony was swinging two swords now; there wasn't any wild swinging like we would've been doing, for he knew exactly how to use them effectively.

These two guys were really doing a great job but even these two brave soldiers were still heavily outnumbered; we had no choice but to help, so we got stuck in; the problem we had was how do you kill something that can't die. I screamed out, "The head, Tony, decapitate the head! If anyone gets hurt, shout out I will get to you." It was not long before the cries for help started to flow as one by one of my lads received some type of blade wound. At speed whilst doing my bit, I was also managing to get to my mates and placing my hand over and on top of the wounds received, the wounds were immediately repairing themselves.

As I was doing this miracle healing, it was clear that we were being pushed back. "Retreat, lads, fall back!" I shouted. No one had to be told twice.

As before, the skeletons' only weakness was speed so we had plenty of time to withdraw. Now we all remembered how Andy was killed, a knife in the back, this time we retreated facing the enemy. After a few hundred feet, we came across some ruins of a building; we were at this time scattered about to twenty feet apart from each other. James then did something rather unfortunate as he had a hole that was covered up by twigs and branches.

He yelled as he disappeared down into it; we all rushed over to make sure he was okay. Tony shouted, "James, you okay?"

James replied, "Yeah, I'm fine, stupid spot to stick a fucking hole."

"What's down there?" I asked; the drop was so deep none of us could see the bottom of it.

James then continued, "There seems to be some sort of a passageway down here; it's hard to work out; it leads off somewhere. Can someone please tell me how the fuck do I get out of here?"

I quickly remarked, "You're not, we're coming to you."

"We're what!" Tony responded in a surprised fashion.

I then turned to him and stated, "Well, if you want to spend an eternity fighting those skeletons, be my guest." Tony looked across from where we had come from, there the enemy were visibly closing the distance between us.

"After you."

Tony waved his arm in front of himself with a beckoning motion. I think the intention was for me to go first; slowly one by one, we gradually lowered ourselves into the hole. I made absolutely sure that the weapons came with us this time. After five minutes, we were all at the base.

Tony produced his phone and turned on the torch and we then began our reconnoitre; the walls were made of brick so someone had taken a great deal of trouble on this passageway; we walked for at least a mile until we came across some steps leading upwards.

Alan moved ahead of us with sword in hand, ready for any foe, and proceeded up the stairs. Soon we had reached a door that unfortunately was tight shut. I looked at Tony. "Can you get it open, mate?"

"Well, that's an excellent question, Pete, let's see what I can do."

Tony raised his sword as the rest of us moved backwards down the stairs as to allow him more access to swing his heavy double-handled broad sword; after several good wakes on the door, Tony had managed to break the door enough for us to pass through; we were now standing in a large room; scruffy place for whomever had lived here didn't do much cleaning, there was dust everywhere; whoever these people were they must have left in a hurry as there was still fresh food and a decanter of wine still unfastened on the table.

I had a rough idea that these people were probably servants as there was nothing of value to be seen anywhere; the battle up above us was still raging as we could hear more and more sounds of cannon fire; we had moved nearer to the battle instead of further away. I was praying that we did not get caught by either side and that we stayed undetected.

I then turned to James. "Can you take Alan and have a look upstairs, and whatever you two do, don't let anyone see you." The two of them moved off; we waited patiently for their return as Tony and the rest of us enjoyed a few bits and a glass of wine; it wasn't that bad as it goes. After a short period of time, they returned, each carrying a reasonably sized barrel.

"What you got there" asked Tony.

James then commented, "Gunpowder what else for this time period; there's tons of the stuff up there; one of those sides above us must be using this place to store its explosives."

"Explosives," I blurted out. After a moment had passed, I said, "Right then, okay, James, you take one down the passageway and blow it to pieces. I don't want those skeletons coming up on us from behind."

"Al, give us a hand," James asked; once more the two of them went off.

The rest of the lads followed me as I went towards the room where the gunpowder was stored. James was right, the room was full of the same type of barrels, at least twelve feet high; at a guess, I would say roughly close to around 500 tons of the stuff.

"Now no one smoke for god's sake." I sniggered. At that moment, I could hear two voices coming from up above; they grew louder as they were approaching our location. "Quick, hide," I whispered.

Shortly after that, these two Roundheads appeared and proceeded to grab a couple of barrels; they left the area, and we in turn came out of hiding. "Fucking hell, that was a close shave," I remarked.

Shortly, James and Alan returned to us. "Thought you were going to blow the passage," I said in a confusing manner.

"You can't blow this gunpowder, Pete, if the powder's wet," Alan replied.

I then replied to him, "What, both of them?" Alan nodded in agreement. "Oh terrific," I responded. "Right, let's see what's happening outside, shall we."

The noises from outside had seemed to stop; keeping our weapons close, we approached the front door; opening the door, we were taken by complete surprise for we were not at Naseby anymore, the weather was ice cold, probably minus six or seven; snow lay thickly on the ground, trees were white; basically, everywhere had snow on it. *Where on earth are we now*, I thought to myself, *and for that matter, what year is it?* "Let's walk on, lads, who knows we may see a landmark that one of us recognises." So that was exactly what we need, another second passed and then it dawned on me, our weaponry had disappeared with the last time jump, none of us had actually realised that they were missing, strange. Anyway, there were some houses that lay ahead of us; they at least looked modern so I knew we were close to our own time period, that was something. We turned the corner; there on the horizon, less than two miles away, we finally got the confirmation as to where we were, we were looking straight towards a stunning view of Dover Castle. Thank God.

"Come on, lads, get warm." With that remark, I quickened the pace to a brisk walk.

As we continued our stroll, Alan whispered to me, "Pete, if the curse had taken all that effort to transport us 400 years back into the past, then bring us here, surely, it's not going to stop its games just like that."

I twisted around to him and said, "Who says it's stopped, just because it has not attacked us for a while, bet you, it's got something ready for us. Questions are where and when will it come from; we just need to be more alert than we've ever been before, come on, let's just keep moving." By this time, I had fallen back a few feet so I was in last position as Alan moved up to chat to the twins; as we carried on with our glorious trek, I could hear a faint whisperings coming from behind our position.

I turned to see if or what it was, it was the old boy. I sighed with relief and stopped; a few seconds later, the lads realised I was not with them; they then too stopped and came back to me.

I was standing there looking at the old boy. It then came nearer to me and I mean inches away, our noses were nearly touching; we were that close I thought at any second it was going to try and give me a kiss.

We were seriously that close. It spoke softly. "Be aware, be aware, the demon be near, aware, the Peter, aware, aware."

I then responded with, "Where is this demon going to attack us?" The old boy then slowly raised his arm and with its finger it pointed to the castle on the hill. It then stated, "Dover Castle, the Dover, be alert, be aware, the Peter, be aware, all." And like a puff of smoke, the old boy left us.

Alan then said, "Well, at least we now know, that's a first." My mind proceeded to try and break down the new information. "Why tell us where the red curse is going to attack?" The old boy has never passed information like that on to me before, so why now? Alan was right, it has never done this in the past. I wonder what it means.

"One thing's for sure, it's going to be bloody dangerous for all of us." I spoke to the lads in a very reassuring manner. "Come on, lads, let's show this bloody thing how to kick arse, shall we." I then broke into a song, the guys looked at me amused; within seconds, we were all singing away, blasting out at the top of our lungs, glory, glory, hallelujah; what a beautiful song; our sound must have made everyone run away from the area.

It was dreadful to be honest; not one of us could sing to save our lives, but who really gave a shit, we were having some fun.

We were off with renewed vigour as we proceeded to Dover Castle, only there would the old boy reveal what the red curse had in store for us; after ten minutes had passed, we were finally at the entrance to Dover Castle.

No one was home at the entrance gate, this wasn't normal practice, people pay here to enter the grounds, so where was the staff? We passed the hut and walked inside; there weren't even visitors, no sound, no birds flying overhead.

"No wonder the old boy had warned us; something seriously is about to happen here, I can feel the stress building up within my chest," Alan said. Guess everyone had gone on holiday and that included the animals and birds; there was not even the sound of children running up the embankments. "This ain't good, Pete."

Looking towards him, I simply muttered, "Keep alert, Alan. Tony, James, you too, stay alert, I don't like this one fucking bit." I had never known this great castle to have ever been as abandoned as it now stood; as my thoughts were going into overdrive, we carried on walking; the sun was still shinning so that in itself was a blessing. I was walking along in front with Alan as Tony and James followed a few feet back; no one had anything to say at this point, but their thoughts were pondering on the warning we got from the old boy, 'be aware, be aware', but aware of what, that was the haunting question.

Every noise that sounded made us all twist and turn around to see what was causing it; we were all becoming nervous wrecks at this point. As Alan and I were walking forward, James then whispered to his brother, "Tone, look, do you fancy doing a runner? This whole situation ain't good, I'm fucking shifting a brick."

Tony responded, "Grow a pair, James, how the fuck can we leave those two here alone? I couldn't live with myself, and neither could you." It wasn't long before we noticed our archenemy raise its ugly head once more.

Walking forwards, the ground started to shudder, a crack appeared within some concrete that lay along the ground. I then stated, "Here we go, lads." The red curse as before raised itself through the crack as a deep red vapour, spurting out like an eruption; debris flew everywhere as it raised itself a good twenty feet into the air; it then began to widen its mass, gradually spreading two metres in width and height; it was roughly 50 metres off from our position. As it was gaining ground on us, it became blatantly clear that it was reducing the distance between us.

My mates started to move backwards a few steps, but I stood my ground. I had had enough of running from this poxy entity. I then started to shout at the thing, "Hoy, arsehole, you don't scare me, why don't you just fuck off?" Its colour grew darker at that point as if it understood what I was saying to it; a stronger blood-red developed; this thing was now seriously pissed; it shrieked an evil cringing noise in anger; lightning bolts were now being thrown at us but not precisely directed, as they seemed to be random like its targeting system was off line.

The lightning blasts when hit the walls, they were causing small craters as splinters of stone and mortar sprawled around like shrapnel. I stood there laughing at it and shouted, "You couldn't hit a barn door, you piece of shit."

Tony shouted at me, "Peter, what're you doing, you're deliberately trying to piss it off." Then the red curse got even darker in colour. Now I had never thought for one second it could become as mad as I had got it, for its accuracy began to improve; lightning bolts were still heading towards us and now getting bloody close.

I then started to step backwards. "Let's get to the war tunnels, lads." We started running at top speed; again the lightning bolts continually rained down on us; the red curse was like a baby having a screaming tantrum; its volume was intensifying. Faster we ran but it kept its pace. In hindsight, I should've kept my big mouth shut. Hurriedly, we turned a corner.

As we did the manoeuvre, I lost my footing and tripped over my own feet. James came rushing over to help me. I screamed at him, "Get the fuck down those tunnels!" James stopped and then did what I asked him to do; as he followed the others, I then stood up and faced the hideous thing. "Come on, you bastard, I'm sick of this shit, you want me then come on, finish it you tub of crap." I then received a tremendous blast as a bolt of energy struck me. I could only describe it as lighting; it bashed me in the chest, as I stumbled backwards but stayed on my feet. "Come on!" I screamed, more and more lightning bolts struck me in the chest, but they were not damaging me, the old boy had somehow made me virtually indestructible; the guys were watching in amazement from a safe distance as they had by now reached the war tunnels. They stood there watching my battle in disbelief as I was managing to shrug off each of its lightning bolt attacks.

Without warning, another red entity came from over the top of the war tunnels from behind us; the curse had split itself into two separate parts, a trick it had done some time ago.

Tony noticed it first, he grabbed the others' attention, and within a nano second, they were in full-on panic as they rushed away; the only way though was straight ahead towards my position; they had to run, but they had very little choice for there was nowhere else to go. As they ran, the lightning bolts were still whacking into my chest. "Is that all you have, you bastard!" I screamed at this demonic thing once more; it was at this moment that any ideas that I was going to plan went haywire; the curse had a change of heart, for it re-evaluated it's aiming power, my friends were now being focussed on. I was no longer its target. I turned and shouted at them at the exact moment I realised what was taking place, "Get down, get the fuck down." At that moment, a lightning bolt struck and plunged itself into James's stomach; the blast was so strong that it immediately lifted him off his feet and threw him up and away into the air like a kite.

Flung with tremendous power and speed for at least thirty feet, the only thing that prevented him traveling further was the stonewall that he had landed up against; he was impaled against the wall. We just stood there; the horror of our situation was clear to see on our faces as the wall took most of the blast with some debris falling away; the poor sod was impaled by the now solidified bolt;

it had resembled a javelin by design. James was dead; we stood there helpless as the curse reached us.

We were only three. At that moment, the old boy reappeared from nowhere; it immediately placed itself in a position that it could defend. God, was I pleased to see it show up; it began blasting away with some sort of powerful beam of energy; the curse reformed back into one then vanished back into the concrete from where it appeared; we were now out of danger, but the cost was great, our second team member had been murdered. How much more could I take, when would this nightmare end?

The old boy came slowly across to us and said, "The aware it was all for, the Peter not alone, time is losing. Ramsgate must you, Ramsgate." The old boy then stumbled forward. I felt emotion towards it for the first time. I couldn't believe it, I was actually caring for it; the entity was starting to grow weak, now this was a first. "Where in Ramsgate?" I asked; before it could answer, it vanished.

We were alone once more. I turned and faced Tony. "Tony, I don't know what to say to you, mate, I'm so sorry." Tony didn't answer me as he just walked over to his lifeless brother, who was still impaled up on the wall.

Alan came across to me. "Leave it, Pete, can't you see he's completely out of it, he's upset; now leave it."

"But it's my fault, I was so full of my own self-importance that I didn't realise that the warning was regarding us all. Like a dick, all I thought of was that the warning was directed for me and me alone. Al, I will never let you down again." I tried once again to talk to Tony, who by this time had tears streaming down his face. "Tony, can I talk to you?"

"Fuck off, Pete, as far as I'm concerned, it was you that killed him, if you hadn't got that thing so pissed maybe my brother wouldn't be hanging up there, don't want to talk to ya, leave me alone."

"Tony," I tried again to start a chat with him. Tony then turned and landed a right punch that connected to my jaw. I hit the ground hard.

I rubbed my chin then stood up off the floor. "Okay, Tony, I deserved that."

Alan came over and asked if I was okay. "What do we do now?" he asked.

"There's only one thing we can do," I replied.

Alan then said, "What's that?"

I responded, "Simple, we go to Ramsgate. It's gonna take us at least a day to walk there, god, I wish I had my bloody car."

Once more, the old boy transported us; this time, we were on the outside of the castle ground, and to my astonishment, my car was there waiting for us. "Okay, Alan, jump in, let's start to make a move, mate, I've had enough of this place." Alan jumped into the car. Turning to Tony, who was wandering around in a daze, I said, "Tony, we're off to Ramsgate now, mate."

Tony twisted around and faced me as he said, "My journey ends here, I'm not coming with you."

Tony then turned his back and began his trek back to his dead brother's body. I looked on helplessly as I watched Tony slowly walk away; it was heart breaking. After a few moments, Alan asked, "What's Tony doing, Pete?"

"I'm afraid, it's just you and me now, Alan. Tony's not coming with us anymore."

Tony's journey ended when his brother was taken. I then just for a few moments completely lost it as I started to bash the steering wheel in frustration and anger. "I should've seen this coming, Al, I should've seen it coming."

"Well, how the hell were you supposed to know, mate, you had as much idea as the rest of us; we were tricked; you were tricked. We were all led to believe that you were being the one threatened then at the last moment it focussed on James; you were then just a decoy; it chose who it was going to focus on; it focussed on James; it could've turned on anyone of us, but James was in the line of fire; he was just bloody unlucky, that's the bottom line. Now come on, let's get out of here."

"Thanks Al." Continuing our drive, I started to speed up a little. "You know something, Al, I have been a total idiot."

"What do you mean?" Alan replied.

"I have spent all this time right up until Andy died thinking that once I had found my five guys that would be it, wouldn't need any more for they were gonna be with me till the end of whatever this is, but no, now we've to find another three idiots who may well die before the end."

"Who knows what's ahead of us, don't beat yourself up, mate; at the end of the day, we're gonna beat this bloody thing. Just keep holding on to that great thought, we're gonna beat it. Saying that, how far is it to Ramsgate exactly?"

I replied, "Half an hour's drive, give or take, depends on traffic really. You know, Alan, during that episode when I was dead, sounds bloody stupid saying that, but those images I saw were so vivid, it was like an out of body experience, or was I a ghost peering in?"

"Must have been scary for ya," replied Alan.

"Yeah, it was, but it was also intoxicating watching people from the past. Following every move, but this bloke, this War-pen guy, now he must have been really bloody intelligent for the work he was doing; you could say he was the father of trans warp technology seeming his son has just recently invented that device, can't think what the bloody thing's called now, oh, that's a point. Alan, is it still in the glovebox?" Alan had a look inside it.

"Yep, it's there, thank god for that." Alan then carried on our decent conversation. "Well, thinking about this device, yeah, you could say his dad was the father as without his work his boy wouldn't have been able to do what he did; let's hope we meet this guy before it's too late."

We gave each other a glance. As we passed a road sign, Alan stated, "Hey, look five miles to Ramsgate." Alan began to grow excited at last and I wasn't that far behind. "You know something, Pete?"

"What's that?" I asked.

"Well, we don't know a damn thing about each other. Have you got kids? Wife? Where do you live?"

"Hey, slow down," I answered, "those are three questions, let's take 'em one at a time. Yeah, well, I have five kids, and yes, I do have a wife, her name's Tracy, and I live in Tonbridge, Kent, your turn."

"Well, exactly the same as you, wife called Lisa. I've three kids and I'm living in Basildon Essex. Well, that was pretty painless I must say."

"Yeah, I enjoyed that," I stated, "We're coming up to Ramsgate shortly."

"Oh, goody, goody," joked Alan.

I glanced at him and said, "Oh, goody goody?" Alan grinned as we continued on our merry way.

"Do you know Ramsgate at all, Pete?" Alan asked.

"I know it a bit, I had to travel here regular some years back, yeah, I know a few places; let's go down to the harbour, you never know we might get lucky and pull a couple of birds." Alan began chuckling.

"Yeah, how bloody lucky it will be, a couple of ugly seagulls." Laughter rippled through the car. After a further five minutes of driving, we came upon the town harbour, beautiful glistening sea as the sun shone upon it, some decent boats lay tightly tied up, a few hundred people strolling around. Alan remarked, "Must be lovely at night here."

"Yeah, it has its moment."

We parked up and got out of the car. Alan then stated, "Oh shit, have you any change on ya?"

I replied with, "Only a few quid, not much really, why?"

"Well, we have to get a ticket otherwise it will be a fine if a warden shows up."

I replied with, "Sod the warden, we get a ticket then the old boy can pay for it." Again, we found some humour. So without further ado, we walked away and left the car in the car park. Walking down the pier were easily half a dozen fishermen waiting to grab a bite as their rods were cast full out. As we approached, I asked one of them, "They biting today?"

"Not a bloody sausage," the guy responded.

"Keep plugging away, mate, keep on plugging away." We moved off.

Alan looked ahead and at the end of the pier stood a building in the ship of a ship. He asked me, "What's that place ahead of us then, Pete?"

"It's a restaurant, mate."

"Really?" Alan replied.

Chapter 5
Welcome to the Party

We moved across to a little coffee shelter. I asked for two mochas; taking our coffees, we then continued on our own personal tour; it wasn't long before we knew why we were here for as we manoeuvred our way back from off the pier we witnessed a commotion taking place within the chip shop that stood close to 200 feet away. The chippy stood virtually opposite the pier entrance; we thought to ourselves, *Nah, we won't get involved with it.* We had cottoned on as to not getting involved with other people's problems; it was none of our business.

We carried on walking past the chippy whilst we did our level best not to eavesdrop or look inside. As we were on the verge of passing completely past the chippy window, a large rubber fish, think it was a pike, came hammering through it; the toughened glass shattered everywhere, millions of pieces flung through the air; we got covered, luckily enough, Alan wasn't cut. I shouted out, "What the fuck!"

Alan at the same time yelled, "Fucking hell!"

As if we didn't have enough on our plates, all we saw because by this time we hadn't a choice but to look through the gaping hole, we watched as a brawl was unfolding between three guys; it was two against one. Alan and myself looked at each for a moment. "Well, what do you think, Al?"

Alan knew exactly what I was referring to and said, "Well, it's not our problem really, Pete, but it certainly looks like he's in need of some assistance."

That precise moment, this bloody stranger pounced through the window and onto us; he totally caught us both off guard as the three of us hit the deck. After we all came to our senses, the stranger spoke. "Cheers, lads, I was hoping I'd have a rather soft landing." Alan and I chuckled at each other. I thought to myself, *The downright gall of this bloke, the cheek of it all.* We took an immediate liking to this stranger, so there we were, the three of us sitting in a pond of broken glass with hands on knees; the two guys that he was fighting with were standing inside the chippy; seeming they were both wearing aprons, I took a wild guess as I believed they were staff.

As they looked out of the now non-existent window, they too found the funny side of the whole situation.

Rising to our feet, I stated, "Well, that was a grand entrance, I must say."

He replied with, "Yeah, you showed up in the nick of time, my name's Geoff, by the way, you are?"

"Hi, Geoff," I politely answered him. "I'm Peter and this ugly brute is Alan."

"Hiya, and not so much of the ugly brute, you tit." Alan cheerfully gave a slight wave.

I then asked, "So, what you doing here then, day trip, or you visiting someone or something?"

Geoff then replied with a puzzled expression on his face, "I wish, I'm not quite sure at the moment to be perfectly honest with ya, can't work out what's happening. I appeared out of the blue inside that chippy virtually on top of the cash till, then within seconds, I had those two jumping all over me, well, more like pouncing all over me."

"What do you mean, just appeared?"

"What you a magician or something then?" Alan remarked whilst taking the piss out of Geoff's so-called story.

"Well, yeah, I must be for I was sitting down with a couple of beers, just about to watch TV. England were about to kick off in a friendly against France, bloody France would you credit it, for god's sake.

"It was then that I saw this mist appear, it came straight out of the tv. I thought I had a fire starting up, so I got up, now here's the really strange part, and you're not going to believe this for a second, cause this mist thing then started to encircle my legs. For a moment, I thought that I was daydreaming.

"I rubbed me eyes, next thing I knew, bang, a flash of something red, and here I was."

I then quickly asked, "It touched you, you just said, did the mist try to talk to you at any point?"

Geoff replied in a very unsure manner, "What do you mean talked to me, how can a mist talk, you've been watching too much sci-fi, Pete." Geoff naturally had no idea as to the situation he had become involved with, which was totally and completely understandable.

I then asked, "Look, okay, okay, besides the sci-fi, which I do enjoy by the way, now it was definitely a mist in the room with you?"

"Yeah, I just told you that, it was just before I got here. Look, Pete, I would really love to know what's going on, that's if you know something. I just want some answers as to what the hell is happening, that's all, what's happened to me, that's all I'm after."

Geoff was totally confused and so he should be. So, I began as good as an explanation as I could. "Okay, right, I will try and be as brief as I can, right, here goes, you've been transported here by a thing we've come to know as the old boy, it's a friendly entity. Now I don't know why it's helping us at the moment, but it is; you also have a second entity that's not so nice, as a matter of fact, it's a killer; it's killed two of our friends so far. Now somewhere in this future, we, well, I say we loosely, there's me and five others; we do or whatever to this thing in our now future, so it's trying to destroy us before we accomplish our task. Whatever that may be, right, so now you know."

Geoff then looked at Alan and asked, "Is he for real, Alan, was what he just said for real?"

Alan responded with, "Afraid so, Geoff." By this time, Geoff was considerably uneasy with what he had just been told.

He then stated, "Oh right, well, now I know, thanks a bunch." He was more confounded than before. "So I'm stuck in some sort of a revenge fuckup?"

Alan then joined in with, "I say, I think the man's got it, give this man a cigar." After Alan took the piss out of Geoff, he then moved into a more serious mode. "Yeah, it's a revenge against us, as Peter's just said; we don't know the ins and out of whatever the future has in store just yet, but we will soon enough, you can be sure about that."

Geoff then stated a fact, "Well, I guess because I'm here I'm a part of whatever this is."

"Welcome to the party, Geoff," I keenly said, then I followed it up with, "Shall we get moving?" So, now we were back to three members once again.

Geoff then mentioned, "Shit, how am I going to pay for this window damage?"

Alan responded with, "Well, who threw the fish?"

"He did." Geoff pointed to one of the employees that he had the confrontation with.

"Then it's not your worry, come on, where to, Pete, you know the area better than us." At that moment, the telepathic hotline began ringing in my head once more.

"Thank god, it wasn't as painful as it used to be."

Geoff asked, "What's up with Pete?" Alan then mentioned the fact that the mist and Peter were in some way connected and that this was part of the process. "Must be fun," Geoff quipped.

"Saying that though, you okay, Pete?" Alan asked whilst placing his hand on my shoulder.

"Yeah, just takes a little time to get used to these links. I'm being told to go over to the Margate Caves now."

"Any ideas as to why?" asked Alan.

I responded with, "Not a damn clue, mate. I guess, we've gone back to the days of crap information."

"Crap information, what does that mean, Al?" Geoff asked.

"Well, mate, this mist, entity, whatever you want to call it, only communicates in little pieces of info, a bit here, a bit there, we never get the full SP, in some ways it feels at times that there are like two entities trying to outwit the other, but one thing's for certain, they're at war and we're the combat troops.

"Now for some unfathomable reason, Peter's been made the general, again, we don't know what he does or doesn't do in the future.

"That's the real puzzle for us to solve." It wasn't long before we were back in the car.

"Wow, nice wheels, who owns this little beauty?" Geoff asked.

In defensive mode and without thinking, I snapped, "I do, why?"

"Okay, mate, I was only asking, chill man," Geoff apologised.

"Sorry, Geoff, but I seem to be just a tad overprotective when it comes to this car. I've had her for so long, she's my baby." I grinned and started the engine, destination this morning time, Margate Caves.

Ramsgate and Margate were neighbours so to speak; they're only around five miles apart, so within no time at all, we were nearly at our destination, driving through west gate at a steady 40; we soon arrived in Margate.

The sea lay to our left side; passing the railway station to our left, we came to traffic lights and carried on as they were showing green, up the hill, which again bearing over to the left, at the top the road it had a reasonably sharp bend to it; there ahead a few hundred yards up were the caves.

I parked as close as I could; we all got out and moved on foot towards the caves; at the entrance lay a small shop on the land that stood directly over the caves themselves; you could buy all sorts there, you know, memorabilia type, from pencils to ornamental pieces, trinkets and postcards, that sort of stuff. It was evident to us that you also had to pay to enter these caves, now guess what, we were not told about that.

We went up to the counter to see what the prices were, but to our amazement, there was no staff, now this we were really starting to accept as the norm, not a single sausage was in the shop; we waited for a few moments, but no one came, so we gave up. Geoff then happily stated, "Oh fuck, this for a game of soldiers, let's go caving, gentlemen."

Without wasting time, Geoff moved off down a single passageway as we then followed close behind; there was full electrical power to this cave, so that was a lovely sight to see; the passage seemed reasonably long and narrow with slight twists to it as the ground slowly dropped lower into the earth; it was certainly big enough for us though; we reached the end and the cave then opened up in all its glory.

It was a massive chamber, probably over a 100 metres high and the same in width and depth; it was big; there were a few areas that were blocked off; this was done within the last ten years as the material used was brick and mortar, the cave's walls were of chalk; we could see drawing on the walls from time to time. The three of us slowly separated but still kept in close proximity to each other; it was excellent, the air seemed a little thin, but well, breathable so no issues there.

Geoff called over, "Eh, look at this." As he looked down, Alan and I walked over; there was a pit or a hole in the ground, surrounded by a small two foot high wall, above and screwed down over it was an iron mesh. Geoff then commented, "I suppose they did not want anyone to fall down it. It must have been bloody deep as we couldn't see the bottom of it."

That told me it had to be at least 30 feet deep. "Fancy falling down there?" stated Alan.

"No, thanks, mate, rather not," I replied.

Geoff then said, "You fall down there, you're in a world of hurt as you're not getting out." The idea of falling down in that pit gave us all the willies.

We moved away with our own thoughts. "I wonder what they used it for," said Geoff.

I then came back with, "Well, I would possibly say that it was either used as a loo, or maybe it was a type of prison of sorts." At that moment, I could hear a faint noise coming from somewhere around from where we were. Geoff and Alan heard it too after a few seconds had past.

"Can you make it out?" Alan asked me.

"No, no, I can't."

"Where's it coming from?" Geoff asked.

I then said, "Let's find out, split up, boys." Geoff moved back over in the direction of the pit as I and Alan went in different directions.

"Hmmmm, lads, I think I know where it's coming from." Geoff raised his voice slightly.

"Where?" I called.

Then Geoff said, "Down there." He pointed to the pit.

"Oh, no, you're bloody kidding me." Alan was not impressed.

We gathered around the pit once more. Geoff shouted down, "Hello, anyone down there, hello!" No sound came from below, except the echo from his own voice. He then tried again. "Hello, if you can hear me, make a sound, hello!" Still no sound came from within except his echo once again.

I then stated to Geoff, "Har, this is shit; it must have been the wind or something you heard, Geoff, there's nothing down there. Come on, let's keep—"

At that moment, I was interrupted by a single word that sent shivers through our bodies. "HELP!"

"Oh shit, there was someone down there, after all." Geoff knelt down and started to communicate with whomever was down there.

"We're gonna try and get you out!"

"It's too deep for that," came the voice from below.

"Any ideas, lads?" Geoff asked.

Alan asked Geoff a really good question. "Ask him how he got down there in the first place, will ya, cause he never went through this grate."

I in turn then stated, "Bloody hell, Alan, good question."

Geoff then called down again, "Can you tell me, how did you get down there in the first place?" No reply came from below so Geoff repeated his question, then he repeated it for a third and final time of throwing down the same question.

Finally came a reply, but not the reply we were expecting. "I didn't."

I then spoke, this guy has to be confused. "Listen to what I'm saying to you, mate, who or what put you in this hole?"

Then this guy started to make sense. "I don't know how I got in here, no bloody idea, but please for god's sake, please get me out." The stranger was getting upset at this point, well, who could blame him?

I then said, "Right, lads, have a look around, see what you can find, we need to get this grid off. Alan, hang on second thoughts, can you and Geoff pop back upstairs and try to find a screwdriver, if not, I've got a few in the car, here take these." I then threw my car keys to Alan for he timely caught them extremely well; off the two went. I then knelt down over the grate and spoke loudly. "We are going to try and move the grate off this pit; we're going to be as quick as we can, how long have you been down there?"

The voice cried back, "Feels like hours, lost track of time. It's so bloody dark down here."

"Okay, mate, look, try and answer this question, how did you get down there in the first place, would it have anything to do with a mist or fog?"

The voice replied with, "How did you know about the mist? I was the only one there."

"Don't worry about that now, we're gonna get you out, just take it easy." Just then, Alan and Geoff returned at the same time. Geoff took a screwdriver from Alan as the pair immediately got to work unscrewing the grate from its fixings.

After a struggle, the grate was free; all three of us then took a grip each and lifted it off and away from the pit, but one major problem then raised its head, as the hole was pretty deep, how on earth were we to get this guy out of there?

I looked at Alan and said, "Well, whoever this guy is, he's with us now."

"With us now, what do you mean by that?" Alan remarked.

"He's aware of the mist," I replied.

"Ha, right, got ya." Alan gave a sigh and then muttered under his breath, "Another one for the chopping block."

Geoff heard his remark and answered back, "What do you mean by that?"

Alan then turned and faced me, we looked at each other for a second, as I then responded to Geoff, "It was only a figure of speech, Geoff, don't worry about it, now let's deal with this, any ideas, lads?"

Alan came up with a fantastic idea. "How about a human ladder?"

"Yeah," Geoff responded, "we could also tie some of our clothing to give us some extra depth."

"Sounds good to me, okay, who is taking off his shirt then?"

Geoff piped up, "Well, you two are wearing shirts, I ain't."

"Well, Alan, looks like we've pulled the short straw on this one." As I finished my line, we started to remove our shirts and bind them together.

Alan said, "I hope this holds together; if it does, it'll give us at least three extra feet."

I then stated, "Right then, we're all around six feet, give or take an inch or so, with the clothing we've got around twenty odd feet."

"Twenty odd," Alan said astounded, "where did you learn to count."

I then reminded him, "You do have the arms' lengths as well or has that slipped that little brain of yours?"

"Har, yeah, I forgot, sorry," Alan respectfully apologised.

"Okay, who is the strongest out of us three?" I asked.

We gazed at each other for a few more minutes, then Geoff opened his mouth, "Oh, what the heck, I will go first." He then took the clothing and began to get into position for lowering himself down the pit, head first.

Alan looked at me and asked, "Do you think this is a good idea, Pete?"

I replied, "No, I don't, but if you have a better suggestion, I will be happy to go with it, well." Alan shook his head to say no. I then stated, "Right, once Geoff has got halfway down, Al, grab his ankles. I will do the same with you. Geoff, once you're down there, get the bloke to jump up and climb."

We started the descent, slowly but surely, we were closing the gap between him and us; after roughly five minutes, the task was starting to feel impossible as the weight of each other was becoming far too strenuous; the effort it was taking began to take its toll on our arms; it was then that I felt the wall begin to crumble; the bricks were beginning to crack and fall away under the strain of my body pushing against it. "No!" I cried out as the wall by this time was virtually cracking to pieces; the wall then fully caved in on itself. I screamed out again, "Quick grab him, Geoff, for fuck's sake, grab him." At that moment, I finished my last word; it was too late; before we knew it, the three of us were falling down this hole.

Within seconds in a heap, we landed with a bloody tremendous crash as our bodies virtually fell onto one another, thank the gods, none of us were badly hurt by the fall.

"Everyone okay?" I asked. Everyone acknowledged that they were okay; the lads had suffered some bruising as some were visible on Alan's cheek as well as Geoff's eye. Alan put their torch buttons on his mobile; we had light; we finally caught our first glimpse of our new recruit. "Well, hello, sorry, but that was not supposed to happen," I said.

"Really, I had no idea, my name's Rob, by the way, thanks for the try. Looks like we're all fucked now."

"No way," I answered, "there has to be a way out of here, one way or another, there has to be a way out."

Hurriedly, I introduced each other to Rob. "I'm Pete, Alan, Geoff." It was like I was late catching the number 9 bus, I then started tapping on the walls. Alan then stated the plain facts of our situation.

"Pete, what you doing, mate, there's no hidden passage or a hidden door down here, just admit it we're fucked."

I was not going to accept our fate lying down as I blurted out, "There's no bloody way we are trapped down here; we have not come this far to be taken out like this. I'm going to try and call for help." Rob then laughed.

"Who you going to call, god?"

"No," I responded, "I'm calling the old boy, you know it better as the mist."

Rob then reacted in a very nervous way, as Alan witnessed his reaction he said, "Rob, calm down, mate, it's all right, this mist has become like a companion for us, when we find we're in deep trouble, it always gets us out of the stew pot."

I then closed my eyes and prayed that the old boy would hear my call. "If you can hear me, we need your help." I opened my eyes and stood there waiting.

Rob then started a conversation with Alan. "Pete does not really think that a mist is as intelligence, does he?"

"You don't understand as yet, Rob, but give it time, you will."

Rob went on to say, "I think someone better tell me what's going on here, my world's been turned upside down.

"I'm somehow zapped from a lovely meal at my local restaurant with my girlfriend and thrown into this shithole for hours, and now I've got you trying to have a conversation with a fog."

"Yeah," I answered, "look, I can see where you're coming from, it's a very long story."

"Well, I'm not going anywhere now, am I, so, I'm all ears, fire away," replied Rob eagerly.

"Alan, you explain it to him, will ya?" I asked.

"Oh, thanks a bunch," Alan replied. I then began testing the walls once again, as I did, Geoff decided to rest his arm against the sidewall; he stumbled forward as his entire arm just disappeared within the wall, within a micro-second, he had pulled his arm back out of it.

He was shitting himself as he was really shaken up as he muttered, "What the fucking hell happened there? Have we just found our way out?" Okay, it was not the way out we had hoped for, but nevertheless, it would free us from this hole we were trapped in.

Every one of us was dubious about what was to follow as they all knew what was going to happen.

I started the ball rolling by saying, "Okay, lads, I'm going through first, that's our way out."

Alan then said, "Pete, let's just think about this for a moment; this may well be a trap, you have to consider that."

I then replied to his concerns, "Alan, trust me, I know what I'm doing, trust me."

I passed through the wall; once I had reached the other side, one by one the others came through and followed, first Alan, then Geoff and lastly Rob; we were all safe and sound, to our astonishment, we weren't on our planet earth anymore, we had been struck dumb, confusion was rife.

We were phase shifted into an animated world, but then saying that, you wouldn't be wrong if you thought you were in a cartoon.

We were now looking around in total shock and disbelief; the trees were pink, elephants were dancing on the branches, the sky was a horrible orange colour. I can best describe this world like someone had administered hallucinogenic drugs into our blood system; we had entered another system or universe maybe, or perhaps a world of nothing but fantasy.

We were still looking around; the one thing you noticed virtually straightaway was the fact that there were no birds in the sky, not a single one, absolute silence fell around us; the colours that we naturally would associate with were all wrong to us, you take the grass, now it was blue, the sky was an orange as I just mentioned, then you had those trees, even the sun was a dark pink colour; everything we knew about life was totally different here. The four of us just slowly walked off staring at everything that our eyes came in contact with.

We had emerged into this world from a gigantic willow tree that we had somehow come through, this would have to be marked as our entry position.

Rob was the first to speak. "Someone wake me up please."

Alan then remarked, "You can say that again, this is one weird shithole." We carried on examining the area in the hope of making sense of this strange new world. I then made a point to the others as I said, "Well, the laws of gravity don't exist here, so it's perfectly reasonable to presume that the laws of physics don't apply either, ergo, every law that we have been taught no longer applies."

Every kind of animal from earth was here though, but they just weren't in the right colour format, they were either a different colour or they were doing abnormal things like the elephants we had seen earlier.

We were coming upon a clearing that overlooked a brown sea; the water was calm and placid in places but choppy and stormy in others, like a gigantic thick line was separating them, weird, man. To our immediate right lay a massive orange building with aluminium tins sticking out of the framework; now these tins looked like tins of baked beans, and as we looked at this building harder, we could see instead of spires on the rooftops, shipwrecks were visible; the windows on the building were scattered all over the place in triangular shapes; further along as we scanned away from the building was another lawn, again blue in colour, and there in the middle of this blue lawn sat a bloke, but again, this just was not right, for he was sitting at a desk, in itself, no issue, but the desk and chair were the size you would expect to see at an infant school back in the day; they were tiny and this bloke, well, he looked normal, when I say normal, I meant to say that he looked human and not animated, but then saying that, what is normal in and around a world such as this one?

As we tried to gather our thoughts and watched this strange man, across the lawn marched another guy, this bloke was more military, more upright than the first figure; he approached us. Alan then muttered as he assumed, "He's got a butler, the lucky beggar."

We began to walk cautiously over towards these two strange people, Rob then asked me, "Do you think they're human beings or something else, Pete? This is just like the twilight zone. I'm really, and I mean really struggling to come to terms with this place."

"Well, I don't believe you're alone thinking that, Rob."

We continued walking; the guy who was marching towards us was dressed in black and white; he looked like a penguin; he then turned from his seated colleague and started to approach us; he had one seriously bad limp on his left side, now his movements were jerky. I was now beginning to ponder on the question, was this guy human or was he some kind of Android of sorts. I guess we'll find out which he was soon enough. Soon we were face to face. "Good evening, I am the colonel, Colonel Smithers; how can I assist you, gentlemen?"

"Well, hello, my name's Peter, Peter Tate, this is Alan Stoppage," I said as I pointed him out. "This chap here is Geoff."

Geoff looked at me, then took the initiative and gave his introduction, "Geoff Townsend, nice to meet ya." Then Rob stepped forward.

"Hi, Rob Walker."

Introductions over, the colonel asked, "Would you care for a P?"

"Sorry, say that again?" I was thrown aback with surprise, what a weird thing to say.

The colonel then repeated his statement. "I said, would any of you like a P, we prefer cups of P, rather than a tub, don't you think, well, there's no need for everyone to speak all at once, welcome, come." He then clapped his hands and rubbed them together.

"Oh, I understand now, sorry, got a bit muddled, you're offering a cup of tea?" I replied.

"Well?" answered the colonel. We all replied with a no thank you. The colonel then started, "I guess we better pop along and see the main man, well, come along then, haven't got all year, people to kill, you know and all that stupid shitty things to say and do." He then shouted out in a very rude manner at us, "WELL, MOVE!"

We immediately looked bewildered at each other and followed like ducklings following their mummy duck; shortly, we were standing in front of this stupid-looking idiot, of whom I had previously said was sitting on a kid's chair.

The colonel cleared his throat. I thought he was going to bellow again, but to my surprise, he whispered, "Excuse me, Chieftain, but we have guests."

The chieftain looked up at us strangers, grunted then started to read his book again, talk about giving the cold shoulder, but strangely enough, his book was upside down. "Can't read this bloody book, colonel," the chieftain frustratedly moaned!

"That's because you've got it upside down, Chieftain."

"Just bloody watch it, you," the chieftain replied. In our minds, he was slightly over the top in the way he spoke, and his manner was not pleasant at all in the way he was talking to the colonel.

Give the colonel his due for he simply twisted the chieftain's book around to face the right way. "Colonel, have you offered them a P yet?" muttered the chieftain.

"They refused a P, chieftain."

"Oh, not they bloody did, what's the matter with my P? I will have you know I have allowed the queen to P here. How dare you refuse my P, my P has a strong aromatic flavour and it's strong anol. I am my own cafe. I will tell you, I'm also suffering from a bad case of flatulence."

I nearly choked as I responded to that last remark, "You have what!"

The chieftain then shouted, "Farts, farts, farts, farts, farts, you deaf pudding of a bean sprout. I fart a lot and do they pong; they do, I tell you. Poo, stinky." Then the chieftain got really mad; he rushed to his feet, knocked over his book, table as well as his desk; everything went flying across the ground.

He was fuming for some strange unfathomable reason; the colonel stepped in immediately. "It's okay, Chieftain, come and sit down, there's a good chap." The chieftain then continually mumbled under his breath, but you could still hear him talking. "My P, nothing wrong with my P, fuck 'em, shit, just farted again."

"Anyone got air freshener, stinks?" The colonel then spoke to me whilst holding his nose; it wasn't long before we all did the same. "Peter, isn't it, tell me, what do you think about our new blue lawn, was thinking of an apple grey me self but got overruled by guess who."

"Yes, very nice, Colonel." I tried not to laugh. "Where did you get it from?"

"We had it flown in from Pompey do do."

"You imported from where?"

The colonel repeated himself, "From Pompey do do, have you heard of it, they sell great peanut and castor oil squash over there."

I responded with, "Right, do they indeed."

The colonel then continued saying, "Yes, we got it from over there." He pointed to the grassless area not twelve feet away. I looked at him in disbelief.

I asked, "Sorry but you had the grass flown in, but you had the grass dug up from just over there." I was astounded, and by this time, I was totally bewildered with this pair of dicks.

The chieftain heard our conversation and butted in, "Oh, yes, and bloody expensive unto me too, cost of the beanery, 35 tins of bean, oh, stinks, Colonel, I just shit my pants I think!" shouted the chieftain.

"Beans!" I cried.

"Yes, beans," the chieftain responded. By now, everyone was holding their noses as the smell was seriously bad. I mean it stunk as if a dead skunk had dropped out of his bum hole; everyone started holding their noses once more as the aroma began to drift towards us. The guys and I were not exactly taken with these two fruit bats; their language was weird to say the least. Just then, Geoff thought he saw a cat way over in the trees.

"Eh, look over there, there's a cat, well, I think it's a cat, our first sign of an animal." The chieftain again sprinted to his feet, gave one massive explosion between his legs, it was like Hiroshima all over again, Jesus, it stunk. "Har, that's better, nothing better than clearing out ya gut." And he once again destroyed everything around him, and instantly, he went into another rage.

"Cat! You say cat, call out the beanery troop, Colonel, call 'em out, call 'em out, I say. I am the chieftain, strength of a thousand beans, call 'em out." The colonel pulled out a long thin whistle from his pocket and blew into it hard.

Now it had to be a dog whistle he was using as it made no sound, then from out of the manor house that stood behind everyone came waddling over four dwarfs, all dressed in blue shorts and t-shirts. Once they reached the colonel, the chieftain addressed them; he screamed at the top of his voice then cried out loudly, "Attention, attention, cat on grounds, up to bottle on a ship today, you What, you go to left, you Where, go right, you When, you go that way, and Why, you follow them all, and get the cat. I never sort after I am. GO!!!!" The dwarfs ran off as fast as their feet could carry them; it was as if their very lives depended on getting this cat.

The colonel could plainly see our confusion so he explained it all. "Yes, well, that's our combat unit, What's the oldest member, then you have Who, Why, and When have been with us for roughly 12 beans now, good bunch of men."

Geoff then bellowed without thinking, "Who, What, Why and When, you serious, they're actually real names?"

"Of course, they are, you wouldn't expect names like apricot, tomato, or arrow head, now would you, oh, come on, be serious here," the colonel remarked.

The chieftain then picked up his book from the floor and faced the colonel. "You know something, Colonel?"

The colonel replied, "What's that, Chieftain?"

"I have really got to learn to read one day."

"Yes, Chieftain," the colonel replied. I tried to change the subject.

"Look, we're sorry for any misunderstandings here, but we're strangers here."

Chapter 6
Insanity

"I was wondering, could you tell us where exactly are we?" The chieftain was now in his element.

"Why you're in Beantopium."

Alan then made his voice heard. "Beantopium?"

"Yes," responded the chieftain, "and I own my own cafe so you better get off my bus I tell you, so near buggers to you."

"Yeah, right, fair enough."

Alan responded as he looked at him with an expression of bewilderment, "What's the name of that place over there then, if that's not a stupid question?" He pointed to the near horizon. The colonel abruptly stepped in as the chieftain was about to let rip with more vocal rubbish.

"Emmmm, we don't talk about that place much."

"Why, what's wrong with it," I asked.

The chieftain then spoke abruptly and shouted, "It's not nice, bad, bad, bad place, rather eat a pancake roll full of dirt."

Rob then piped up as he hadn't said much so far, "What's wrong with it, looks like a decent castle to me; looks all right from here."

The chieftain continued, "It's called Peabodium Castle; the area's run with a firm bum, I'm afraid; it's the leader, really not a nice female at all, at all, at all. Now what's her name again" – chieftain paused – "Colonel, you tell 'em, I can't say it, what a dickers she is, she can't even tie her horse's head to a barn shed; her boobies drop to the floor like heavy tuna fish cans, stupid cow."

"Very well, Chieftain, her name's May Owen. A dark, hideous character, fangs as long as her fingernails; she's really good at back scratching; she's also very good at getting the dirt out of your—"

The chieftain immediately stopped the colonel and said, "Steady, Colonel, steady, man. I will take it from here, Colonel, you just have a shit, I mean sit. She would even eat her own stuffed porcupine if she had some mustard cake and an apple sauce to go with it, vile creature, I must say. Whatever you lot do whilst you're in this world, never, ever, never, I beseech you, don't go there."

"Sounds fun."

The chieftain replied, "Well, it ain't right." Rob had tried to humour the moment; the chieftain didn't have a sense of humour though, he wasn't having any of it. "Stick your bum in a fried egg, mister, I will have you know that I had this May Owen around for a P and roasted bean farts bread, mmmm, bloody tasty. Colonel, make a note, need more farting bread."

"Yes, Chieftain, how do you spell it?" The chieftain looked at the colonel and said, "Fa, tin her."

Rob was just about to correct the chieftain as I stepped forward. "Leave it, mate, just leave it." The chieftain continued with talking his usual crap.

"Do you know what she did?"

"Did she eat them?" Rob was being sarcastic at that moment.

The chieftain then responded, "Yes, she bloody did; she ate every single bloody one, ate 'em all she did, bloody bitch ate 'em. I didn't get one crumb. Colonel, make a second note. Buy more farting bread. But I got the last laugh though, she didn't get her hands on my kitty pudding, not my kitty pudding though; she never got that. I hide 'em all, you see, no way she was going to get her sticky fingers on my kitty pudding. I tell you, she didn't, she didn't, Colonel."

"That's so true, she certainly didn't, Chieftain, very, very naughty of her, wasn't it? Do you want to have your usual six-hour snooze, Chieftain, it's gone midnight, you know; it is past your bedtime."

The chieftain said abruptly, "I want to play cricket, so fuck off, tart shit bum, you boys fancy a game of cricket, don't you?"

"Not really," I replied whilst trying to make up a reason as to why we didn't want to play. "We haven't any whites, sorry."

"Whites, whites, what you on about, man? We don't use whatever that is, just use the colonel's pants."

"Use his what?" I was astounded by the suggestion and for that matter so was the colonel.

"I say, Chieftain, that's going a bit too far, don't you think?"

The chieftain responded, "Stick your finger up your bum, Colonel, please yourself. I'm going off to play cricket, gonna play with myself for a bit. Only way I get to win around here, yes, and by the way, Colonel, when Who, What Where and When return, send 'em across, haven't got a cricket ball now, What bloody ate it, stupid git, didn't even use a sauce, must have been as dry as hell, any way up to bottle, and shit to all, send 'em across, need their heads to play, going to create a new game. Head but cricket, oh yes, maybe I will start a Beanery Tournament, right, I'm off, and up yours too, Colonel." The chieftain walked away, again in this weird-looking jerky movement.

The colonel politely stated, "Have a good game. Now that he's piped off, how can we be of service to you lads?"

I then thought, *Thank god for some normal behaviour at last*. I then said, "Well, we need some answers because we have no idea as to where we are."

"You're in Beantopium, I thought I had already said that to you."

"Well, yes, you did, but where exactly is that?" I politely asked.

"Well, it's here, you're not stupid, are you?" replied the colonel.

Rob then butted in, "Colonel, look, what Peter's trying to ask is that we've been pulled out of our time and, well, we have—"

Immediately, the colonel interrupted him with the realisation, "Oh, my dear boys, I do apologise, you're the Peter, you're the Peter!" The colonel started to grow very happy.

I immediately responded to him. "Where did you hear that from?" I asked keenly.

"Why I heard that from Mr Mist; he told us to expect you."

As I was about to reply to him, Alan interrupted, "This Mr Mist bloke, what does he look like?"

"Oh, right, you want a description, I take it, well, he's thin, wears a piece of string for a belt and he has a monocle."

"Where is he now, Colonel, it's very important we meet him," I eagerly said. The colonel paused for a moment.

"Let me think, hang on a moment, now I last saw him, now where was it, oh yes, he was going to find you if I remember, Peter."

"Yeah, he found me, all right, but the question is, where is he right now."

"Right, okay, give me a minute, yes, I know now," stated the colonel, with great importance.

I eagerly blurted out, "Well, WHERE!"

"Sorry, didn't I say, he's behind you." The colonel laughed. "Well, I'm going off now to join the chieftain for some head butting cricket, have fun, cheerio." The lads and I spun around.

There, true to form, stood our old boy, standing there as if he was a statue, but there was something strangely different with his appearance this time. I guess it was that he appeared more humanlike as his eyes had a sparkle, life to them, whereas before, they were dead and lifeless.

Now he seems happier, more energetic than before; it was really good to see it, the old boy then spoke to us all. "Welcome to my imaginary universe, gentlemen, time is seriously moving on, and there's not much of it left.

"That's one thing that is totally out of my control, not even I can alter that, time will end our adventure."

At that point, I said, "Oh, right, you call this an adventure, do ya? I've already lost two of my mates, how many more will I lose, can you tell me that?" The mist didn't reply, it just continued to say what it was saying as if it was blatantly trying to ignore me.

"You need to be informed of certain matters; this is now the time for you to know your past, your present, but not even I will or can tamper with your immediate future."

The old boy stood and directly faced me.

"Peter, you are the one."

"Why, why does everyone refer to me as the one, one what, and are you going to answer my question?" I asked.

"It was you and yours that created my existence, you are my creator."

"I'm your what, how?"

Alan jumped in with, "You need to be more precise with the information you pass on to us, we need to understand these things, how the fuck are we supposed to keep ourselves out of the shit if you can't tell us what we need to know, for Christ's sake?" Alan was getting a little frustrated at this point, and who could blame him; he was right.

The old boy continued, "Your present time I removed you from, placing you in my past, your time has not altered, you're just not in it at the moment. You must understand this point, if our enemy manages to remove your existence, I am unable to re-conjure you."

Rob said, "What, conjure who?" What the old boy had just said went completely over Rob's head. Geoff then decoded the message into English.

"Rob, basically, you die, you stay dead for the rest of time, there's no returning."

"I cannot alter this fact. I only wish I could for all of your sakes. Peter, your main purpose is to release me from existence, your creation is not what I want, you need to destroy my timeline.

"This would without doubt destroy my presence, if I am destroyed, it will also cease to be, our enemy will become obsolete."

I responded quickly, "You mean the curse?"

"The red curse," blurted Alan.

"Yes, Alan, the red curse," replied the old boy, "it loves its time manipulation powers; in time, it will grow too strong for me to deal with; on that day, I will be unable to help you; on that day, I will become a possession, slave so to speak.

"You must destroy us both, Peter, and your timeline will return to what you perceive as normal, that goes for all, if you do not, eventually, every universe through existence will fall into the entity's power and control.

"At this moment, I have placed certain devices that when the time is right, you will have with you, all these items of five must you find, you already have one.

"I will create an emission of light on each piece; it will glow once you're near to it; this should make your tasks easier, once you secure them.

"Our mortal enemy cannot harm you and yours directly, so it will use its power to manipulate others, other creations, you must secure these items; the enemy must not destroy these, you have to collect as I am forbidden to recreate them, the, as you aptly call it, curse, they are being hidden from its sensors and the struggle to keep them that way is slowly decreasing my strength.

"Once you have these five pieces, the time would become the now, the time for non-existence would be upon us all; the curse and myself are split entities; this is the creation that should never have been allowed to be.

"Destroy me, Peter, destroy it."

"Where do we go?" I asked.

The old boy then said no more, instead he just pointed into the far off distance with his raised arm; he was pointing towards the place we were warned not to go, Peabodium Castle. The old boy then revealed once again using its telepathic link to me where the second device was to be. "Go, you must go now, find and secure."

Alan then stated, "That makes absolutely no sense to us, what on earth are you talking about, can't you just keep talking straight?" With that remark, the old boy then like always disappeared.

Rob started an avalanche of verbal diarrhoea forced directly at me. "Right, so now we know all this is down to your fuck up, what did you do?"

He was quite rude, immediately followed up by Geoff. "You fucked up big time, well, what did you do for fuck's sake."

I tried to reply to them as best as I could. "Don't know, okay, I don't know. I'm as clueless as you lot. If I knew, don't you think you would have been told by now?" I was seriously getting pissed off. "Al, why you keeping quiet, don't you wanna give me your penny worth?"

"No, Pete, I don't. I'm with you hundred percent. I know you're as much in the dark as the rest of us; these two are just as scared as we are; we're all looking for answers; at least we own one of the devices; we also know that there's four more devices still to find.

"Secondly, we know the old boy wants to be taken out, third, an experiment that goes wrong, and four, there's still two more guys we still need to find."

"Technically, yeah," I answered.

"What do you mean, technically?" Alan was puzzled.

"Well, we know that Professor War-pen's son's involved, seeming he invented the warp thingy, so I'm presuming he's in our number. So really, we've only one more guy to find to make the numbers up."

"Yeah, see what you mean," Alan agreed.

Geoff and Rob then apologised for being dicks; they genuinely realised that Alan was right. "Well, gents, it's to Peabodium then." Everyone looked towards a large castle that was lying amongst a forest towards the horizon; above the terrific looking structure was a terrific storm, lightning clashing through the clouds, it was like a horror film from Hammer, a horrific sight, but for some strange reason, it really looked lovely to watch, saying that I was glad it was in the distance.

Now strangely enough, the storm was only over the castle, and nowhere else; everywhere else was lovely, like a summer's days; it was so weird to see.

Our trek was now in full swing as we were walking. Guess who we bumped into, yeah, you got it, it was those two bloody weirdos, the colonel and chieftain. The colonel spotted us first. "Hello, again," he stated.

"Hello," I replied.

The colonel then asked us, "Where you off to?" Rob then opened his big mouth.

"We're off to Peabodium Castle."

"Oh no," the colonel cried.

The chieftain then butted in, "Why are you lot walking around with poo in your eyes, Peabodium is bad, it's worse than the bad, it's baddish. How about playing some cricket instead? I've got a spare bat, oh, come on, we can have some really good fun here, and I promise that I will not cheat. Did I tell you I own my own I?" The chieftain then finally shut up.

"Sorry, but we really don't have enough time," stated Alan.

"Oh, come on, we can be on the same team," stated the chieftain.

"We just haven't got the time, sorry, but no," stated Rob.

The chieftain then had verbal diarrhoea once again. "I'm trying to be up to the bottle on a ship today here. I am my own boss anol; when I first came here, there was no bean at all. I created everything you see.

"I especially enjoy the blue grass outside my place, but right now, I really want to play cricket with you lot; if you don't play, I'm going to smack the colonel in the head and then he's going to eat his own foot.

"I am the chieftain, strength of a thousand beans, oh, come on, I will be your friend, well, if you don't want to play with me, we're going to come with you. Colonel, I'm bored, I fancy eating May Owen's bum. I hear she has honey on it. I do like chewy honey, did you know that, Colonel? Oh, yes, I do, haven't had a bit in, oh, such a long time."

I was virtually at the point of blowing a gasket as this twit wouldn't shut his fucking mouth, just to shut him up I then turned to him and said, "Right, fine, if you want to come with us, then be our guest." It then ran through my mind, have I just made one big balls-up, but how else could I get him to shut his mouth? The colonel moved up and walked along with Alan whilst I got the short straw and had the chieftain walk along with me.

Rob and Geoff followed up in the rear. Rob and Geoff started chatting first out of the three twosomes we had going. "What do you think about this place then, Rob, it ain't that bad once you're here for a bit."

"Yeah, it's not bad, just wish the colouring was in the right order though, after all, who the hell creates a blue lawn, it's like someone's gone around with an aerosol can and sprayed the entire planet."

"Jesus, he must've been colour blind."

Geoff and Rob had a little giggle with each other, then came the colonel and Alan. "So, Alan, why is it so important to go to the castle? We've already seen it several times ourselves, some bits are nice mind."

"At the end of the day, Colonel, we have to find some items; it's like a jigsaw of equipment that we need. Problem is we don't know what these pieces look like."

"I see, I think it's a bit of a pickle looking for something for when you don't know what it is you're looking for, yes, pickle indeed, you must have some idea though surely?"

"It's machinery, or it could be computerised."

"Computerised, what's that when it's at home?" the colonel was really puzzled.

Alan said, "You don't know what a computer is? Okay, I will try to explain it to you." It was at that moment the chieftain and I started our conversation.

"How long have you known Mr Mist then? I bet I've known him longer than you, ha, ha, ha," the chieftain boasted.

I replied, "We haven't known him long." My thoughts at this point were why on earth did I agree to take him along; he was doing my nut in.

The chieftain continued, "Yes, it's been a long time; have you any idea on how you're going to pass her boobies?"

"Her boobies, chieftain, what you talking about?" I was totally taken aback, what was he on about, was he talking about her chest, or what?

"You know, those boobies she has got scattered all around the grounds; last person I heard of had his bum cut off, blood everywhere, I hear, must have been a bloody good booby I tell ya."

I then realised what he was trying to say, as I corrected him. "Got ya now, you mean booby traps."

The chieftain continued, "There was the time I tripped over her booby, I actually cut off my fingernail. I cried for a week. Have you ever cut a fingernail, Peter, bloody really hurts, I tell you, oh well, up to bottle on a poo bum." The chieftain turned his thoughts in the blink of an eye and asked me, "What do you think of my trousers, Peter? I had them made especially from cactus plants; they're a little bit prickly under the crotch though, still beggars can't be choosers—"

I then interrupted him within seconds. "Look, chieftain, I'm truly enjoying our little chat, but is there a shortcut to this castle?"

"Oh, yes," the chieftain replied.

I gasped for a moment, then said, "Well, where is it?"

"Why, do you want to get there quicker?" the chieftain answered back.

"Well, yes," I replied.

The chieftain without pausing said, "Well, follow me then, you should've said something earlier, I haven't got exceptional secure percussion you know, had a PhD once, that was painful, then there was an eco, that tasted shit." By this time, I was gradually going insane with his continual verbal diarrhoea.

I also knew what he meant to say when he stated ESP, he should've said, extra sensory perception, but I just didn't have the heart to upset him, yet again.

"This way," the chieftain called out as he marched straight into a strangely shaped edge row; it was some sort of yellow private. "Come along and mind your feet, this area is full of cattle prods poo, very, very, very stinky poo. I had stinky poo for cleaning my beans once, called it curry, my dwarf squad loved it. Do you like curry poo poo, Pete?"

"No, I bloody don't, Chieftain."

I started to walk ahead; I had just taken all I could take from the crap he was spilling.

Alan came over to me. "What's up, you okay?"

"Alan, if you ever hear me about to say something stupid again, like let's take an idiot along with us, you have my permission to shoot me, okay?"

Alan understood perfectly. "Right, got ya, I take it you're referring about the chieftain?"

"Yeah, you got it in one," I answered.

Alan then questioned our route, "Why have we come through here then?"

"Well, apparently," I answered, "it's a shortcut to the castle."

Alan then responded with, "Right, and you trust him, do ya?"

"If he's true to form, this shortcut is going to take us at least a week, and that's just so we can find out where the fuck we are." We then turned to hear the chieftain singing.

"Up to bottle on a ship today, saw a bake bean on the Milky Way. I've got a bus so fuck off too, this is my song and it's not just for you. I'm the chieftain, strength of a thousand beans. I'm the bean so up your trousers with a munch king or two."

"Peter?" Alan called.

"Yes, mate?" I replied.

"The bloke's completely gone, doolally; he's lost it big time."

"I know that, Alan, I know that, excuse me, Chieftain, sorry for interrupting your great vocals, but when do you think we'll get there?" I asked extremely nicely.

The chieftain replied, "It doesn't take long, well, maybe it will be a good days' walking; it all depends on the type of year you're having."

"Chieftain," screamed the colonel, "how long!"

The chieftain then said, "Oh, sorry got carried away. I do love a good sing-song, we're here Colonel."

Rob then stated, "I don't mean to be rude, Chieftain, but where's here?"

"There." The chieftain pointed through a small gap through the trees; the castle lay in front of us; everyone stood and looked in amazement at the massive stonewall that encircled Peabodium Castle, stood in all its fabulous glory.

Geoff then moved forward. "Right, now what do we do? I suppose we just knock on the door, do we?" Alan, Rob and myself including the colonel and the chieftain looked at him. "Well?" blurted Geoff.

"Yes!" blasted the chieftain right back. Before you could say boo to a goose, the chieftain marched off, through the gap in the trees he marched, and I do mean marched as he moved.

We had to start running at a decent pace just to keep up with him, what with his march and our run lasted that took us at least 15 minutes; we had finally got to our destination; the chieftain without any patience walked straight up to the castle drawbridge and bellowed, "Hey, you lot inside the castle, I am the chieftain, strength of a thousand beans, open this fucking drawbridge or I will do you right up the bean. If you don't, I'm gonna get me bus now, fuck off and open up. There you go, Colonel, that should open the door all right, well, I never did."

The colonel then answered, "Great one, Chieftain, and may I say, very well done too."

The chieftain replied, "Yes, I thought I did decently pretty good too, think I will write what I said in my memories, just remind me on what I have just said again, will you, please? I was too busy saying it to be thinking of what I was stipulating, Colonel, you see, Peter, I am the chieftain—"

"Yes, we know," I quickly got that in.

Geoff then mumbled under his breath, "Yeah, and we all wish you'd shut the fuck up." Within a few moments, the drawbridge began to lower; its creeping chains struggling with all the weight as it slowly lowered itself; with a heavy thud, the drawbridge hit the ground; below the bridge were bright blue creatures that swam in the deep moat that surrounded the castle; they must have been from the same species of shark, well, that's what they resembled to me. There standing directly in front of us was a hideous-looking dwarf; he wore a long tatty grey beard, dressed in a pure black worn-out suit; on his head, he wore a pointed hood.

It ranted, "Welcome to Peabodium Castle, gentlemen, oh and you, Chieftain. My name's Alpine McGregor."

The chieftain bellowed once more, "He's got my hat on, Colonel, look, look, that's my hat, how did you, you titty bum outrage, get my hat? Give me my hat or the colonel will piss in it."

The colonel whilst in complete dismay replied, "I will not, Chieftain. I don't feel like I need to go."

The chieftain promptly said, "If I say you will go wee wee, you go wee wee or I will, will do you to too, just watch it, right."

Rob blurted out, "Forget about the stupid hat, Jesus, mate, you're not all there, are you?" The chieftain then looked at the colonel.

"What did he say, Colonel? I'm not all there, well, where am I? I thought I was here with you lot, have I gone somewhere I don't know? You better just watch who I am to be, Mr Poo Bum, eh, Colonel?"

"Yes, Chieftain."

I moved forward. Alpine moved nearer and said, "Well, what do you want here, it's harvest time and the trees won't like being disturbed."

Rob then responded whilst looking around the area, "What trees, there ain't any, look around you."

Alpine then bellowed, "I have not any nobly bits, how can I help?" His attitude had totally changed. Rob then spoke again.

"We would like to see May Owen if that is at all possible."

Alpine snapped, "Well, you can't, so up yours, well, not yet anyway."

The colonel then asked, "Why is that then?"

Alpine replied, "She's having a poo, follow me, and wipe your feet please, I hate cleaning the floors. I'm taking you to the big hall, and do yourselves a big favour, when we go in, duck, for there isn't a lot of headroom inside."

"Sorry, but didn't you say it was a big hall?"

Alpine replied, "Did I? I meant to say, it's not a big hall."

As we walked along this corridor to the so-called big hall, the suits of armour that stood upright on pillars of rock on both sides of our troop gave the impression that they were looking at us. I was getting some weird feelings. Finally, we reached the big hall door; it stood at least ten feet in height and a good six feet wide. Geoff said to Rob, "How is it that we're told to duck for lack of headroom, Jesus, look at the size of this door, it's huge."

"Yeah, begs the question" replied Rob. Alpine unlocked the door. Alpine was right after all as just because the doorway was large, the hall wasn't, simply because the door was only an illusion for once opened, the opening to the room was only four feet in height; everyone had to virtually get on their hands and knees apart from Alpine; we moved down the big hall, and gradually, the height began to grow and we could at least stand up; in front of us lay a massive throne.

Fit for the greatest of all monarchs, Alpine turned and addressed our troop, "Wait here."

"Where?" asked the chieftain.

"There," repeated Alpine.

"Oh, right here, not there, but here." Alpine looked at him and walked away.

We waited and waited and waited for some more, eventually, May Owen entered the room. Jesus, I thought her nose was longer than the Eiffel Tower; the best way to describe her was of the wicked witch of the west in *Wizard of Oz* but without the hat, ugly bitch too; two servants rushed across to her and helped her onto the throne; she needed the help as she was a dwarf herself. In a squeaky voice, she said, "Oh, it's you," looking at the chieftain. "What do you want this time?"

The colonel then spoke in his stead. "Your Queerness, Your Queerness, the chieftain and I have come here today—"

The chieftain interrupted him by bellowing once more, "Shut up, Colonel, you look here, I have serious matters for you and I to sort. I have grievances that need to be sorted, and sorted they to be him."

"Right, fine, go on," replied May Owen in a depressed mode. I guess she knew what she was in for. Then the chieftain was vocally fired.

"Right then, May Owen, my issues are these: first, I want my stick of rhubarb back. Second, Alpine's got my hat, I want it back. Third, I want my quaternary of pork scratching that we agreed on. Fourth, where's my pancake roll gone?"

"Is that it?" asked May Owen.

The chieftain was getting upset for some reason as he stated, "My god, woman, have you no heart? I want my hat, my pancake roll, my pork scratching, my god, and you mark me here and now, you won't get my bus, so stick a burger up your bum."

Geoff than whispered to Alan, "God, he talks bollocks." Alan let out a snigger of laughter. May Owen and the chieftain then immediately spun their heads and gazed at Alan for a few seconds.

The colonel then looked straight to Peter. "Get him to apologise now, Peter, now."

Peter than said to Alan, "Apologise for laughing, Alan, do it,"

Alan then red-faced remarked, "May Owen, Chieftain, I'm sorry for the ill humour. I apologise unreservedly." May Owen glared at him.

"Right, don't do it again." The colonel then stepped forward.

"Your Madge, may I introduce strangers to our world?" As he called out each of our names in turn, we stood one step forward then one step back.

"So, you're the Peter, are you?" she stated.

"Yes, I am," I replied. I had the strange idea that she knew our reason for being there. "You say that as if you're aware as to why we're here and what we need to find."

"Correct, very astute of you, Peter. But I am afraid you cannot collect for I have needs of my own. Do you think I want to remain here with him?" She pointed at the chieftain and then continued, "I need to stretch out, embrace other time dimensions; now go before I change my mind and secure your futures for the rest of your timeline."

"I believe it's time we went on our way, gentlemen," stated the colonel.

The chieftain then came out with, "Well, I must say, female creature, that was harsh, I must say, what about my P? I always have my P everywhere I go, down right rude you ask me." The chieftain was not at all happy with May Owen's verbal attack on Peter.

"Burt, come here!" shouted Owen. From the next room entered Burt Jones, a stocky 6 foot 8 inch bloke, built like a Frankenstein monster; he walked like one to.

"What?" he abruptly answered.

"Get them your P, then you go. I'm off now as I'm needed in the loo again." May Owen jumped off her throne and out of the room; that left us six with this huge mountain of a bloke.

"Right, come with me," Burt said as he was moving extremely slowly; we followed this big lump into another room; everywhere you looked were pictures of May Owen in all sorts of poses; she must seriously love looking at herself.

Some of us sat down whilst others stood as there wasn't enough chairs in the room. I turned to the chieftain and thought that this could be the perfect opportunity for the chieftain to actually be useful to us for once. "Ummm, Chieftain, I need a favour."

"Oh, do you now, what is it? I do love a good favour, my aunty done me a favour once, yeah, blocked her bum hole with an orange, took twenty men to pull it out, weird bitch; carry on, Peter, what's the favour then?" he asked. I looked at him with a dead expression on my face.

I paused and then asked, "Well, I need you to distract that hulk for a few hours."

The chieftain gazed at Burt and said happily, "Certainly, I can, just watch this. Oi, Burt, just thought I would let you know to be the git you are and up to the cattle market we can go, the colonel thinks you're just a big shithead with the brain of a maggot." Burt immediately faced the colonel.

The colonel stood as he witnessed Burt's approach. The colonel responded, "I say steady." But Burt Jones was raging, his eyes slightly closed as he frowned, like a wild bull in a chip shop; he kept moving towards the colonel's position, then all of a sudden, he lunged at the colonel as all hell broke loose; the colonel easily managed to side step him as Burt passed him; the colonel picked up his speed. For a big guy, this Burt Jones had some decent speed on him, as the chase developed.

It wasn't long before they were scurrying all over the room, furniture flying all over the place, items being knocked over. The colonel screamed out, "What in god's name did you say to him, Chieftain? HELP!" The chase then went to the next level, out of the room they ran, for the colonel it became a chase of survival around the castle.

Once they had left our area, I faced the chieftain and said, "Well, excellent, Chieftain, now for your last assignment. Can you keep May Owen occupied for a few hours as well?"

The chieftain responded, "What about me P?" The chieftain wasn't happy at this point.

"I will make you your P when you come back, how's that?" After a few moments, the chieftain agreed.

"Has to be strong P, but okay, see you all later, skippy da poo poo." The chieftain left the room.

Alan remarked, "Thank god, he's gone."

I then reacted by saying, "Let's be thankful for small mercies. Okay, lads, I know what the objective is."

Alan was so keen, he just jumped into the conversation, "Okay, what is it?"

I then stated, "It's a time stabiliser. Now it's going to release an energy pulse once one of us gets close enough to it; in other words, it's going to glow, so it should be easy for one of us to locate it. Geoff, I want you and Rob to start your search from over there.

"Alan and I will start from this side. Whatever you do, don't let anyone see you doing it. Oh god, I sound like the chieftain, oh no, he is rubbing off on me now.

"Okay, lads, good hunting, stay safe; we can meet back here in say thirty minutes or so. If on the other hand we find nothing, guess, we'll be doing it all over again, but if you do find it, collect the others and we can get the hell out of here. Right, let's move."

After a few moments had passed by, Geoff and Rob are now walking down the west wing; the lightning was still in full swing, flashes of light blasted the stained-glass; this time, it was accompanied by the thunder; thunderous bangs echoed the corridors. Rob then spoke to Geoff. "Is it my imagination or are these pictures watching us? Their eyes are moving, hang on a second, they're holograms."

"Yeah, you're right, Rob. Jesus, so this place does have technology, after all; it makes sense now, that's why this Owen wants our device, crafty cow." Just then, you could faintly hear the screams of the colonel as he was still running from Burt Jones. "Hark at him, Rob."

The two of them thought it was funny and had a little chuckle over the colonel's misfortune. Carrying on with their uneasy hunt, they soon became more comfortable with their situation; they were now becoming more less concerned with their surroundings. Meanwhile, back with Alan and myself. "So now we are alone, Pete, what do you think about our chances of getting out of this world alive, try and be honest, I would like a rough idea."

"Well, Al, I think pretty fair; we're certainly better prepared than we were; we're on the verge of collecting our second device. At the moment, if we use them well, we've our two distractors."

"What you mean by distractors, oh, you mean the colonel and big dick?" replied Alan.

"Yeah, the big dick." We gave ourselves a little laughter. Back with Geoff and Rob at this moment, we're doing well in covering the ground; they noticed a glow that was illuminating from another passageway. Rob nudged Geoff's arm to get his attention.

Pointing without a word spoken, they then proceeded to follow this pulsating flashing. Rob then said in a whisper, "What do you think, Geoff, should we get the others, well, what do you think?"

"And say what, Rob, all we've got are flashes of light, be serious, let's see what it is first, we can make the decision later, yeah."

"Yeah, okay," he replied; the flashing appeared to be coming from up on another corridor; a set of steps lay in front of them as they climbed, hoping that they would soon find out what this strange light was. Once they had found themselves on its level, they could then see that the flashing light was coming from within a room, as it shone from under the door. Rob stood in front of the door whilst Geoff stood a little back of him. "Ready, mate?" asked Rob.

"Yeah, do it," replied Geoff.

Rob slowly released the doorknob; with his arm outstretched, he pushed the door slightly ajar, and seconds later, the door was opened fully; they were unable to see anything from within the room as the light was so intense; it was as if the sun itself stood in front of them. Rob stated, "At times like these, you wish you had sunglasses." Rob stepped forward in the hope to see a little better.

Geoff then said, "Hang on, Rob, what're you doing, come back here, we can't see shit. Rob, did you hear me? I said stop." Rob couldn't hear a thing, he was in some sort of a trans-like state; he by this time was fully in the room. SLAM, the door closed solid, separating the two. Geoff rushed to the door and tried with all his might to get the door open again. As he was pulling and punching the door, he was screaming, "Rob, can you hear me, Rob, you okay?" There was no noise coming from the room; the flashing of light had stopped.

At this point, Geoff continued to do what he was doing before, yelling, kicking and punching whilst pulling at the doorknob; he just wasn't getting anywhere. He then stopped and took a deep breath; at that moment, his eyes glanced down to the bottom of the door, a red liquid began to slip from the room out into the corridor. Geoff stood back a few steps in horror, it was blood; it was Rob's blood. "Holy shit." Geoff was horrified. Without any more waiting, he moved away and ran back to find us. Meanwhile, Alan and I were struggling to see or hear anything.

"This is like looking for a needle in a haystack. Pete, let's give up."

"No," I replied. "We have to keep looking, it's here somewhere, come on," I blurted. My thoughts then wondered on how the other two were getting on. As I prayed that their luck was better than ours, it was just then that we both heard a commotion coming from behind us, it was Geoff, out of breath and sweating profusely.

Geoff, once he had reached us, fell to his knees. I knelt down to him; holding onto his shoulder, we started to chat. "Geoff, Geoff, what's up, mate, are you okay?"

Alan then looked around and stated, "Where's Rob?"

"No, oh, no." I knew what was coming. "He's dead, Pete. Rob's dead."

"What happened, Geoff, take it easy, nice slow breaths, now what happened?"

"Well, we knew we had to look for a glowing light; we saw one and followed it—"

Alan interrupted, "Why didn't you come looking for us?"

"And say what?" shouted Geoff.

"Carry on, Geoff, then what?" I asked.

We followed it to a room up on the next level; the light was coming from inside; we assumed it was the device glowing, you said it would glow, Pete, you said that. Rob opened the door, but the light was too strong. Rob started to walk inside. I called him to come back, but he couldn't hear me, Pete, I tried; he just didn't hear me. The door slammed behind him; he didn't close it; something slammed it shut. I tried to get the door open, but it wouldn't budge.

I then witnessed blood seeping from underneath the door. I knew it was Rob's. I then came back here, sorry, guys, I tried to stop him. I tried.

Alan then put his hand on to Geoff's shoulder, "Okay, mate, okay, come on let's get you to your feet."

"That's fucking three we've lost now, no more, I tell ya, no bloody more." I was cursing. At that moment, Alan and I were witnessing a shimmering light emanating from the edge of one of the wall panels around ten feet away.

We approached once Geoff was on his feet; slowly, we walked up to it. I examined the wall panelling with my fingers. Alan then stated, "Be careful, Pete, for god's sake." Pressing hard with my fingertips all around the panel, I somehow released the holding mechanism, the panel came forward then moved across to reveal an opening.

There it was in all its glory, our second device.

It was small, smaller than I imagined it to be; quickly, I put it into my pocket. "Right, lads, as far as everyone's concerned, we've found absolutely nothing, okay. Rob's lost somewhere in this castle. Whatever is said or done, that's our story; let's just pretend for a bit so we can get the fuck out of here and get back home. We can grieve later. It's not the time, you lads okay with this?"

Alan and Geoff agreed with the nodding of approval. "Right, let's make tracks."

Alan then said, "Pete, the panel."

"Shit, nice one, Alan." I then secured the false panelling. Once done, we started our walk back to where we originally set off from; once there, we sat down and waited for someone to come into the room.

The colonel came back first; he seemed pretty calm and relaxed for a man who had just run a marathon. "Hello, once again, gentlemen, everything okay, did you get what you came for?"

I then respectfully replied, "No, afraid not, this place huge, never realised it would be so massive, never mind, hey."

Chapter 7
The Pit Beckons

Burt Jones then entered the room seconds later. Neither the colonel nor Burt Jones reacted when they came across each other again. So naturally, we all presumed that they had let bygones be bygones; all matters resolved, so to speak.

The chieftain then came back with his stick of rhubarb. "Well, hello, every up to bottle. May Owen and I are going into business together." The colonel was startled.

"You're what?" said the colonel.

"Yes, funeral business, to be precise." I, Alan and Geoff looked at each other with uncertainty as to what was he going on about this time.

"I'm truly sorry for this, but you must explain that last remark to me again, you're going into business with May Owen, what happens to me?" The colonel was getting rather angry and upset at this point. "Well, Chieftain I'm waiting for your explanation."

"Well, it's like this, Colonel," the chieftain replied, "May Owen and I had a chat, it wasn't a bad chat as it goes; we had a lovely P, really tasty, and a great big poof of Cornish pudding topped with bean, you should try it, Colonel, it's yummy poo poo."

The colonel reacted, "Chieftain, explain where I come into this so-called business venture. Well, I'm waiting." We hadn't seen the colonel this upset before; he was really showing some balls for the first time.

"I was rambling, wasn't I, right, sorry, Colonel, I can't drive, ha, ha, ha, we're going to need your expertise in that field."

"Oh, I see, you want me as a chauffeur, I like that."

The chieftain continued, "Yes, Owen's going to the funeral parlour shortly; we're gonna drop off the body, you're also sorting out the paperwork for this castle as we're buying this place tomorrow. Did I mention I own my own cafe and I've got a bus too?"

"Are you telling us May Owen is dead" asked the colonel.

"Yes," responded the chieftain, "I am. She just keeled over after eating my special bean that I dropped in her pudding; she did shout out two words though before she went."

"And what were these two words," I asked.

"Oh, yes, the two words, what were they now? Oh yes, the device, that was it. Around fifteen minutes ago, she just hit the floor, poor cow, oh well, anyone for a quick game of cricket, baggy batsman first, who is bowling?" The chieftain then gazed at us all.

The idea of her death and us grabbing the device made me consider the possibility that they may had been joined somehow, but no, that's a ridiculous idea, unless the curse had made the deal. Just seems weird how she would drop dead around the time we had grabbed the device.

But then, she knew what we were here for, and she also refused us to have it. Oh well, she's dead so who cares anyway.

The chieftain certainly didn't as he then practised on his stroke play; all we did was look at him. The colonel noticed something odd and asked, to be honest it was about time, "I say, wasn't there another one of you, isn't there someone missing from your group?" I then jumped in immediately as to cover our tracks.

"Yeah, it's Rob; he still thinks he could find the device by himself; he shouldn't be too long now."

The chieftain once he had completed his play acting asked, "Right, Peter, my P please, want my P nice and strong, that was the deal, and I want P, did I ever tell you that I was eaten by a large reptile last week?"

"Oh, you were, were you?" I answered.

"Yes, it didn't like the flavour of my bean farts so it spat me out."

The chieftain was still talking crap as usual, then the colonel to everyone's surprise said, "Yeah, spat him out all over my new boots too. I was not impressed, was I, Chieftain?"

The chieftain then replied, "No, you was not, was you, Colonel." I had taken enough as I then moved across to the chieftain. As I did, I received one hell of a shock, for in front of me stood a windowsill, the window was ajar, slivering through and down the wall. Entering the room came this mighty cobra, hissing as it moved.

Its tongue swishing around, its eyes were like glass; the thing must've been a good thirty feet in length. "Jesus!" I cried out; this thing was huge.

I and the others gently proceeded to move backwards to increase the distance between us and it. The colonel and chieftain stood there just looking at it; it lifted its huge bulk as it came to within two feet of the chieftain; we all assumed the worst.

I shouted out with sheer panic, "Chieftain, look out!" The chieftain just stood there as if he was frozen in time.

The colonel wasn't one bit interested as to the danger his companion seemed to be in as he sat and grabbed a book that lay on the table beside him.

I thought that this was just an illusion or a daydream; it couldn't be real; the chieftain then, to my amazement, moved his head to within an inch of the snake's face, looked directly into its glass eyes and said to it, "Now where have you been, you naughty boy?" The snake then wrapped itself around his body. Alan and Geoff turned away as they didn't want to see what was about to happened next. The chieftain then said to it, "You jam tart, what are you, you're a jam tart. Now off you go, see you at P time." To our astonishment, the snake unwrapped itself and slithered out the way it came in.

We all took a deep sigh of relief as the chieftain just brushed himself off. Geoff looked at the colonel and stutteringly said, "What the fuck was that all about?"

The colonel smiled and replied, "As if it could eat the chieftain, he's had that snake since it was a puppy."

The chieftain then responded as he heard what Geoff had to say, "I'm strength of a thousand beans. I am my own boss a nol, I tell you."

Burt Jones then saved my bacon as he left to create the P for the chieftain; it was at that specific moment the colonel looked over to the entrance to the room and said, "Oh, it's all right now, your friend has returned. Did you find the device, Rob?" We suddenly turned towards the doorway, there he stood, red eyes aglow; it was Rob.

Well, the shell of Rob anyway and there were no prizes as to who was operating its strings.

Alan, Geoff and I were totally dumbstruck; the colonel and the chieftain were none the wiser. The Rob-like thing approached Burt as he had just returned from making the chieftain's P. Burt politely asked Rob if he would care for a cup.

Within seconds, Rob lunged forward, grappled with Burt then raised him off the floor; without any effort, he flung him clearly through the large pane of glass.

Burt Jones was no weakling himself, and it was a fact that you would have to have the strength of Superman to do what this thing had just done to him.

Everyone was on full alert by this time.

"Peter, what's the matter with your friend?" asked the colonel.

I responded by saying, "That's not my friend, Colonel, it may look like him, but it's not."

The chieftain then took it upon himself to prove me wrong. "Of course, it is, look, I will show you." The chieftain was about to walk ahead and confront this Rob, but the colonel stopped him in his tracks.

"Sorry, Chieftain, but I do believe Peter is right on this point. Shall we adjourn, gentlemen, say somewhere else?" The colonel immediately ran, the rest of us followed, that just left the chieftain. He walked up to the creature. "Now see here, you thingy, I'm the chieftain and I have the strength of a thousand beans." The thing then turned to attack the chieftain, but right at the very last moment before it struck, the colonel came rushing back and grabbed hold of the chieftain by his hand and forced him out of harm's way. "Colonel!" shouted the chieftain. As he was being dragged along by his arm, the chieftain didn't take his dragging all that well. "Now see here, Colonel, if you don't stop what you're doing, I'm gonna tear off your trousers and eat 'em. I am the chieftain—"

The colonel then replied, "Yes, I know, I chieftain, chieftain, I know." Shortly, we were all in the grounds and out of the castle.

The chieftain turned to Alan. "You person thingy, what's happening here? I never until I did." The chieftain was adamant he wanted answerers.

"It's the red curse, Chieftain."

Alan tried to explain, "You know of Mr Mist, the old boy?"

"Yes, carry on," the chieftain answered.

"Well, the curse is its twin, they're both entities of the same being."

"Are you telling me they're both tits?"

The colonel then intervened, "Chieftain, look, Mr Mist and the curse thingy are one of the same, one's nicer than the other, bad, bad."

The chieftain then said, "Why didn't he say what I was thinking, stupid person thingy."

Geoff stepped in with, "You get it now, the bad bad has taken the form of our dead friend."

The chieftain then said, "Fine, no need to gobble d gook. I have not to be deaf. I heard that it was understanding now, dick thingy person." The chieftain muttered under his breath.

At that moment, Alan yelled out, "Oh hell, it's coming again."

"It's Frankenstein's monster!" I shouted.

The chieftain, who by now was totally baffled, said, "It's who and the monster, Colonel, what's going on, whose monster?" The chieftain had by this time lost any rational thought, but with saying that, he never had much anyway.

"It wants us dead, Chieftain, understand that!" I shouted.

"Okay, lads, just keep moving so it has no clear target to aim for, start swapping places!" I shouted out; the chieftain then slowly raised his head as his thought process improved; he then understood.

"Colonel, give me the bean mobile!" the chieftain shouted.

"Why do you need that?" shouted back the colonel.

"I'm the chieftain and I'm getting cheesed off, so burger bum to you, Colonel." But true to form, the colonel threw the phone towards the chieftain.

The chieftain then made his call. "Who, is that you, oh, it's What, right, now listen to me very carefully, grab your weapons, yes, the special ones, get the combat team together, take the beanery on the special route and get here yesterday; do you understand me? Drop everything and get over here pronto, okay? The cavalry is on its way, now can we play a game of cricket, please?"

I thought for a moment and shouted over to him, "Let's play a different game. I know, let's play, catch me you dickhead!"

The chieftain responded with, "Mmm, sounds right up my alley passage. Any rules?" he asked.

I replied, "You get three points for each time you kick that thing in the nuts. But if he grabs onto you, he's allowed to kill you!" I shouted.

"Kill the chieftain? There's no game where they have the bottle or can, for that matter. Kill me? How ridiculous. I am the chieftain, stand aside, I'm going to teach you lot how to win, charge." The chieftain went off like the clappers.

The chieftain kept kicking the monster bloody hard every few moments; the monster, whose movements were slow to say the least, had no chance in catching the chieftain. I faced Alan and asked, "How long do you think he can keep this up, Alan?"

"Knowing him, I'd say all bloody yearlong; he's got the mind and body of a child. He can't see danger for one, so that's a great advantage." I wondered how long this combat team was going to be. An hour had passed, the chieftain in fantastic form was still going strong as the rest of us just watched in awe.

The combat team came across through the woods and stood in a line directly in front of the monster.

They knew exactly what they were doing, thank god. The chieftain saw them and broke off his game; he rushed over to them.

They were standing roughly 50 yards away from the monster, then the chieftain came into his own once more. "Gentlemen, your weapons." Each one produced his catapult.

I looked at the colonel and said, "You have got to be kidding me, Colonel, catapults, really?"

"Watch," replied the colonel. Back with the chieftain, he then shouted; it was like the British thin red line at the battle of Rorkes' Drift all over again.

The chieftain called out, "Gentlemen, your beans." The monster was closing the gap on them in decent time, then came the chieftain's final command. "Stand by, at my command, FIRE!" The combat team fired their beans all in one moment; the monster was hit each time, it dropped to one knee then rose up and continued its forward movement. The chieftain then shouted, "Reload, FIRE!" Again, the monster received the full amount of beans; this time, it was harder for it to stand and move forward. "Reload," shouted the chieftain, "independent rapid fire, fire at will!" Who, What Where and When released bean after bean after bean, for they were finally taking effect.

They had taken out the monster. I rushed over to the chieftain. "How?" I was lost for words.

"This is my domain, Peter, my reality is far simpler than yours, besides I am the chieftain." He gave me a smile. I smiled back.

I then went up to Who, What, Where and When. I reached out to shake their hands, then they all started to growl and snarl at me.

I moved back slightly as I was slightly startled; the chieftain then shouted his command, "Sit!" They immediately did exactly what they were commanded to do.

"I give up." I said as I turned away.

"Yes, I know the feeling, Peter, I gave up a long time ago." The colonel laughed.

The chieftain started to walk off back towards the castle. "Colonel, come on, want to look at my new property, goody, goody?"

"Coming, Chieftain." Well, that was it, both of them just pissed off without a 'bye' or 'your leave'. *Ignorant gits*, I thought, *didn't even say good bye.*

Alan and Geoff looked over to me; the three of us stood there thinking as to what to do next. Geoff came up with, "Well, I suppose we can always start walking around, explore the place a little, you never know, that old boy of yours might even show up."

Alan then said, "Yeah, you never know, Pete, we might even get zapped out of here."

"Yeah, get back to my car, besides I have to put this device in a safe place." I said.

Alan then mentioned, "We have a second way to go; we could always go back to the castle, have a better look around."

"Not with those two dicks, I have had my fill of those two," Geoff stated.

Now that I understood. "But give him his due, lads, the chieftain did come good when it was needed though, Geoff." I made sure I gave the man some appreciation; after all, he probably saved our bacon.

Looking up and away, I noticed on the horizon. "Eh, lads, look at those clouds over there." Geoff and Alan then joined me; we could see what seemed to be a strong black cloud, moving around in a vast circular motion, definitely not the motion you would normally see from clouds.

Alan spoke. "Pete, you sure that's a cloud we're looking at?"

"It doesn't look like a cloud to me." Geoff paused for a moment as the realisation of what it was came into his thoughts. "Fuck me, they're locusts; we better get under some cover, Pete. We get caught in that and we're all dead men."

I made my next line very clear. "Get to the castle!"

We ran as fast as our feet could carry us; soon, we had reached the drawbridge. As we rushed over it, we were in severe panic mode.

The locusts were by now virtually all over us; they were moving at a tremendous speed. "Crap, find a way in, lads, or we're dead. Move it!" I yelled. The locusts were not changing their direction at all, for all intents and purposes, they were being controlled by, guess who? The three of us were bashing at the main door. Geoff was trying to use his shoulder by barging at it.

Alan and I were shouting at the top of our lungs, "Colonel, Chieftain, Colonel, Chieftain!" We weren't getting anywhere, could we be heard from the inside? At that moment, we had no idea, all we could do was exactly what we were doing now, so Geoff carried on barging the door and we continued shouting as loudly as we could. The locusts were now virtually on top of us; the first few of this large mass were now reaching us as we started to brush them off ourselves whilst still trying to get into the castle. At the last possible moment, the colonel opened the door as we all fell inside. "Colonel, shut that bloody door, now!" I screamed. He did so; the three of us were shaken up pretty badly. Geoff had received a few bites to his neck and face.

Alan had a trickle of blood running down his cheek; the fear we felt was overwhelming. During that period, I had plum forgotten that I was immune from any physical damage to my body, not even the locusts could harm me. The old boy had rearranged my DNA structure of which had left my skin virtually damage-proof.

"Everyone okay? What seems to be the problem, gentlemen?" the colonel asked.

"You what, you gone blind since we saw you last?"

Alan was really starting to get cheesed off with him at this time. "There're bloody millions of locusts out there trying to get in here and you're asking if there's a problem, what's wrong with you? Surely, you could see them when we rushed through the door?"

"Well, no, I only saw you three. I presumed one of you was in need of the loo," replied the colonel.

I then abruptly stated, "Are you telling us that we were hallucinating the whole locust thing, what, all three of us?" I was astounded by the accusation.

Alan then stated, "No bloody way was that a hallucination. Hallucinations don't cut your skin, Colonel, look at Geoff's face, he's got bite marks, for god's sake, and my face, just look at me face, go on." The colonel looked puzzled.

"Well, I'm sorry, but I only saw you." Just then, the chieftain came out from the study.

"Now then, now then, what's the commotion, I'm trying to P."

"Sorry to disturb you, Chieftain, but Peter and his friends have just been attacked by locusts, millions of them." The colonel by now was convinced due to the injuries, concerned for the bites and blood.

"Attacked by whocusts, what's a whocust, never heard of 'em, wasting my P time, are you?" The chieftain was getting everything mixed, well, that was normal, or he had a hearing defect.

"No, Chieftain, locusts not whocusts, la, la, locusts." The colonel was plainly getting frustrated by now.

"We haven't had locusts here for, oooh, ages. I ate them all up, I did, had a big stew if I recall, got the bits in my teeth, yeah, went to the dentist. Yes, that's it, Colonel."

"Yes, Chieftain."

"What exactly are locusts, flowers of some kind, maybe?"

The colonel then screamed at him, "No, they're not bloody flowers, you stupid chieftain, they're eating machines, the grasshopper family; they eat anything organic; they leave nothing behind; they eat everything, and these two nearly got eaten."

The chieftain responded with, "The grass hopper family, you say, any relation to you, Colonel? I don't know them myself."

Geoff then said, "Oh, come on, this is going nowhere fast. I'm not going back out there, Pete, no bloody way."

I then asked, "Right, okay, you lot stay put. Colonel, will you come with me? I'm going back out, want to see if the locusts are still out there."

"Yes, I will come with you, Peter, but I'm afraid, you won't find anything," the colonel remarked.

I then remarked, "Well, you've nothing to worry about then now, have you?"

The colonel eased forward; he moved nice and easy. Gently, he opened the door; once he had opened it enough, he popped his head around the door, and immediately, he said, "You see, there's absolutely nothing to see." At that second, his mouth dropped. "Mmmm, I say, Peter, what's that?"

"Oh shit," I said, "they must have circled and come back around, locusts, Colonel, locusts." The colonel slammed the door hurriedly; he then began running around like a headless chicken, who just had its head chopped off in the farmyard. "We, we, we need to do something, something, what, what?" He had lost it; he had really lost it; the chieftain walked straight up to the colonel, twisted him around so that he could look at him face his face.

The chieftain then slapped him reasonably hard across the face. "You are my colonel not a raving Alpine McGregor. Smithers, pull yourself together. I never did, and that's saying something, unto the bottle of blur."

The colonel stood there for a few seconds in total shock; he then returned to normality. "Thank you, Chieftain, I don't know what happened to me. Sorry, gentlemen, I have never felt that before. What would you say it was, Peter?"

"Well, that's obvious to us three, Colonel, it was simply fear."

"Fear," the colonel gasped, "what a horrid feeling."

"Yes, Colonel, it's not nice at all."

Geoff then stated, "That poxy curse won't give up till we're dead, Pete, you know that, don't ya?"

"Yes, Geoff, I know, question is what do we do now?" I thought for a moment. "Chieftain, have you any fire extinguishers?"

"What, who, Colonel, what did you say, fire what?" The chieftain was totally oblivious to what I was asking for.

"Jesus, you ain't got a clue, have you? Don't worry about it, for god's sake, okay, the answer's no, got it, right, fine, rules that out, so we can't burn them, can't trap 'em, can't eat 'em."

Alan then realised something and shouted out aloud.

"Bollocks, they're coming under the door, oh Christ, what do we do now!" The colonel then thinking ever so quickly made a suggestion, "Run!" The five of us looked at each other then we ran like hell down the corridor; each room we passed had an inner door.

The whole castle was built like a maze; there were no areas that we could get trapped in for there was always an exit; by this time, the locusts were inside the castle and giving chase; we continued our evacuation as fast as we could.

It was soon becoming apparent that all we were doing was wasting time for how do you get out of a situation like this? We were fast growing out of options, let alone rooms to run through.

The colonel made another suggestion, "We could try the dungeons, May Owen was running experiments down there, well, that's what I heard."

"Do you know the way?" I asked hurriedly.

"Well, no, it's my first time here actually. Chieftain, you have been here before?"

"Of course, I have, Colonel, bean twice for him."

"Well, can you get us there?" Alan yelled.

"Yes, yes, I can. Follow me."

The chieftain was in his element; he took us down passages, corridors, hundreds of steps that just kept leading down, down. The locusts you could hear swarming about for they weren't just moving on our position, they were extremely busy whilst devouring any and everything they could eat.

Well, it was their nature after all, and not even the curse could fight that. Eventually, the chieftain had managed to find the dungeons of the castle, more like luck, if he was honest to himself and us.

But as usual, he took pride in his own achievement. The dungeon looked a miserable place; sod being a prisoner down here, it must've been hell on earth; it was cold, dark and miserably damp; rats were freely running around the place, scurrying from cell to cell.

The chieftain opened his big gob and said, "Here we are." He then produced a box of matches from his trouser pocket and ignited a straw-headed piece of wood that was mounted upon the wall; it immediately erupted into flame.

Alan removed it from the wall so we could now use it as a torch.

We then walked ahead until we came up to what seemed to be a dead end.

Geoff then stated, "Oh bloody terrific, fuck our luck. Pete, he's only brought us to a dead fucking end; he's really fucked us up, Pete."

"Chieftain! What the hell have you done?" I wasn't a happy bunny.

"Oh, poo bum," said the chieftain as he looked over the dead end facing wall.

"I thought you knew where we were going," cried the colonel.

"Trust is a word of love, Colonel, if I was to be where I wasn't, I would be there."

Alan then said, "You really do come out with some bollocks at times, Chieftain, what do we do now then?"

Alan was nowhere near impressed, none of us were. The chieftain then made a strange request that involved me. He said, "Peter, do you see that orange button on the wall over there? Would you care to press it?" I turned as I looked at this button. I then looked around at everyone else.

Geoff said, "Don't, Pete, the chieftain hasn't really shown himself to be trustworthy."

Alan agreed with Geoff, "He as a point, Pete."

I looked at the pair of them and responded to their remarks, "I need to find out, one way or the other. I just need to know what's on the other side, lads." I closed my eyes. God, was I on edge, full of apprehension as I pressed.

Total disbelief fell upon everyone as the button released a sliding door; the door slid open to reveal a sealed experimental chamber that May Owen had created over a long period of time; we entered the room and the door sealed tightly shut behind us.

"There you go, we're safe now." The chieftain was very happy with himself at that moment.

"Oh, bloody great," I said, "We're safe, all right, we're also trapped in here, we have a swarm of locust just itching to get in here and eat us all, and right now, they are waiting outside for the dinner bell."

"Just listen, Chieftain, we could plainly hear them through the door."

"Har, bless their little hearts, they're trying to come in with us." Geoff was being so sarcastic, he then said as he gazed around, "Jesus, Pete, Al, look at all this stuff." The three of us looked around the chamber.

It was a scientist's dream, probably every piece of equipment ever invented was here, from gyro compasses to microscopes; it was magnificent; we moved around the room with amazement. "Is there anything you would like for your journey, Peter?" the chieftain asked.

"Yeah, everything, Chieftain." I just couldn't believe the amount of stuff May Owen had acquired, no wonder she had said no to me taking an item.

"If you want, take it," the chieftain said.

"You serious?" I was flabbergasted by the chieftain's generosity.

"No use to me or the colonel; for that matter, we can't even boil an egg."

"Well, I can," stated the colonel.

"Well, thank you, thank you, Chieftain, this will really help us out a lot. Right, lads, see what you can dismantle, and please be gentle. Don't forget the adaptors, leads, plugs, USB sticks, whatever the connection, take it."

The colonel looked at the chieftain and whispered into his ear, "Why have you given them all this equipment, Chieftain? We're trapped in a sealed room, one way in and out, locusts at our door, we haven't a chance in hell of getting out of here."

The chieftain then said, "They're happy, ain't they?" The colonel smiled at the gesture, but he was right, where could we go?

Even that though didn't interfere with us detaching as much as we could carry in our arms.

Alan then remarked, "Tell you something, Pete, that May Owen wasn't stupid, she's still got the equipment's details on each piece."

Geoff then said his piece, "Yeah, brill, we can make an inventory now. Save having to guess what each one is, what a time saver." After roughly twenty minutes, we had managed to dismantle a good amount of gear. Alan was keenly writing each named piece of equipment onto a piece of scrap paper that was in his pocket.

Geoff said, "You know something, Pete, there must be two to three thousand pounds worth of stuff here, what do we do now?" I looked at him.

"Alan, what have we?"

"Well, there's the two we already have in the car, now we've got one catalytic isolation control panel and accessories; we've a universal transmit stabiliser unit, magnetic decoding oscillator, four transponder units, and six micro core induct valves, keep us going for a bit, wouldn't you say."

"Yeah, I would, but there's still three more items we need to find, remember that."

"Three more?" stated Geoff surprisingly.

"The old boy was to identify them remember?"

"Oh yeah, sorry." Just at that moment, my brain then had a realisation trip that ran up and gave me a good kick up the backside. I was so focussed that I just totally forgot that we were fucked in all the excitement.

I stood there and whispered to myself, "Old boy, please come in, I need you now, please we need you." Then as if by magic, our friendly old boy materialised.

"You are doing well, the Peter, soon the end and peace will be free; you have all you have. I am forbidden to remove you and yours from this place. I am also forbidden to give precise information, you are, the Peter. I am to afford you the phase, the phase will remove you from the danger of the swarm, you will be taken to the original place of entry. Once inside the phase, the locust swarm cannot harm you in any shape, way or form; it is unable to penetrate its shell.

"Nothing can penetrate the phase unless I will it so; once you are engulfed by it, the phase will focus on to you, Peter, your mind, your thought patterns will entwine and control the phase's path, your thought waves will guide you three back to the large willow tree.

"Your point of entry into this world you will then be returned to the pit from whence you came; do not alarm, I will come to you." The colonel and the chieftain stood there gormless, just looking at the old boy for as they looked, it lifted its hands and began summoning the phase bubble by chanting something that none of us could understand. From deep within itself, a black mass gradually came into view; slowly, the mass began to form into a translucent bubble.

It grew and grew; eventually, it was large enough to accept three fully grown men, and the equipment. As this was taking place, the swarm of locust began to compress area of the door, you could hear them going crazy outside trying to get into the chamber. I looked at the chieftain and then the colonel, the two of them just stood there and waved a goodbye. The old boy then faced us. "It is time, enter the phase." We stepped into it.

Within a micro second, we were phase-shifted from the chamber to the willow tree; as we touched down on the grass, the phase bubble just evaporated. The entire journey took us less than a second; it was unreal. I without pausing stated, "Let's find the phase wall, lads, think we've had enough of this place, don't you?"

"And how do we find the entrance?" asked Alan.

"You'll soon find out once you have found it, mate, trust me, you'll know," said Geoff giggling. So off we went prodding and poking everything on the tree.

Alan was the lucky one for as he touched a section on the tree, his hand slipped straight in; he yelled as he immediately withdrew his arm. "Hey, found it, come on!" Alan yelled. You could see the locust swarm was in hot pursuit; we didn't have a great amount of time in which to get everything into the tree.

We moved like we had a purpose. I mean nothing was left behind, and it was all done before you could say the chieftain was a stupid dick, then we left the miserable place and our friends behind as we all jumped through. The old boy must've sealed the gateway as no locust came through after us.

We were back in Margate Caves, trapped but alive; we gazed around at our situation. Geoff then said, "Hope he's not too long, I hate this hole."

I then replied, "You ain't the only one, mate."

"I suppose the only thing we can do now is sit and wait." So, that's exactly what we did, but to praise our entity, the old boy, we had to give it its due for it appears every time we're in need of it. There was an instant flash of light that illuminated the entire hole that we were in. Next minute, we were all sitting in my car; it was at that moment that I wondered where was the equipment we had with us, was it transported as well? I flung myself out of the car and rushed to the boot, opened it up; lo and behold there was everything neatly packed.

Right down to the smallest of leads, I returned and sat in the car. "We're okay, lads, everything's been placed in the boot; it's all safe and sound."

"So, where we off to next then?" asked Geoff.

"Hospital," I replied.

"Why, what's the matter?"

Alan was slightly anxious. "No, not me, I'm okay. I have just been told to go to the QEQM in Margate."

"What for?" asked Geoff.

"I have no idea; we never get told more info than that, it's the norm," I replied. We drove away. Now the hospital was only a few streets away so it wasn't long before we had arrived; we made sure we parked outside the hospital car park as none of us had the parking charge fees.

Once out of the car, we crossed the road and walked over to the hospital; we went inside. I then mentioned, "Just remember, if you're challenged by security, you're visiting."

"Sorry to be a party pooper, Pete, but who exactly are we visiting?" Geoff asked.

"Bloody hell, Geoff, we're not visiting anyone. It's just a cover story, come on wake up," I answered.

"Oh, yeah, sorry, just having a blonde moment," Geoff remarked then gave himself a little chuckle.

I walked up to the information boards that lay upon the wall in the hope that I would receive some more information as to why we were sent here; the psychiatric ward started to glow and pulsate, but this was for my eyes only as no one else could see what it was doing.

"Right, let's get going, lads, follow me." Nothing came from the other two as they just accepted the fact that I knew a bit more than I was letting on. At around this time, inside the psychiatric wing, within one of the small side rooms, one of the psychiatrists was sitting with the two new arrivals.

The two sat on one side of a long table whilst the doctor sat opposite them. "Hello, gentlemen, let's get the formalities out the way before we start our little chat, shall we? Now my name's Doctor James Anderson, you can call me Jim if you're more comfortable with that, and your name's are?" asked the doctor.

"Well, I'm Colonel Smithers, this is the chieftain," remarked the colonel.

"I see, emmm, when you say colonel, is that an ex-military title? I mean were or are you in the armed forces at all? I'm asking as I just want to be clear as to why you've given yourself that title, that's all."

"No, it's my name, it's always been my name, ever since I was born; it's a normal name from where I come from," stated the colonel.

"I see, so no military experience, whatsoever?" replied the doctor.

"No, no military experience," stated the colonel once again.

"Right, okay." Now during this interview, the doctor was frantically jotting down notes on his clipboard. "Right, now, Chieftain?"

"I am that, I believe I am to what the others would say I am," muttered the chieftain.

"Excuse me, I haven't asked you anything as yet." The doctor was stumped for a few moments.

Chapter 8
Welcome Back to the Fold

"Right then, do you remember the police officers that brought you in here?"

"Yes, I do, very nice chaps, I must say, yes, very nice." The colonel was rather jolly for his situation.

The chieftain immediately also responded to the doctor's statement, "I thought it was a burger van we travelled in, Colonel, you sure, well, it smelt like one." The chieftain was astounded.

The colonel replied, "Yes, Chieftain, do you also remember the farting completion we had at McDonalds, oh, that was funny, do you know that fart of yours smelt like a sausage and egg McMuffin."

"I did enjoy those," the chieftain replied, "Of course, I do, Colonel, it was one of my best; they evacuated the place; they thought it was a stinky bomb, yes, I was quite proud of that one. Did you know, Doctor, they only use the coffee bean?

"When they're making that brown liquid thingy, do you know, Colonel, if they used my variational bean, that could seriously increase their profits by at least £1.50." The psychiatrist was amazed as he was helpless in shutting these two up; he tried valiantly to intervene on several occasions to get back on track with his consultation, but the colonel and the chieftain were just rabbiting on like kids in the playground. At this moment, he had had enough; he slammed his hand on the table so hard, it stung as he shook out the sting.

"That's enough, you two, settle down. I'm going to start again."

The colonel then asked, "Starting again, what are we starting then, we going to be watching a film?"

The chieftain butted in, "Oh, certainly, we always enjoy a good film, don't we, Colonel? What're we going to watch, Andy Panda, or I'm not a fairy, now that's a very good film, that really is a good film. Did you know, Colonel, I peed my pants watching Andy Panda, when Ted lost his dummy, very sad moment indeed, very sad."

The chieftain started to get upset as the colonel then responded, "There, there Chieftain, do you feel better now?"

The psychiatrist again just sat there as he once more slammed his hand on the table. "Enough, enough, I say, Jesus, what's wrong with you two, can't you ever just shut up for five minutes?

"Now, now according to this police report I have here, you Chieftain, you kicked over a table and chair, can you tell me what you were thinking of at the time?"

The chieftain said nothing as he just gazed at the doctor; the doctor repeated, "Oh well, maybe you didn't quite understand. The table and chair incident, Chieftain, you kicked it over. Why did you do that, what was running through your mind at the time?" The chieftain again said nothing.

The doctor looked at him in a muddled fashion; he then said, "Look here, I don't know what game you two have cocked up, but it won't work on me.

"Now, Chieftain, will you please answer my questions, it's important for us so that we can come to a diagnosis to assess your condition." The doctor then turned to the colonel. "Will you get him to talk to me, please?" The colonel was as quiet as a mouse, not a sound came from either of them as the doctor lay back against his chair in full dismay.

He faced the colonel, "Look, I don't understand what type of game you two are playing here, but let me assure you that unless you start cooperating, then I'm afraid, it will be a long time before you smell fresh air again."

The colonel and the chieftain looked at each other; the chieftain then said, "Right, the five minutes are up now, now what was the question again?"

The doctor withdrew in his chair as he stated, "What five minutes are you referring to, Chieftain, may I ask?"

The chieftain replied, "You told us to shut up for five minutes."

The doctor responded, "Oh no, I didn't."

"Oh yes, you did," replied the colonel.

"No, I did not," replied the doctor.

"Did," remarked the chieftain as he then quoted, "oh, bugger me."

The colonel responded, "What's the matter, Chieftain?"

The chieftain replied, "I've just done a poo poo in my pants."

The doctor then stated, "Why are you doing this to me? I've been nice and polite with you; do you know I've been in this job for thirty eight years? I've met all kinds of mentally ill patients, but you two are absolute idiots."

The chieftain responded, "Well, what can I say to you, that outburst was bloody beautiful, thank you, emmm, you did say you were a doctor, didn't you?" Just then, the chieftain lifted one bum cheek and let off a massive explosion that rippled his trousers; it stunk to high heaven, as the aroma spread; it reached the doctor's nose; he immediately stood as the stink grew stronger with its intensity.

Holding his nose he shouted, "My god, sausage and egg McMuffin, oh my god!" Hurriedly, he left the room, green-faced and weak at the knees; it was as if he was about to vomit all over the place.

Every few seconds, he was retching whilst holding his stomach and mouth. The colonel looked at the chieftain and said, "That's a shame; he was nice. I thought we were getting on reasonably well for a moment there; by the way, Chieftain, that's a lovely aroma to your farting capabilities, yes, very well done I must say."

The chieftain stated, "I need some pants."

At that moment, two more psychiatrists entered the room; this time, they looked like they meant business; they weren't showing any sign that they wanted to be friendly at all.

Just stern looks on their faces. "Right, my name's Doctor Gerald Fitzpatrick and this is my colleague, Doctor Patrick Fitzgerald. Let's get one thing perfectly clear from the start, we expect cooperation from you two, okay? Now Doctor Anderson has had to leave the hospital for a short while due to a nervous breakdown he has just had." The chieftain and the colonel looked out through the glass panelling as they could see two white coats trying to assist Doctor Anderson out of the wing, the poor sod was hysterical.

"They're idiots, I asked them, I did. I asked them, but they're idiots!" Tears were streaming from his eyes as he was screaming out; he couldn't even stand on his own steam; he was a complete wreak as they took him off the wing.

Doctor Fitzpatrick asked, "Right, we've got the police report, now which one of you is the colonel?"

"That'll be me, I'm the colonel, ain't I, Chieftain?"

The chieftain replied, "I think so, that's unless you've changed into a pollock fish-eyed monster called Cedric."

Doctor Fitzgerald then shouted in a deep authoritarian voice, "Right, that's enough, just answer the questions, okay, no verbal detours of any kind from now on, is that understood? Right, you, emm, the colonel, in your own words please, why do you think you were arrested this morning by the police and brought here to us?"

"Well, personally, I strongly feel that it was due to the chieftain, he must've caused a scene when he let out a bootie burp, sausage and egg McMuffin, did you know, that's a delicacy where I come from?"

"I see." Everything that the two guys said were eagerly written down by whichever doctor wasn't speaking.

Doctor Fitzgerald then asked the chieftain, "So, Chieftain, did you mean to break wind or was it by sheer accident?" The chieftain looked at him in a weird way.

"I never had an accident, did I, Colonel? I did have a bootie burp though; it was one of my best, wasn't it, Colonel?"

"Yes, Chieftain, it certainly was. Do you remember when you bootie burped when you sat on May Owen's face that time?"

"STOP!" cried out Doctor Fitzgerald. "I thought we had got this part perfectly clear to you, there is no verbal chitchat, okay? Now where was I?"

"Why you asking me," replied the chieftain, "don't you know? This one's a total dick, Colonel."

Doctor Fitzpatrick then stood from his chair, faced his colleague, and said, "Can I have a word with you outside, Doctor?"

Whilst they were out of the room the chieftain and the colonel started another chin wag.

"Do you know something, Colonel, thinking back now, do you know it could've been the bean they served me? It must've been that caused my bootie burp, its colour, texture, its entire design wasn't right, you know; it was totally insulted to the bean and everything that I, sorry we, had created there.

"My beanery would never make that type of bean, you know? The bean has to be egg-shaped with a crunch to it and has to be bright orange, otherwise, it doesn't get passed in section."

The colonel then leaned forward and spoke softly in to the chieftain's ear. "Try to understand, Chieftain, when these white-coated people come back in, please shut up."

"You trying to kiss me, Colonel? Well, I never did, up to bottle on my ship and all that. I say steady, maybe later, you weirdo." The chieftain was rather taken aback by the colonel's advances.

The colonel then said in self-defence, "No, I wasn't trying to kiss you, Chieftain, the accusation is totally preposterous."

"I must say, well, you started it, Colonel."

"Oh no, I didn't," the colonel responded.

"Oh yes, you did, monkey face." The chieftain was getting rude at this point.

"Stick your fingers up your bum poo breath!" shouted the colonel.

"Hi, say, Colonel, steady. You've never asked me to do that before." The chieftain began to cry.

"I'm sorry, Chieftain, things just got out of hand, sorry."

"Yes, oh and by the way, fuck off." The chieftain was extremely rude once again.

The chieftain then stood and stuck his hands down inside the rear of his trousers; seconds later, he pulled his hand out and stated to the colonel, "It's okay, Colonel, I've only done a bootie burp, thought it was a poo."

He then had a little chuckle at that point. "I'm the chieftain, strength of a thousand beans. I eat bean and drink P, so ner to you and double the poo stains on your pants." The chieftain was pleased with his verbal diarrhoea.

"Oh, Chieftain, well done, blinking well done." The colonel was just about to put his hand to his forehead and was virtually ready to burst into tears as the doctors re-entered the room; they had overheard the chieftain's last remarks.

They immediately gazed at him, then said, "Right, so you have the strength of a thousand beans, and you eat baked beans, I take it and you drink P, I see. Now, Chieftain, take me back to when you were younger, what's your first memory as a child?"

The chieftain then replied, "Eating of the bean, Mummy didn't have mushy peas at the time, no ice cream nor Scandinavian chipmunks, so we all just ate the bean. He is very stupid, Colonel, and I will tell you this for a fiver, Doctor. I am my own cafe, and my own boss anol. I was five, or was I six, so put that in your pipe and eat it."

"You mean smoke it?"

"Put that in your pipe and eat it, I say."

Doctor Fitzgerald then stated, "I think you'll find the correct phrase is stick it in your pipe and smoke it, Chieftain." Naturally, the doctor was spot on. "So let's have a look at this police report once more then, shall we? Yes, here we go.

"Now the police arrested the pair of you for breach of the piece, was that before you broke wind or after the shop was cleared out?"

The chieftain was rather confused at that point as he said, "What do you mean before, Doctor? I could only produce that explosion between my bum cracks only once, four indeed, you're really stupid. Colonel, he's off the planet, fancy a game of cricket anyone, and I promise not to cheat." Then the chieftain mumbled under his breath, "Well, just a little."

Doctor Fitzpatrick once again looked at the chieftain. "You seem to be able to switch your mind off and on, Chieftain, one minute you sound rational."

"Well, thank you, Doctor, it's been a pleasure; he then stood expecting to be let out." The chieftain had totally misunderstood.

Doctor Fitzgerald then spoke. "'em, Chieftain, please sit down, we are far from finished here, so Colonel, you tell me about this man, where did you meet him say?"

The colonel stated, "Well, I was working at the beanery for at least one day when a young man came up to me, introduced himself as the chieftain; you see, I had made a foul-up on the line; there should have been three beans per millimetre square to the inch. I got it wrong and so the chieftain sorted out the problem."

"Oh, interesting, how did he sort the problem out then?" the doctor asked.

The colonel carried on, "He smashed the conveyor belt." The doctor then wrote down 'limited mental ability'.

"So, Chieftain, let's get back to your childhood, can you remember any moments when you got afraid of anything?" Doctor Fitzgerald asked.

"Yes, course I can, May Owen's bum, scared the crap out of me. I remember it well. I was planting my first bean plant when as I stood up, there it was looking right at me, all black it was."

"What was?" asked the doctor.

"The soil, try and pay attention, Doctor, please. Colonel, I think he's a fruit bat, you can't follow me, can you, doc?"

"Okay, okay, this isn't getting us anywhere," exclaimed doctor Fitzgerald. "Let's change the topic, have you any pets?"

"Yes, of course, I have. I've also a snake called Cedric; the dwarfs I named them after my aunties, uncles, cousins, and niece; there are four of them, you know, named Who, What, Where and When."

Dr Fitzgerald then stated, "I asked you if you had pets, Chieftain, dwarfs are human beings."

The chieftain took that as offensive as he stood up from his chair and raised his voice. "No, they're not, they're my pet dogs, Who, What, Why and When." Both doctors were extremely baffled as they looked at each other astounded.

Doctor Fitzgerald then responded, "Who, What, Why and When are your dogs? But you stated they were dwarfs a minute ago, this is rather confusing, gentlemen."

The colonel then tried to ease the confusion by saying, "The dwarfs are our companions; they were born human, but overtime, they altered to dogs."

"Right, so you're implying that they're werewolves, are you? This is very interesting," said Doctor Fitzgerald. "You two are pretty unique, well, that's your interpretation, isn't it, Doctor Fitzpatrick?"

The chieftain then stated, "Where and Who are lovely putti kinships. Why and When are from the Buttons family; my favourite is Who."

"What!" The doctor found this difficult to follow. "Who is the what?"

Replying to the doctor, the chieftain continued, "Who and What, they're my favourites."

The two doctors were totally confused by this time as Doctor Fitzpatrick stated, "Well, I'm sure they're nice dogs, Chieftain, Colonel, well, I'm sure you'll appreciate that there's going to be at least another full session that we're going to need, so tell me, where do you two live, what's your address? Can you tell me that as I don't see anything written down on these police reports?"

"Certainly, doc, we live at the beanery."

"Oh right, and where's that then?" Doctor Fitzgerald asked.

"Beantopium, Number 2345, Beantopium, in the land combined with the P."

"I see. Well, thank you, for the chat, it has been very instructive; now you two sit there and chill for a while, we're just going to pop off and have a few words with our people. Would you two like to have a drink of something, maybe some waters, you must be thirsty by now."

The doctors seemed very polite, but not as to the meaning, the chieftain really took offence. "Water! You're trying to kill me for the ship to be, you hear that, Colonel, he wants us to drink water. I never did to poo this way before, Colonel,

I never did, up to the ship it could have been. I will have you know water is an illness; everyone should drink P, or bean juice."

The chieftain was most upset; the colonel then asked the doc, "Haven't you any bean juice in this place?"

"Well, I'm, I'm not sure. I will try to get you some from our canteen."

"Yes, and jump to it, we haven't got all the day, you perhaps some." The chieftain wasn't happy as everyone could plainly see.

"Yes, this is going to be a long day I think."

Doctor Fitzpatrick then answered back under his breath, "They're absolutely barking mad, the pair of 'em; this is fantastic, two real fruit bats; this is great material for my forthcoming lectures next month. Right then, we won't be long." The doctors then stood up and used their swipe cards to get out of the room. Meanwhile, back with me and my mates, we had just got outside the psychiatric wing.

There stood a vending machine to our far right. Alan checked it out, coffees were free. Within seconds, we were enjoying a cup each; we sat down to think of our next move. "So now we're here, what's the plan?" Geoff asked.

Alan jumped in with, "Yeah, Pete, who are we here for, we have to be here for someone as why would the old boy want us to come here in the first place?"

"Okay, okay, get your heads around this if you can, we're here to get the colonel and—"

I was immediately interrupted by Geoff, "Oh god, no, please tell me we're not here for him."

I responded with, "Geoff, he did us a favour, remember that; after all, the old boy couldn't just leave those two there to be eaten by locusts, come on now, we've got to think of a way we can get them out of this ward, as well, as past the security."

Alan then said, "Well, we're gonna need access cards, passcodes, and an invisibility shield to get past the cameras without being seen."

"In that case, it should be child's play," stated Geoff.

We sat there still pondering; after a few more moments, my brainwaves finally kicked in. I used my telepathic link for assistance, three access cards, nametags and the passwords of this psychiatric wing; we also needed three white coats; it wasn't long before the three of us had access cards.

The passcodes were now firmly embedded in my head, and with that, we were automatically transformed with a white coat; we actually looked like doctors; the old boy has done us proud once again; we even had a stethoscope each, fantastic.

"Right, this is what we're going to do, Geoff, you find the security control room or where ever the security hangs out, get some distraction going.

"I don't know, say something like there's a fight on the grounds somewhere and make it convincing; if luck is with us, they won't have camera for that area. I think the old boy can deal with that. Alan and myself, now we're gonna go inside the ward and get those two fruit bats out."

"Is that it?" asked Geoff.

I then replied, "Well, have you a better idea then cause if you have, that will be great, if not, get going. Alan, you're with me."

Geoff moved off as Alan and myself approached the ward; using my access card, we stepped onto the ward.

I approached the reception desk, "Afternoon, nurse, we have two new arrivals on the ward, a colonel and the other calls himself the chieftain, what room are they in please?"

The nurse replied, "Room 5, Doctor, just over there."

"Thank you, nurse, Doctor Stoppage, grab the notes please."

"Certainly, Doctor Tate." Alan did exactly that; we entered Room 5; there sitting down in front of us were the chieftain and the colonel; they looked up and saw us; the colonel was the first to react.

"I say it's you. Chieftain, look it's them."

The chieftain then stated, "Well, bugger me with a pitchfork, well, it's certainly nice to see you two again."

"Have the doctors given you two any medication yet," I asked.

The colonel replied, "No, not yet, but we've had a lovely chat with three men in white coats, two of them have just popped off to chat to their friends."

The chieftain wasn't as loving. "One of them only wanted me to drink water, the do do person. I wanted P. I never did."

"Right, okay, Chieftain," I answered, "let's just get you two out of here before they decide to dissect your brains."

"That would be fun," Alan quipped.

Alan and I walked out of the room with the colonel and chieftain at our sides; we moved towards the reception desk where the nurses were stationed.

Alan and I broke into a conversation as we passed the two nurses who were heads down typing away on their computers. Alan came out with, "I've arranged for a CT scan for Mr Anderson, should be reasonably interesting to see the results, Doctor."

"Certainly, will be," I responded. Within seconds, we were off the ward.

Geoff was successful as he had the security guards chasing after three factious foes. Geoff came running up the corridor and said, "We better move before the security guys realise they've been duped."

"Well done, Geoff; come on, you two, now move."

I was very eager for us all to get off the hospital grounds as soon as we could. Shortly, we were across the road and into the car once more. "Tell ya something, Pete, it's pretty neat having an entity on your side, ain't it?" Geoff remarked.

I replied with, "It has its moments."

"Oh shit!" I shouted.

"What's up?" asked Alan.

I replied with, "The police have just been informed that these two are now missing, well, when you think about it, it makes sense when you consider it is a high risk area being at the psychiatric ward; we better burn rubber, lads, before we're all nabbed."

I drove off out of Margate as quickly as I could but without grabbing the attention of the law; my direction was the motorway.

The chieftain was looking rather down in the dumps as the colonel asked him, "Are you okay?"

The chieftain replied, "Well, no, I am not okay, Colonel. I'm confused, what happened to us? I am not collating information all that well."

"That's not a surprise," mumbled Alan.

"Peter, do you think the understanding will be clearer if you were to open your mouth and explain it all?" the chieftain really needed some clarity at this point.

"Yeah, okay, Chieftain, I will try." I then said, "Well, it seems like the old boy did its bit and removed you two from that swarm of locust and transferred you to this time period, well, Westgate anyway. I guess you scared a lot of people by showing up as you did; the police were called and they took you two to the hospital after chatting to you both, I guess. They started their examination by the psychiatrists there; we were informed of your dilemma, we got you two out, now you're here with us once again, hope that helps."

"Yes, it does, Peter, thank you," stated the colonel.

Chieftain looked at him. "What did he say, Colonel, the police, who are they? This place is not like my home, don't like it, Colonel, want to go back to bean and have a P." The chieftain started to try and open his car door to get out; this caused a commotion within the car.

"Chieftain, pack it in!" Alan yelled.

I then stated, "We're doing 60, do you want to get killed? Colonel, restrain him, will ya?"

Geoff then assisted the colonel. Slowly, the chieftain calmed down. "Want to go home, I never unto the bottle anymore."

The colonel then stated the obvious, "I do believe the chieftain has had enough of this adventure, Peter."

"Well, if I'm any type of judge, Colonel, he will just have to get with it cause we're no way finished in this yet, what did you call it, adventure," I replied.

The chieftain responded with, "Get with it, get with what? Who is he referring? I am chieftain, not a pee bum. I never did, I tell you, bar humbug to you with knobs on."

The chieftain wasn't feeling great; the colonel was doing his best to pacify his friend as he said, "Where we off to then, Peter?"

"Well, at the moment, I'm trying to get us onto the M2, we're off to a place called Reculver; it's about eleven miles away. Saint Mary's Church, to be precise." I kept driving.

Alan then remarked on how beautiful the setting was as he witnessed this low fog that was drifting its way across the countryside; it was far off in the distance, just below the horizon on our left-hand side.

It was just like a mist you would normally see over the fields in the early hours of a spring morning. He remarked, "Look at that, beautiful!"

"Yeah, pretty decent," Geoff agreed. Something then dawned on me as I too watched this strange mist like fog.

I started to question myself as I thought, *Was this thing increasing its speed, and was it now changing its direction and heading towards us?*

As I drove, I had one eye on the road and the other on this fog. "Alan, do me a favour, will ya?"

Alan responded, "Yeah, sure, what is it?"

"Can you look at that fog and tell me that I'm seeing things? I could swear it's changed course and coming our way."

Instantly, Geoff and Alan twisted and gazed at the fog; the pair of them then looked at each other as they both said together, "Shit."

"No need to say any more, lads, okay, make sure all the windows are closed please. I think we've got visitors coming our way."

Geoff then said, "What do you mean guests, Pete?"

"Look at it." I pointed across at the fog; it was like a sandstorm over the desert; its speed was tremendous.

Within minutes, the fog had reached us and covered the car, pounding on the car's shell, like a knocking on the door; the situation shortly began to become impossible to drive as the fog then started to thicken and change its colour tone; a deep blackness overcame the area.

I immediately stopped the car but kept the engine running. "Whatever you lot do, no one opens any windows." I made myself very clear on that point. The knocking on the roof now became harder and more concentrated, pounding and pounding. The chieftain began to get frustrated with it as he started to punch the roof above his head. "I like this, this is fun, come on, Colonel, get punching."

I turned around to him. "Chieftain, this is no game. Do you understand me?" At that moment, the car's engine just cut out; everything was a dead eerie calmness.

"Oh crap," Alan called out, "what now, Christ, no." I then continually tried to restart the engine but to no avail, the engine was completely and utterly dead; the black fog slowly began to find its way into the car through the vents.

Alan and I tried desperately to hold it back, but how do you stop the wind? "Cover your faces!" I shouted. Within minutes, we were engulfed, struggling like made in trying not to inhale any of this, whatever it was.

Geoff broke first as he needed to breathe, taking in a quick gulp of oxygen; the blackness seemed to be able to think as it instantly and dramatically closed in on him; it changed in its direction and flowed into Geoff's ears, nose and mouth.

The impact simply knocked Geoff out for six; he was really out cold; the fog immediately then disappeared.

We sat there mesmerised for a few moments. Alan and I came to our senses. "Geoff, Geoff, you okay, mate?" I called out; there was no movement or sound coming from him. "Colonel, help him, will ya?" I asked. The colonel examined him the best he could.

132

"Sorry, Peter, but he's fast asleep. I can try to wake him or do you want me to leave him?" the colonel asked.

"No, leave him be, let him rest. You now know how beautiful the bloody mist is?" I said in a sarcastic manner.

"Well, how was I to know it was gonna do what it did? It looked harmless when I said it."

"Come on, Pete, this ain't my fault," Alan replied.

"I know that, Al, I know." Shortly, Geoff began to come too; he was stunned for the first few moments.

After a few minutes, his memory started to return. He then stated, "What the fuck happened there?" I asked.

"What do you remember, Geoff?" Geoff replied.

"I don't remember a bloody thing, well, tell a lie, there was this fog that somehow got into the car, that's it, did I miss anything?" Geoff must've had some sort of amnesia or something like it; he had no memory of what he had breathed in.

That in itself must be treated as a gift from god, as at that moment the engine restarted all by itself.

"Strange, the engine was as dead as a dodo."

"Keep an eye on him, Alan." I drove off down the road; it wasn't long before trouble would raise its ugly head on us once again.

Alan noticed that Geoff was acting in a strange manner for his hands began to tremble, not a great deal but enough for him to grow a little concerned. Alan then put his hand on to Geoff's shoulder; it was then that Geoff started to have violent convulsions; it was as if he was having some sort of seizure; everyone on the back seat tried to restrain him so he wouldn't damage himself or damage any other. Alan did his utmost in trying to get Geoff back with us. "Geoff, Geoff, it's Alan, can you hear me; are you okay, mate?"

Geoff miraculously then calmly looked at Alan and responded with, "What you on about? Why you lot looking at me like that, what, did I miss something again?" It was quiet clear that he had had no recollection of what his body had just suffered.

Alan looked across at me and whispered, "Pete, we better find somewhere to stop soon, Geoff's in some trouble."

"Why what's up with him, I can't exactly see what's going on, mate. I'm driving."

"Well, he's shaking violently, but he does not know it. I'm really worried about it, something's seriously wrong."

"Right, okay." We drove a little further; there was an abandoned country house coming into view; as we approached, we could see that it was boarded up, so I thought to myself, *That's ideal, it's secluded and open to us.* But at that moment, Alan once again remarked on Geoff condition, as on Geoff's face were rings of inklike marks, blotches of sorts, like a plague had started to fill his face; the odd one seeped blood, a dark congealed blood that slowly ran down his face.

"Come on, Pete, he is getting worse, put your foot down, mate." Alan was by now fully worried about Geoff. Within seconds, Geoff's eyes had turned a hideous black; he then instantly flung himself and his arms around my neck and was trying to strangle me. Alan and the colonel moved within seconds, as they were desperate to free me from him, whilst all this was going on I struggled in controlling the car. The chieftain, the poor sod, was trapped between Geoff and a forward leaning colonel.

"I say steady Geoffrey, I'm getting, oh, I say steady, get your elbow out of my crotch. I am Chieftain. Colonel, get off my back, I tell you unto me. I never did." During the chieftain's verbal crap, Alan managed to use his karate to knock Geoff out. Geoff slumped to the floor. I was then rubbing my neck after the attempted throttle, core!

"Thanks, lads," I said.

I drove up the short driveway and passed the front of the building, finding a spot to park. "Right, lads, let's get him inside." The chieftain came into his own at this time for he knew exactly what was needed.

He had Geoff over his right shoulder as he approached the rear door, and with one great almighty kick, the door swung open.

Alan then stated, "Well done, Chieftain, great kick." We all entered the house. As we did, I then gave out the orders.

"Alan, can you try and find what you can for Geoff's hands and feet, we need to make sure he can't hurt anyone."

"Yeah, sure," Alan replied and walked off.

"Chieftain, you and the colonel get some windows open, please, let's get some light in here."

"What are we going to do with him?" the chieftain asked, as he was still holding him over his shoulder.

I then bluntly stated to the chieftain, "Just drop him, Chieftain." The chieftain true to form wasted no time, he literally just dropped him where he stood to the floor. Geoff fell like a ton of bricks.

Dust clouds came flying up to our waists. Shortly, the chieftain and the colonel had managed to open the living room windows.

Alan in the meantime had found some material for us to use in securing Geoff up with; he also had got his hands on a chair for us to use.

Alan and myself got Geoff onto the chair and secured him to it; it wasn't long before Geoff came to; it wasn't a pretty sight.

Geoff's face had now been twisted and deformed into something hideous; it was as if he had been taken over by a demon; it screeched, snarled and kept repeating over and over again the same phrase, DIE-TODAY, DIE-TODAY. It was like trying to listen to an old recording on one of those old cassette tape machines; the tape was on a loop for it just kept repeating the same over and over it spoke; it was driving us nuts. We left Geoff there and all entered the kitchen area. "What are we going to do?" asked the colonel.

"Kill him," answered Alan. There was no way I was about to do that so I responded to what Alan had just said.

"That's enough of that shit, Alan, no one's killing anyone. I'm sick of losing friends, no more, you hear me, there's got to be another way to free him from whatever this is; besides, we all know it's the work of that red curse."

Alan then replied, "Yeah, maybe, but the curse is always showing up as the colour red, this thing's jet black, has to be something else." The chieftain then made a wise statement.

"Well, call Mr Mist, surely, he will know what it is."

The colonel stated, "Yeah, call it," Alan agreed, so without fail, I called it telepathically. Within thirty seconds, the old boy came.

"We've a problem," I stated to it; the old boy looked at me then went into the other room and observed Geoff's shell of a man.

"Save you no, save you no, the Peter, possession has destroyed the Geoff, destroy option is all to do."

"There has to be another way, there has to be," I said. Alan came to me.

"Listen to what it's saying, Pete, Geoff's been possessed, there's no going back; it's done. If it can't save him, it's done." Alan and I looked at each other as I knew they were both right. I then looked at the old boy.

"Okay, okay, do it." I felt sick after that. I felt useless and defeated; the old boy moved towards Geoff. Geoff was screaming at him, snarling and dribbling from his mouth; the old boy placed his hands onto Geoff's shoulders.

The old boy and the demonic creature glared at one another, slowly a glow began to reveal itself around Geoff's body, and gradually the glow increased in heat. Soon Geoff's entire body ignited; flames spread all around; there was no sound from Geoff's demonic demon. Shortly, it was over, no more demonic demon, no more Geoff, all that remained was a pile of ash where Geoff had sat.

I was gutted and engulfed with failure. As the old boy whispered to me two words, Daryl Hawkins, I looked at him, but as usual, he would vanish like a vapour. I then looked at the pile of ash that lay on the ground, our friend was gone. "Come on, let's get back on the road." I was in a really low frame of mind.

I just kept thinking of what if, once in the car we drove off to Reculver, we arrived there at around 2 pm in the afternoon, parked up and started to stroll along the shoreline. There on top of the hill stood the ruins of St Mary's Church. I turned to the chieftain and colonel and spoke for the first time. "There's a canteen down that way, lads."

"Canteen, what's a canteen?" the colonel asked.

"You can buy food there, or the bean, I suppose."

"Buy, what do you mean, buy?" The colonel was puzzled. I produced a ten-pound note out of my pocket and gave it to him.

"Just go into the canteen, ask for what you want, like beans on toast and a drink say, hand the tenner over to him or her, you sit, they bring, you eat, simple."

"Eat! I say, the bean, come on, Colonel, I'm starving. I could eat a thousand beans." The chieftain with that stormed off; the colonel gave chase

"Wait for me, Chieftain!" the colonel cried out.

"You okay, Pete?" asked Alan in a caring manner.

"No, not really, mate. I'm gutted, to be honest with ya."

"Why did you send those two off?" asked Alan.

I replied "Well, they need to eat, mate, we don't, besides we're here to find a bloke called Daryl Hawkins."

"Daryl Hawkins, who is he then?" Alan asked.

"I have absolutely no idea as yet, mate. We're just going to have to find out, like always. Come on, let's go up to the ruins, you never know what we'll find."

"Yeah, probably a mob of skinheads after our blood," Alan stated. We walked off. Meanwhile, the chieftain and the colonel have got to the canteen.

The chieftain walked in first and up to the counter. "I am Chieftain, I want bean, you got that?" The member of staff took immediate offence by the way the chieftain had spoken.

"Excuse me, but why are you being so damn rude?"

The chieftain not understanding that his manner was too aggressive then went on, "Now look, me as hungry as a lamppost and the bean need to eat, now move it, will you, me hunger." The manager hearing this customer's rude and abusive attitude approached.

Chapter 9
Mythology

"Excuse me, but is everything okay here?"

"No, it's not, Mr Shanks, this man's being extremely rude to me." The manager then spoke to the chieftain.

"Now see here, I do not tolerate abusive or bad manners towards my staff, tone it down or get out."

The chieftain looked at him and said, "Now you just listen to me, bar humbug, sit on it here. I am chieftain and me hunger, me want 'em the bean. I never did, now feed me, Colonel, I am car filleted."

The colonel then stepped forward in the hope to ease the tension that was brewing. "Hello, look, there seems to be some confusion here, he doesn't mean to be unreasonable or unpleasant, he just wants some bean. As you can see, he is not well, you know."

"Right, well, then sit down and I will take your order. I'm telling you two now, one more outburst, and unwell or not, you will be out of here." The manager really drew the line in the sand; the colonel and chieftain sat down. The chieftain had no understanding of why people always took offence when he spoke. The manager came over. "Right, what can I get ya?"

The colonel answered with, "Have you got beans?"

"Course, I've beans, you trying to be funny, this is a café, you know." The manager was abrupt but firm.

"Good, can we have two beans and a P, please?" the colonel asked.

The manager threw down his writing pad on the table and shouted, "That's it, you have had your last chance, get out!"

The manager was furious with the pair. The chieftain stood up and stated, "I say to you bum is bum, I say. I am chieftain strength of a thousand beans, I never did."

The manager again shouted, "Get out of my café!" Well, that was it, the chieftain then went into more verbal diarrhoea. "My own cafe, I own my own cafe, you are up to bottle on the ship today. I saw a baked bean on the Milky Way, I did, so there, come on, Colonel, we're leaving. I never did, who am I, Colonel? I will not be addressed like a pregnant fish."

"No, Chieftain, let's leave."

The colonel was in full agreement; the pair of them left the canteen with the member of staff and the manager looking on through the window. The colonel could see us on top of the hill in front of him within the ruins; they headed our way.

Alan and myself were looking around the gravestones as tourists do; the sun was shining down on the ruins of the church; it really was a beautiful day, well, weather wise anyway. The chieftain and colonel came to us. "Hiya, eat well, did ya?" Alan asked.

"No, we didn't," cried the colonel, "they kicked us out of their canteen. I think it was the chieftain who upset them with his manner."

"Oh, munch on a fig leaf, Colonel," the chieftain bellowed.

"You see?" The colonel was always having to take the flak from the chieftain's gigantic troublesome mouth.

Alan and I broke into a short laugh, then we started to carry on surveying the area, and as we did, the colonel then managed to trip over a large stone that was virtually covered by soil and grass, but enough of it was still visible from the surface; he fell with a thump; we all went to his aid. "Get up, Colonel, you orangutan poof." The chieftain really insulted him at that moment, but the colonel didn't take offence to it, which was something of a surprise.

Alan and I looked at the stone that tripped him up.

I noticed that there was some light coming from beneath it; there was a gap, not much of one but there was enough of an area to grab our curiosity. "Alan, take a look, will ya?" I asked. The two of us started to move the grass so as to get a better look; the ground wasn't too hard around where we were as the stones had created some sort of loosening of the soil.

With our combined weight and strength, we managed to move a few more large rocks. Now we must've caused the ground to sink a little; without any warning, a sinkhole just opened up underneath our feet.

Alan and I looked at each other at the same instant; we used the magic word together, "SHIT."

We fell through into the depths of this hole, at least thirty feet we fell. Luckily for us, the sinkhole fell at an angle of maybe 45 degrees, that was more than enough to prevent us from having any major injuries.

At the base of this whacking big hole was a stairwell leading further down. The chieftain and the colonel walked down to us as they used the angle of loosened dirt; we started to walk down these steps. Shortly, we were approaching a doorway. I faced the chieftain and said, "There you go, Chieftain, your type of job; break it in will you, please."

"With the much of my pleasure unto me!" the chieftain cried out as he rushed forward. The chieftain smashed his shoulder against the door; it immediately shattered into splinters and fell apart onto the ground.

We entered a damp freezing cold area; it dawned on me that there was a twinkling of light that we saw when we started to clear the ground, but where was it coming from? I couldn't see any type of light down here.

Once again, we had managed to discover another crypt. "Have a look around, lads, and for god's sake, please be careful, don't want any more accidents." We all separated, the crypt was interlocked with six other rooms and passages; we carried on looking around. As I entered one of the rooms, there was a flashing of light coming from a deep crack within one of the caskets buried within the wall space.

What the fuck now, I thought. I called the guys together; we gazed at each other. I moved forward slowly.

Alan then joined me; we in turn took a firm hold of the casket and pulled gently. The chieftain and the colonel came across and assisted. Gradually, we removed it from the wall and placed it oh so gently onto the floor.

Whatever was inside was humming and flashing streaks of light. "What do you think it is, Pete?" Alan inquired.

"How the fuck should I know, Al? Let's just get it open and have a butchers, shall we? Well, who is going to do the honours?" No one was keen to open it so I then stated, "Okay, we'll all do it together. Take a corner each; when I count to three, we lift, okay? One…two…three!" We lifted the lid off the casket, and to our amazement, there lay our three missing components that we were searching for, at least that side of our journey was complete. "Oh yes, yes!" I was ecstatic.

"What are they?" asked the colonel.

"They're the three missing items we have been eager to find for a while; we were asked to find them by the old boy. You see, they had to be hidden before the red curse could destroy them."

Alan then mentioned the simple fact, "And so now we've got 'em, which means they're in the open now, so the entity can track 'em."

I looked at him, and replied, "You're such a bundle of laughs, Al, ain't ya? Well, don't just stand there, you dummkopf, grab that one."

I took another as the colonel lifted the third.

I stated, "We really need to get these items to somewhere safe."

"And where's that supposed to be? There isn't any place on earth that's safe against this bloody curse," snapped Alan.

"Oh yes, there is," I replied. I then called the old boy. Once more, the old boy had appeared. I then remarked, "There you go, you can put these items with the others; we can't hide them in the car now." With that, the devices and the entity disappeared.

I turned to my friends. "Right, all it leaves us to do now is try and locate this Daryl Hawkins."

Alan then remarked, "And who is he, may I ask?"

"How the hell should I know, Al? Now come on, stop asking stupid bloody questions, will ya, maybe he can answer what we need to know. Come on, let's take a break for a few hours." As I rubbed the top of my head, we strolled along the shoreline.

"I need to clear my head, let's walk." The thing was that the old boy had informed me as to our next destination and the possible perils that the red curse may have in store for us to face up to ahead, but it wasn't in anyone's interest that they knew at this particular moment. So, I wasn't about to put the fear of god into them. I just knew that there was going to be a lot of serious problems when we got to where we needed to go.

I prayed to myself that this Daryl would be worth the sacrifice that lay ahead; some of us were not going to be walking out of this one; thing was, I didn't know who, when, or how. Anyway, we managed to clamber down the rocks onto this little clearing. We were close to the shoreline; the waves caused a lovely crashing sound as it burst over the small rocks. Luckily, the tide wasn't high; a few crabs were crawling their way in between the crustacean that the sea was leaving behind.

It wasn't long before we came up against an entrance within the rock face. "Here we are, lads," I stated.

Alan looked at me with curiosity; he looked at the entrance, then he looked at me. "You know more than you're letting on, don't ya, Pete?"

I gave him a sorrowful look and muttered, "Just watch yourself in there, okay, keep alert."

Alan then remarked, "Yeah, yeah, yeah." He seemed to find something funny about the whole situation.

I responded very swiftly with an aggressive tone to my voice, "I mean it, Alan, you stay alert, you understand me? That goes for everyone."

"Okay, chill out, Pete. God, you're acting as if one of us is going to drop dead or something; it was only a bit of fun," Alan said. I looked at Alan. Alan then had an expression come over his face; it was as if he could read my thoughts.

The chieftain then decided to open his big gob whilst shouting in the direction of the cave entrance, "I am to be first; I love being first, don't I, colonel? I won the egg and bean race once, didn't I, Colonel?"

"Yes, Chieftain, you stuck your bean on with glue, yes, I remember."

Without further time delay, the chieftain entered. "Fuck off to him, Colonel, are you with me, oh, poo humbug I say."

"Yes, Chieftain, I'm with you. I'm always with you!" cried the colonel. Slowly, but surely, the chieftain and the colonel crept inside, followed then by Alan and myself.

It was as you would've expected, damp, cold and dark; the deeper we moved, the colder, darker and narrower the passage became.

After forty to fifty feet or so, the passage had narrowed so much that it was now only a foot in width; the light was growing extremely low; it was almost impossible to see; then to our amazement, the walls began to glow; a phosphorus algae had woken up, as the entire passage began to lighten up it was glorious to say the least, I raised my voice towards the chieftain who was leading our troop, "How's it going up there?"

"Up there, what, how dare he say that to me, up there indeed, Colonel, I am Chieftain, up yours be him."

The chieftain was extremely abrupt and erratic as he blurted out his verbal diarrhoea, but then that was the norm. The colonel then replied to my question in pure fact, "Good here, bit tight for space, but we're pushing ahead, Peter. Come on, Chieftain, push your bum."

"I say, Colonel, steady, not P time yet." We all pushed on.

Now it wasn't long before the passageway began to increase in size. Before we knew anything else, the passageway had disappeared as each one of us came out and away from the narrowness.

We had found ourselves in a massively beautiful, well-lit cavern; a small river ran along a narrow ledge over to our right-hand side; it was spectacular; the current ran at a decent pace.

The ceiling of the cavern stood a good two hundred feet; the length of the cavern seemed to be never ending; it gave the appearance that it never stopped. The chieftain and the colonel continued their trekking along; as they did, the colonel, who was strolling mindlessly, tripped over on a small mound that was slightly raised from out of the ground surface.

He fell over the edge, but luckily for him, he had managed to grab hold of the chieftain's leg. Within seconds of all this going on, the chieftain found himself flat on his back; he then began to scratch at the ground in the hope of stopping himself from plunging into the river.

The colonel was still holding onto his leg with fear gripping through his face.

The colonel started to shout in a very frantic manner for help. Alan and myself leaped into action and scurried over to assist; gradually, we managed to get the colonel onto safe ground; the danger had passed without any of us being killed; we all relaxed for a few moments to catch our breath; it was then our first predicament arose.

The mound that the colonel tripped over must've been a trigger of some kind for it was a trap set out by the curse.

Released from high above our position, rocks of all shapes and sizes began to rain upon us; we had inadvertently started an avalanche.

The first rocks were small in number, so they weren't an issue as we ran for cover under a slight over hang then came a hail of rocks; the avalanche was having a field day, hundreds of rocks of all shapes and sizes rained down around us; we were in some really dangerous shit.

The over hang too that we took shelter under gave way; we had no choice but to scatter, and scattered we did; our biggest mistake was that we had separated in different directions.

We were trying desperately to evade the falling debris. I was struck several times around the head and shoulders; the force from the first rock had sent me flying a good four feet. I was then rained upon by more rocks.

Alan received small gashes to his legs from the fragments of rocks that were shattering as they destructively hit the rocks that had already fallen to the ground. Strangely enough, the colonel and chieftain were unaffected; they were easily able to dodge any and all rocks that fell; not one scratch did they receive between them; well, that was what we assumed as neither of them made any complaint of being in pain. I got to my feet and brushed myself down as the avalanche subsided.

Alan lay in a seated position for a little whilst rubbing his legs and trying to see how much damage he had sustained, grimacing from time to time with the pain.

I rushed over to Alan to check him out; the chieftain and the colonel stayed over towards the far side.

Neither of them attempted any sort of approach towards us; they didn't even ask if we were okay; this wasn't like those two I thought to myself. Sarcastically, I shouted over to them, "He is okay, thanks for the concern, lads, very much appreciated." There was no response from them; all they were doing was looking at the floor. I shouted again at them.

"What the fuck's wrong with you two, will you get the fuck over here?" Again, there was no movement.

Alan remarked, "Maybe they're suffering from chronic deafness, Pete."

I then stated, "I will give them chronic deafness in a minute. You two!!!!" It was as if they were frozen solid. I made sure Alan was okay and walked across to check these two selfish sods.

I couldn't believe what my eyes were seeing; there was more damage than wounds; the chieftain and the colonel weren't human, after all. They were perfect cyborgs as instead of blood seeping from the wounds to their backs, there was some sort of thick green lubricant; their circuitry was all fused together; sparks of broken circuitry were flaring out of control, talk about damage; there were massive areas of skin ripped off their upper backs, small electrical explosions from inside their outer shell were still igniting.

"Jesus! Alan, you've got to look at this; no wonder they didn't try to help us, they're robots."

"You what?" Alan remarked as he hobbled over to me; we gazed inside the chieftain's back as Alan remarked, "Oh my god, that explains why the chieftain spoke the way he did; he must've been short circuiting for ages."

144

I replied, "Poor sods, but it's still as I said to you before, keep your eyes peeled, ears open, there's only you and me left now until we get our hands on this Hawkins bloke. How are the legs? You know we've got to keep moving, don't ya?" I became like Mother Theresa as I stated the question sympathetically.

"Yeah, I will be okay; they're more superficial than deep, just don't expect me to do many marathons."

"Okay, Al, we'll try and slow the pace down a bit. I can tell you this now though, there's still a few problems ahead of us, but once we're over them, we should be at the end of it."

"End of what?" Alan asked puzzled.

"This poxy cavern what else. We've also got another bonus, that's if we get to meet this Hawkins bloke; the curse has him secured somewhere down here; it's using him as bait for our benefit."

"Well, how thoughtful of it," replied a sarcastic Alan.

We moved off and away from our now decommissioned troops; we didn't have long to wait for as we walked easily due to Alan's legs, a segment of the river began to swirl, the current began to speed up; within seconds, it was the beginning of a whirlpool, gradually growing larger and its strength increasing with every minute that passed.

Alan and I just kept moving as we continued to watch this phenomena grow and swirl; we gazed down towards the centre of this mass of destructive power; something was forming within it just beneath its surface, but whatever it was, our curiosity was now taking over. As we stopped walking without either one of us noticing, we were in full suspense mode, transfixed into what this thing could possibly be. At that instant, a massive explosion of water came from out of the centre of the whirlpool; the speed that it controlled was out of this world; the strength and agility of this thing was unbelievable.

With a gigantic thud that shook the very ground, it stood within ten feet from us. Twelve foot high and built like a shithouse, this thing must've had a sixty inches chest and arms to match; it was a Minotaur.

This strange-looking beast just stood there, simply standing with a deep anger strewn across its face; its body was that of a muscle-bound man and its head was that of a white bull, two massive horns loomed over its forehead directed straight ahead, and in our direction.

A blast of some type of thick gaseous cloud bellowed out from its nostrils; what a magnificent sight it was; it was such a shame this thing wasn't in a friendly frame of mind; it would've been an honour to have this beast on our side.

Alan and I stepped back a few paces. I then called for the old boy to show itself.

As soon as I began to think of asking for help, Alan and I both then found that we had each received an eight foot lance and an oval shield.

Alan shouted in surprise once his shield and lance appeared, "What the fuck is this, we in *Jason and the Argonauts* or what? I was hoping for a light saver or a laser maybe. What the fuck are we supposed to do with this junk?" We were amazed by the entity's thoughts as to our protection.

All we did for a few moments was to stand and look at the weapons issued; shrugging off our shoulders, we prepared for battle.

We twisted our bodies to confront this beast; we must have looked like two Spartan warriors ready to take on the Persians at Thermopylae; we had a great fighting stance, I must say.

There we were face to face with this Minotaur, this was from the time of ancient Greek mythology.

Alan manoeuvred himself around to the Minotaur's far left. I went over to its far right; we did this in such a way that if it then approached one of us, it would naturally open its back to a full attack from the other side; the Minotaur kept its aggressive posture charged, snorting and scuffing up the ground as if it was about to charge, stepping forward towards Alan.

We surged ahead with our lances poking this thing's body; it was as tough as old boot leather, the Minotaur would then re-direct its attack towards me; again, we would surge forward, probing for any weakness; the fight was going on and on like a Mexican standoff.

No way were we going to defeat this thing unless one of us made a dramatic move and took a chance. I looked over at Alan and smiled. Alan's face dropped as he knew I was about to act. I threw my shield to the ground, this caught the Minotaur's eye as it slowly manoeuvred itself around to me, but it never forgot where Alan was. I then once I knew I had its undivided attention, I threw my lance away and slowly moved towards it. Alan shouted, "What the fuck are you doing?"

I then responded by shouting back, "What the fuck are you waiting for!" Once more I stepped closer towards it.

146

Alan continued to monitor the situation; the Minotaur stepped ahead and moved closer towards my location; the gap between us was now getting too close for comfort; it was at that moment Alan lunged forward and with great strength rammed his lance into the Minotaur's neck. The Minotaur turned, and at that split second, he swung his arm out and around himself; this waving movement connected with Alan's lance and it was flung away from his grip! At this moment, neither of us had our lance as they both laid upon the ground; the sudden shock and realisation made Alan stepped back with surprise at this thing's speed.

Stumbling, he tripped and fell backward. As he collided with the ground, he managed to strike the side of his left temple on a boulder.

Alan was out cold; the Minotaur charged at Alan's position. I picked up my lance and screamed out, "Guide my lance!!!!" I flung my weapon as hard as I could at the Minotaur, as the lance penetrated the Minotaur's throat and passed through it, it stopped and dropped to its knees. A few seconds later, the Minotaur fell forward hitting the ground dead.

I walked up to this gigantic monster. I gathered my thoughts and looked over at Alan unconscious body and went over to him; he was still well out of it. I twisted myself around and sat down beside him.

Looking around and looking at Alan once more, I then had a sudden realisation of my situation that I had never felt before, if Alan doesn't wake up from this, I would be alone. The feeling sent a shiver down my spine, the thought of that was the worst horror imaginable.

I know it sounds selfish, but who in their right minds would want to go through this shit on their jack jones, so I sat and waited for Alan to awaken. As I sat, I began to grow tired. I relaxed and laid back. At that moment, the whirlpool began to come back to life. "For fuck's sake, give me a fucking minute, will ya?" This time, whatever was coming out of the water was accompanied by a terrific noise, sounded like a swarm of locusts and I hadn't forgotten the last episode we had had with them. I turned to Alan. "Alan," I shouted, "for fuck's sake, mate, wake up, wake up, Al! I need you!" There was no response from him. I got to my feet and grabbed hold of my lance and shield. Again, with a tremendous gush of water from the whirlpool rose another Greek mythological creature and came crashing onto the ground; this time, it was more terrifying than the Minotaur, for this thing had three heads. I remembered back at school when we did Ancient Greek mythological creatures, this thing was called Cerberus; it was a three-headed gigantic hound, teeth as sharp as razors; it was extremely noticeable that he was seriously pissed off. "Holy crap," I spurted out.

I took my stance once more as I stood between it and Alan. Alan's only chance of remaining alive was two-fold, one was that he needed to wake up bloody quickly, and the other was that the Cerberus doesn't get past by me.

The Cerberus just stood there growling; each one of his three heads worked like they were three separate dogs; their eyes were all a strong deep beetroot colour, with snarling four-inch fangs, saliva dripping from his three great jaws; it was barking its head off, a humongous creature.

Bigger than any Great Dane that I had ever seen, its head must've stood a good six feet high, the height of a fully grown human male, more muscular than a gorilla, a magnificent animal if you visited one in a zoo.

I took a gulp of saliva as my throat started to dry up, a common thing when a human being becomes scared shitless.

My adrenalin was pumping around my body as if my life depended on it.

The Cerberus started to patrol around us. I mean it began to walk very slowly, encircling our position like a lion or a tiger in the wild, stalking its prey. Now this creature was far more dangerous than the Minotaur we had just got rid of. I didn't want to make it any more pissed off than it already was.

I stood patiently awaiting its attack. Within moments, it pounced at us. I managed to veer it away with my shield; it then pounced again, and again I managed to deflect it whilst it was flying through the air; it was looking for a weakness. Again, it pounced for the third time, and once more I managed to fend it off. How much more can I take in defending its attacks, all it needs to do is get the upper-hand just once, just one bite or scratch would be enough for it to then kill us both.

I shouted again at Alan, "Wake the fuck up, Alan! I need you, Alan!!!!" Alan never stirred a muscle. I then, to my horror, could see a trail of blood slowly start to flow from his head wound. I thought the worst at that moment.

I was determined to defend my mate no matter what the cost to my safety.

It was at that moment I then began to think the worst, was Alan already dead? The Cerberus could smell the blood as it attacked; its gigantic jaws struck their teeth into the edging of my shield and the shield went flying away and into the river with a splash. I grabbed my lance with both hands and awaited for what could be the last charge.

I was not a betting man but I knew I didn't have a great chance in hell of surviving this. The Cerberus came at me once again, snarling viciously; it pounced once more. I defended myself as best I could, a second lance came then out from nowhere as it pierced the chest of the Cerberus. The Cerberus went down, but he wasn't dead. Alan had come to and seeing what was taking place had immediately flung into action. "You took your fucking time," I said as I smiled at him.

"Yeah, sorry, I was having such a lovely dream," Alan replied. I then focussed my full attention on the Cerberus; with as much might as humanly possible and without taking any unnecessary risks to ourselves, we both plunged our lances deep into the wounded animal; it squealed through the pain.

We had killed it outright; we had our victory.

I fell to my knees exhausted. Alan looked at me and said, "Well, come on then, get up."

I glanced back at him and without thinking blurted out, "Go fuck yourself, Alan." I then paused, thought for a second then said, "Sorry, mate, but bloody hell, I've fought my guts out here whilst you were having a kip, give me a break, just five minutes, yeah?" Alan grinned and strolled away but not too far. After a few moments had passed, I got to my feet. We collected our weapons and moved onwards; the cavern was really showing some beautiful sights; the formations of rocks and the colours from the fluorescent algae were stunning; trickling water gave it an atmosphere all of its own.

We manoeuvred around a bend that was just ahead of us; we immediately could hear a deep humming sound coming from somewhere; it was immediately followed up by a low-toned singing voice, well, that's if you were tone-deaf that is. Alan remarked, "Where the hell's that crap coming from? Wish he'd shut the fuck up, it's doing my head in." We scurried on in quiet mode.

We soon came up on a massive rock formation that stood smack bang in the middle of the cavern floor; its height must've been close to touching the ceiling, a fantastically sized chunk of rock. Within seconds, we heard this crap voice trying to sing, its footsteps were like the sound of a brass band's drummers. There stomping out from behind the rock stood a humanlike creature, to be more precise, it was a Cyclops, one eye in the middle of his forehead above his nose.

He stood around fourteen feet tall whilst carrying an enormous wooden club; he wore furs that covered his lower regions and an off the shoulder strapping; whilst giving out grunting noises he started to walk towards us.

After a few feet, he stopped; we gazed at each other; it felt like a lifetime. As we continued our surveillance, I whispered into Alan's ear, "Go around the rock, Al, come up on him from behind, I will keep him occupied here."

Alan agreed with 'okay; and he moved off. The cyclops watched every step Alan made as he moved out of sight. I during this time was making chanting grunts to keep his attention focussed on me; with any luck, his brains were the size of a peanut and he won't have a clue what Alan's up to.

Well, that's what I was banking on anyway.

The cyclops started his approach towards me; as he did so, he was whacking the club against whatever he found close by.

Every bash knocked out chunks; this was one strong motherfucker I thought. I could see Alan had managed to get behind him at that point; he had made good time. Alan shouted out, "You have to see this, Pete!" I thought to myself, oh, you stupid arsehole. The plan was scrubbed as the cyclops had heard him and without wasting time immediately turned to face him.

Being that was that, I shouted back, "What the hell are you going on about, what the hell's wrong with you?"

Alan then shouted a sentence that excited me. "We've got a guy here, but he is in some sort of shielding." *That has to be Daryl Hawkins*, I thought.

"Is he okay?" Alan gave the thumbs up. The cyclops then started to pick up whatever he could see on the ground and started to pelt them like missiles in Alan's direction. Alan immediately retreated behind the rock formation.

That gave me time to move up as quietly as I could without being heard or seen. I thrust my lance at it and hit him in the stomach; the cyclops screeched in pain then swung his club at me. I ducked as it flew over my head.

Alan then used his lance; again, the cyclops screeched as the lance penetrated his flesh; after half a dozen or more lance thrusts from each of us, the cyclops strength failed as it fell to the floor dead; we rushed back to see this Daryl Hawkins; the red curse had secured him inside a force shield.

He looked healthy enough, but we couldn't hear whatever he was trying to say as he was continually getting tried talking; we looked around, but as expected, there was no way of getting him out of there without the old boy's assistance. "There has to be a power source that's creating this, Al, there has to be."

I contacted the old boy with my telepathy, "We need you." The old boy appeared through the rock structure like dry ice, low fog; it materialised in front of us. "We need to release him, can you do anything?" I asked. The old boy stepped forward and placed its hands on the force field; it then dropped its head as it closed its eyes; rays of energy surged through its body and out of its hands; the electrical shielding started to shudder through the air; it was at that moment the red curse then decided to join the party for it too materialised from the depths of the rock formation; the deep redness of evil was calling once again.

The old boy as soon as it felt the curse's presence stopped immediately from what it was attempting to do; the two entities faced off once more.

I called to Alan to get over to me, and we shielded ourselves out of harm's way; the entities grew their enormous powers and started bombarding each other with blasts of plasma pulses and streams of alien blast formations of what I can only discreet as lasers of some kind; the battle raged on and on. After what seemed like an eternity, the struggle to destroy each other was starting to tell on the two entities as their strengths began to weaken.

But it also started to drain the strength of the shielding that had trapped Daryl; soon the shielding was sufficiently weakened enough for Daryl to leave his confines and slip out of the area.

Daryl looked at me and was about to say something when Alan piped up and shouted, "Come on, let's get the fuck out of here before we get another creature wanting a piece of my bum." The three of us then made tracks, running as fast as we could; it was a struggle for Alan with all the damage he had sustained earlier to his legs, but he managed to keep up with us; we got out of the area and back out through the narrow passageway.

Once through, we finally reached the cave's entrance. Whilst on our trek you could still hear the conflict raging between the two entities as the old boy battled with its dreaded evil twin.

Chapter 10
One Step Closer

We stood there whilst taking a breather, hands on knees. Alan went over to a boulder and sat down to massage his wounds. I looked at Daryl, at the same time as he looked at me. Daryl then asked in a blunt manner, "Where the fuck did you piss off to then?" With his outburst, Daryl pushed me backwards a few feet.

I was startled by his violent reaction towards me. "You can pack that shit in, we just saved your fucking life, what do you mean where did I piss off to? Have we met then?" Daryl then gave the expression as to how I felt, confused and dismay filled the air.

"Yeah, you heard me, where did you piss off to?"

I then responded with a firm tone, "Right, just calm down for a bloody minute, will ya? Now I don't know what the hell's going on here, but we have definitely got off on the wrong foot, Daryl, honestly, I've never met you before."

"Oh bullshit, what's this, amnesia time then? Nothing changes with you, does it?" Daryl was getting really pissed off with me for some unknown reason.

"Daryl, let's cool down and sort this misunderstanding out, yeah, what do you say? Come on, let's just chill for a mo, look, I'm in need of a sit down, let's go over to Alan and then you can explain to me and him as to why you think you know me."

Daryl then moaned once more. "Right, fine, but it's not just you, I know him too, and then maybe afterwards, you can explain to me what the fuck's going on." Daryl was taking no prisoners.

He was extremely confused with everything; we sat with Alan. I then opened up the conversation. "Right, come on then, Alan, you have to listen to this, he thinks he knows us both."

Alan laughed then responded with, "You what! He thinks he knows me, where from? Look, just listen for a mo, my friend, I don't know you, okay? I don't know what planet you're from, but I have never met or seen you before in my entire life, well, come on then, we're all ears, this is gonna be good."

Daryl stood up; we watched him just in case he has got more aggressive tendencies to us both; he then spoke in a more calmer tone. "Around an hour ago, there was you, me and Alan. We were waiting for our mate to show up with our last device so we could then start running the final sequence to end the experiment—"

I stopped him mid-sentence. "Hang on, question, what mate are you referring to? What's this experiment? And what device are we talking about here?"

"Just wait a minute, let me get this out first," Daryl replied. "Anyway, our mate showed up; he had been working on this time displacement unit; you thought it was great, Pete; anyway, he finally showed up and connected the unit into place.

"Alan went to get his notepad so he could have a written record as to what was happening. Pete, you operated the mini camera unit that encased the specimen to be transported.

"He was hoping to transport an apple from one secure pod to the other one; he called it his treks pods, as you know he's a *Star Trek* freak, or maybe you don't, anyway, the experiment was started once Alan was ready to take these notes; we had two more lads, for some reason, I can't remember their names, but they were there, there were six of us.

"Anyway, during the transportation sequence, there was a power surge; it must've shorted some circuitry, well, something inside one of the new devices that Harry had installed earlier in the day, it was probably the anti-protons that he was creating, I guess. I don't know exactly what happened as I'm no scientist.

"There was this explosion inside the entire system; you tried to shut the experiment down.

"You had no idea as to what you were doing. I was busy hiding from all the debris, but something created this thing against a wall. I think Harry called it a vortex, if I remember correctly; there was something inside it, you could see it struggling to break free, crazy to watch. It was like a dominos effect; everything, and I mean everything, went mad, one by one, pieces of equipment were sucked into this vortex thing, chairs, cups, anything that was not nailed down started to go. Before we knew what was happening, you and Alan just went, you just disappeared like a puff of smoke; one minute you were there trying to sort out the mess we were in, next nothing.

153

"I remember now, there was a flash of something across my eyes, a deep red blinding flash; next thing when I opened my eyes, I was in that fucking cave surrounded by some sort of invisible wall, a gigantic cyclops was gawping at me. Initially, I nearly shit myself, that was one scary moment.

"One ugly son of a bitch, then you two showed up, got me out, and here we are."

"Wow," Alan exclaimed, "what a mouthful of crap."

"No, hang on, Alan," I responded, "let's take a minute here, you take this crap we have had to deal with, I mean everything that's happened to us lately, I believe him, Al, it's like the entities have somehow managed to twist everyone's timeline inside out. Anyone that has a connection with that explosion, or there's another answer to the question, and that would be a parallel universe."

"Excuse me, Pete, but what on earth are you going on about, you have to explain what you have just said. I have just spilt my guts explaining what's occurred with me, now I'm waiting for you." Daryl wasn't in the mood for party games.

"Okay, this is our story, here it is, now I'm just gonna give you the overall state of play, okay? Okay, here goes. I was transported out of my timeline by something in the form of a mist, well, sometimes, it appears in the form of an old man, now this thing is helping us to defend ourselves against the red curse.

"It turns out that there are two of the same entity, that explosion enabled this entity to split, on one side you have the old boy, well, that's what we've come to call it, that part of the entity doesn't want to exist, the other half, well, that's a different story; it's full of hate and revenge, we call that bloody thing the red curse.

"It wants absolute power and it's doing what it can to destroy me and any other poor sod that joins up with me.

"We've already lost a few guys because of it.

"At this moment in time, we have already found multiple devices, they are all safe and sound, probably the same ones as those that were zapped from your experiment and thrown into this timeline.

"The old boy has them in a safe place, right, okay, now are you with me so far?"

Daryl was bewildered. "Yeah, course I am."

"Good, now the old boy and I have a two-way telepathic link, that means it can communicate with it and it can contact me, believe it or not, it's come in useful a few times.

"I was once virtually dead, but it revitalised me, and there was a side effect, I now have impenetrable skin; it had altered my skin's structure right down to my DNA strands; everywhere the old boy sends or directs us, you're guaranteed to see the red curse there; it will either show itself or it will transform or use another thing or object in trying to take us out, so here we are, as it stands at present. We're here to find this bloke, what was his name again?"

"Oh, you mean Harry Tar-pen?"

"Daryl, look, you have to accept the fact that in this time we haven't met him yet; there's been no experiment, nothing has taken place in this timeline that took place in yours; the curse is out there and trying desperately to destroy us all. If it can't, it will just grow stronger and stronger till it crushes everything, and that's going to include all of us.

"It has a supreme hatred especially for me for some reason, and as I have said, the old boy is doing what it can to assist us, so, there you have it, in a nutshell so to speak."

Daryl responded with, "Well, blow me down with a feather, so nothing's happened in this timeline that happened to me in the other one?"

"I just said that, didn't I?" I replied.

"Yeah, sorry, I was just recapping my thoughts," Daryl remarked. You could plainly see Daryl was having a hard time trying to digest the new info.

"Now who is this Harry?" Alan asked.

Daryl replied, "Oh, did I not say, it's Harry War-pen, Professor War-pen's son."

I screamed with delight, "I knew I was right! I knew it! It's his son, yes, I knew it. I was right all along. I said that, Al, let me think for a moment, right, we know that there's to be six of us there at the time of this experiment, we've already established that, there's an explosion event, we also know that us three were also there, but then saying that, we can't take whatever happened as guaranteed."

Daryl then being more confused than ever stated, "But I was there, I saw you two."

"Yeah, I know that, Daryl, but remember the timelines, the entity has altered time itself and that's why we can't be certain of anything anymore, you getting

155

that?" Daryl just gazed like a three-year-old trying to work out how to suck a lollipop. I continued saying, "Right, what do we know for sure? One, there are two entities, two, the devices, and three, we need to find Harry and these two other guys. Question now is, where ever are they? Time's on the curse's side so pray we find them before that scum destroys each and every one of them. Hopefully, we can destroy this thing before it claims us."

Daryl looked at Alan and said with a gulp, "He's not kidding, is he?"

"No, I'm afraid, he's not kidding at all, mate, wish he was though." Alan became deadly serious at that point; he kept chatting away. "So, I guess, it's back to the car then?" His tone then turned and became more sarcastic. "Oh, the joys of the adventure continue; can't wait for the next instalment."

"Eat yours," I said. We moved away from the area towards the car. As we walked, I asked Daryl the fundamental question, "So tell me this then, where did this fucked-up experiment take place?"

"Scarborough, 36 Station Road, why?" Daryl replied.

"Ha! So that's why, yeah, makes sense now. Scarborough was the first place the old boy sent me to. Pieces of the puzzle are growing clearer right now. So what are your views on this Harry War-pen bloke then?" I asked, as my curiosity grew regarding this bloke.

Daryl replied, "He's a bloody genius, Pete, he really is. It all started a few years back following his dad's death; his dad was convinced that time travel was possible; he spent his entire working life on the idea; it was the strain of that I think that finally killed him.

"It just got too much. Once he passed away, Harry picked up the mantle and carried on; it was a couple of months ago when Harry had a great breakthrough; he had managed to finally figure out what the time distortion process really was. I guess you could say that he discovered a new form of travel.

"Since that day, he's been like his dad, he hasn't stopped working, but then came the experiment; it was a strange explosion thinking about it." My curiosity went into overdrive.

"How strange?" I asked.

"Well, the vortex that sprung up initially only focussed on the scientific devices. It was as if there was some sort of method to an attack, just seemed to focus on them. I'm sure as I ponder on it that there was as an intelligence at work."

"Well, you saying that, Daryl, that would tie into why we have been on the hunt for the devices, the old boy must've been here and removed them at that time to prevent the curse from taking 'em? That has to be it. Now let's think about this for a moment, the old boy wants to basically die, so it's collated the equipment from your time and then placed them in this one with only one purpose."

Alan then jumped into the conversation and said, "It wants the experiment to run again so it can reverse time itself."

"You got it in one, mate, it has to be," I replied.

Reaching the car, we all jumped inside. I started the engine and drove away. "So where to, suppose it's back to Scarborough, yeah, after all that's where the experiment took place." Alan seemed pretty certain that he was on the right track, but unfortunately, I soon ruined that idea.

"Yeah, but it doesn't necessarily follow that explosion will happen there again, that's one of our major issues." I then had a message come through on my telepathy phone line. I then blurted out two words, but I wasn't surprised by our destination. "Elvaston Castle."

"Har, no, not again, you're bloody kidding, Pete. What another poxy castle? What is it with castles and this fucking entity?"

Alan was cheesed off by our next adventure, well, so he called it.

Daryl jumped in to our little chat that we had got going. "So this is the famous old boy bat phone, is it? Sorry, Pete, but how the hell do you know it's not the other one giving you false information? It's possible, you know?"

"Yeah, it's feasible, all right, but highly unlikely, Daryl, it keeps a heavy dampening field over the telepathic link, well, it's more like a cloaking device really; it's there to prevent the curse from entering the same thought process."

Alan popped up with a little humour once again, "So there's a one percent chance then."

I looked at him and said, "Alan, do me a favour, don't get smart with me, you jerk off. The odds are astronomical, Daryl, there's absolutely no bloody chance." In hindsight, I should've kept my mouth shut for as I spoke the last word in my sentence, the external area around the car suddenly developed over us a deep pure red sheeting of some kind.

It was as if someone had thrown a red tarpaulin over the car. Alan and I both knew who was responsible, the curse was doing another one of its party trick on us; we couldn't see a damn thing. I instantly slammed on the brakes, producing an emergency stop; we shuddered to a full stop.

Alan cried out, "No chance, Pete, really." The three of us gazed out of our closed windows; there was nothing but redness; it was at that moment the old boy appeared from nowhere and sat beside Daryl. Daryl instantly reacted by jumping off his seat and away from the old boy; the sudden appearance had him leaping against the car door scared shitless.

"What the!!!!" Daryl cried out. "It's all right, Daryl, it's all right, calm down, it's our mate; this is its chosen form when we meet up."

"Oh right, is it?" Daryl replied.

"Just relax, Daryl, chill, man, you'll get used to it soon enough, may take a little time, but you'll be okay, took me a while."

Alan managed to get a laugh from that one. I faced the old boy and asked the question that we all wanted the answer to, "What's going on?"

The old boy looked straight into my eyes and stated facts that none of us wanted to hear, "Entity stronger grow, broke telepath seal, no more communication, limited strength can use, destroy entity soon, the Peter, growing weakened, limited help can give."

"Right, okay, but what's going on now, what's this red shit?"

"Curse transported you, bad place here, no out of car, will try to remove, Derby, time short." It was at that moment the entire car began to rumble and shake; for all intents and purposes, we felt like we were in the middle of an earthquake; the car started to bounce violently.

The three of us were being tossed around like ragdolls; at that moment, the old boy summoned up all its strength and blasted us out of danger; we were plunged one day backwards.

Derby was to be our next destination; we landed with a thump that made the three of us hit the roof of the car. Rubbing our heads, we looked out of the car windows; we had landed in a field of wheat. Luckily, the ground was firm enough to take the weight of the car.

Struggling to get out of the car as the wheat was pressing against each door, we finally managed to escape. I walked around my wheels and examined my baby's body work; the damage was minor, thank god, but then when you think on it, the pressure build-up had only just begun. The old boy had done us proud freeing us when it did. Alan then stated, "Well, we're certainly in the shit now. Guess we need to find this Harry and these two others pretty sharpish."

"Well, I'm game; we still going to that castle?" Daryl asked.

I responded with, "Yeah, unless someone has a better idea."

"It was only a question, Pete; besides, don't you think we should talk about what's just happened in the last five minutes?"

Alan agreed with him, "Yeah, that sounds like a good idea, Daryl."

I didn't feel like chatting so much so I responded with, "Okay, if you wanna chat, let's discuss it, a great help it'll be." I seriously didn't like the idea of standing around in one place for too long. "Okay, who is getting the ball rolling then?" I asked.

Alan broke the ice, "Well, I think we need to chat about what we've lost here, i.e., no more telepathic link, what do we do now?"

I remarked, "Well, we still have the old boy's help; it's still going to keep us up to date with what the curse is going to do. I just won't get the information as quick."

Daryl stated, "Yeah, fine, but we've lost the advantage it sounds like."

"Well, there's nothing we can do about it, we just need to accept the fact and move forward as best as we can. Any other points you want to go over, Alan?"

Daryl then popped up again, "Yeah, wanna discuss this point, now this entity has just stated that it's growing weaker while this curse thing is maturing. What happens now?"

I answered with, "Look, all we can do is continue doing what we're doing. I've just said that the old boy will do what it can, we just need to keep focussed, think clearly, and most of all, we need luck."

"Oh right, we need to be lucky, do we." Alan seemed to dismiss my last sentence.

"Yeah, at the moment, mate, we have no other means of doing anything, just thank your lucky stars that this entity can't just swipe us out of existence."

Alan replied, "Yeah, I think you'll find the operative words are, not yet," Well, Alan hit us out of the park with that factual piece of the English language; we stood there for a few minutes feeling sorry for ourselves.

"Right, we've wasted enough time, now can we get back in the car? I don't want to be standing here giving this entity an easy target, get into the car." I really didn't want to push these guys, our self-belief was dropping way too low for my liking.

I drove off gently as to make sure we didn't get bogged down in the field, gradually, we emerged out of the wheat and back onto the road.

As luck would have it, the old boy had managed to pass the route that I would've needed to get to Elvaston Castle; we were making good time.

Daryl then asked, "What are our chances of finding these guys, Pete? I mean has this mist thing mentioned anything before your link was cut?"

"That's an excellent question, Daryl, nice one, the answer to that is very simple."

"Well, come on, we're all ears," Alan said erratically.

"One word, yes, fingers crossed, we're going to collect our two chums pretty soon."

"Yeah, fingers crossed," replied Daryl.

After a short drive, we could clearly see the castle ahead of us; we drove towards it; you really couldn't class it as a castle anymore as it was just a bunch of stones, only the shell of a magical building remained; the windows were gone; the sun glided through the remains of its once gallant walls; it was also closed to the public due to all the structural damage it had suffered from over the years.

"My god, look at it," Alan expressively stated.

Daryl then said, "Must have been a stunner in its heyday." I took the car into the car park, pulled up the handbrake and we all got out of the car and began our reconnaissance.

"Please no walking, wandering off, lads, remember, strength in numbers." I made that sentence very clear; the curse knew where we were as it could read the old boy's thoughts; it wasn't long before the curse showed itself once again.

We had reached the first corner of the ruins; we turned around on the next elevation; there in the middle of the grounds stood a fair ground.

We stood there, all three of us stumped as to what the hell was a fair ground doing in a historical place such as this.

It was obvious to all that this was no ordinary child's playground. I tried to move off but just couldn't move my feet; it was as if I had fixed my feet into the old adage used by gangsters in America in the 1920s and 30s; in our language, it meant that when they wanted someone dead, they would set their feet into cement blocks and they would be thrown into a river, hence concrete shoes.

Alan and Daryl both had the same issue; none of us could move an inch, all we could do was wait for whatever was in store for us. Suddenly, it was then as if we were on a conveyor belt, a forward motion took over us; we were now sliding towards the fair ground.

We desperately tried to break free, but it was useless, just a wasted effort. Daryl just stood there as if butter would not melt in his mouth; as if he had just calmly accepted the situation. Once we had been placed inside the fairground, the concrete shoes just disappeared.

"What the fuck!" Alan shouted! In front of us from deep under the ground rolled out the curse in its usual form of a mist, the deep red mist was swirling like a typhoon at a hundred miles an hour, rising itself to a height six feet in the air; it slowly materialised into an old man dressed in a ringmaster's costume; his voice was a hideous, evil low-toned thing; it's laughter echoed as it sounded out; it was like we were facing a demented demon; it's face, all twisted and deformed, gazed in our direction.

It then grunted, "Compete, compete or you suffer defeat, the Peter." Its laughter was growing more louder now as it screamed with delight; screams of laughter continued as it slowly vanished back from whence it came.

Daryl spoke. "I don't think I care for this, Peter."

"Me neither, mate," I responded

Alan then muttered, "Pete, I'm scared." His usual sarcasm was gone for he genuinely felt fear as we all awaited for what was to befall us.

I stated, "Everyone, stay calm, and stay together, if we can get through whatever this is, then maybe we may well have a decent chance of getting out of here alive. Alan, no heroics, you got that?"

"Yes, sir," replied Alan. We waited for a good five minutes for something to occur; we didn't have to wait much longer for the concrete shoes once again appeared on our feet.

We were once more being dragged away; we came to a sudden and abrupt halt outside the ducking pool. As we looked at this contraption, all we could see was a swing sitting over a large glass container filled to the brim in some type of liquid.

I was praying that this liquid was water. Now I had seen this contraption before; there is a target just above the swing area, a beautiful woman would sit on the bar of the swing, and the idea was that someone throws something at the target, once hit, the woman falls into the water, but what has this curse got planned for us? Whatever it was, it wasn't going to be a pleasant experience.

The creepy ringmaster reappeared from behind a tent that was on our right-hand side.

Chapter 11
Reunion

From where its legs should've been, to our total shock, it was slithering like a snake, an ugly half-breed creature stood before us.

Pausing as it raised itself to head height, it spoke as its snakelike tongue hissed. "Who is to drop in the drink, which is to drop, I say, the way is open" – the thing waved its arm towards the ducking pond – "the way is now closed for you to sink." Instantly, Daryl found himself sitting on this swing.

Utterly mesmerised by the shock, none of us was expecting this event. I faced the thing and said, "Right, so we're playing, what are the rules?"

It replied with, "Save or drown." He laughed his stupid silly head off.

"Hang on a fucking minute!" Alan shouted at it, but it was too late.

The bar on the swing gave way, Daryl went straight down and under the water and the casing from just above his head slammed shut.

To my reckoning, we had about two minutes in finding a way of getting him out from inside this container; we surged forward and tried to lift the lid; it was as tight as a duck's arse.

I mean it was more like screwed down, it was that tight. We struggled like mad. Daryl was in an extremely dangerous situation. At that moment, I felt something in my trouser pocket. Putting my hand inside, I removed whatever it was. To my amazement and gratitude, it was a glass cutter of all things. I eagerly started to use the cutter on the glass by drawing a large circle.

I then drew Daryl's attention by banging on the glass. Giving him hand signals to follow, I wanted him to hit the lines drawn by the cutter; he cottoned on to what I was telling him and so he did, water started to seep out. I then drew more lines inside the circle in a criss-cross formation; again, I told him to hit them. Within seconds, the glass was falling away, water was pouring out.

Alan and I lunged forward and dragged Daryl out of the death trap. "You bastard!" I screamed as the ringmaster stood there laughing his stupid head off once more.

Alan stood up and violently threw a punch at this thing; it waved its arm and Alan went flying through the air, not one body part from either man had touched each other; he had no chance.

I made sure Daryl was okay after he had stopped coughing and retching for breath; he lay in a heap for a short while. Once I was satisfied he was okay, I went to assist Alan who was dazed but okay. "What are we to do, Pete, what are we to do?" Alan asked in a sorrowful manner.

I whispered to Alan as if to make sure that this thing couldn't overhear us, "It will be okay, Alan, where do you think that glass cutter came from, it's the old boy doing his bit; it can't do major stuff like appear any more, well, not in this place, so it's now doing guerrilla warfare on the bastard."

"What, undercover so to speak?" Alan replied.

"Yeah, undercover work. Can you stand?" I asked. Alan got to his feet, a little wobbly but he was okay.

We returned back to Daryl as of then he was sitting upright and breathing normally once again. "Fuck that, don't want another one of those, fucking hell, thought I was a gonna for sure; saying that, Pete, where did you get that glass cutter from—"

"Shut up, Daryl," I rudely interrupted him, "talk later."

Daryl looked at me strangely as Alan gave Daryl some facial expressions with his eyebrows and a quick nod of the head.

Once all three of us were on our feet, the curse gave us no opportunity to rest as it once again used its transport method to drag us to the next misadventure.

We were now outside a bloody shooting gallery; we looked at the firing range. Now there were five manikins featuring historical figures from the Second World War. There was Adolf Hitler, Winston Churchill, Franklin D. Roosevelt, Joseph Stalin and Benito Mussolini. Each were set on a revolving platform; each one had a target over their hearts. "What now?" I muttered. The ringmaster again laughed his arse off and once more gave its poetic speech.

"Five of the best is for you to choose, if you fail, it's the Peter to lose." Its laughter was really starting to gnaw into our heads by this time. It was my turn to face an ordeal as I was removed from Alan and Daryl's company.

Within a blink of an eye, I was tied and gagged up with a stinky piece of rag, hate to think where it had been.

I had been replaced by one of the manikins on the firing range. I had no idea as to which one it was, but for where I was situated, there was no way Daryl or Alan could have known or could see me, for that matter.

Alan looked at the ringmaster and said, "What have you done with Peter?"

The ringmaster just grinned, that hideous look of evil flushed across its face as it muttered, "Five bullets you have, Peter be free, target hit three." Its laughter grew louder and even longer than before.

"Answer me, where's Peter!"

Alan's anger at the ringmaster's arrogance and ignorance was growing stronger by the minute, another micro-second had passed, both Daryl and Alan now held rifles that were fully loaded; the ringmaster pointed at the targets and stated one last time, "Hit target three times to free the Peter, if you can."

It then vanished into thin air and into the soil beneath. "What do we do, Daryl?" Alan asked.

Daryl then replied, "There's nothing we can do but shoot the stupid targets."

"Right, I wonder if Pete's okay," Alan remarked. The revolving platform began turning, along with the historical manikins. Daryl fired first, the bullet made a loud pinging sound as he struck Mussolini's target. The next shot was Alan's, he aimed and fired; another ping struck Stalin's target.

Daryl's second shot was released; this time, there was no ping as his shot missed the target. Alan then jokingly stated, "Thought you were good."

"Just fire, will ya; it ain't over yet," Daryl replied.

"Game on."

Alan grinned; his second shot came up, again a ping as the Hitler was struck. Daryl's third shot was now ready. He fired and hit the target, but to their surprise, there wasn't a ping. "Strange," stated Daryl, "I hit it."

"Yeah, I know you did," Alan responded. "Oh well, must have been a dud, my turn."

Alan didn't give it a second thought as he fired once more. Alan waited for that same manikin to reappear before firing. Once it came into view, he fired, perfect shot, but once again, there was no ping. "Now this is strange," Alan muttered.

"Right, two shots each, fancy a bet on the side?" Daryl asked.

Alan remarked, "Just take your shots, Daryl. I wonder what Pete's getting up to, hope he's having as much fun as we are." Daryl fired once more at his appointed target, this time it was Churchill, a ping this time. Alan then put his rifle down and stopped; he shouted out in the hope of drawing the ringmaster's attention. "I've hit this bloody target three times now, where's Pete?"

There was no ringmaster's appearance, this time in its place an evil demonic voice that gradually increased in volume rose up into the atmosphere and cried out, "Peter free, Peter hit two times, Peter free, go." Alan and Daryl looked at each other. Alan then realised what the no ping meant.

"Oh, Jesus, there was no ping." The lads looked at each other, as the light of day hit them; they both realised what had happened, the fact that there was no target sound.

They ran around the back of the firing range. I was slumped forward, the only reason as to why I wasn't on the floor was the fact I was still tied up. Hurriedly, they rushed to my aid. "Ha, no, shit, we've shot him!" Daryl shouted out.

"Quick, get these bloody ropes off him!" Alan shouted in a caring manner.

"Watch his head," Daryl stated. Keenly, I was released from my bondage and laid down on my back.

Daryl put his head to my chest to listen for my old ticker. Alan then stated to him in a very faint voice, "It's okay, Daryl, give him a few minutes, he'll get up in a minute."

"What're you talking about, he has got two bullets in his chest," Daryl stated in a confused manner.

Alan then explained, "What you don't know, Daryl, was that he died a few days ago; the mist rejuvenated him at the DNA level; it had a side effect that made his skin impregnable."

"Well, why the fuck did you not tell me that before?" Daryl wasn't impressed.

"When did I have the time to say something, may I ask?" I started to come around. I was groggy and a bit bruised from the bullets, apart from that, I was okay. After a few moments of me rubbing my aching chest, the lads helped me to my feet.

"What's happened then?" I asked.

Alan looked at me and said, "We shot you, sorry."

"Oh, terrific, charming," I said.

"Well, how were we to know that the bastard put you up against one of those targets, sorry, Pete," Daryl exclaimed.

"It's okay, really, it's okay, so what's happening now then?"

"Well, we've just been told to go," Alan said.

I looked at him for a moment and said, "What just like that? We can go, yeah right. I bet you it's got other plans for us." I wasn't about to accept that; we walked out from behind the firing range only to find a house within a few feet; it was the old familiar ghost house you always get. I then stated, "Yeah, we can go, really. I guess we're going in, after all, it's not that we don't have a choice now, is it?" The house stood there looking eerie, cobwebs covered all over it; dim lights shone from the partially blackened-out windows; a few steps lay in front of us near the entrance.

We started to move and walk up them; the floor creaked as we strolled. Soon we had entered the desolate dwelling; our way ahead was already pre-arranged as great big illuminated white arrow signs were fixed to the floors.

Slowly, we edged ourselves forward; it was bloody quite scary as we had no idea as to what was waiting for us; we got to our first corner.

A large manikin fell from the ceiling dressed as a bat, yeah, a bat; the three of us jumped backwards with fright; clutching our chests and looking at each other, we laughed and moved on.

Alan moved ahead first followed by myself, Daryl followed up. Alan walked straight into a huge spider's web suddenly released itself from its moorings; it fell and engulfed his face; he screamed like a little girl as he hurriedly wiped the web away. Again, we found it funny; it was pretty obvious that the web wasn't real as it was soft and brittle. "What in god's name's going on here, this ain't real, Pete!" Alan shouted.

"You know what it's up to, don't ya?" I remarked.

"What?" asked Daryl.

"It's killing time, that's what it's up to; it knows its counterpart is growing weaker, so it's trying to waste as much time as possible. The old boy can't defend us and itself anymore."

"That crafty son of a bitch," Alan stated.

"So, what can we do about it?" asked Daryl.

"I don't know, Daryl, why have I got to have all the answers? I'm just like you, mate, taking this one step at a time; all we can do is carry on doing what we're being told to do. I'm sure the old boy will sort something out; it always manages to come up with something." Alan moved off. As we continued, I quickly grabbed his arm and pulled him back.

"What are you doing?" Alan shouted.

"Take a look, you blind git," I replied.

Lying in wait just a foot ahead of him was a whacking great hole on the ground, a hole just waiting for one of us to fall into.

Alan gulped as I then stated one more time, "Keep focussed, will ya, for fuck's sake, Al, switch your brain cells on, will ya?" The three of us moved around the hole by clinging onto the sidewalls and sliding by; it was growing darker the deeper we went. Alan as he couldn't see a great deal walked straight into a wall and broke his nose.

"Fuck that." Blood poured out as he held his nose tightly to try and stop the flow.

"You okay?" I asked.

"Yeah, I'm fine, broke me fucking nose, poxy wall." Turning to our right, the floor began to rise a little; it wasn't long before the level stepped up to a forty-five degree angle; it was becoming a struggle to reach the landing ahead. Gradually, we managed to reach it; ahead of us were rows of spikes which were scattered along the walls, floor and ceiling.

"Oh, fucking great!" I shouted.

We gazed for a moment, each one of us were studying this problem and looking for a way through.

Alan then stepped backwards and moved in behind me. "After you!" he cried.

"Oh, thanks for nothing." I couldn't believe what he just did, but I did understand it. "Right then, let's see what happens now." I moved ahead gently, carefully making sure I didn't touch the spikes in any way shape or form; it seemed as if there was nothing really to worry about until Alan dropped us all in it.

He was following me as his ankle managed to touch a spike; we heard an almighty clank, and gradually, the walls and the ceiling began to move.

Daryl, who was coming up the rear, screamed out, "Move!!!!" We didn't need him to say that twice. Luckily for me, there was only four feet between the spikes and clear ground. I jumped and got safe; the area was reducing at a decent rate of speed.

Alan managed to get across shortly after; the height had diminished to around four feet. Daryl was having to virtually get on his hands and knees to get through.

Alan and I soon got to the edge of the dropping ceiling, and with all our might we were attempting to keep this ceiling from dropping any further. "Hurry up, Daryl, for fuck's sake!" I screamed, as Daryl finally removed his last remaining foot from the spiked area. With our loss of strength, the ceiling came crashing down, not even a rat would've been able to squeeze through those spikes now; we were so fortunate that time.

"Try calling the old boy, Pete, please, just once more?" Daryl asked.

"Why, you heard what it said, there's no point," I stated.

Alan piped up with the same, "Try, Pete, what have we to lose, try."

"Right, fine, but nothing's going to change, you're just holding onto hope."

I concentrated hard, and within my thoughts, I said, "We need help, can you hear me, get us out, please." Within the blink of an eye, the three of us were instantly transported back to the castle grounds and free from the fair ground.

The old boy re-emerged for as though by magic he stood in front of us once again. "What the hell is going on, you informed us that you were growing weaker and the curse was growing stronger, our link was severed, you said." I was bewildered to say the least; the old boy was in a seriously weakened state.

Its form was dishevelled, showing that of an old boy's human age for he was more crouching over as you do as age creeps up on you. "Entity stronger growing, the Peter, enough strength to help when can, not enough to stop entity, you the Peter, you." The old boy as usual had done its disappearing act on us.

"We really needed a break; we need to find these other two and bloody soon."

"Yeah, we know, but we're looking for a couple of needles in a giant haystack, where do we look?" shouted Alan; frustration was clearly taking hold.

Daryl then stated the obvious, "Well, they must be around here somewhere otherwise why were we sent here?" We began to wander slowly, each of us pondering on our own thoughts when to our amazement one of our old pals emerged from around the far easterly corner of the ruined castle.

Alan spotted him first and grabbed my arm in astonishment as he shouted once again, straight into my ear, "My god, look, Pete, look at this!!!!"

I shouted back whilst grabbing my ear, "Fucking hell, Al, take it easy!" I looked ahead in the general direction; my jaw dropped to the floor, I couldn't believe what my eyes were looking at, it was Tony. Tony had turned his back on us some time ago when his brother James was killed, it was unbelievable that he was here.

Tony, once he had seen us, started to walk over; we did the same. Soon as we were all together once more, Tony looked at us; he was fuming. I mean he was ready to burst if he didn't calm down. "What the fuck am I doing here, Pete, I was out of this shit for good, you bastard." His voice was overflowing with aggression; walking up to me, he grabbed my collar with his left hand and began to shake the hell out of me; with that, he used his right fist and followed up by a second thump, he laid into my jaw. I hit the ground pretty sharpish.

Tony stood over me with fists clenched. I was still feeling guilty over the death of his brother so I did nothing. I didn't retaliate. I just laid there for a little while.

Alan and Daryl had other ideas, as they moved forward and stopped him from trying to do any more damage to me by grabbing his arms and pulling him backwards. "Get your fucking hands off me!" Tony screamed at Alan and Daryl as he struggled to free himself from their grips.

Alan shouted at him "Calm the fuck down, what's the matter with you?" Once they released their grasps and Tony was free, he stood there breathing heavily, like a deranged bull. I then said to him, "Tony, look, if I could go back in time, I would. I'm sorry we lost James. I really am; there's nothing on this earth I wouldn't give to see him here with us right now. I'm sorry." Even whilst saying that, it was so good to see him again. I was so remorseful towards him as I felt the build-up of emotions.

Tony's gaze deepened towards me and he stated the horrible statement, "Have you any idea how tough it was for me to bury him; it was virtually impossible trying to explain to the police as to why your brother had a lance through his gut, let alone how he had managed to be twenty odd feet up in the air impaled to a wall. I was sectioned for three fucking months." Alan looked bewildered.

"But it was only a week ago, weren't it, that James died?"

"Yeah, well, it might've been in this timeline, but it wasn't in mine. I went through fucking hell, what with the police investigation that took a lifetime to complete, then you had the pathology department, the coroner just kept putting back the body release date; they just wouldn't release his fucking body, then there was the funeral, try explaining his death to our family. I tell you, it was a nightmare." Slowly but surely, Tony's aggression grew more sombre and placid; the more he spoke, the more he cooled down.

Tony asked, "Who is this then?" He pointed to Daryl.

"I'm Daryl, pleased to meet ya."

Daryl raised his hand to greet Tony with a handshake. Tony looked at his hand for a moment then looked back at his face; after a few seconds, he acknowledged him with the handshake. "So he's got you into this as well, has he?" Tony was still cheesed off.

"Well, there wasn't much choice really; it's certainly interesting," Daryl stated.

"So, what's been happening since I have been away, or shouldn't I ask," Tony said.

"Best if we just get away from here, I will tell you in the car."

I threw my arm over Tony's shoulder as we walked off towards the car. Tony didn't throw my arm away, that was a good sign that he was able to accept it wasn't all my fault; hopefully, we had buried the hatchet, or at least for now. We approached the car. Daryl shouted, "Jesus, Christ, look!" Alan, myself and Tony gazed around and saw nothing.

Alan then muttered, "What! What are we looking at?"

Daryl then stated, "It was him."

"Him who?" Alan quizzed again.

"It was Harry."

I then turned to Daryl and said, "What, our Harry?" Daryl nodded a yes as he stood in shock.

Alan then said, "You'll be seeing pink elephants next, look, there's nothing here, it's just us."

Daryl was convinced. "Pete, I'm telling you Harry was over there, then he was gone."

Alan said, "So, what was he doing then, playing hopscotch, oh, come on, Pete, he's dreaming, for god's sake."

"I'm not so sure, Alan, the one thing I know in this timeline is believe everything you hear and see until it's proven wrong. Now, Daryl, tell me, what was he doing?"

"Well, it looked as if he was whacking something and yelling."

Alan then with his usual sarcastic comments said, "Yeah, I suppose he was also in a force field, oh, come on, Pete, this is shit."

"Yeah, possible, Alan, but let's just say that Daryl did see him, just suppose, then that would mean that the curse was showing him to us, but why?" It was at that exact moment that we all saw this mirage as it re-emerged, again Harry was

170

beating hard at something, some invisible screen that was in front of him and shouting at us, and once again, he couldn't be heard. We all stopped dead in our tracks in amazement as each one of us witnessed it. "You see, I'm not mad, there he is!" Daryl shouted at Alan, but then as soon as the visual effect had occurred, it vanished.

"Who the fuck is Harry?" Tony blurted out.

"Right, Jesus." I couldn't believe it. "Right, Tony, a few hours back, we had managed to free Daryl from a force field that the curse had put him in, now in another timeline, we were there with Daryl and this Harry War-pen bloke—"

Tony interrupted me and said, "Oh right, so this Harry bloke is the son of that professor that James spoke about in the car?"

"Yeah, now we all thought initially that it was the professor who invented that device I showed you and James if you remember, but it was his son; he's the one that does the experiment, and it's down to him that the experiment went wrong, hence the two entities."

Daryl then spoke. "No, Pete, you can't just say it was down to him, we don't know what exactly went wrong, now do we?"

Tony replied to my last sentence that I had said to him before Daryl stuck his little whore in, "Right! that explains things a little better."

Alan once more voiced his assumption, "Well, this Harry could well be placed within a force field of his own, that would explain the shouting we couldn't hear and the banging away we just saw, you may well be right then, Pete, and if so, that can only mean one thing."

Daryl then joined in the conversation, "Yeah, that poxy curse has him."

Tony then followed up with, "And it's now showing us that it has him secure, but secure where? And in what timeline is he in, now that's an interesting problem."

Chapter 12
Consciousness

So now that we had Tony back with us, we were still one short, but we were up for the fight of our lives against the most sinister creature that ever existed, moving off towards the car the curse struck once more; as fast as you could blink, everything changed. Instead of us being outside in the fresh air, we had been transported away; there was also another problem that now existed; the curse had thrown another problem into the mix, they had been separated from each other.

I had no idea as to where my mates had been removed too. I prayed that they were still alive. I looked around, it was like a mouse sterile unit, the type used for experimentation on rodents.

I was able to stand with plenty of headroom in this sterile place, no toilet facilities, no bed, no windows; my position was dire. I approached the walls and slowly examined each wall for any breaks as there may have been a door that I wasn't able to see. On one wall at the base was a slit, like a minuscule cat flap.

I was puzzled as to what this was. I sat down on the floor, knees forward and just gazed at this flap; it felt like an eternity, just sitting with my own company, mumbling to myself as I continually prayed that my friends were okay. The cat flap flung open, a tray of food came through it.

Someone had to be on the other side of this wall. I started to bang the wall with my fists whilst shouting at the top of my voice, "Hello, can you hear me, hello!" There was no reply, for all I knew was that this person, well, I assumed it was human, was deaf, and that was why it didn't communicate with me. I looked at the tray, it had an apple, some cheese and two slices of bread and butter. I picked it up, glanced at it for a few more seconds in dismay and threw everything against the wall as I shouted, "What do you think I am, you bastard! I'm no rat, let me out of here!"

There was no sound, this could drive a man mad. I then sat wondering what was next to come through this flap. I waited and waited but nothing else came. Once more I started scanning the room; this time for some strange reason I hadn't seen this earlier, simply because it wasn't there.

Towards the upper far corner near the ceiling, I witnessed a white screen materialise; the screen was segmented with ten individual compartments, you know chamber like. Each one was enclosed with black lines showing the room size within it; it was like a surveyor floor plan of a building; within just two of those chambers were four black dots, one in one chamber and the other three in another. Now this chamber with the three dots within were moving around, but the one on its own wasn't.

As I stood and moved over to the screen, this black dot seemed to copy every movement that I was making. It soon became transparent to me that that moving dot was me. I also then realised that the other dots were of my guys; the seriousness of my situation slapped me in the face.

We were in some kind of a maze, an experiment may be, or was it a bit of fun for this entity to see us freak out, what did it want to find out about us? Or maybe it was just plain and simple insatiable curiosity, or something worse.

I had no idea, all the other dots then thankfully started to move around within their own segments. "Thank god," I muttered as I knew that they were all reasonably okay; all I could do now was wait for something to occur.

It also dawned on me that it wasn't interested in killing as why would it feed me? At least, I got piece of mind on that point.

It must have been ten to twenty minutes that had passed by without anything taking place. It was then that it crossed my mind as I was sitting there, was I going to have to get to them, or were they to free me? I stood up and once again looked at the screen; there were eight chambers that now showed on the screen that separated us; we were at the fullest distance apart; there was no way on this earth that I would be able to get to them. I had no tools, no weapon; it was a hopeless situation, but I wasn't put off as I knew that the old boy wouldn't allow us to fail. I placed myself as near to this cat flap as possible in the hope that when it was opened again I could grab hold of the thing, well, whatever or whoever was there, so I sat and waited, and I waited some more, just looking at the flap. When I thought to myself that I couldn't take much more of this, above the flap, a crack started to form and open up; to my amazement, it grew as it appeared in front of me.

Watching as the crack enlarged, it soon became big enough for a man to slip through; cautiously, I peered through it into the next ugly chamber; it wasn't the same as the one I was imprisoned in; the base of the floor had a maze of large tunnel sections like drainpipes throughout, just enough room for an adult to crawl through, so I edged ahead. Slowly and quietly whilst observing my surroundings, I entered this tunnel maze, as I passed through a section, there must've been some sort of a device that would drop a shutter behind me.

My retreat was being cut off after each section I went through. I then knew then and there that no matter what lay ahead, I had to go up against it; each corner I turned, I expected something to be in the way, but so far, I hadn't encounter anything; it was at that moment that I came across my first problem. Flame bursts leaped from the ground, very similar to a gas burner system in a cooker turned full on; jets of flames erupted up and into the tunnel just ahead of where I was, but at segmented intervals of roughly six feet apart and at a height of at least a foot, looking down the tunnel, I could see that there were at least six of these flame things. I was a foot away from my first flame.

As I watched this burn for a good period of time trying to work out my next move, I realised that the timings between each flame burst were lasting six seconds; it would flare up then switch off; it seemed like it was on an automated system.

It was then I felt a feeling of euphoria; it was going to be a piece of cake. As the flame blast died off, I hurried and scurried over the burner and stopped just before the second flame blast.

The timings for each of the six were exactly the same; it became simple to go through this challenge; it wasn't until I had reached the sixth burner that I abruptly stopped dead in my tracks.

This last burner was different; the timings weren't cooperating with my plans, as the flames were sporadic. "SHIT!" I cried. "Bollocks, now concentrate, Pete, you need to focus." I examined the burst for ages, well, that's what it felt like, in actual fact, it was only a few minutes when again I worked out what it was doing; its sequence was burst for six, then off, then I would drop to a five-second burst, followed by a three, two, as it would then go full circle and restart at six. I waited for the cycle to reset to six.

I then scurried over the line, and taking a pause, I relaxed for a bit and took a rest bite; shortly, I was back crawling through until I had reached the end of the tunnel system.

It was then that I thought about who it was that gave me the tray of food; it was compellingly interesting. I wondered if I would ever meet him; the third chamber was awaiting my entry; this one was much taller than the previous, but a great deal narrower, ropes lay all over the place, twisted over each other running from wall to wall. Now I could see the floor below, there was a swirling mist covering the ground. As I watched, I could plainly see an image of something swimming around in it, but it was impossible to see what it was; you could only see movement down there. I knew the way forward would have to be these ropes as they were taut. *They have to be fixed to something*, I thought to myself.

On the far sidewall opposite my position was the exit; it was roughly around eighteen feet from the ground, but saying that, I didn't go much about the dangers involved here; the mist started to clear a little.

Water was now rising and replacing the mist; to my dismay, I realised that the water wasn't stopping for the soles of my shoes were now starting to get wet. I knew time was against me so I had to push on. Now some of the ropes were tightly compacted close whilst others weren't.

I took a gamble as I thought to myself, *Why?* I managed to manoeuvre myself into a decent position in which to leap on my first rope. I then suddenly caught a glimpse of a few other ropes; these weren't fastened to anything but to one another as I deliberately yanked on one of them.

It just went tumbling down over my head and into the water. I knew what I needed to do; looking at each rope before I grabbed, I was able to work out which was safe and those that weren't.

The water was increasing in depth and height at this point, climbing its way towards me; it felt like the water had a will of its own as the faster I moved up towards the exit, the faster the water rose up. I had to make a decision, do I take my time or throw caution to wind.

I threw caution out of my mind and started to quickly move myself from this watery death trap. I reached the exit point and crawled through, straight into the fourth chamber.

I immediately felt uneasy with this one; there was no light; it was pitch black. I could see where I was going regarding the other chambers but this one was gonna be a nightmare; all I could do was carefully place one foot in front of the other in the hope I didn't trip or fall down a massive hole, step by step was the plan. Slowly, I proceeded into the depths of darkness, and as far as I was aware, it was just me in here. I was alone with my thoughts, maybe this was my biggest challenge, and believe me, that's a scary thing, you try closing your eyes and having no sound or light to focus on, it was then, BANG! I had hit something with my foot.

Luckily, I stayed upright, carefully, I stepped over whatever it was. I was feeling physically sick; this was the worst chamber I had yet had to face so far. Now don't get me wrong, it wasn't the darkness so much that terrified me, it was my own thoughts, my own imagination, now this is the ultimate enemy. "Fuck that!" I shouted out as I once again walked into something.

I had walked straight into a bloody wall, but luckily, I had used my nose to stop myself. I gave my nose a tweak," traffic, not busted," the pain thou made my eyes water as I felt the wetness drip onto my cheek. I moved off. I must've turned six or seven bends, then like a bad dream a flickering light began to be seen just ahead of where I was standing; two shivering figures began to form. I was horrified to see my old mates.

Andy and James standing side by side, each one was pointing at me as they spoke, but I couldn't hear them. I was frightened to death as I got nearer to them; it was then that their voices became clearer as they continued to repeat the same line over and over again. "Why did you let us die, Pete, why did you let us die, Pete?" I grabbed my hands and covered my ears.

"I couldn't help you, I tried." I tried answering back, but it was as if their voices were fixed, there was no consciousness with them, just the images of their past selves, ghosts. I felt tears falling from my face with hurtful shame. As I moved towards them, I had got to touching distance from their forms; they disappeared. I was once again completely alone.

I had to get out of here; it was now the worst of all had come, every bloke that I had met since this nightmare began started to appear then vanished; it was just their faces that were zooming in and out at me as large as life then shrinking as they faded out; all they did so they were laughing; it was hysterical laughter, their eyes were streaming tears.

Jesus, was I going crazy, is this how I meet my end I thought. At that moment, my reasoning took hold of me as I realised what my enemy was, it was my own conciseness I was fighting against. I stopped and screamed as loud as I could. "ENOUGH!" I was no longer in the darkness, as if by magic lights immediately filled the chamber; hurriedly, I had to close my eyes. Slowly, I opened them. It was bliss, the thought of it being once more in daylight was like all my birthdays coming at once; it was like a blistering hot summer's day; the heat and light were now beating above my head; it was so bright, the walls were gleaming like sheets of glass. I had to squint my eyes and cover them slightly just to see where I was going.

Was I in another chamber or was this the same one I thought. I didn't know, but at least there was light now.

As I walked through along this narrow passageway large long swordlike things came swishing across my face; luckily for me, I managed to catch a glimpse of it as it came seriously close to my forehead, that gave me a second to jerk myself backward; in front of me stood what I could only describe as an ancient Roman gladiator; he was in a fighting stance, wearing all the mod cons for the time period, the helmet, short sword and a reasonably decent-sized oblong shield. I think that the name for this type of gladiator was known as a Thracian. Now the only Thracian I had ever heard of was Spartacus way back in my history lessons at school. I think it was from around the year 73 AD; he was killed by Crassus and Pompey's armies in Italy, a bloody long time ago. He came towards me staggering his foot work. I stood there thinking, *What the fuck do I do now? I ain't even got a sword.*

Within milliseconds from out of nowhere, Thracian body armour of the same time period came flying through the air from all different directions! As each piece came towards me, it clasped itself onto my body; all I could do was watch in amazement as I got kitted out with the same weaponry as my enemy, with one important exception, there was no helmet. Clutching this sword as tightly as I could, I stood there in dread for if this was a true gladiator, then I'm already dead, for these guys were seriously trained in the art of killing.

The Thracian came to within striking distance and began swinging his sword left to right, up and down. I prepared for the attack; he swung his sword high, I ducked and lashed out; my thrust made contact with his helmet as it flew off his head and into the air; to my horror, I knew my enemy, it was Tony.

I dropped my guard and said, "Tony, it's me Peter, how did you get away?" Tony shouted back at me in Latin. I had no earthly idea as to what he was saying, but whatever it was, there came a great deal of aggression in his voice. He once again launched an attack; immediately, I defended myself and then I tried to reason with him in an attempt to get through to his logic. "Tony, stop, listen to me for a second." Either he didn't want to listen to what I had to say or he just didn't understand English; there was no hope of me trying to talk him down as he just kept attacking. "Tony, please, I don't want to hurt you." He swung his sword yet again; this time he showed his left side.

I swung my shield and connected with his rib, he was cut and fell to one knee. Instantly, there was rapturous applause screaming and shouting from a non-existing audience; it was as if thousands were cheering the sight of blood. I felt like I was in the arena of ancient times.

I stood there listening to the chanting and screams of 'kill him', 'kill him'. Tony wasn't finished as he rose up once more, staggering but moving forward. Again, I shouted at him, "Tony, stop, for god's sake." He again screamed in Latin at me. I had no choice but to do the crowd's bidding.

It was now a simple choice, kill or be killed. Tony's rage was seriously growing in strength as he attacked, but this time, he attacked with plain simple aggression, no thinking as to what he was doing; he attacked sword high, I twisted and plunged my sword into his chest.

Tony stopped instantly, looked at me and fell backwards; before he hit the floor, he had vanished into a puff of smoke; my weapons and armour disintegrated from me; there was no bloodstains on the ground; it was as if it had never happened. Had I just dreamt that or did it actually take place, now that was a quandary. Looking ahead, I saw a doorway creep open. "What now?" I cried as I moved towards it.

Slowly, I opened the door and peered inside, to my amazement, it was a bloody big army training assault course, like the old circuit training we did at school; now I was bloody good at that. As I looked, I could plainly see what the circuit consisted of and what was involved for me to complete; there were hurdles, looked like the hundred metres, two low nets that lay sprawled across the floor, you had to crawl under those, two rope swings you had to get swing across, it was then a mad rush for the finish line. As I continued my observations, a voice came from out of the blue; it was the evil curse's demonic voice; a gigantic stopwatch appeared in front of the first obstacle; it just sat there in mid-air; there was nothing holding it in place apart from empty space. The voice cried out, "Fifteen minutes, fifteen minutes, fail, you stay, fail you stay." The clock began to tick down the allotted time; the demonic voice just laughed its stupid head off as it always seemed to do.

I ran like a bat from hell. After the first five minutes, it soon came to my attention that I was not sixteen anymore, I had to try and steady myself instead of going at this circuit like I was still a schoolboy. I steadied my pace, I only had ten minutes to finish. I had completed the 100-metre hurdles and the two nets, all I had left were the two rope swings and then the dash for the line; every minute would feel like an eternity from now on. Two more minutes had passed as I climbed where I needed to be. I started the second rope swing, another five minutes had elapsed. I only had around three minutes of time to get to the finish line. I ran my heart out, as the clock was counting down the seconds, 5...4...3...2...I passed the line.

I was exhausted as I fell to the ground absolutely knackered; a devilishly strong roar of anger ripped the atmosphere as the curse knew it had lost that particular battle.

After I had caught my breath and calmed down, another room beckoned as its door swung open; all I kept on saying to myself was, *Keep strong, keep strong.* I moved through and entered the next chamber.

To my surprise, this one looked quite pleasant, it had all the trappings of a poker club, you know cards, stud or draw, who cares, now this was my cup of tea. I was totally transformed clothes-wise into a black suit, complete with a dicky bow tie; everyone else wore the same; a male steward approached me and showed me to a particular table. Five men were already seated; they all had drinks so I asked for a double whisky. I sat down and watched each one in turn. Once I had sat down, the area then changed; there was no one, everyone had disappeared; it was just me and those five men. A gun then miraculously appeared in the middle of the table. One guy said as casually as asking for a bacon sandwich at a grill bar, "Russian roulette, gentlemen." I slumped back in my chair for I knew what was about to unfold. To people who don't understand what Russian roulette is, it's where you have a group of, say, six, like here, you take it in turns to pass the gun around, each player puts the gun to his head and pulls the trigger. Rules are simple, gun fires, you lose, well, you're dead, that's it; you then start again until one man is left alive.

I thought that this game looked quite pleasant when I first walked in; I should've realised well before this.

The steward appeared from nowhere, he picked up this gun, opened up the chamber and placed one bullet within it, he then closed the chamber and spun it so no one was aware where the bullet was; the gun was then passed to the next man to the steward's left. The first man picked up the gun, he looked at each player, placed the gun to his head and pulled the trigger, nothing, no shot was fired. Now I was number five in line; the gun was passed on. The second guy did the same, pulled the trigger, nothing once again. I was beginning to think the worst.

The third guy then took the gun, fired, again no shot rang out; it was now my turn. I looked at the gun, then I looked at the others, they were all smiling as if they knew that the bullet was meant for me.

I tried to stand, but I was secured to the chair by something. After a brief struggle, I knew that I had no choice but to play! My hand was shaking like mad. I raised the gun, closed my eyes and fired, no shot rang out. The fifth guy had no luck, I'm afraid; he held the gun to his head, pulled the trigger, we watched as if in slow motion, half of the side of his head blasted out across the floor; blood and brains flew everywhere. The other four guys raised their glasses and toasted to his death; the steward then loaded the gun with another bullet.

The game continued in this fashion until all that remained was the last two players, me and this guy.

A coin spun through the air in front of the two of us, I guess the winner would choose to either fire first or second. I called heads and won. I chose the second shot; my nerves were at breaking point. The guy picked up the gun, immediately without hesitation, he pulled the trigger, bang!!!! The shot rang out, and again, the demonic roar of hatred rang out.

I was truly convinced that the old boy was watching over my shoulder somehow, it had to be. The second from last chamber revealed itself as a further door opened. I stood up as my restraints broke away.

I walked over and into the chamber; in front of me stood a massive climbing frame, one gigantic vertical wall with tiny stupid little grips strewn all over it. The demonic voice said, "Climb, climb, when you fall, this shall be fine." The laughter was really starting to piss me off big time.

"Go fuck yourself!" I shouted.

Without equipment of any kind, I began to climb; the top of this vertical wall must have been at least five hundred feet for I felt as if there was no chance I could climb this; it was hard work trying to grip on to these grips, but that was all I had. Gradually after the first ten feet, my foot gave way as I slipped off the grip. I came tumbling down, sat on the ground and thought, well, rather now then two hundred feet up. I stood, brushed myself down.

Looking at the wall once more, I then started climbing once more.

As before I was having a bad time climbing, I was fifty feet up, so far no more slips this time; after another fifty feet, I once again lost my grip as my right hand gave way; luckily for me, I had managed to grip onto the other grip that was close to me. I took a little breather, and again, I started the climb. After what felt like an eternity, I had reached halfway; there was no turning back now, it was do or die. Three hours later, I had reached the summit. I had made it to the top, what a relief, for at that moment, I was no longer on the wall but in a courtroom dock surrounded by coppers. There were courtroom barristers, ushers and a judge, wig and all, but, and this is a gigantically big but, they were all canines.

Every single one of them within this so-called courtroom were animated dogs, and that also included me, well, at least, I was a human animated character. The judge was a cocker spaniel, the cops were bulldogs, the barristers were Alsatians and the usher was a pit bull. The judge then started to bark, but the words were in English; he said to me, "Are you guilty or not guilty?"

I stuttered and with total confusion, I uttered, "What, what the hell, where am I?"

This has to be a dream, someone wake me up for fuck's sake. I couldn't believe what was happening; nothing was making any sense. I was feeling extremely uneasy whilst unsettled. This time, the bulldogs all shouted in unison, "You guilty or not guilty?"

Again, I just couldn't understand as I said, "But you're animals, what's happening? Where the fuck am I?"

The cocker spaniel then barked at the jury who were twelve different breeds of cat, as he said, "Find him guilty for swearing and I will hang him."

The head cat stood up on his back legs and said, "Guilty." The cocker spaniel then laid down the sentence.

"Peter Tate, it is the judgement of this court that you be taken hence to a place of lawful execution, there to be hung by the neck until you are dead, so is the judgement of this court; bulldogs, do your duty." I closed my eyes, and shook my head.

This was ludicrous, absolutely fucking ludicrous. It was then that once again everything changed around me.

As all this was taking place, old boy had somehow managed to keep the curse occupied as it cleverly removed my mates one by one and without the curse becoming aware out of their chamber and into a secure location; it replicated and substituted each as it worked its magic; it then focussed its attention onto me. I was transported out of this animated courtroom as the bulldogs were dragging my screaming carcass.

Seconds later, I was smack bang in the middle of my teammates. The scene was so joyful, everyone grabbed me in one big team hug, as we were congratulating each other for all still being alive. The old boy showed itself as it emerged from the flooring. As usual, it resembled the old boy; it spoke to us all, "Entity growing, time running out, reduce I will for you safe you will, your Harry awaits, reduce for you safe shall be for time short."

I then looked at it and asked, "Why the animation?"

The old boy looked at me and stated, "In animated form entity can destroy the Peter."

"Then why didn't it?" I asked.

The old boy then responded with just two words, "Play time."

Tony then asked, "This shrinkage you just referred to, when is it to happen?" The entity smiled and then simply evaporated from whence it had come.

Whatever the old boy had in mind about shrinkage, we had no idea, but it did say that we were going to finally meet this Harry War-pen and that would also mean destroying the entity once and for all.

My worry was that I didn't lose any more friends. As we stood chatting in our secure location, Tony mentioned a small fact that none of us had yet noticed, well, not right at that moment. He stated, "Is it my imagination or is this room growing?"

I looked back at him and replied, "It's not the room that's growing, mate, it's us, we're shrinking, so that's what the old boy was talking about."

Alan looked at me and blurted out, "Oh bollocks." As Alan's words echoed around us all, we were slowly but surely being reduced down in size; every second that passed, we reduced still further until we were roughly around an inch in height. "Har, this is really bollocks, Pete." Alan wasn't a happy bunny as he grunted. At that moment, once again, we were transported. This time, it had placed us within a military compound; we stood there just looking around for a few moments as we gathered our bearings.

"What in god's name," I gasped.

Tony had totally lost the plot when he came out with, "Holy shrinkage Batman." He was bewildered to say the least.

Alan then said, "This is still bollocks." Daryl said nothing as his mouth had dropped around his chin.

I said, "Well, at least we'll be safe from the curse for a while. Let's hope when we do return to normal size, the old boy will have gathered enough strength to fight alongside us."

"Why would it do that?" Daryl asked.

I then replied, "Well, it's simple really, it wants to not exist, Daryl; it doesn't want to be, and we're gonna make sure it gets what it wants, right, lads?" We all cheered. Now all we really needed to do was to keep our heads down and pray that the old boy could actually return us back to normality.

Chapter 13
Imagination

Tony was now starting to search the area. I had no idea as to what he was looking for. I, at that moment, had a massive realisation, everything around us was at the size you would expect to find in comparison with your own size, but we had been reduced in size, so why wasn't everything a thousand times bigger than we were? The answer hit me like a bolt of lightning; it was so obvious, the old boy had put us smack bang inside a bloody child's toy, on closer inspection as I touched a few walls and other pieces that lay about the place, I was right, everything was plastic; it was some sort of military barracks. I also knew that if we were going to survive whilst in this state, we were going to need weapons for one.

I asked Daryl if he could pop over with Tony and see if they could come up with any ideas. Alan was examining part of a wall for some strange reason. I left Tony and Daryl for a moment and went over to him and asked, "What are you doing?"

He replied, "Not a lot, just looking at these scratches." He brushed them with his hand.

"What about them?" I inquired.

"Well, what made 'em for one? I think you're forgetting one major issue, we now have, Pete."

"Oh really, and that is?"

I was extremely interested in his answer as he said, "Well, whatever has made these scratches was a hell of a lot bigger than we are now; it was probably a cat, or even a big rat; it's defiantly some type of animal. Now these are going to be our real enemy now; if we're not ready for 'em, we're gonna be lunch." It was clear that there wasn't much thought processing going on when we were miniaturised.

"I see what you mean, Al, you do know we're in a model, don't ya?"

Alan replied, "Yeah, it did cross my mind; right, get the boys together, we need to discuss what we're going to do."

"Right, will do, captain."

Alan then moved off to get Tony and Daryl back, shortly we were together. "Right, here's the state of play, lads, we're in a model army barracks. I hope you're all aware of that fact by now. Alan has mentioned that our main enemy could possibly be pets or rodents. Our predicament will be having no defence. We have to create some sort of a plan in which we can defend ourselves if needs be. Now here's what I think we need to do, due to our size.

"There are going to be more dangers to us than the old boy had realised; maybe it didn't even think about this kind of danger, you know, cats, rats, kids even. I suggest that we start to fashion whatever we can get our hands on into weapons."

Daryl then said, "What about matches, they may work?"

Alan then jumped in with, "And you're going to do what with a match, that's a bloody stupid idea."

Daryl defended himself by stating, "They're not for killing, you dick, they're defensive, you jab something in the eye, they're gonna run off." I then defended Daryl as I agreed with him.

Tony then put his thoughts into action and came out with an excellent suggestion, "What about catapults and slings, now those could be useful."

"Oh yes, now we're cooking."

I was getting excited with these ideas as we continued our conversation. "Right, so here's what we're gonna do. Alan, you and I will see what we can find and hopefully put something together, as long as it works, who cares, Daryl, you go with Tony and see what you two can find."

We separated and proceeded with our tasks.

Daryl and Tony moved off at a decent pace and entered another area as Alan and myself moved off towards another; when you think about it, none of us had actually asked the question as to where the old boy had placed us, okay, it's military barracks, but where on god's earth are we?

Apart from it saying to us we will be secure here, we knew nothing else. Oh well, at least we'll be safe for a bit, well, that was the hope anyway. After a short time had passed, Tony and Daryl came back; they were carrying some shiny items. Alan and I had no luck finding anything we could use for weapons; finally, we reunited. I didn't waste time as I got straight to the point and asked, "What you got there?"

Tony replied, "Paperclips, there was a bunch of 'em in a heap over there in the corner of the compound. Now if we were to straighten 'em, they will certainly do the job."

"Sounds good to me, let's make a start." Each one of us took a paperclip and began straightening. Slowly, we managed to get the clips into some sort of a spear-like shape, granted they didn't look like much, but god help the creature that gets one of these in their eye.

Tony then came out with an excellent suggestion, "Has anybody bothered to have seen what's behind those gates yet? I only wondered as it may be a good idea."

Alan replied, "Well, no, we didn't. I can always go back if you want me to."

"Why not?" Tony responded.

Alan asked Daryl if he fancied a stroll, he nodded a welcoming yes and both men wandered off. "I'm going to check the layout of this place; it'll certainly be interesting to see how well this place has been designed, looks like a World War One barracks to me," I eagerly stated.

"What you into history then, Pete?" Tony asked.

I replied with, "Yeah, I'm not bad as it goes, let's go in here."

I pointed to a main building and we walked inside; what a waste of time that was, the only thing in there was the shell of the building. We soon materialised back into the compound; it was at that moment, Alan and Daryl came rushing back over to us; they were running as if their lives depended on their safe return to us. "Eh, slow down, where's the fire?" I moaned.

Daryl shouted out, "Voices!" I then raised my voice as fear began to drift into the atmosphere.

"Voices, where from?"

Alan yelled back at me, "I don't fucking know where, but I'm telling you this, whomever it is, is a lot bigger than us."

"Shit." I turned around and shouted once more, "Come on!" We moved like lightning back into one of the barracks and hid.

Tony and Daryl went over to a smashed-up window frame to see what if anything. Alan got behind the doorway, and I stood on the back wall. "Can you see anything, Tony?" I asked keenly.

He replied, "Not yet, hang on, hang on a minute." Halfway through his sentence, we could hear a door handle turn; you could then hear a group of children laughing as the door swung open. I whispered very softly to the lads, "We must be in someone's bedroom, what are they doing?" I was so eager for Tony to tell me something interesting.

"I can't see anything, Pete." The door then closed as the children's voices slowly drifted into silence.

Alan came out from behind the doorway and spoke, he was seriously pissed off. "Secure location, yeah, right, what a load of bollocks, this entity couldn't run a piss up in a brewery, Pete, how the hell is this secure?" I replied to him as I defended the old boy.

"No one's perfect, Alan, not even you."

"Oh, up yours." Alan then went back behind the door and sat down holding his hands over his head, knees up and mumbling to himself.

I then said to him, "What are you mumbling about?"

Alan abruptly stated, "We were lucky that time, maybe next time we won't be." I just looked at him.

Daryl then popped up and changed the atmosphere with, "Well, at least we know a bit more as to where we are; we know it's probably a house or maybe even a flat; we also know it's occupied with kids, so they're for it's reasonable to assume that there are to be adults. Maybe that was what the entity meant by secure."

"Who knows, Daryl, who knows," I replied.

Tony then stated the obvious, "We better make bloody sure we don't get spotted; if we do, we're gonna be in some serious shit, oh, and by the way, Daryl, how can you assume?"

"For all you know, those voices could have come from other things than children; we can't even see outside this fucking compound." The group looked at one another as we all knew Tony was right.

Daryl then asked, "So what now, we can't just wait here, could be hours or even days before the old boy shows up again."

I then made Tony wish he kept his big mouth shut as I suggested, "I think we should follow Tony's guidance and see what's out there." Tony looked at me with dread.

"Now hang on a minute, I didn't say that, did I? I just said that we don't know what's out there."

I replied to him with, "Well, there's only one way of finding out now, isn't there?" I looked over to Alan and asked, "Do you fancy a reconnoitre, mate?"

"Reconnaissance, you bet," Alan replied.

"Right, Tony, Daryl, you two stay here out of harm's way, Alan and I won't be long. Alan, do me a favour and grab two of those spear things please, mate. Right, let's now get a glance of what's behind these walls." Alan and I moved out whilst making sure we wouldn't be discovered; we would drop behind any obstruction that we thought would give us the best protection from it.

Shortly, we reached the furthest wall from where we thought the voices originated from; luckily, the walls were only around four inches in height. There were a couple of toy cars that lay nearby so we used them to climb; it wasn't long before we could look over the wall. To our astonishment, the barracks were on the floor, right up against a humongous window.

Well, it seemed to me that it had been deliberately positioned there to create as much distance between the barracks and the door; we clambered over the wall one at a time. I went over first as Alan passed the spears over. Once we were on the other side, we stayed close to the skirting boards and moved around; as we did, we received one almighty shock for out of nowhere appeared a household spider; it must have reacted to our movements; it stood looking at us. God, it was one ugly motherfucker; it was at that moment it charged.

Alan and myself used our spears and began jabbing them at the creepy crawly; it was great timing that we got help from an unexpected source. Daryl and Tony had been watching from the barracks and rushed over as soon as they witnessed the spider, and now all four of us were jabbing this monstrosity; the spider just kept moving towards us. I shouted, "The eyes, aim for its eyes!" Tony and Alan were successful as they both landed blows to the spider; it miraculously stopped, moved back a few steps then moved off, and within seconds, it was crawling up its web.

Alan calmly looked at Daryl and Tony then said, "What took you so long?" He was joking, of course; it gave us a release valve as we all had a little chuckle.

I took the lead, as I did, I said, "Take it nice and easy, lads, we could well have a few more surprises on this little trip." Slowly and once more, we eased forward; as we did, another surprise loomed over us.

A couple of flies were swooping over some food remanence that was stuck into the carpet fibres; it must have been bubble gum or something on those lines;

the flies were going nuts, luckily for us, they weren't paying much attention so we eagerly moved around them.

Daryl stopped and froze as Tony walked into him. Tony then blurted, "Come on, Daryl, what's up with ya? At least, say you're…Daryl, you okay?" Daryl was just steaming into mid-air. "Pete, there's a problem with Daryl," Tony blurted. I turned and doubled back to them. Alan followed.

"What's up with him?" Alan asked. Daryl was shaking.

I held Daryl's shoulders, looked him straight in the eyes and asked, "What is it, Daryl?"

Daryl looked at me and shakingly he replied, "Harry, it's Harry." He pointed over to his right-hand side about twenty feet up in the air; we all took a look. To our amazement, we could see Harry pounding on something; it was exactly like it was before; he was shouting, but no sounds were coming out.

It appeared like we were watching a silent movie or something like it; the image was floating in mid-air; we were mesmerised by the mirage. "He's got to be close by, he has to be, that's the seconds time now," I said.

Tony responded by saying, "Well, the old boy did mention him, but why's he trapped?"

Alan then jumped in. "Well, if he is trapped, the question has to be answered, who has trapped him." The apparition then began to fade away and disappear.

Daryl, came back to his senses. I asked, "How you feeling, you okay now?"

Daryl replied, "Yeah, I'm okay, Pete, just gives me the willies seeing him like that." I grinned as we moved off; we hadn't gone fifty yards when we heard a rustling, it was coming from what looked like an overturned shoebox.

The four of us then lined up within seconds; we were like Ancient Greek soldiers in a phalanx formation.

Spears facing slightly to the right and ahead of us, we were ready for whatever came out of it; within moments, it had pounced out of the box and was running at full speed towards us; we aggressively took our stance and braced for impact. It was a rat, a bloody big one at that.

Alan shouted, "Fucking hell, look at the size of this bloody thing!" It was growing very angry when Alan shouted once more, "Pete, it's getting bloody close, do you really think these things are going to stop that thing?"

The rat was now only a few feet away when I screamed out, "Hit the deck!" No one needed to be told twice as they all did what was instructed.

At that moment, the rat had the opposite idea as it leaped over us like a horse jumping at the Grand National; the rat was as much afraid of us as we were of it. The rat once it had jumped over us continued its run as it just scurried off and out of sight; we stood and pretended we weren't scared with how the situation had developed; well, that was bullshit, trust me, the adrenaline was pumping; you could smell it, it was that strong. After a few moments had elapsed, I began to move onward. Alan followed, then Daryl and Tony moved in behind. Shortly, we had passed the shoebox; once again, the voices of children were heard. Hurriedly, we hid in the best place possible, the shoebox. We hadn't lost much time, for once inside it, the door to the room swung open once again, in came four kids, roughly six to seven-year-olds, rushing around the room like kids do, pushing each other over onto the bed, screaming; sounded like lots of fun; they were like they had just had a strong sugar fix.

A woman's voice echoed in the air as she screamed out, "Dinner!" The kids moved off at speed, but they forgot to close the door.

I peered out of our hiding place, the way was clear; we then moved away from the room and entered the landing; it had gone extremely quiet. Huddling the skirting, we began to continue our dangerous trek along the landing, because it was so quiet it became eerie. Everyone was on full alert for if anyone had started to come upstairs, we would be in dire trouble.

We approached another door. Alan whispered in my ear, "Fancy having a butchers in here, Pete?"

"Why not?" I replied. Keenly, we all knelt down and slipped under the closed door, looked like a bomb had gone off in this room.

It had to be a young girl's room as there were plenty of clues laying around, baby dolls, miniature plastic teapots and cutlery, clothing were strewn over her bed and floor, well, at least we knew we were in a family home.

Daryl mentioned a small point, "I've been wondering, why did the old boy state we were in a secure location, doesn't make sense to me."

"Well, I guess we're gonna find out soon enough," I replied. It was then we heard another commotion from the stairs, without thinking, we scattered in four different directions. I made it under the bed, Alan jumped inside a loose sock, Daryl slipped behind a few toys, and Tony couldn't choose where to go, he just laid close to a toy in between the doorway and the bed. Into the room, they came.

I was in a rather reasonably decent position to see these kids for the first time. I gasped, as to my horror they weren't kids at all, they were Who, What, Where, and When, the chieftain's old comrades. What the hell are they doing here, I thought to myself, what's going on? This just didn't make any sense to me. Who then noticed Tony, who was lying on his chest, slowly trying to get away and under cover; it was too late. Who picked him up and shouted, "I've got another one, I've got another one!" He pranced about like a fully grown idiot.

The four of them then rushed out, as they did, Where was heard to say, "Put it with the other one, Who."

"Yeah!" Who shouted back. I rushed out from under the bed; the rest of the guys joined me within seconds.

Alan then said, "Christ, Pete, did you see who they were?"

"Yeah, I did. Come on, we've got to see where they've taken Tony."

Daryl then mentioned, "They're gonna put him with another one, it has to be Harry, bet ya."

"We'll just have to wait and see, won't we? Now come on." The four dwarfs hadn't gone back downstairs as we would have heard them clamber down, so that must mean they're in another room up here. The door started to open. I was right as they began to appear one by one; by this time, we had managed to get behind the door out of sight of these ugly gits.

As luck would have it, they didn't bother to close the door behind themselves, that was fortunate for us. We charged out from behind the door and into this other room; the three of us split up to cover more ground. As we scanned the room, over in the far corner was a large domelike glass! It was then that I saw them. Daryl was right, it was Harry, and thank god, Tony was with him. We rushed over to them; the glass was resting on three books. Once again, this was lucky for us.

Tony and Harry, once they had seen us, stood and waved for help. It wasn't long before we were all trying to lift this thing, god, it was so heavy. I then had an excellent idea. I said to Daryl and Alan, "Can you two go over there and grab some books?" There was not any questioning as they moved off. Harry and Tony looked bewildered as they didn't realise what I had in mind.

Soon enough, we had collected four books. I placed one near the glass. "Right, Daryl, we're gonna lift this, when you get enough room, shove that book under it. Ready, three…two…one, go." We lifted the glass with all the strength we had.

Daryl then slipped a book under the glass, everything was really looking good until all hell broke loose. As we were preparing to lift once more and get the boys out, we had another intrusion, no one had seen this thing before. From the edge of the carpet beneath the window a twig grew. As I said just a moment ago, no one had seen it, but this twig grew massively fast; like a mind of its own the twig grew and spread. Seconds later like a giant squid, it pounced on us. Its twigs engulfed us all, either by the ankles, or stomach, it was everywhere. We hadn't a chance of escaping this plant; it was like the film I saw once before, years ago, *The Triffid*, but thank god, this thing wasn't carnivorous. Instead of eating us, it proceeded to lift the glass and fling the rest of us under it. Within seconds, we were now all trapped within a glass dome. The plant then returned to its original starting position as if time had reversed itself somehow. The five of us stood looked around then looked at each other. Daryl said, "Pete, meet Harry." I shook Harry's hand.

"Great to meet ya, Harry."

Harry looked bemused and said, "What do you mean pleased to meet ya, you know me."

I then stated the facts to him, "Yeah, in another timeline, now this is going to be difficult to understand, but the fact is this, Harry, the experiment that Daryl has spoken about, well, it just hasn't taken place yet, mate. This timeline we're in isn't ours. You see, in another timeline we had a tiny hiccup during this so-called experiment, we created an entity or allowed an entity to come into our time; there are two parts to it, one wants to stop us, the other wants us to destroy it."

"So, you have no idea of the experiment, the chamber?" Harry confirmed.

"Not a clue, mate, all I know is what Daryl has mentioned."

"Now we need to find a way of getting out of here," Alan then said. "Can someone please tell me what the fuck just happened to us? And what was that bloody plant?"

Tony agreed with him, "Yeah, I'd like to know as well." Alan and Tony both faced the twig.

Alan then mumbled, "Do you think it's dead?" We then all looked at it, whatever it was, it was dormant at the moment.

Daryl was standing there looking very puzzled and confused, so I asked him, "What's up, Daryl?"

His answer threw us off for he stated a scary statement, "I think I brought it to life, Pete."

"What do you mean, you think you brought it to life?" I eagerly asked.

He then said, "I was thinking of a plant that could move, and don't ask me why, it just popped in there."

Alan wasn't impressed. "Oh, do me a favour, how can you think something and there it is? It's just coincidental, that's all." I took a few minutes to sound out what Daryl had said; well, maybe he did, like the chieftain's idiots earlier, how did they get here? I then decided to test the theory out for myself. I then decided to think of a couple of cyber men from *Doctor Who*.

Harry looked and asked, "What are you thinking of, Pete?"

I replied, "*Doctor Who*, wanna see if there's any truth to Daryl's thinking." I had just stopped my sentence when to our disbelief, two cyber men actually did walk into the room. They approached and stood over us; they were of normal size but seemed like giants to us in our current state. We all moved backwards to the rear of the tumbler. "Jesus, it's true, please, lads, whatever you think about, please try not to think about anything dangerous, okay? Now thoughts do come true here, so nothing bad."

Alan said, "Har, right, so you just thought about cyber men, yeah?"

"Yes, I did," I replied. The five of us just watched these cyber men walk around and around like mindless zombies. Laughing again was heard, we assumed it was children's laughter, who knows what it was now. Alan all of a sudden had a smile come up on his face; he began to grin like a Cheshire cat who just had some whipped cream.

Harry asked, "What's up with you?"

I looked at Alan too and said, "Oh shit, come on, Alan, what's running through that nut of yours?"

"You'll see." Moments later, a laser weapon appeared within Alan's hands; he immediately aimed it at the glass and fired; there was nothing, no blast, no sound.

With that, Alan shook it hard and then pressed the trigger once more. "It's busted, how the hell can it be busted?" Alan was not happy.

Harry then made a suggestion, "Maybe we can't use weaponry here; we can think of things that then appear, but weapons are a no no."

"Well, that's bloody pathetic then, ain't it?" Alan was slightly pissed off, but then I realised something.

"Now this is making sense, that's why this place or time or whatever this is, is secure; the old boy has put us here so the curse can't take us out."

Daryl then said, "Are you saying we can't leave here then?"

"No, I'm not saying that; it's like he is biding his time, preparing his strength. We've just got to find a way of getting out of here."

Harry then took charge. "Right, I've got a great idea. Everyone form a circle, hold hands."

Alan remarked, "Oh right, ring a ring a-roses, is it?"

"Oh, shut up, Alan," I moaned. We held hands, even Alan reluctantly held my hand.

Harry then put his plan into action. "Right, here's what we do, everyone after three, think of lifting this structure up and over to our right and onto the floor. Now think hard, all ready? One…two…three, think." All of us had our eyes closed as we all focussed on the task in hand. As seconds ticked by, a rustling of the structure was heard. Gradually, the glass dome lifted itself up into the air.

Slowly, it lifted itself higher and higher until it was at a decent height, enough to cross over each and every one; a few minutes later and the glass dome was away and resting on the floor beside us. "Now here's our weapon, Pete, teleportation. We get into difficulties, we just move it out the way, simple as pie." Harry was extremely pleased with his effort, and to be honest, so were we. "Right now, that's out the way, what now?" Harry asked.

"We get under cover then decide what we do next," I replied. Swiftly, we left the room, and cautiously, we moved back into the army barracks and into the barrack room.

I then turned and asked Harry, "Harry, this experiment, do you remember anything about it, anything at all?"

"Well, I do remember something trying to enter our timeline you mean, yeah, I do, it was coming through a time vortex that I had created with my boy; it was a serious blunder, sheer accident.

"But what a sight it was, really amazing to see, then I had a lot of precise equipment just go, I mean vanish; it was astounding to witness it. Every time I looked at a piece of equipment, poof, gone.

"A flash of red light and I was in that glass dome, that's it. Why?"

I responded to him, "Well, you can relax about your parts, we've got 'em safe and sound."

"Where, that's great." Harry was overwhelmed by my statement.

"Well, we haven't got them exactly, our old boy has them, but they're safe," I replied.

"The old boy, who is that?" A puzzled look appeared over Harry's face.

"Sorry, mate, that's what we've come to call the entity who is helping us, you'll meet it soon enough," I replied to his question.

"Can't wait," Harry eagerly replied.

Tony then asked, "So, I don't suppose there's any chance that you can have a go at contacting it, you know, getting us out of here?"

"I guess it wouldn't hurt to try, let's give it a go, see what happens," I answered.

I moved away to get a little piece of chillout time and concentrated on contacting the entity. After a few minutes, the strain of my thoughts was growing heavy as I began to grow dizzy. I stopped and returned to the lads and then said, "There has to be some kind of a blockage in place, I can't contact it, sorry."

Tony then said, "Well, we can't stay here permanently." At that moment from well above our position, we could hear an aircraft swimming around overhead. As we all looked at each other and left the barrack room, to our amazement, we were witnessing a World War One air battle; the planes were in scale to our size; there were three British by plane fighters in a dog fight with a single red-coloured German fighter plane. Now if my memory stood firm, the only plane painted red at that time in Germany was what the British called, the bloody Red Baron, his real name was Manfred von Richthofen; strangely enough, he was never shot out of the sky by another fighter pilot. The story goes that a soldier took a pot shot from ground level, hit him and the plane then crashed. Anyway, I turned to the lads and asked, "Okay, who is the bright spark who thought up this one?" Daryl raised his arm slowly whilst keeping his head down.

Tony then looked over at me and said, "Oh shit, Pete, sorry, it just slipped in my nut. There's a toy plane outside the barracks, it reminded me of the film I once watched, think it was called *The Blue Max*."

"Your scaring me, Tony, what the hell have you conjured up now." I wasn't impressed.

Chapter 14
Fearsome Ones

Tony replied to my question with two words, "King Kong." All of a sudden, you heard the gorilla roar as Kong came out from behind the barracks, jumping up to a great height, in a feeble attempt to grab a plane or two. Luckily for them, he missed the grab. Once he had landed, he just kept beating hard on to his chest and roaring out aloud. This was getting out of control by now, for as we watched, three stunningly beautiful brunettes came strolling along in the room with the smallest bikinis known to man.

It was a man's paradise, they were stunning. Two were carrying beachballs and the other a towel, but where was the beach? "Right, lads, that's enough!" I shouted; it was like school kids running riot without control. "Everyone think of a small block of ice, all of you, Alan, that especially applies to you."

Within a millisecond, all the apparitions had disappeared. The only thing that was still in view were the half dozen or so ice cubes that lay on the floor in front of us.

Now these thoughts were getting out of control, it wouldn't be long before they came to be bloody dangerous to all of us; it was then that the old boy appeared to us, once again as always it was in vapour form until it formed into the old boy. Harry looked at me and asked, "The old boy, I presume?" I nodded back a yes. It approached us all with a gentle grin on his face.

Now this had to be a good omen for us, god knows we need some good news. Before it could start communicating, I asked it, "Why did you place us here? And why is this place secure to the curse?"

It looked at me and said, "Imagination secure your within the minds, contact he can no complete, interference from without, we go now." Like the waving of a magic wand, we were once more being teleported from the realms of imagination and back into reality, and thank god, we had been restored back to normal size.

We found ourselves standing on what looked like a balcony overlooking the sea. As we turned around, I immediately recognised to where we were; it was a lookout view of the sea; we were in the war tunnels inside the grounds to Dover Castle.

Tony and Alan also knew where we were. Daryl and Harry though, had no idea. "Any idea as to where we are?" Harry asked.

Tony stated at lightning speed, "War tunnels, Dover Castle."

"Oh right, tell me is it me or do you lot feel a little queasy?" Harry held his stomach.

"You'll get used to it, Harry, we did," Alan remarked.

I then said, "Come on, let's make a move." We moved inside the entrance, and as we did, we could plainly see a small canteen area, but the place was empty.

Usually, this place would be full of visitors as they did guided tours here; they also had a radio play that would run along at the same time as the tour guide to give the visitors more insight as to what it must have been like during the Second World War. It was also here that the Dunkirk evacuation was planned and put into action; the place had an eerie feeling to it.

But I guess that was because there wasn't anyone around; we kept on walking deeper into the tunnels, at least the lighting was still operational.

Daryl and Harry were clearly on edge as all this was brand new to them. Tony and Alan were taking things pretty well by now; they had a calming way about them, more carefree to be more precise.

Happily, they carried on with small talk as they walked together. I was out in front. Daryl and Harry kept watch from the rear; a clang came out of the blue that echoed through the tunnel passages.

The sudden sound sent shivers down our spines. Daryl and Harry nearly had a baby each; they were virtually shitting themselves with fear. "What the fuck was that!" Harry shouted out. I tried to calm the situation down.

"It's probably a piece of masonry, the tunnels echo the noises; it's fine, mate, relax."

"Relax, he says, taken out of time, transported through time, monsters, noises, Jesus, how the hell do you relax, Daryl, you tell me that." Harry was having a rough time.

"I know, Harry, I feel the same," replied Daryl.

We had only gone a few hundred feet more when we heard a familiar voice call out, "Where do you think you're going?" We looked towards the direction of where we assumed the voice had come from. Tony's mouth dropped open; his eyes filled up with tears of joy, as he screamed out, "James!" It was his dead brother.

Tony was virtually about to rush towards him when Alan and I grabbed his arms and stopped him.

Tony started to struggle to get free as he couldn't understand why we were holding him back. "It's James, take your hands off me, it's my brother, let go."

I then said, "Tony, it ain't James, mate, look at him, just look at his face." James's face looked like what you would expect from a body being underground for a few months, grey and thin; his eyes were jet black, demonic even.

Alan then said to Tony, "Listen to us, mate, that ain't him anymore."

Tony composed himself and stood up straight, tears strolled down his face. "Hello, Tony," James remarked, "you've come to give your brother a big hug, scum bag." You could plainly see now that this was not the James he once knew. Slowly, he proceeded towards us as we stepped back, keeping the same distance from us and him at all times. Out from another blackened-out tunnel passage another known voice called out to us. This time, it was Geoff, another colleague that we had lost.

Again, he came out with the same phrase as James did, "Where do you think you're going?"

"My god, it's Geoff," I called out.

Alan moved quickly. "Pete, you know it ain't him, don't ya?"

"Yeah, I know, it's just a bitter pill to swallow, seeing people you cared about and losing 'em. Let's get back, no one touch 'em, come on, keep moving!" I shouted loudly. Another twenty feet had passed whilst James and Geoff slowly followed us. Once more, there was another voice from the past, from a dark recess came Andy, our first casualty.

"Where do you think you're going, leave me for dead, will ya, Pete, we're gonna rip your heart from out of your chest, yummy, yummy." Each one of them carried the same expression, the same blackened eyes, the gaunt features; it was like that all had gone to the same plastic surgeon.

"Move, lads, move!" I shouted once again.

As we ran, Harry shouted to me asking, "Here, Pete, why did this entity put us in the shit if it's so keen to help us, tell me that?"

I replied, "The curse is growing strong, it knows what the old boy knows now, even before the he thinks of it, but it comes good when we need it, trust me!" The fearsome threesome was still following as they struggled to keep the pace up.

Tony shouted, "Being dead slows you right up, poor bastards."

Daryl asked the question, "Where are we going?"

I answered, "No bloody idea, just keep moving, will ya." After forty to fifty feet, we entered what was the operations room. To our horror and surprise, the threesome stood, somehow, they had managed to get in front of us. They stood in mid-shadow way over in the far corner of the room.

They gave out a really demonic chant in unison, "Death will be coming, oh, so soon, laugh if you want." The room went ice-cold; our breath as we exhaled nearly froze on us. As we shivered like ice pops, James moved forward one step and faced his brother. Now Tony was seriously having problems with seeing his brother standing in front of him, even though he knew that James was dead and his body was being possessed. The demon then spoke in a calm but hideous manner, "Come over here, bro, come over here, we can talk about the good days before the bastard killed me, come on, Tony, you know you want to."

"Go fuck yourself, you bastard, you're not James, let him rest in peace, you piece of shit!!!!" I put my hand onto Tony's shoulder and gave a light squeeze; he must be going through hell I thought. James grinned then began that pathetic demonic cackling laughter. After a brief moment, the other two of the threesome joined in.

Tony grabbed his ears and tried to block out the noise; we keenly moved out of the room and scurried off like rats in a maze. The threesome stood there motionless. Harry spoke to Tony. "How did James die, that's if you don't mind talking about it."

"Nah, it's okay, it was here on the grounds of Dover Castle a few months back, we, I mean us, lot were in a fight with the curse; it was throwing lightning bolts at Pete, it wasn't having any effect so it changed tactics.

"Next thing I was aware of, was James receiving a bolt through his stomach; it was so strong it had lifted him off the floor and impaled him against a wall; it was bloody horrible."

"I see, sorry for your loss, Tony, I really am; he must have been a decent bloke," Harry stated. Tony smiled, as we continued our way.

Once again, the dreaded threesome was close by, but this time, their focus was on Daryl for some strange reason.

Tony I could understand, even Alan, but Daryl, Daryl wasn't around when these three died, so why were they so keen on him? Daryl started to move backwards as the three focussed their attention; it was like we were all in a trancelike state; we were frozen as the threesome just walked by us.

We couldn't do a thing apart from look like a bunch of manikins.

Daryl shouted for help as he ran back down the passageway; once he and the threesome were out of sight, we came out of the trancelike state. Harry was the first to speak. "Oh my god, what just happened?"

Alan then said, "They could've wiped us out there and then." I just thought, well, why didn't they and why focus on Daryl?

"Come on, boys, let's get back, we need to help him." We ran as fast as we could backtracking our steps. Every twenty to thirty feet one of us would shout out Daryl's name, but every time we did, we got the same response, nothing coming back from him, no voice, nothing but silence.

We soon found out why Daryl was so quiet, for as we turned into another part of the war tunnels, we could see the threesome just standing there motionless. Tony took one more step than the rest of us, his face was raging with anger. Luckily, we saw this and prevented him from getting any closer. At that moment, James and his entourage then turned around and faced us.

Again, they screamed out their demonic laughter and then disappeared; what we then saw would haunt us for the rest of our lives.

Daryl was pinned up on the wall, a few feet off the ground; he had been crucified, his clothing was shredded, his stomach torn open, his intestines were already strewn over the floor beneath his feet.

Daryl's blood was everywhere. Harry, once he had seen the devastation of Daryl's body, moved away, put his hand against the wall as he bent forward and began throwing up. Alan, Tony and I just stood there stunned, motionless; all we could do was look in horror, opened mouthed and speechless. "Oh, Jesus!" I cried out. Alan moved slightly ahead of me. "He didn't deserve that, you bastards!!!!" Tony then just fell to his knees looking up at Daryl's body.

Once Harry had stopped being sick, the four of us then slowly moved up to Daryl's lifeless body and tried to get him off the wall; it was as if he had been stuck there, he just wouldn't move.

I then shouted out in the hope that our friendly entity would hear. "That's four we've now lost, how many more do I have to lose before we get the chance to destroy this poxy thing?"

Alan came over to me and spoke. "Come on, Pete, you still got us, mate, there's Harry, he's got the brains, we've the brawn, we'll, sort it out, come on."

I looked at him and just responded by saying, "That's four we've had to say goodbye to, Alan, fucking four deaths. There hasn't been one opportunity in all this time for us to kick this thing's bloody arse, in all this time, not one bloody chance."

Harry then spoke gently. "I'm sure Alan's right on this point, Peter, we will get our chance eventually. We had a go once before, okay, it wasn't successful, but at least we learnt from it, trust me, we will kill it."

Alan then said, "Hope you're right, Harry, I really do."

I followed up with, "When? That's what I want to know." Once we had gathered our composure and with one last look at Daryl, we left the area. At that moment, we didn't know if this threesome would return or not, and if they did, who would they go for next?

I guess, we're gonna find out soon enough.

Our next area we approached and walked into was the operating room; they had surgical tools of the time period on display lying on a side unit next to the operating table; a massive light stood above the table, well, when I said area, I meant to say it was more like a walk through.

It was exactly the way it would've been back in the 1940s. Now if memory serves, when visitors would pass through here on the tunnel tours. Now as I said earlier about the radio play, it would follow a wounded RAF pilot who would have needed surgery; it was brilliant to listen to. As we moved on, the operating lights started to glow and flicker; we looked at them, the lights were now starting to get brighter and brighter. At that moment, one by one each individual light exploded, shattering minuscule pieces of glass everywhere.

Instantly, we covered our faces best we could as we cowered our way past them; the eerie sound of demonic laughter poured into the air once more; this time we had no idea as to if it was coming from where we had been, or was it ahead of us, as we passed the light.

The surgical tools began shaking in their tray that was on the unit; the surgical knives then began to, as if by magic, fly through the air at great speed; it was as if they were being thrown at us; each knife would penetrate the walls around us. Luckily, none of us got hit. Dodging and weaving, we managed to get out of there. As we came away, James, Andy, Geoff and now Daryl, one by one walked along the same route as we had just done; they were close by.

We knew they were closing in on our location so we picked up our speed. After a small period of time had slipped away, we somehow managed to find our way back to the balcony that the old boy had transported us to; it was now a dead end. We turned once we realised our situation; it was too late for the demons stood there side by side, blocking any possible chance of our escape; they were all grinning like Cheshire cats. Daryl spoke. "Time isn't very good to you, is it, Harry?"

James then followed up with, "Tony, wouldn't you prefer to die at my hand, come on, what do you say?" Geoff then took his turn and looked towards Alan.

"Would you like to describe how you want to die, Alan? I can accommodate you." They then moved a step forward. At that exact moment, we all took a fighting stance as we knew this was going to probably be the last fight.

Glaring at each other for a moment or two, we began to move closer to them; they in turn moved towards us, as if by a force of magic an invisible force field flashed in between them and us; it was the old boy up to its old tricks. I took a great sigh of relief as the demons continually pounded on it; the four of us began to laugh at the so-called supermen; their attempts to break through were pathetic as it was futile. It was then that something began to happen to the force field. "Oh crap, look, the force field's breaking up!" Alan shouted. The old boy was struggling to hold the curse's strength back. I knew we didn't have a great deal of time, keenly I rushed to the balcony's edge and looked over.

There was a narrow ledge about ten feet below; now if we kept tight in, we stood a chance. I faced the lads. "Right, come on, over you go."

Harry stammered, "You what?"

"You heard," I said. Alan then looked over the ledge, then looked at me.

"You're serious, ain't ya?"

"Yes, I bloody am, now keep tight in; when you're down on the ledge, move to the left, come on, the force field's breaking down."

Tony then stated, "You three go, I'm staying here. I can buy you some time." I looked at him whilst Alan and Harry crawled over the balcony.

"What's fuck wrong with you? I lost your brother, I'm not losing you now, get over that fucking balcony."

"I can't!" Tony shouted out.

"Why?" I screamed back.

Tony then bellowed, "I'm scared of heights, for fuck's sake."

"Is that all? I'm scared too, just don't look down." It was at that moment the force field finally broke, and the demons came forward. I grabbed Tony by the arms and shouted, "Get the fuck over onto that ledge or I will throw you over!" We looked once more at the demons and took our chances with the ledge, over we went.

After three minutes had passed, we were all down. "Move!" I shouted, and so we did. Alan was in the lead, Harry followed behind, then Tony who had his eyes shut. I knew that for he was shuffling his feet and feeling his way as he went. Naturally, I was last, and to my horror, the demons were coming over the balcony in pursuit. I blurted out, "For the love of mike, shit, Alan, they're chasing us!!!!"

Alan shouted back, "Okay, Pete, there's a passage up ahead, about ten feet from now." We keenly moved as quickly as possible; the demons were making ground on us thanks to Tony's fear of heights. After another five minutes had passed, Alan and Harry had made it safely into the darkened passage.

The demon zombies were only around eight feet away from me; the old boy came to our rescue as it worked its spell, a blinding flash erupted between myself and the demons; the ledge that was between us blew out.

No way could the demons span that area unless they could levitate. Tony and I reached the passage and went inside. Once we were all together, I muttered, "Right, let's see where this goes." We moved off.

Alan asked what happened back there. "All I saw was a flash of light," I answered him. "The old boy blew out the ledge."

"Good old boy," Alan cheered.

Harry then remarked, "Well, let's hope that's the last we see of them."

Tony responded with, "Oh, don't kid yourself, Harry, the curse has more shit up his sleeves than that lot, trust me."

"Why thank you for those kind words, Tony, much appreciated."

"He is right though, Harry," I explained, "we can't afford to get complacent, mate. If we drop our guard for just a minute, we're dead."

"Okay, Pete, I hear ya," Harry remarked. The passage was narrow but wide enough for us all to pass through it safely.

Shortly, we had found a stairwell that led up; we followed one by one. After two flights of stairs, a door lay ahead. "Try it, Al," I asked. Alan tried the door, it was either jammed or locked. Tony moved past Harry.

Alan and Tony looked at each other and in unison they said, "Shoulder barge." They charged the door with all their might; dirt and a small amount of debris fell from above the door. Again, they barged, more dirt and debris fell. After a third and final shoulder barge, the door gave way, so did the doorframe and half the surrounding wall; the dust filled the air in an instant. We did our utmost in preventing the dust from getting into our lungs as we staggered through the now non-existent doorway.

In front of us stood more stairs, we began to climb them. After a further two more flights, we could see a glimmer of hope as daylight shone on us once more. Soon there was enough light and we could see a lot clearly. The shining lights were from cracks within a structure. It had to be a wall, I thought. "Alan, Tony, do your stuff again please." The two of them looked once again at each other. With that, they both charged, the wall must have been extremely thin for they virtually ran straight through it, and again, tons of dust filled the area.

The dust soon diminished; it was becoming very clear that we had entered a room. The room was old fashioned in its design and furniture; this was at least the 1700s. There was even a harpsichord sitting in the far corner; a piano was near the Georgian windows. Now naturally, there wasn't anyone around unless they were a good 300 years old.

Tony directly went over to the brandy bottle that sat on a dresser, he blew into a glass and poured out some brandy. "Anyone want one?" he asked.

"Why the fuck not, yeah, pour us all one," I quickly replied. The brandy went down a treat, bloody strong though, well, after 300 years what did we expect.

"Corr, Jesus, they don't make it like this anymore, do they?" Tony remarked as he tried to take a breath!

"This stuff should be outlawed," Harry said as he cleared his throat.

"Tony, you're closer to the window than the rest of us, can you see anything from there?" I asked. Tony had a look outside.

"Can't see a damn thing, mate, too many shrubs in the way. No one has touched this place for centuries, and that includes the grounds."

"Okay, cheers, right then, let's have a look, where's the bloody door?" I had said that because there wasn't a door in plain view, the room was surrounded on all sides by panelling; it was a good three to four minutes before Harry found where the door was. The doorknob stood out from the wall, but you had to be near to it to actually see the bloody thing.

Harry gently turned the doorknob and opened the door; it creaked as it came open. Once it was opened enough, we all moved and walked through into the pantry area; another door stood over to our right, this one had the old fashioned latch on it, the type you just press down and the bar lifts up; it had to be the entrance or the exit. I guess it all depended on which way you were going.

Harry opened the door as the daylight shone into the area. I was right. We walked outside and into the fresh air.

The castle wall stood over to our left-hand side; the walls were covered in foliage, and what's more, there were no signs of those dreaded evil bastards either.

Chapter 15
Two Guns Go to War

As we strolled along, all I could think of was the loss of Daryl. Now that was the most vicious attack that the curse had handed out this time; things were going from bad to worse; on top of that, there was still a further three guys that we were in need of, or maybe we didn't really need them, after all?

My head was full of what ifs. The way things were going at this rate of loss, I wouldn't be surprised if I was the only one left to fight this bloody curse. I just knew for certain that we had to keep up the search until I knew for sure what was to happen.

In front of us, say twenty feet away, a space on the ground began to shudder. Now it was no earthquake. Within seconds, the ground began to give way until a hole had emerged; we all paused and wondered what was to happen, would something rise up through it. We watched closely for a few minutes.

Nothing was coming out of it. Slowly, I moved forward, making damn sure that no one followed me just in case. I rested on my knees then I laid onto my chest. I was really close to the edge at this time. I peered into the hole.

As I looked, I witnessed something moving; it was dark so I couldn't see too much. Gradually as the darkness started to clear and my eyes adjusted, I was startled and jumped back to my feet. Slowly but surely, the figure developed and began to levitate up towards me. I gave a huge sigh of relief; it was the old boy as it once more appeared to me. Once it had reached eye level, it came across and landed beside me. The rest of the guys came over; the old boy sorrowfully spoke.

"Time against the Peter, redness growing the stronger, time limited now, two must find and destroy, anger will rage, fire will fall, death will come, fight will follow, stand and prepare."

I then asked it, "Why can't you just tell us what to do, why so cryptic all the time? We need help." The old boy gave its standard grin then evaporated in front of us.

Harry said, "Right, so that's the friendly entity, I take it, bloody good warning I'd say."

Tony remarked, "We're gonna be in some serious shit soon enough, Pete, any ideas as to what we do now?"

Alan then remarked as I just looked bewildered, "All right. Tone, leave him alone, we'll think of something." At that moment, we were transported away, and within seconds, we had found ourselves in what looked like another military place. Across the yard was a decent-sized information sheet fixed to a couple of posts; we approached and Harry took it on and read it.

"Well, gentlemen, it appears we're in Essex, Tilbury Fort, to be precise."

I wonder what's to happen here. We looked at each other and just gazed around the grounds; the place looked empty, okay, you had a few military vehicles on the training ground, which was a large flat piece of concrete, and couple of gun emplacements now surrounding them on all sides were billets, I guess, you know, living quarters. I stood there and told the lads straight, "There's gonna be no wandering off from now on, lads. The old boy has made it bloody clear we're in for a lot of crap; let's just have a look around." And so we did; we began by going onto the ramparts. We had the Thames River on our west side as we peered over the wall. As we were preoccupied with seeing the so-called sights of the area, there was a massive blast from outside the main gates.

It was that loud that we all jumped out of sheer fright; straightaway, we were drawn towards the gates; they then burst wide open; the strength of the gates opening blew dust into the fort causing tons of the stuff to engulf the area; as the dust slowly began to dissipate, we got the shock of our lives for there in the entrance to the fort stood the three demonic bastards that had mutilated our mate Daryl, not fifteen minutes ago.

The stage was now set for a real bust up; the odds were seriously stacked against us; the problem we had now was the fact that we had nowhere to go except fight or die. We immediately got down from where we were and stood on the parade ground, watching these creepy demonic things as they started to approach us. It was like a scene from a western where gunslingers come face to face for a gun fight; you could say we were slightly apprehensive as to the outcome. As the demons got to within ten feet of reaching us another surprise came forth, and thank god for it, it was our old boy, a huge smile came over us all as we then knew we had a decent chance now of surviving.

It stood in front of us like a brick wall, what a sight, talk about giving us inspiration. Now we were really up for it. The three demons immediately went on the attack, throwing bolts of energy at him. The old boy in turn returned fire. For around three to four minutes, this continued, blasting at each other without a victor. James was slowly moving off as it tried to outflank our position. Tony spotted his move, and with Alan, they then mirrored his manoeuvre. Harry and I stayed behind the old boy as protection and carefully kept a good view of events. It was at that particular moment that the old boy saw what was about to unfold, it generated a terrific blast of energy from way down from the pit of its stomach; you could see the force as it rose in strength like a translucent glowing then erupted, the blast was directed straight at James; the power hit him with a massive whack; the impact lifted him off the ground and sent him soaring through the air. As he travelled towards one of the barrack room, a large spike then suddenly materialised on a wall. James was heading straight towards it, Harry and I watched with excitement as we were jumping up and down with hope that James would meet this spike. Within moments, our dream came true.

For the second time, James had his body impaled; he struggled like crazy to free himself, screaming with rage. I felt no remorse this time as my memories came flooding back, for I knew this time it wasn't my friend dangling high up.

We turned to where the old boy continued its fight. As the blasts of energy continued to flow back and forth, the tables were slowly turning in our favour; as the demons who were left started to lose ground as the persistent missiles of energy became more frequent, more powerful. We started to goad the demons calling them whatever we could think of in the hope they would fuck up in some way so we could finish them once and for all. Our excitement was short-lived as our nightmare came onto the scene, a segment of air just above these demons began to shimmer and swirl around, the curse was slowly materialising.

Once formed, it began to come forward, placing itself just in front of its demons; its size was at least three times larger than the old boy in comparison; its form was cloudlike, a deep hardened redness engulfed itself. The old boy did no more than turn towards us; its shape altered into the mist like vapour, engulfing us as it formed a shield over all of us. Its protection was comforting, we all knew we hadn't a chance in hell of defeating the curse without our entity.

The curse began its attack, bombarding the force field with all sorts of energy blasts, but the force field stood strong; the battle raged on and on.

It was clear that the mist couldn't keep this force field intact forever.

After a solid five minutes of nothing but defence moves, the old boy was slowly being pushed backwards; we were now getting into a dangerous position, if the mist didn't manage to achieve something miraculous shortly, we were in real trouble. It was at this moment we witnessed something I had never seen before, a second shimmering of air began to form; its structure started to swirl and spin on our right-hand side, then to our astonishment, we could see it gradually form into a vortex.

It was like a swirling whirlpool but vertical, like a gateway of some kind. From within the middle of this thing, two men emerged.

Harry and I from another timeline period stepped forward; they had each in their hands a strange new weapon, some sort of gun that no one had seen before, definitely not from our timeline but more they seemed more futuristic. These two guys then opened fired at the curse; the blue pulses of energy pumped away; the blasts must have caught the curse off guard as it immediately stopped its assault on us. It turned to face this new threat; as it turned to face the guys, it simply dissipated; its evil scream of rage echoed for a few seconds. The area went into a still calmness; the fort gates were closed as if nothing had taken place, even James was gone; the mist returned to its old boy form.

We stood and looked at this futuristic Harry and Peter. I faced up to myself like looking into a mirror; this was nuts. Harry was right by my side. I spoke to myself. "What the—" I hadn't any words to say. I was just flabbergasted.

My other half then said, "We're leaving these here for you, now time's short, keep fighting, Pete, we really ain't got time to explain, just take care." The two men then stepped back into the vortex; everything went back to normality; the vortex was no more.

Tony and Alan came over to us. Alan blurted out in an astonished manner, "Pete, that was you."

I looked at him and replied, "No really, I didn't know that, Alan, tell me something I do know." Harry picked up one of the weapons.

"This is fascinating, another timeline, there's definitely a time link here, this is going to really increase our potential in turning the tide of fortune; this is what we've been waiting for, Peter, now things will start to turn in our favour at long last."

Tony asked a good question, "What are they?" He pointed to the guns. I then picked up the other one and examined it.

Harry replied to his question, "Well, if you can give me a good five minutes, Tony, then maybe I will be able to answer your question, now there's a good chap." Tony then laughed.

"Sorry, Harry, got a little excited, mate, sorry."

The old boy came to me and said, "Time is short, the end soon to come." It smiled then vanished like vapour in the wind.

As I gazed at our new weaponry, I said, "This is amazing, Harry, another timeline helping us now, Jesus, how many timelines are involved do you think?"

"Well, that's an impossible question to answer without more data, Peter, probably millions of them. If this entity came through the first vortex that was created in the accident of ours, yes, I'd say all of them. If we don't destroy it in our timeline, every other one is in serious trouble."

Alan then piped up, "Well, now we can hand out some shit of our own, shame there's only two of 'em."

I looked at him and said, "I'd rather have these two than none, mate, we've got the bastard now. Did you see how it was shaken up and how quickly it fucked off?" At that moment, there in the not so far distance came the sound of a pride of lions; their roars sounded like a stunning concerto, a beautiful sound. I had to pinch myself for if you closed your eyes, you could've been forgiven if you thought you were in Africa. The beauty didn't last long though, for as we spun around, there they were, six hungry, fully grown, massive-jawed lions.

Alan shouted, "What the fuck, ha, Christ!"

Tony let loose, "I think we better find some cover. I don't think they want to chat much." Harry held onto his new gun, I immediately did the same.

"Everyone behind Harry and me, move!" I shouted. I didn't have to say that twice. As we watched this magnificent group of animals, two of them just casually strolled away as if they weren't interested, another two stepped forward to our right, the last two strolled down our left side.

It was a plain case of separate and conquer. Alan and Tony clocked the two lions that had separated from the pack earlier as they pounced onto some barrack rooms and flanked our position; the other four, who by now had shortened the distance, had begun to encircle us.

The two that were high then pounced. Harry and I immediately opened fire on them.

It was like a brilliant flash of pure light as when each one of them were hit, they were gone. Tony screamed out, "They're coming!" Harry and I then reacted as we opened fire against the rest. Again, as soon as they were struck, the same result, like a puff of smoke and they were gone.

Harry and I looked at our new weaponry. Harry spoke first. "My god, they're ingenious devices. I wonder if I could possibly replicate them."

"Well, that would help, Harry."

Alan jumped in at that point. "Bags first one."

I then replied, "You'll get what you're given, now behave yourself."

Within seconds, we could clearly hear another roar, but this was coming from outside; it also didn't sound like an animal's sound, more mechanical. We slowly moved across to the gates.

Alan and Tony opened them slowly. Harry and I both had our guns at the ready just in case. I nearly dropped the gun as I fell onto my knees, I was that ecstatic; my Capri was sitting there, engine revving, doors open.

I rushed over to it and touched the bonnet, seconds later, we were inside and driving away from Tilbury Fort. Harry was extremely interested in this new gun as he closely inspected it once more.

The future finally had started to brighten up for us.

We hadn't gone twenty feet when we saw two guys being pushed around by a gang of six skinheads outside the pub; strangely, it was called the World's End, and these six didn't look as if they were very friendly.

I pulled over for a few moments. Harry then said, "What're you doing, Peter, please let's not get involved, don't you think we've greater concerns?"

I looked at him and said, "Harry, I've never enjoyed bullies, wouldn't you want a Good Samaritan if you were in their position?" I got out of the car and moved towards the commotion. Alan and Tony then followed swiftly behind. Harry, good old Harry, stayed in the car to look after our newly required goods.

Now the odds seemed a lot fairer, as five against six instead of two against six. The leader of the gang of six spoke, in a friendly skinhead fashion. "Fuck off."

Alan then remarked, "Now that's not very polite, mate." Within moments, the punches started to fly from both sides.

Alan went over one of the benches with one of the enemy. Tony sent another straight over another bench. I tried to put one down, but he was lucky and missed my punch bins were flying around as people fell over them.

Black eyes and a broken nose were found on the skinhead gang leader. Our fighting skills had dramatically improved as we sustained no injuries. The fight was over within minutes; the skinheads crawled away leaving the five of us standing there breathing reasonably heavy. I faced the two that we had rescued. "You guys okay?"

"Yeah, we're good, thanks."

"So, what was all that about then?" I asked.

"Ha, it was nothing, they just wanted my darts."

"Your darts?" Now I wasn't expecting that answer. "Right, okay, well, introductions then, my name's Peter, this is Tony and Alan, that guy in the car is Harry, and you two are?"

"Well, it's nice to meet ya. My name's Jim and he's Lawrence."

I then asked, "So what are you two doing here? I can't see your car and we're miles away from town."

"Well, it's funny you should ask that, you see, we were having a kick about near the shops in Tilbury town and some old boy came up to us and asked if we could do him a favour."

"What was the favour then?" Tony asked.

"Well, Lawrence said yeah, we could, next thing I knew was that we were here and we had those six dicks in our faces pestering us for our darts, weird though."

"Why weird?" asked Tony.

"Well, I left mine indoors, as I said, we were just minding our own business kicking a ball about. Do you have any idea as to how we got here, cause I don't," asked Jim.

I looked at Tony and Alan then said, "As a matter of fact, Jim, we do know how you got here."

Tony then speedily interrupted me and just spurted out, "You were transported here, yeah, by an entity, you're here to join us and kill it."

"Oh nice, Tony, well said, well, bloody done," I replied. Jim and Lawrence then thought Tony's remarks were a joke as they then had a little chuckle between themselves.

"That's a good one, mate, you nearly had us then, no seriously, how did we get here?" Lawrence commented. I then had to put him straight.

"Well, I'm sorry for the way you've been told, but the fact is, it's true, there is an entity, well, two actually, and you're now involved with it."

"Do me a favour, Peter, think we're stupid or something?" Jim wasn't impressed.

"This is no bullshit," Alan remarked, "You're in serious shit now so get used to the idea." I began to walk over to the car, Alan and Tony followed.

As we were nearer to the car, I turned and asked, "Well, you two coming?"

"Hang on a mo, look, we've got some questions we need the answers to first," Jim called out.

"I bet you do, look jump in and we will explain it all to ya." After that, Jim and Lawrence came over, what a squeeze they had. Alan was in the front with me. Harry, Tony and Jim were sitting on the back seat, well, when I say sitting, more like squeezing and poor old sod Lawrence who got the long straw had to be content with the floor. I then asked Harry, "Any ideas as to what makes those guns tick yet, mate?" Jim got rather alarmed when I mentioned the word gun.

"You got guns in here, what's going on, you doing a job or something?"

Harry then jumped in and tried to calm Jim's thoughts. "It's all right, Jim, I can explain it. Erm, not really. Pete, all I can work out at the moment is that they work, sorry, I've just never seen or heard of anything like this before, they're fantastically incredible."

I drove off then asked Harry once again, "Look, do me a favour, Harry, bring these guys up to speed, will ya. We can't have them thinking we're bank robbers or something like that." Harry then started explaining our history.

"Well, you see, Jim, it's like this..." An hour had passed by. Jim and Lawrence were now fully aware of the precarious situation we were in. Now by this time, the sun was getting low in the sky as it was getting rather late.

Jim and Lawrence had crashed out, god knows how Lawrence could sleep in the position he was in, but he was out like a light. Now at some point I must have been daydreaming for I found myself driving through a small village; there were no traffic lights, no warning signs anywhere around us, which I found extremely odd; we had an extremely low mist that laid itself upon the road and surrounding fields. This village didn't really give out great vibes for on top of that, if that wasn't enough, every street that we could see was abandoned. The streets were just deserted. Okay, time was getting on, but to see no one around, this village was really starting to get my old trouble senses tingling.

Tony and Alan were intensively monitoring everything that we passed or approached. Within a few moments, we could see an old church up on a hillside. What a beautiful setting, the sun was going down behind it, as it lit the church up like a Christmas tree. Now inside the church, we could clearly see light, so there must be life in this place, after all. I mentioned to the lads, "I'm going to drive up there, these two are shattered, let's see if there's anywhere they can get their heads down."

"Yeah, not a bad idea, Pete," replied Alan. Off I drove. Now the church wasn't that far off, as we got closer.

We could now see movement from inside through the stained glass windows. I pulled up in their car park. "Wake 'em up, Tone," I asked. Tony obliged as he gave them both a shove.

"Hey, come on, wacky wacky, rise and shine!" Tony yelled. Both Jim and Lawrence took a couple of minutes to come to their senses.

"Where are we?" Jim asked.

Tony replied, "No idea, mate, come on, we're getting out." After a few moments, we were all out of the car. Harry covered the new weapons and placed them behind his seat; we then crossed over to the church entrance; the door was open and so we walked straight in. The priest was in his pulpit preaching his sermon to his ninety-five percent congregation.

He stopped in mid-sentence as he noticed us. "Ha, strangers in our midst, welcome to the congregation, come on in, come in, sit yourselves down, all are welcome in the house of our high lord, praise be to him." I nodded and acknowledged his gesture; we moved across to some empty seats that were nearby. There were exactly six spare seats, each had a weirdly coloured bible placed on top of them. I'd never seen deep blood red bibles before. I raised my bible up and showed the lads, our curiosity was high. We sat down and listened to this priest; my senses were tingling once more, why were there exactly the correct amount of seats available, why the blood-coloured bibles? The priest then continued his speech, "Our lord wants us to be free, to be able to stand up for yourself and say, no, why should I do as I'm told, your lord loves you, break off your shackles of being the good…"

As he kept on, Tony then said in a whisper to me, "Why is he just referring to, the lord, he hasn't mentioned Jesus or God yet."

"Well, give him time, here wait a moment." I suddenly noticed the weirdest thing yet, something that was really unsettling and disturbing.

Tony asked, "What is it?"

I replied to him with, "Where are the usual things you find in a church?"

Alan inquired, "What usual things?"

I again replied, "Well, the cross for one, you know, the crucifix, statues of Jesus, there aren't any." My group just looked puzzled.

The priest continued his sermon. "Our lord wants us all to be free, you are all his children, the thousand years are ending, his disciples, his followers, throw away your fears of being judged; after all, your lord wants you to be happy; we must spread the word that the lord is coming; the day of judgement is nearing; the thousand days are ending, praise be, praise be to our lord praise to the one; he is your lord, praise be to Satan."

The six of us immediately lifted our heads with astonishment; we all looked at each other and in unison, we said, "Satan." The doors to the church that we had come through immediately shut with a loud clang.

The priest looked down from his pulpit at us and said, "Yes, my children, Satan. I fear you are not believers."

Alan looked around and gave an excellent response to our situation, as he said, "Oh crap." The congregation stood, turned and faced us; we finally caught a glimpse of the village population, they all had a grey complexion, a dull tone to their skins; all the men had grey hair, even the youngsters; haggard wrinkly old faces were gleaming at us; the women, young and old, all wore a dark covering which covered their entire face, except for the eyes. I felt like a father trying to protect his kids as I deliberately attempted to stand in front of my lads.

From out of nowhere, Lawrence began to shout out so all could hear, "I'm a believer! I'm a believer!"

I tried to shut him up by putting my hand over his mouth, but he shrugged me away like a child trying to escape a parent; he then quickly moved forward. Before we could react, some of the mob came across and Lawrence was scooped away and placed near the priest.

We moved ahead and tried to stop him, but there were just too many people. We just couldn't get past them; all we could do was hope and pray that nothing bad was going to happen and that he was just trying to buy us time so we could all get out of here. The priest looked down at Lawrence and asked him, "You're a believer, my son."

"Yes, Father, I am. I always have, always shall be."

The priest raised his arms high and shouted out, "Rejoice, rejoice a son of Satan is here with us." He then paused and once again looked at us.

"My son, and your friends, why are they non-believers?"

Lawrence then turned around and faced us, his face was happy. It then hit me like a brick. I couldn't believe it for I then knew that this wasn't any kind of wind up, no trying to gain us time, this bloke was genuine in his belief of satanic beliefs; he stood there then smiled like a Cheshire cat who had just had some cream. Without a single hesitation, he stated. "They're non-believers, Father."

The priest stood upright, his tone of voice then began to grow dark as he shouted aloud, "Sacrifice, sacrifice, the strangers in our midst will be sacrificed come the striking of midnight, the glory hour of our lord, to the honour of our lord Satan." We were then immediately rushed; the guys that grasped us were terrifically strong.

Far stronger than we were. The priest then shouted out once more, "The crypt, my children, the crypt." We were dragged like sheep to the slaughter through the church and thrown one by one down the steps that lead to the crypt.

We fought as hard as we could, but it was a hopeless situation as we all found ourselves thrown into the crypt door.

With a loud thud, the door was slammed behind us; we were in serious crap.

Once the dust had settled down after our fall created a dust storm, we started to brush ourselves down.

We soon began to explore our new home, looking for any possible exit from what may be a deadly situation.

Chapter 16
The Papers

Jim stood there, shoulders dropped. "I've got something to say, and it's directed to all of you. Firstly, I need to apologise to each and everyone. Peter, I'm sorry, Alan, Harry, Tone, I truly am sorry. I had no idea Lawrence was like that, you know, a satanist; he never spoke of it."

"It's all right, mate, it's okay." I calmed the situation slightly. "Now we need to find a way out of here."

I gently tapped Jim's shoulder in acceptance. "Anyone got the time on them?" I asked.

Harry replied, "Eight pm, Pete."

"Eight pm, that gives us four hours before they drag us back up there for you know what, oh shit, I just thought of something, oh shit. Harry where did you put the weapons?"

"They're safe, Pete, don't worry about them. It's the here and now we're concerned with."

"You're sure, yeah?" I needed to be convinced.

Harry repeated once again, "I'm sure, they're safe and sound, now can we get on?" An hour had gone by and we had still found nothing; the only way out was from where we came in; it was hopeless; it was at that moment we could hear singing from above us. The priest had stopped his babbling and now there's a sing-song going on.

We looked up the stairwell, there was still light shining under the door, but then something strange took place, the light changed from normal light to a deep red type. The singing stopped as there was now chanting going on up there; we gazed at each other wondering what was going on. The door swung open, in the doorway stood someone we had never seen before; he stood tall, clean shaven, jet red long hair, he was dressed in a red cloak.

He entered the crypt and started to walk down the steps.

We watched this stranger as he stopped dead still, then gazed at each of us, his attention halted as he witnessed me. He walked straight up to my face, his eyes slightly closed as he grinned. "The Peter, at long last, the sight is exhilarating. I will enjoy your death, do you like my present state?"

I looked at him bewildered and confused as I asked, "Who the fuck are you?"

The stranger then set us all backwards with fear as he stated, "You can call me Mr Curse, if you wish, surely, you recognise my voice, the Peter. Or perhaps you would prefer this form?" The stranger then immediately returned to the deep red mist that we had always fought; once it appeared to us, we now know who it was; it then returned to its humanlike form.

I then said in a nervous state, "What is it you want now?"

Mr Curse then said, "That's obvious, your death, nothing else, you're a hard one to destroy, you and yours. I did enjoy Dover Castle. I enjoyed that one, the pain was extremely enjoyable. Daryl, wasn't it?" He laughed as Alan went completely mental, as he rushed towards the curse without any thought for his safety.

Sheer rage was all he felt; the curse just raised his arm as if he was swatting a fly away. Without contact, Alan went flying across the crypt. I rushed over to him as Tony and Harry assisted. The curse just stated, "Midnight, not long to wait, the Peter, you will be delighted to know that I will be doing the honours with you, the rest of these things I will allow the dogs to eat, should be so much fun; see you soon."

The curse left the crypt in a slow but positive manner; all we could do was look at him leave.

Jim just stood there and bluntly came out with, "Can someone please tell me what the fuck was that? What's happening now, please?"

Tony then nudged me. "So that's what it looks like in the flesh, one ugly bastard, no wonder it chose to go around as a mist."

Harry then stated, "How the hell can he call us dogs, what a wanker, can't wait to see it fall." Alan slowly came to his senses, as he came to, he immediately assumed that he was still attacking the curse as he tried to speedily get up; we held him firm so he didn't hurt himself.

He looked around and said, "It's gone then, fucking bastard."

Harry then asked me, "Why do you think it changed form now, Pete?"

I replied, "That's simple enough, Harry, it's an easy form in which to actually communicate with us; it wants us to know who it was that's gonna take us out; it's finally getting its revenge."

Alan looked at me and stated, "No fucking way, Pete, we're gonna kick its arse back to where it came from."

Jim then asked again, "Well, is someone gonna answer me?"

I looked at him and remarked, "Sorry, Jim, that was the entity who wants us all dead in human form." It was then that something upstairs had taken place.

Tony grabbed my arm and whispered a single word, "Listen."

"What, I can't hear anything," I answered.

"Yeah, I know, that's my point."

Alan looked towards the doorway and said, "Oh crap."

Harry took the initiative and moved up the stairs to see if he could hear more clearly; he then called down, "It's dead quiet in there."

"Try the door handle," I asked.

Harry then twisted the door handle, the door wasn't locked, we calmly moved ahead and walked the flight of stairs, sneaking our heads around the door. To our dismay and surprise, the priest had gone, the congregation had vanished, all that was visible were blast marks around the walls, the blasts looked like heat marking with silhouettes of the remains of the human body.

I called to Jim, "Check the main door." Immediately, he moved over to it.

"It's still locked, Peter, but there's something else."

"What do you mean, something else, what?"

"Well, it's bolted from the inside, no one left through this way."

Alan then nearly lost it, "Har, do me a favour, what they just farted and walked through the wall, out the way, I'm gonna look." Alan moved to the door, he then looked at Jim. "Emmm, Pete, Jim's right. No one has left this way." We immediately started to search the entire place from top to bottom as there had to be a logical explanation as to where they all went. After ten minutes had elapsed, we all returned to the same spot.

It was clear that something out of this world had just taken place here for people just don't vanish into thin air; there had to be an explanation somewhere.

I scanned around. "Tony, that sheet or sacking over there, check it out, will ya. Harry, you got a minute?" Harry started to walk over to me.

"Yeah, what's up?" Harry asked, as Tony lifted up part of the sheeting.

He couldn't help to make a stupid noise; he just grunted in shock, then froze in his tracks as to what he then saw took his breath away. "Errrrr, Harry, Pete, you might want to have a look at this. I think Christmas has come early."

Harry and I looked at each other and walked over to Tony. Jim also followed. As we walked, I then asked, "What's with Christmas, mate?"

Tony then remarked, "Just take a gander at this lot!"

Tony with that remark removed the whole of the sheeting, there in two piles were four more of those gun-like weapons, a reasonably sized cardboard box, and two metal containers that stood around six inches high, probably ten pounds in weight each; they were engulfed in polystyrene containers for safety reasons I guess. There was also a thick envelope, a digital disc enclosed within a transparent cellophane packet; the envelope had just one name on it, it said 'Harry'.

Alan came over and instantly started to jump up and down for joy as he caught his first glimpse of the weapons.

"Oh, bloody yes, now we can really give that entity a good kicking." Alan grabbed one of the guns.

He was like a six-year-old with his first toy. "Don't point that thing!" I shouted. I then focussed onto Harry, the letter and disc. "You going to open that then or are we gonna be in suspenders all night?" Harry shrugged his shoulders and opened the envelope. He then proceeded to remove a thick amount of folded paper. As he started to read, he then fell on his bum whilst still reading; his facial expressions changed. After he had gone through each single sheet, he spoke.

"They're schematics, Pete, we've got ladder logic sheets, wiring diagrams, block diagrams, and what looks like electrical engineering plans. This is fantastic, Pete, my god, if I only had my hands on this material two weeks ago, Jesus, this is amazing."

I then grabbed his arm and said, "Harry, Harry, calm down and listen to me for a second, now imagine this scenario for a moment, yeah, now we, and I mean all of us, we ain't scientists, okay, nor do we hold diplomas in hydro physics, so please, just tell us in straight forward English, what the fuck are you gibbering on about!" Harry began to laugh loudly, like a nutcase, and then he spoke.

"Peter, oh, Peter, I'm sorry, I believe I got carried away with excitement. These drawings in my hand, if I'm right, this will totally transform the human way of life; this is going to open new doors for us all; we will be able to travel through time itself." Harry once again lost control of his composure, as he was fingering through the papers in a demented state of mind.

A single sheet slipped out of his grasp and floated down to the floor. Jim was the first to see it; quickly, he moved in and collected it from the floor. After a short glance at the paper, he then stated, "I believe this is addressed to you, Harry."

"Thank you," replied Harry.

"Well, well," I too began to lose my composure.

Alan remarked, "You never know, we might even find out what the fuck happened here." Harry then started to scan the letter for a few moments instead of reading it. As he did, his excrement grew and grew; again multiple facial expressions formed across his face as he read on; his brain was in the clouds.

I once again abruptly spoke. "For fuck's sake, Harry, who is it from?"

Jim then said, "What does it say?"

Harry looked up and away from the letter, and looking directly at me, he said in total disbelief, "It's from me, Peter."

Alan then jumped in with, "How the hell is it written by you?"

I then snapped at Alan, "Shut the fuck up, Al. Wait a minute, Harry, what do you mean, it's from you?"

"This letter was written by me, but the me in another timeline."

Jim interrupted with, "What, an alternate universe-type thing?"

Harry continued, "Yes, Jim."

I was so enthralled I just blurted out, "Well, go on read it to us then."

Harry then raised the letter and started to read it out aloud; it was like being at Sunday school. As he started to read, we instinctively all sat around him, we gathered around the teacher with an intent of listening hard.

"Hello, Harry, this isn't easy writing to one self, you may be wondering what happened in that church, well, some time back I with some help from others stumbled over the concept of time travel, a vortex; the vortex is how we appeared to your team some time back and kicked the entity back into another timeline, that was when we gave you two our pulse disrupters, you now have issued you with six in number; be very careful with them; you have full details in section six about these weapons, that includes their powerpack designs and their energy rejuvenation.

"The blasts on the walls you can see are all that remains of the human body once hit by these weapons, so in god's name, please be extremely careful when handling them. Now the vortex can only be used once a month; its rejuvenation process takes around 30 days as it's still only a prototype, that's why we only have seconds within your timeline before it closes on us.

"That's the reason why you have this letter; you have schematics and other plans, use them well. I have put together a large number of capacitors, inductors, connectors and transistors, so you shouldn't want to find any other components. You also have two containers, one container carries anti-protons, the other container has anti-mater, take special care when using these items.

"There are designs and schematics that will give you great insight; you have in your hands all the knowledge you will need. In my timeline, we have successfully got rid of this entity once and for all, but we have not managed to destroy it. What it is trying to do is remove any person of whom could cause it harm in whatever way possible. I presume you have lost friends. I hope Peter, Tony, Alan and Jim are safe; they are here with me at this moment as they all want to say hello to you and everyone else. Harry, you must make sure that this entity is taken out of time.

"I mean totally destroy it; this entity, given enough time, could potentially destroy time itself if it is not stopped within your timeline.

"Stop it, Harry, stop it, we shall be seeing you, that's it." Alan looked at Tony, Tony looked at me, Harry looked at Jim; we were all mesmerised by the words in this letter. Harry then said, "I need time to study these papers, Pete. Do you know of any place that's suitable and safe?"

"Sorry, Harry, but no, not in this timeline; you just read that the entity was wiping the floor clear of its enemies, it's aware of a lot that goes on.

"That's another reason why we keep falling into its bloody traps; we need to be patient, we'll find somewhere, don't worry just yet. Right, let's get those doors open and get this stuff in the car.

"Tony, Alan, can you two grab the containers please?" Tony and Alan acknowledged and moved to them. Alan bent down first; he grabbed the container, but it was too heavy, he couldn't lift it.

Tony nearly wet himself as he saw his friend struggling; he then went to lift the other one, again, it was too heavy. Alan then said, "Wanna work together, Tone"

"Well, yeah, why not." That was the macho Tony, still trying to be bigger than the rest. The two of them after an initial struggle managed to lift the containers.

Jim led the way to make sure that the way was clear for them. Harry and I collected the disrupters and carried them outside to the car; the low fog still lingered as we loaded the equipment once everything was done.

I drove away, leaving the eerie village desolate and alone; the time was closing in on midnight. Jim was shattered. Harry closed his eyes and fell asleep as well. Tony, Alan and I still had no need for sleep. As I twisted to see if Harry was okay, I could see his grasp was firm around the papers he now possessed; nothing on earth could have removed them from his hand.

The fog began to lift and fade away the further we drove from that place; we drove all night. As the sun began to rise once more, Jim and Harry started to come back into the land of the living. "What time is it?" asked Harry.

Alan replied, "Nearly six am, mate, had a good nap, did ya?"

"Not bad actually, thanks, Alan, where we bound?" he asked.

I replied, "You wanted time to study, well, we're going to the safest place I know of."

"Are you joking, Peter, not four hours ago you stated to me that you had no idea as to where such a place was, so where's that?" Harry asked.

"Yeah, we'd like to know the answer to this one too," Alan remarked.

"You'll find out in good time, firstly, let's deal with this," I answered. I slowly slowed the car down to a crawl.

"Why are we stopping?" Jim asked.

"Look out there," I answered. The lads looked out of the windscreen in front of us; there in the road stood a mob of around fifty guys, each one of them carried some kind of a weapon, from a knife to a lump of wood, chains to a hammer, seemed like anything that could cause damage to the human body was being waved about.

"I don't think they're very nice people," stated Harry. Tony and Alan just looked at him, even Jim didn't seem very impressed by his opinion. I stopped the car.

Jim then shouted, "What're you doing, drive through 'em!"

I then said hurriedly, "Everyone." I then immediately got out of the car and dashed to the boot. As I opened it up, I removed one of the disrupters at that moment the rest of the lads came around, each one then in turn removed a disrupter.

We stood there for a second or two then moved away from the car. "Let's do this in military fashion. Alan, Tony and Jim, drop down on one knee, facing the enemy."

Harry looked at me and said, "You're enjoying this, ain't you?"

"You bet, it's payback time." Harry and I stood upright and standing behind our other three as we waited; the mob just stood there growling at us.

Alan said, "What the hell are they waiting for?"

"Patience, Al, patience," I responded. It was then that the curse materialised into its human form, a massive cry from it rang out. Then this mob took flight and charged at us like possessed madmen. "FIRE!" I yelled.

Within micro-seconds, the five of us opened fire; we were scoring hits with every shot. Tony shouted, "It's not working."

"Keep firing," I shouted out. Two to three more seconds later and the first of the mob fell to his knees, then a second one fell, then a third; it was like watching dominoes fall.

The wounds we were inflicting were strange to witness, for as they fell, each one grabbed the spot of where they were hit; a second would fall by before a minuscule hole would form; you could see daylight through the body, the hole would then enlarge; their bodies were riddling in agony as the hole would grow until the entire body form disintegrated from existence.

It was horrific to watch, but we just kept pumping the disruptors into them; the firing continued until they had all either been hit or dead. The fight was over in minutes; none of us were hurt; the mob didn't even get to within twenty feet of us.

Mr Curse stood there, stretching at us whilst pointing. "Time is short, death will come slowly, painfully, enjoy." With that, Jim and Alan, who were thinking in unison, shouted, "Go fuck yourself, arsehole." They opened fire on it; the curse vanished once more.

We had won our first victory without the help of our friendly old boy. Our first major victory; it felt great. "My gun's empty," moaned Tony as he shook it.

"Careful, you dick!" I shouted firmly.

"Mine's empty too," stated Jim.

We had fired till the charge from each weapon had been drained. I then said to Harry, "Well, here's your first task."

"Oh yeah, what's that then?" Harry replied.

"Sort out how we recharge these beauties."

"I hear ya," replied Harry.

Tony then said, "Well, we've still got one fully loaded."

"Yeah, true," I answered. "We use that in an emergency, agreed?" Everyone acknowledged.

"Right, okay, let's pack up and ride, cowboys." My humour hit the spot as we all finally had something to laugh about.

Seconds later and we were back on the road once more; it was an extremely happy team within the car; smiles wouldn't die down, it was as if we had just found some happy pills and taken six each; talk about getting stoned, what an electric feeling; we knew that we were now turning the corner.

We really had a decent chance of destroying this entity. Tony gave me a nice reminder as I drove along. "So, Pete, where's this place you had in mind, you know, this safehouse?" Now everyone within the car stopped doing whatever they were doing and looked at me.

Without hesitation, I said, "Well, that's up to Harry really."

Harry looked gobsmacked and responded to my sentence, "What do you mean it's up to me?"

"Well," I said, "That experiment you and I supposedly did that went wrong, now within these timelines this place must exist, so I was thinking maybe we could give it a go and see if it's still on the map, if it is, then maybe the entity could throw a flatulating damping field around the place.

"That way if the field mutates every whatever, it will prevent the curse from locating us, well, it will give us enough time to build whatever those plans are, well, what do you think?"

Harry then stated, "Why not, it would certainly give me enough time to study these designs, so yeah, why not."

I then asked Tony for his opinion. Tony stated, "I'm up for it."

Alan then said, "Yeah, sounds good."

Jim then followed up with, "Anything sounds good, but don't you think it's a gamble though, Pete? We don't even know if this place exists."

Harry then replied to him, "Well, I personally think it's worth a shot."

Alan then said, "We've nothing to lose, have we? If it ain't there, at least we gave it a shot. Do it, Pete, we're all with ya."

I had got the approval from all the lads. I asked Harry the fundamental question, "Right, okay, so we all agree, right then, that's what we're gonna do. There's only one thing I need to know from you, Harry."

"What's that, mate?"

I replied with, "Well, what's the bloody address?"

We all laughed as Harry then stated, "68 Station Road, Scarborough, do you want the post code?" He laughed.

"I would, but I haven't got a sat nav." Then I burst out an almighty laugh of my own.

The car then filled with more joy. "I guess it's hello good old Scarborough then, let's get cracking, shall we?" The stage was set, all we had to do was get there, develop all that was needed from the instruction sheets, crush an evil entity, not too much to ask for now, was it? It was mid-morning as we finally hit Scarborough.

The town was bustling with people. Within a further twenty minutes, we had found the station road. Counting the street numbers down as we moved along, we soon came across number 68; the house had been boarded up for years, as the boarding around the windows showed their age.

Even the front door had had marine ply fixed to it. Now I thought, *Shit, I wanted this place to have electricity at least.* But then Harry seemed quite optimistic, that was a real surprise to me.

Anyway, I parked the car up as close to the house as I could get. Harry said, "Now this is good, Pete."

I looked at him in shock as I replied, "Excuse me, good, but we haven't even got electricity."

"I know," answered Harry, "but at least, we won't be seen from the outside. The electricity issue isn't a problem, Pete, believe me. I can get around that, don't worry about it."

"Okay, cocky, if you say so," as I replied, I too then started to feel decently optimistic as I stepped out of the car. At least the house was detached, that was a good start. I moved off around the back of the building to the rear garden to have a decent look around.

Now luckily, one of the boards wasn't fixed very well as one of the screws had dislodged itself; the boarding had come away from the framework. I immediately started to try and remove the boarding.

Once I had removed the boarding, I could then peer inside, it was the kitchen area. By this time, Harry and the others followed me, each one coming around the building; it was like a scene from the *Snow White and the Seven Dwarfs*, okay, there wasn't seven of 'em, but it was funny the way they came around.

Our luck had seriously changed for the better as the windows were all smashed in. Jim couldn't wait as he was the first to clamber inside. Within a few more minutes, we were all inside having a good look around.

Harry, went out into the hallway on his own; he had a small torch on his person.

Chapter 17
The Heat Is On

He soon called out for me, I moved off to meet him. Beneath the stairs was a door that he had just opened; they were leading down. Once we had got into the cellar, Harry shone the torch around, there he could see a fuse box hanging on the wall directly inside a small alcove; he opened the fuse box up. As he shone the torch over it, he stated, "Yeah, should be no issues here, yeah, nice." It was then that I realised the car wasn't locked.

"Oh shit!" I shouted as I immediately rushed away, up the stairs and out the kitchen window. I got to the car as soon as I could, thank god, everything was okay.

Tony rushed around and followed. "You okay, mate, what's up?" he asked.

"I didn't lock it," I replied. The rest of the guys were standing by the front gate bewildered, except Harry, Harry hadn't left the cellar.

I opened the boot of the car and started to grab what I could. Tony in turn did the same. Alan and Jim then crossed over the road to copy us. As we passed each other, I said to Jim, "Can you wait by the car for one of us to come back, mate?" Jim nodded a yes, the journey back and forth took three trips.

Each time one of us would be waiting alone so that we didn't have to lock the car every time; this took around ten minutes to complete; everything was in the front room, yet still there was no sign of Harry.

I decided to check him out to make sure he was okay. As I began my descent down into the cellar, as if by magic the power came on; we had electricity, but we only had the electricity for the cellar. I then knew what he was doing all this time, so I forgave his laziness.

I went straight up to him whilst looking around; the area was as wide as the house was. On the far wall were a load of shelves, some tables; we also had a decent table with a few chairs that were on their backs laying in deep dust, a couple of desktops lay against the far wall in the corner; these were lying one on top of one another. I thought, *Now this lot can be useful at some point.* It was a lovely size to do what we needed. "Oh, yes, Harry, nice one, what did you do?"

"Har, that would spoil the magic. Are we going to get the stuff out of the car then?"

"You cheeky sod," I answered, "What do you think we've been doing for the last ten minutes, it's all upstairs."

"Well, I need it all down here, bullock brains," responded Harry.

"Charming," I replied.

With that, we both left the cellar, so there we were again, but this time, we were carting equipment into the cellar.

The old boy must've known what we were up to as it once more appeared to us; as usual it initially appeared as a vapour then it solidified into the old boy. I approached it and asked, "Can you produce a mutating dampening field around this place, we need time in which to prepare for the entity, so we're also going to need those devices you've been keeping safe." Within that micro-second, our entity had transported all the devices that I had just asked for.

Harry's jaw hit the floor as he totally forgot about our entity standing there; he just rushed straight through the entity as if it never existed and over to the equipment. I thought he was going to burst into tears, he was that ecstatic with delight. Christmas had come early.

I then spoilt his excitement with, "Right then, miracle man, I suggest you forget your Christmas presents for a while and focus your attention on getting these weapons charged, I've a feeling we're going to need 'em, maybe if you find time, you could also produce some additional dampening fields so we've maximum protection around here, yeah."

"Okay, Pete, but honestly, I never thought I'd ever see this equipment again.

Jim was surprised with his statement as he asked him, "What, this lot yours then, how did you figure that?"

Harry responded by saying, "Well, when my experiment went tits up, everything you can see now vanished, just disappeared, this entity of ours must have known then that this lot would be needed once more. Pete, you okay if I can have Jim helping me for a while, speed things up a bit?"

"Yeah, sure, you okay with that, Jim?" I asked.

Jim replied immediately with, "Yeah, too right, love to."

Our old boy once more left the scene as its vapour dissipated and floated away into the atmosphere above our heads.

Jim then without waiting moved over to Harry, he in turn and with papers still grasped firmly in his hand, they walked over to some old desks and started to manoeuvre furniture so they could get on with working on whatever it was. I just left them to it.

I then turned to Alan and Tony. "It may be a good idea if we organise some of this stuff. Right, okay, first things first, let's separate the used blasters from the good one.

"Tony, can you put our good one to one side? Al, give us a hand, we can take these ones and put them over here." So, that's what we did; we then placed the two containers closer to Harry and Jim. The box of electrical stuff went with the devices; all this took about five minutes.

I then called over to Harry, "Right, if you're okay, we're gonna get out of your hair for a bit." Harry was so engrossed in his studying, he just raised his arm into the air. I had a short giggle to myself.

I then went over and collected the only available disruptor, the three of us then left the cellar, went out of the house and over to the car. Tony then asked me, "So what's the plan now then?"

"Well, first things first, I need to find a street map so we have some routes we can follow if things go tits up; it's just a precaution so don't panic," Alan replied.

"Why panic, it sounds logical to me," Tony responded with.

"Yeah, I agree, better to be safe than sorry." I placed the disruptor in the boot and locked the car; we were now on foot for a short spell.

We strolled along looking for a newsagent so we could buy ourselves a street map; it wasn't long before we found one and entered the premises; it only took a few seconds for us to find what we were looking for.

I took it off the shelf and went over to the counter, placed the exact amount of money on the counter to pay for it, then to my amazement, the shopkeeper looked straight at me and said, "Thank you, the Peter." That sent a shiver down my spine as I stepped backwards a few feet.

Tony and Alan both at the same time focussed on the shopkeeper. I said, "How do you know my name?"

The shopkeeper replied, "Good guess, yeah, I try that on all new faces that pop in to my shop."

"Really?" There was no way I believed him.

We quickly left the newsagent, got at least five yards, as Tony asked me, "Did you believe his explanation?"

I said, "Do me a favour, the curse has to know we're here, I suggest we double time it back to the house."

It was at that specific moment when at least ten skinheads walked around the corner and blocked our path; they stood in a wide line at least twelve feet away from us. One of them then said, "Where do you think you're going, Peter?"

Alan then commented, "Oh crap." We turned around and began to walk reasonably quicker than we had before; we were far too late though as another five skinheads came out of the newsagent, this also included the shopkeeper.

Tony remarked, "Wish I had that fucking disruptor."

It was then that I shouted, "Follow me!" I sprinted around a parked car and ran as fast as I had ever run before. Tony and Alan were in hot pursuit. Instantly, the skinheads gave chase; we were running as fast as our feet would carry us.

As we ran, the poor innocent pedestrians that were just walking were being pushed aside.

Tony accidentally caught a stranger with his shoulder that sent the poor sod to the floor as he ran past. He shouted at the bloke, "Sorry!" Running hard, we turned into the town shopping centre; again trying to dodge the shoppers, it was intense; luckily for us, the skinheads had no Linford Christie on their team, the distance between us and them hadn't altered.

We alternated which way we ran, left, right, left and right. As we turned into our fourth street, there in one of the gardens stood a skip, half full of all kinds of household rubbish.

None of us spoke as we all got the same idea; in turn we jumped inside it and covered ourselves as best we could; we then listened for the skinhead gang; it wasn't long before they came and we heard them storming past the skip.

We listened as their footsteps grew less softer and softer, this continued until we couldn't hear them anymore.

I popped my head up from the rubbish and peered over the skip. I just managed to see the last skinhead disappear into another street; a great sigh of relief came over me. "All clear, lads, they're gone."

Slowly, we emerged from the skip, covered head to toe in wood shavings and dust. Tony said, "Thank fuck for small mercies. I'm bloody knackered."

Alan then mentioned, "I ain't run like that since my 800 metres back in my school days, Jesus, no more."

I then stated, "Sorry, lads, but I think they've clocked on to our little trick." We all looked down the road, there came one by one the skinheads.

As they emerged from around the corner, Alan shouted out, "Fuck's sake!" It was then that we started our run once more; backtracking our already frequented streets, we soon came back to the shopping precinct.

It was fortunate that there weren't as many shoppers as previously; this gave us more than enough time to increase the distance between our two parties. We continued our run, but after another couple of streets, we had finally reached home base; we were extremely out of puff and nearly exhausted. Slowing down our run, I then said, "We need to get into the car." Tony and Alan stopped quickly.

Tony asked, "Why, what's wrong with the house?"

Alan agreed with him, "Yeah, what's up?"

I then answered them. "Look, the house is a safe zone for us, the curse isn't aware of where it is cause of the dampening fields. I want to keep it that way for as long as possible. Now get in the fucking car before they come around the corner and spot us."

I unlocked the car. After a few seconds had passed, we were all inside. I started the engine and began to drive off.

It wasn't long before the skinheads had reached our street; they then stood side by side in the road to block us. Alan shouted out, "Go through 'em, mate, for god's sake, don't slow down."

That's exactly what I did, bodies went flying as I drove straight into them. I must have caught at least four. As the car drove past and away from the scene, Alan looked through the back window; the rest of the skinheads were not chasing after us, we had finally shaken them off our trail. "Nice one, Pete," Tony said.

Alan then asked, "How long do you think we're gonna take before we head back then, Pete?"

"Well, let's give it an hour, yeah."

Alan replied, "Yeah, that sounds good, mate."

We drove around as I decided to go along the seafront; there were at least six or seven gangs of skinheads wandering around; the gangs must have been in groups of at least eight plus.

I paused for a few moments and collected my thoughts, was this how you start becoming paranoid or were these guys genuinely here for a good time?

I pulled the car over to the side of the road. Tony asked, "Are you okay, Pete, why have we stopped?"

I looked at him and said, "All these skinheads."

Alan replied, "What about them, oh right, let me guess, you think they're all after us, don't ya?"

"Well, yeah, it had crossed my mind."

Tony then jumped in with, "Sounds like a bit of paranoia to me."

"Well, let's hope you're right, Tony. I guess there's only one way to find out."

Alan then said, "That's a hell of a gamble, Pete, if they are after us, there's no way we can outrun away from that lot, na, it's too much of a gamble, Pete, we can't."

"What do you say, Tony?" I asked.

Tony then stated, "I agree with Alan, mate. If we're wrong and make the wrong judgement call, we won't be seeing our mates again, this lot will kill us for sure. I say drive on, let's just be paranoid for a bit longer."

"Right okay, paranoia wins."

I moved off once again. As we drove, my mind began to wander again, this time I was thinking of how Harry and Jim were getting on, were they safe, has the curse broken the dampening field.

My mind was like a washing machine on full spin, going into overdrive. I suddenly decided on what I was going to do as soon as possible. I did a U-turn and headed back towards the house.

Tony asked, "We going back, I guess?"

"Yeah, we are, mate, I just can't hack it anymore. The not knowing what's happening back there, it's doing my nut in."

Alan then responded with, "I know, we've probably been thinking about that as well if the truth be known; we're with ya."

It wasn't long before we reached our street; we pulled up outside the house; the way was clear, no skinheads in sight. Out of the car we got and straight around the back and into the house. Once down into the cellar Harry's first words to use were, "Where the fuck have you three been?"

Tony replied, "Having a sunbathe."

I then remarked, "We had a little problem we had to deal with, how's it going here?" We could clearly see that the disruptors were on charge, that was great to see.

Harry stated, "Well, the disruptors are charging well so that's an issue resolved, but I'm going to need a few days to get everything else in operational order; you do realise this isn't something I can just throw together, it's gonna take time."

"That's fine, totally understand, you take as much time as you need, but have you managed to look at creating a dampening field yet, now I'm only asking before you bite my head off."

"No, not yet," Harry replied, "as I said, I can't just throw things together, just be a little patient with me, we'll get there."

"Okay, Harry, excellent work on the disruptors though, nice one," I answered.

Tony jumped in with, "So how long before these beauties are fully charged then, Harry?"

Harry replied with, "I'd say an hour, maybe two. They've been on charge for around two hours already now, so yeah, I'd say four hours for a full charge, five hours at tops, marvellous creations these toys."

Alan responded with, "Toys! what the hell type of games did you play when you were younger then?"

Harry replied with, "I didn't really have a childhood, my dad used to bring his work home, I used to play with that lot, learnt quite a bit."

Alan then stated, "I bet ya did, thank you, Dad."

Without warning, there was a sudden clash of something from upstairs, the five of us were startled and looked directly at one another. Grabbing whatever we could find laying around, we were within seconds on our way upstairs.

Ten of those skinheads from earlier had smashed through the window frame and were now in the kitchen, some had knives, others had hammers; it was clear that they weren't here to say welcome to Scarborough.

Alan called out his favourite saying, "Oh crap."

I faced him and shouted loudly, "Get the disruptors, Alan."

He replied to me with, "But they're not fully charged yet."

"I don't give a fuck if they're charged or not, grab what you can!"

Alan immediately returned to the cellar, at that moment, the skinheads charged, a terrific fight then ensued. We were having to fight with sticks and broken table legs, Harry had a stupid little looking hammer. We were being forced back by sheer numbers. Seconds had passed as Alan returned; immediately, he opened fire hitting three of them, killing them outright.

The rest of them doubled back and out the window. Tony and Jim both had slashes across their left arms; luckily for us, they weren't deep. Harry had caught a hammer blow across the outside part of his kneecap; limping and clutching his knee whilst obviously in pain, he said to me, "I thought this place was fucking protected by a fucking dampening field."

I replied, "It is, mate, but the bloody dampening field is protecting us from the entity. Shit, we weren't expecting visitors, right. We're gonna have to take turn on watch; give me the disruptor, Al, I'm taking first watch; you lot get back downstairs, see what you can find for those wounds." So, that was what we did. I stood around feet away from the smashed window, totally focussed on killing anything that came through it.

The lads retired to the cellar. After a further twenty minutes had passed by, thankfully no more visitors came.

Tony then came upstairs to give me some company, "You okay?" I asked.

"Yeah, not too bad, we're using pieces of cloth as bandages at the moment, seems to be doing the job. How are you feeling?"

"To be honest, Tone," I replied, "I feel like an idiot, why didn't I think about this. I should've had a watch on this window at the start, bollocks!"

"Hey, come on, none of us thought about it either, let it go, you're not responsible for every bloody thing that goes tits up around here. We're all adults for fuck's sake."

I then asked him, "Where's the cut?"

"It's here." He pointed to his left elbow. I placed my hand onto it and the cut healed instantly. Tony moved his arm around, there wasn't any pain.

"Correct, lovely one, mate, I forgot you could fix cuts up. So, where do you think its next attack will come from, that's if they do."

"Well, if I was the entity, I would be looking for finding another way in here. This window's now obsolete, oh fuck, right, get the lads up here, mate, and make sure they have a disruptor each."

"Roger, captain," replied Tony, as he left me and went downstairs. A few moments later, Tony had returned followed by Jim and Alan. Harry stayed where he was as he had enough to be getting on with.

I spoke to the troops. "Right, here's the plan, whilst Harry's building whatever it's gonna be, we need to keep alert in searching through this place; they got in here once, let's make sure they don't get a second opportunity.

"I'm gonna stay here by this window. Tony, can you patrol the upper floor, yell out if you need support. Jim, I need you to patrol the middle floor. Alan, I'm gonna need you to alternate between floors and be their back up. Just keep this in mind, if you find that you need help, yell out, Alan will be with you in seconds. Okay, right, let's go." As the lads went, I asked Jim to stop and come over to me, as he did so, I placed my hand on his cut, and once again, it instantly healed itself. Jim stood there flabbergasted. I then stated, "It's a long story, mate, go on." Jim looked at me and went off wagging his arm around.

The house was dead calm, you could've heard a pin drop as the only sounds I could hear were the footsteps of the lads walking along the squeaky floorboards above my head; it was a good half an hour when there was another sudden crash from somewhere upstairs. I was immediately facing the window. Tony began to call out. Alan was right on cue and with him within seconds; glass was all over the floor from the skylight. Alan and Tony had their weapons aimed at it. Strolling just underneath it, Alan opened fire at a face that appeared through the skylight; the blast removed some woodwork, but missed the bloke who tried to look in on them. At that moment, another two skinheads attempted to get in through my window.

Their immediate attack was for them to start to throw rocks into the room in the hope of pushing me backwards, this would allow them time to gain entry.

I positioned myself to within a few feet from the doorway and I had the perfect view; it was then that the intruders began to physically climb into the kitchen. I opened fire. I hit the first one directly in the chest, the blast knocked him clearly out of sight; he was dead as soon as he was hit.

The other one witnessing his buddy's demise ran off with his tail between his legs. Next thing we were aware of was Jim blasting away; he was firing at two more skinheads who had already managed to break into the next room without him being aware. Jim shouted for assistance. Alan immediately left Tony and was by Jim's side within moments.

Jim landed flat on his belly like a commando as he flew inside the room within the doorway as Alan stood above him; the two of them released a hail of shots that totally obliterated the two intruders as they were thrown across the room violently as the disruptors tore into their now lifeless bodies. Blood was scattered everywhere; the battle was over.

This was the second attempt the skinheads had had at trying to penetrate the house within the last hour, but for now, the house was once more at peace with itself. Silence fell all around; each one of us sat down or stood still in their respective places and took a well-earned rest, well, that was what I presumed they were up to as the squeaking of the floorboards relaxed its eerie empty noises. It was then that Harry came up the stairs carrying what resembled a small round cylinder, whilst still limping; it was shaped like a ball. "How're things?" he asked.

"We're okay at the moment, thank god, what's that?" I asked.

Harry replied, "It's another magic trick of mine. No, seriously, I've got to come clean, I found it in the bottom of the box we were given."

I responded with, "So are you going to tell me what it does or do you want me to ask twenty questions?"

Harry smiled and said, "Well, according to Timeline-Harry, it's a field projection unit."

"It's a what?" I replied.

"Field projection unit, what's that then?" My curiosity was growing stronger and stronger at this time.

"Yeah, and?"

Harry then came back with great enthusiasm, "Right, here's what we do, it's so simple, this Harry's a bloody genius. He's by far more intelligent than I could ever be, do you know—"

I cut him off in mid-sentence as I said to him, "Harry, sorry, mate, chill okay, now take a deep breath, and in plain English, just tell me what it does, okay, relax, you'll give yourself a coronary." Harry laughed.

"Sorry, Pete, this is so marvellous, right, right then, we've got five of these beauties. So, what we do is place it where you want it to go; there's a little connector switch on it; it's like an on/off button just here, you see it? Once activated, you have around a second to get the hell away from it, say a good five feet, no closer than that, for god's sake." Harry then took a pause.

I looked at him and replied, "Harry, what the fuck does it do, for fuck's sake?"

"Oh, didn't I say, it protects the area it's in within a ten foot radius, it omits a force field, you see. This field will vaporise anything organic that enters the protective field; it also mutates its impulses so it's virtually indestructible."

"You're kidding me." I held the device in my hands. I was shaking with fear as I was scared that I could drop it.

"It's okay, Pete, watch." Harry picked the ball up from my hands and threw it against the wall.

Immediately, I crouched and fell to the floor shouting, "What the fuck are you doing!"

Harry replied, "Demonstrating it, mate, it's perfectly harmless until you activate it." I stood up, went over to the ball and picked it up.

I was buzzing; looking extremely happy, I asked a very good question, "So once we have activated them, how long do these things stay alive for?"

Harry replied, "Indefinitely, Pete, they'll keep alive forever. You see, they have their own power source; the only way to cut them off is from a remote code sequencer" – and as if by magic, Harry miraculously produced one from his pocket – "Here it is, we have, one code does them all."

"Well, thank you, Harry."

"My pleasure," Harry replied.

I then responded with, "No, not you, Harry, I meant the other Harry." We managed to have a few moments of joy. I then asked him, "How's the knee?"

"It's fine, mate, why?"

"No reason, as long as it's not a problem for ya, right, getting back to these field units, I guess, we'll only need two of them at the moment, so if we were to place one at the base of the stairs on the bottom landing near the cellar and one more here on this window sill that should give us ample protection. What do you think?"

Harry replied, "Sounds good to me."

I carried on, "Right, Harry, can you go upstairs, explain it to the lads, get 'em down here? I will activate this one by this window, you can activate the other. I will meet you down in the cellar."

"Yeah, no worries. Just give me a few minutes to pop downstairs and get another one." That was it; Harry went down into the cellar as I remained at my post.

Once Harry had returned and walked upstairs, I activated the field protection unit in front of the kitchen window frame; once done, I walked down into the cellar and waited for the guys to return and meet me. After around five minutes had passed by, my friends finally began to walk down the stairs. "Can we have the disruptors on charge please, lads?" I asked politely. Harry was the last to arrive in the cellar, once I saw him, I asked, "All okay, mate?"

"Yeah, all good, Pete."

Harry and Jim then proceeded to get back to work. Tony asked, "So what the hell do we do now then?"

Alan responded with, "Well, we could always play snakes and ladders, or snap; snap's a good game."

Tony replied, "Get serious, will ya, we're stuck down here, we can't do anything."

I then looked at the both of them and stated, "Well, let's see, I know you could always asked Harry if he needs some assistance." Alan and Tony then shrugged their shoulders and moved over to Harry. I snuggled up by against the wall that was near the stairs leading up to the kitchen area and dropped to my bum. I then started to contemplate on our situation and what events had already taken place. As I looked around, Harry was really getting immersed in his work, you could see he was enjoying every minute. Jim, Tony and Alan were moving equipment around, putting devices on the shelving as Harry was directing every move that they made!

Chapter 18
My Boy

It was nice to see them all working well together. It was then that I assumed I had heard something once more coming from upstairs, but I just brushed it off as it was my imagination playing tricks, but seconds later, I heard the same noise; it was faint, but I knew something was amiss.

I stood up and decided to take a walk and investigate. I climbed the stairs without the boys noticing as they were so tied up in their work. As I looked straight ahead, I couldn't believe my eyes. It was unbelievable.

There were skinheads everywhere trying to get into the house from the kitchen window, the projection unit was really working fantastically well. I actually started to feel sorry for these poor bastards as they were instantly being vaporised. I knew they were being controlled like robots; every one of them that vaporised drew a flash of light; it was like watching sparklers on bonfire night going off; they just wouldn't stop coming on, there had to be close to fifty of them.

This was what I heard from downstairs, all I could do was watch the carnage unfold; it was horrific, but strangely enough, I had mixed emotions for with the regret that I was feeling also came enjoyment of the victory. As the seconds fell by, the slaughter gradually diminished as the entity gave up the fight.

The area went calm once more. I returned to the cellar, the lads hadn't even realised that I had left them.

There wasn't much point in explaining to them what had just happened so I just went to relax and return to my original position. Our entity slowly began to re-emerge, it wasn't long before it floated over to me. I stated, "We're doing well here, Harry's really progressing well." The entity telepathically transmitted that he wanted me to go with him, but it didn't tell me why or where our destination would be, and would it be okay if I brought someone with me this time. the entity said nothing, so I just assumed that in itself, that was a yes.

Thinking quickly, I tried to decide whom do I choose, Tony, Alan or Jim; without another moment's thought, I called Jim over. "Jim, here a minute?" He came across.

"Yeah, what's up?" He looked at me and the entity.

"We're popping away for a bit, grab a disruptor, will ya." Jim without questioning took a disruptor off charge; as soon as he did, he passed it onto me. Moments later, we were gone, god knows where we were going to end up this time. As fast as we had been transported, I had found myself alone within a building; to my surprise, I was dressed in an all-white boiler suit. I immediately turned to Jim. To my horror, he wasn't there; he wasn't anywhere in sight.

I then began to search for him hastily; the entity transferred the dreaded news to me that the curse whilst we were being transported reached out and snatched him from its grasp; even our entity had no idea as to where he was taken or even if he was still alive.

I stopped dead in my tracks. I was gutted; looking around, I slowly began to walk. I was as miserable as sin, all I was thinking of was Jim; it soon dawned on me that I was in some sort of a science building; everything around me was sterile, my suit for one thing, pure white glistening walls and flooring.

I then noticed slightly ahead of where I was were laboratories set either side of me so I started to walk through them; they were separated from the corridor by glass panels; there was a floor plan on my right-hand side. I stopped and looked at one of them; as I looked, I noticed there were six levels, I was on the lowest one. Luckily, this level wasn't occupied. The question popped into my nut, would whoever I bump into be a friend or foe, guess I'd find out soon enough.

I had more questions than answers running through my mind, where was I? Why am I here? Where's Jim? As I carried on walking, I approached a door; it was leading me to the next level. Getting closer, the door opened automatically, was this the work of the entity? Was it showing me the way? I had no idea. Entering the landing, I walked up the stairs to the next level; my hands were shaking as I held my disruptor close like a machine gun.

Once again, the door opened automatically; walking through, I bumped into a young lad, he could only have been around eighteen years old; he was carrying a tray of enclosed spiders; he too was dressed in the same type of white boiler suit. "Sorry," he said as he nearly dropped his tray. "That's a nice toy, level five, is it?"

"Yes, it is," I replied, thinking quickly and without a moment's pause. I asked him, "You been here long?"

He answered with, "About six months, don't know why I'm here really, no one says anything, just been told to run tests on these spiders, got to try and get them to sleep, god knows why they want spider to sleep, oh well, see ya around." He walked away and entered one of the labs. *Interesting, level five*, I thought. I carried on walking and watching everything I witnessed.

It looked like everything was undergoing some sort of experimentation, for as I came towards a second lab, another young lad roughly around the same age as the other one came out; now everyone wore a white boiler outfit. I asked him, "Hi, mate, look, I was wondering what's the fastest way to get up to level five, is there a lift in this place?"

"Yeah, sure, just around the corner, like the toy, by the way, cheers, it's something level five cooked up." I gave a short nervous laugh and quickly walked off. As I was approaching the corner, the young lad called out.

"Where's your ID badge, by the way?"

Thinking fast, I touched my upper right chest pocket, and stated, "Oh shit, I must have dropped it back there."

The kid responded with, "Well, make sure you see someone and get a replacement, they're really strict about ID in this place."

"Yeah, no worries, where do I go for that then? I've only been here a few hours. I don't know my way around this place as yet."

He replied, "Level five, mate."

"Cheers," I answered. I walked away and around the corner, immediately, I came upon the lift; it didn't take very long before I was on level five. Walking out of the lift, three more white boiler suits walked past me. I was totally ignored as they were all in a deep conversation.

I managed to hear something about the j experiment; walking along, I heard a voice call out from directly in front of me; it was an elderly man around fifty years old, "Where's your ID badge, sonny?"

I replied with, "I've just recently lost it, sir, I was told to get it replaced as soon as I could."

"Right, okay, Room 12." He closed the lab door and left me. I took a great sigh of relief as I moved away; the entity transferred some more news about the third floor, Room 8, but that was it.

I then doubled back to the lift and went down to Level 3; once out of the lift, I approached Room 8. I knocked on the door and entered the room; to my amazement, the entity was in the room with the young lab guy who was told to test the spiders. "What's going on here?" I asked as I approached the entity; the entity then faced me and spoke.

"Team member."

I immediately responded with, "No way, he's just a kid, my time's better spent looking for Jim, who the bloody hell is this guy, old boy, I'm not here to babysit, look, sorry, mate, no offence meant but this really isn't what you're looking for." I faced the old boy. "I need to locate Jim, okay, he is what I need right now; besides what's the connection here, there's no connection between him and the entity; it's not happening."

The entity once more stated, "Team member." Now by this time, I was getting rather pissed off with its attitude.

"Right, okay, once again, mate, no offence meant, but what's with the team member bit, what's the connection then?" There was silence as no one spoke. I then said to the kid, "Do you know of the entity issue then, mate?"

"Well, no, not at the moment, these gentlemen wanted to ask me some questions about my tests, what's this about an entity?"

"You see?" I raised my voice. "He knows absolutely nothing."

The entity then just said two words that stopped me in my tracks. "Harry War-pen."

The young lad looked straight at the entity and asked, "Is he okay?" I was gobsmacked.

"You know who he's referring to?" I asked.

The young lad then responded with the surprise of the year, "Yeah, I should do, he's my dad. Look, if he's in trouble, I want in."

"Oh no, no bloody way, there's no way I'm getting you involved with all this. Harry will fucking kill me. I need to find where Jim is."

The entity stated, "The enemy is known, find him will easy, keep safe not dead, will return, the Peter,"

"Just wait a moment—" It was too late.

The old boy transported us both back to the cellar. Harry looked over when we appeared. "Oh no." Harry was dumbstruck as he saw his son standing there.

"Hi ya, Dad." Harry was not impressed with his boy or with me, for that matter.

"What the hell are you bloody doing here, why did you bring him here, Pete! What's your bloody game?"

"Don't start on him, Dad, it was my choice to come here," said his son.

"Pete, explain this will ya?" Harry demanded.

I was on the verge of opening my gob as his boy then came out with, "Dad, will you listen to me for a minute, it was this old boy that found me. Pete had nothing to do with any of it. I knew something was wrong any way as you weren't answering my messages."

Harry looked at him, then stated, "Gents, let me introduce to you my son, Richard." Everyone acknowledged the greeting with a 'nice to meet ya, Richard'.

Tony then asked the fundamental question, "Where's Jim?"

I replied regretfully, "We were in mid-transportation when the curse somehow managed to intercept us, he was snatched; our entity doesn't even know where he is."

Alan responded, "Oh crap."

Richard then asked his dad, "So, what's going on?"

"Well, I guess there's no point in holding anything back from you now. We're here to destroy what I now believe was the result of the experiment that we did last week. You remember the experiment, don't ya?"

"Yeah, I do," answered Richard.

"Well, what you didn't know as I kept it from you was that something came into our world as a result of it. This entity thing, well, it's altering multiple timelines as it's trying to kill anyone that was involved with its existence; we've already lost a few lads, but we are going to kill it."

Richard then asked, "But why did that old boy—"

I interrupted him in mid-sentence, "That old boy you're referring to, Richard, well, it too is also an entity, that's the form it takes when it's communicating with us humans. You see, that experiment managed to separate the entity into separate parts; the evil side of it wants us all dead as it wants to grow and become so deadly there won't be anything on this earth that can stop it. The friendly part doesn't want to exist, so that's why it's doing its level best with helping us, the old boy disappeared without uttering a single word."

Richard asked another question, this time it was directed at his dad. "So this entity, what is it exactly, is it a ghost?"

Harry replied, "No, mate, not a ghost exactly, more like a poltergeist!"

Harry then gave me really dirty look; all I could say to him was, "Don't look at me like that, Harry, I said no to him. Did you really think I'd put your son in danger like this? Besides that, how long do you think he would've survived out there without our protection? If we could find him, how long would it have been before the curse got to him? He's actually safer and better off with us."

Harry hesitated for a moment as he pondered on what I'd said. "I guess," he replied. It was then that Harry went over to his boy and gave him a hug; the rest of us moved in and greeted him properly.

Richard then gazed over his dad's shoulder, he looked at all the equipment on the shelves. "What's all this then, Dad?" Harry turned back around after the emotional embrace with his boy and faced his new lab.

"It's our new experimental lab, Richard, what do you think?" Richard looked at him with a doubtful grin. Harry responded, "Yeah, well, it's early days and I haven't had a lot of time to work with, and yes, I know it needs a few more tweaks, but in theory, it's still good enough to do what we need it to do."

Richard then asked, "Can I help?"

"Thought you would never ask, why not," Harry replied. "Come over here, you've helped me before, tell you what, why don't you have a look at those disruptors over there? I'm thinking of a multiple phase shift to increase its power output, let me know if you have any ideas."

"Yeah, okay, Dad." Richard took a disruptor off charge and started to examine it.

Harry then proceeded to work on whatever he was doing before we interrupted him.

Tony and Alan came over to where I was. Alan whispered into my ear, "What's going on, Pete, you shoot off with the entity and Jim, now we've got Harry's boy, you do know that Harry won't forgive you if we can't keep his boy safe, don't ya?"

I looked at him and said, "Well, that's your job."

Tony then remarked, "No way, no way are you going to put his safety as our responsibility, Pete, we're not taking responsibility for him, that's your job."

I glared at Tony and said, "Look, I can't be dealing with everything that goes on around here, all I want you two to do is keep him behind everyone else; surely, that's not an impossible task, is it? If you can do that and he'll be fine; we're in this situation now, so please do me a favour and back me up for Christ's sake."

Alan then asked, "So what about Jim then, what do we do about that?"

"I've no idea, Al, we don't even know if he's still alive; all we can do is hope and pray we can get him back with us. Tell you something though, that bastard entity's gonna pay for all it's done to us."

Tony responded with, "Too right. With any luck, it'll suffer before it dies." It was at that moment we heard the start of a heavy thudding sound coming from upstairs; it had to be the kitchen; we all gazed at each other.

Richard already held a disruptor. Harry then grabbed another and passed two moreover, one to me and the other to Tony. As Richard moved forward Alan took the weapon from him and said clearly to Richard, "You stick to my back, you got that?"

"I hear you," Richard replied. We gently crept upstairs.

Harry disconnected the field unit at the top of the cellar steps as we passed through the area. The shock over what we saw was horrific; there in front of the window about eight feet from the ground was Jim, his clothing was in spreads; he had cuts and slices all over his body; it was like Daryl's death all over again. His face was like someone had been using a knife for slashing practice; he was covered in blood; there was some kind of an invisible force keeping him hanging there. We knew the curse was here and doing its thing with him. Jim's arms were tightly outstretched above his head and his feet were tight together by his ankles; it was as though he was being crucified on an invisible cross.

We looked on in horror as his body twisted and turned as each slash appeared on his legs, arms, face and torso; screams echoed all around as his torture continued. It was like the Middle Ages all over again. Fresh blood would seep from all over as a fresh cut opened up.

Jim looked into the kitchen area and his voice seemed to focus on me as he said, "Peter, kill me, for god's sake, kill me." Something wasn't right as he spoke so calmly, there was no aggression, no sorrow, no pain.

He then let out an almighty scream. Tony looked at me then he looked at everyone else. "Pete, we can't leave him like this, we have to do something."

I in return said, "What do you want us to do, Tone, open the field so it can come in and do to us what it's doing to him?"

Alan then said, "Can't we drop the field tone, not even for Jim?"

Harry then said, "No, there's no way we can drop the field projectors; it would be suicide. Peter, we can't help him." I looked at Jim in a pitiful way. I knew something had to be done.

A voice came out of Jim's mouth, but this was not the voice of Jim but that of the curse; it was playing with us as it jokingly said, "Oh, Pete, kill me, kill me." It's voice then started to demand, "Open the field, the Peter, open the field or this puny little human dies, come on, the Peter, you know you want to, come on, open the field."

Jim's voice returned as he then said, "Peter, kill me."

It was at that moment I knew what had to be done. I moved backwards and out of the kitchen. Harry then inquired, "What're you doing?"

I in turn replied, "Everyone, come over here." Within seconds and without any questions, they did so.

Alan whispered, "You got something in mind?"

From this moment on, all our conversations were in whispering mode as in the hope the curse couldn't pick up on our intentions. I answered him with, "Yes, I think so, look, this is what I want us to do and I know it's not gonna come hard for some of us, but I think it's the only way forward."

Harry then said, "Okay, what's the plan?"

"Right, this is it in a nutshell, here's how I see it, for all we know, Jim's already dead.

"Now we've heard the curse talk from within him, if he's not dead, then he's possessed, so either way, Jim's gone.

"There's no way of getting him so this is what I want to do.

"I want to drop the field projector units, fire everything we have, then raise it again, questions?" Harry threw one straightaway.

"If we drop the field, we're dead, I've already said that."

"Yes, I know you did, but we're only talking about a micro-second here; all I want is for all you to listen to my countdown, as soon as I say the number three, we fire, and I mean everyone fires.

"We need all the fire power at our disposal. Now as soon as the number sounds, cause once I finish saying the number three, the field projectors going to come back on, we're talking less than a second here; it will be too busy defending itself from the attack, won't be expecting a full on blast; it thinks we're going to do what we can to save Jim. Harry, how long does it take for the field projector to drop?"

Harry replied, "Instantly, mate! And so, you're banking on surprise as your plan." He paused for a moment then stated, "It's possible, I suppose. What do we do with Richard? I don't want him involved in any of this, Pete, it's far too dangerous."

Richard instantly replied, "Dad, we haven't got a choice, stop treating me like a kid, I'm not a kid anymore." Harry looked at him and smiled.

I then said, "Look, sorry, but this isn't the time for a family squabble, we're doing this or not?"

Harry then said to his boy, "Well, I guess you better get downstairs and grab the last disruptor then." Richard grinned and went down to the cellar; he within moments returned to the group.

"Any more questions before we act?" Everyone in the group fell silent for a few moments.

Alan then broke the silence with, "Where're we aiming, is it random or are we to target an area?" I looked at him in surprise.

"Bloody good question, Alan, I suggest Jim's heart." Again, the group went silent. "Right, let's get back into the kitchen, remember, the number three, and blast this bastard to hell." I reiterated as to the make sure that we all knew what had to be done.

We found ourselves once more standing in front of the window frame as Jim's body was continually being torn open; the curse then materialised into its human form once again as it lay besides Jim. "Drop the field, the Peter, I will give you this Jim; he needs a plaster." Jim's screams were increasing, as they became more frequent.

Alan then remarked, "I hope you're right, Pete." Richard stood behind him; it now fell to me.

I shouted out, "Three!" Immediately, the field projector dropped. At that exact moment, all hell broke loose.

We poured every single ounce of energy into it; all the fire power went directly into Jim's chest; the blasts were thundering fast and furious. As my voice fell away from saying the number, Harry raised the field. An almighty flash of glistening pure white light flew through the air as we all got thrown backwards for a few feet; it was as if we had been hit by a nuclear blast. Once all the light had slowly dissipated, we all looked keenly out of the window frame.

The curse was nowhere to be seen; the coast was clear; the disruptors were perfect. A gutted feeling came over us all as we thought of Jim and not the beating of the entity.

Tony remarked, "Thank god," as we went back down into the cellar. Harry tapped me on the shoulder as he switched on the field projection unit behind us, he then said, "Nice one, mate, let's hope it doesn't like the taste." Once downstairs, Richard went over to the charger panel, and gradually, we passed our disruptors over to him as he put each one on charge.

Richard then spoke to his dad, "Dad, are you okay if I called you by your first name, it's a bit embarrassing calling you dad in front of everyone."

"Course you can, mate," Harry replied.

Richard then mentioned, "Earlier, you mentioned you wanted to alter the power output on the disruptors, did you mean its firing sequence or its charging capacity?"

"It was the multiple phase shift I was referring to, Rich, but that sounds a really good idea, good, well done. Why don't you have a crack at that and their charging capacitors?" Harry replied.

"Will do, Harry." They both had a little father and son banter.

I thought Richard could well end up being a bloody good asset for us to have; he seemed to be grasping everything his dad had to say and do reasonably well, and he also learnt quicker than we did.

Maybe it was just down to our age. I watched him go to work on the weaponry, his enthusiasm was commendable.

Richard then started a chat with his dad about the equipment we had or needed to get whilst Alan, Tony and I were over the other side of the area just chatting. "Dad, sorry, Harry, what are we intending to do when we get to grips with this entity thing?"

"What do you mean, Rich?" asked Harry.

Richard then continued, "Well, I presume you're gonna want to catch it somehow."

Harry then stated, "There's no way we're going to want to capture it, it's a case of destroying the bloody thing."

Richard then said, "Well, how? Surely, if we're out to destroy it, we're going to need a containment plan, then once we've got it, we're then going to kill it, but if that's the case, we ain't got one." Harry then after contemplating what Richard had said then realised what his son was saying.

He looked around the place, then stated, "You know that hadn't crossed my mind. I've been so engrossed in setting all this up, sorting out the charge on those disruptors." He then called to me, "Pete, you got a minute? Richard's got something new for you to ponder over."

"Oh, really, right," I approached and said, "so what's this new information then, young man?"

"Well, I was just saying to Dad, if we're to capture this entity, so we can destroy it,

Chapter 19
The Rodent Infection

Well, surely, we're gonna need something to trap it in, we haven't even got a chamber, there's nothing."

Harry agreed with him and said, "He has a point, Pete." I looked about the place and then looked back at Richard.

"You clever little sod, you know it didn't dawn on me, what with everything that's gone on, good on you, Richard, good on you."

I gently slapped him on his shoulder as Harry did the same. Richard couldn't stop grinning. I then said, "Right, me and your dad will bang our heads together while you get back to work." Richard looked at me, then looked at his dad.

Harry then said, "Well, what you waiting for, you heard him, off you trot, well, off you go on."

"Charming," Richard replied as he wandered back to the weapons charger unit. Once Richard had departed our company, I then said to Harry, "Jesus, you have one intelligent youngster there, Harry, you should be a proud man."

"Thank you, Pete, and for the record, I am, very proud. For a lad who is still under twenty years old he has got a bloody good head on his shoulders. So what are we going to do about this chamber?"

I then said, "Well, I guess you better work alongside Rich on this one, seems like I'm out of my depth against you two brain boxes; you decide on what type of chamber we're gonna need first of all. I will then see if the old boy can magic one up."

"Okay, Pete, will do."

I left father and son to work as I went back to the others. Alan asked, "Everything okay?"

I smiled and said, "Yeah, couldn't be better, tell you what, boys, this Rich may be young but he's got his head screwed on."

"What do you mean?" asked Tony.

"Well," I replied, "have any of you two thought on how we're going to secure this entity before we get a chance to destroy the poxy thing?"

Tony and Alan gazed at each other with a look of complete and utter emptiness within their brain cells; they then in unison said, "Well, no."

I then gave my response, "Well, Richard did."

Tony then remarked, "Good on him, you know, he's all right."

Alan joined in, "Yeah, I like him too." I then sat down on the floor as Tony and Alan did the same.

"Right, so let's have a recap, shall we? What have we got going for us at the moment?" Tony was first to react.

"We've six disruptors, the curse has been pushed back by them a few times."

Alan then said, "Yeah, we've also got the field projection units, now they're fantastic."

"Anything else?" I asked with interest.

"Don't think so," responded Tony.

I then came out with, "Well, I think our greatest assets are right over there, those two." I nodded in the direction of Harry and Richard. "Can you just imagine how it would be without them, we'd be in all kinds of shit without their brains."

"We've a really good chance now, Pete," Alan commented.

"I just pray to god that we've lost our last member."

"A-men to that," responded Tony.

Alan then stood up and had a good old stretch on his legs; he then said, "Well, that was a good recap, I must say, what happens now?"

I replied, "Well, I guess that's down to the curse, the ball's in its court now."

"Why's that," asked Tony.

"Well, it knows it's got to either get in here somehow or get us out. It knows we're secure in this place, and it's also aware of the fact that we've had our metabolism altered; we're not in dire need for food or drink, none of us want the loo; we're in need of nothing; we don't even get tired."

Alan stated, "We're more like the living dead." He gave a short outburst of laughter.

I had to be honest, it did sound pretty funny. Tony then inquired, "So what's this chamber thing we're in need of?"

Alan responded, "I guess it's some sort of a cage."

"Well, yeah," I answered, "but it has to be ridiculously bloody strong cause this entity won't appreciate being confined. It will do whatever it has to do to get the hell out of it; it will need at least three or four compartments, I'd guess."

Tony remarked, "We could always do what the Nazis did back in the Second World War."

Alan then inquired, "What, what the hell are you going on about, Tone, bloody idiot."

"Well, they used gas amongst all their other atrocities, they slaughtered around six million Jews that way, evil bastards they were; they would tell them they're going for showers, herd them like cattle into types of massive enclosed buildings, slam the door, job done; they would then fill the place with gas."

"Jesus, did they really do that?" asked Alan.

Tony continued his history speech, "They were murdering everything that wasn't blue-eyed and blonde, the Aryan race they called it, must have been terrifying times for those poor sods."

Alan responded with, "So the Germans were real bastards."

Tony responded, "No, Alan, don't confuse the two, the Nazis, and the standard German were decent people, brilliant soldiers." Once Tony had stopped his monologue, it then dawned on me the canisters we were given, they could be converted into our own gas weapons. I stood up, and with great enthusiasm, I walked over to Harry.

"Harry! I've an excellent idea!"

As I shouted, Tony remarked to Alan, "The gas was my idea, cheeky sod." Harry stopped his work and turned around.

"What's that, Pete?"

I responded with one word, "Gas."

"Explain yourself?" Harry seemed a little confused as he remarked.

"Those containers over there, could devise something, say like a release mechanism. The lads and I were just chatting about the gas chamber in WWII, how the Nazis based the Jews. I think we've hit on a bloody good idea to wipe out this thing once and for all.

"We could have, say, three or four separate compartments in this chamber, the last one we could adapt into some sort of safe zone.

"We persuade the entity through and into it, seal it, bombard it with whatever those containers hold. Well, what do you think?" Harry looked at me in a thoughtful mode. Richard came across as he had overheard our conversation.

Richard and Harry brought their heads together and began whispering to one another.

After a short few minutes, Harry then stated, "You could have something, Pete, leave it with us, this lot's virtually ready. How're you doing with the disruptors, Rich?"

Richard said, "Well, I've altered the frequency modulators. I was about to test one."

"Great, let's see it." Richard moved across and took a disruptor off charge.

He aimed towards the far wall away from anyone and fired; the disruptor fired a spray of pulses this time instead of single pulses reaction; the weapon was firing more like a submachine gun than a laser. "Oh yes, Rich, beautiful job, well bloody done." Harry and I were over the moon.

Tony then gently thumped Alan in the upper arm and then mumbled to Alan once more, "The gas was my fucking idea, what a bitch he is."

Alan then said to Tony, "Oh, eat me, we're a team, remember, who gives a shit about whose idea it is, if it kills the poxy thing, who really cares? I certainly don't."

Richard then mentioned one good problem with this fabulously new concept. "I don't want to spoil things here, Harry, Pete, but we've got a problem with this whole thing."

"Problem?" I was intrigued. "What problem?" I asked.

Richard then said, "Well, this thing's not just gonna go into an enclosed space like a chamber now, is it, we're going to need bait."

"Yeah, I see your point," Harry replied. I then had a few moments of a pause to gather my thoughts as for then I had the worst idea of my entire life.

"We use me, I will be the bait!"

"You're not serious, Pete." Harry wasn't at all interested with my suggestion. "You can't, there's no way I'm going to allow you to walk inside a sealed area with this bloody thing chasing after you, no, that's a fucking stupid idea; we'll have to think of something else; it's preposterous, you'll be dead in seconds."

Richard then stated, "Not really, Dad, if like Peter said a few minutes ago, we could design another extension to the chamber at the rear, but will be the safe zone, all Pete would have to do is get there as fast as he could.

"Seal it behind himself, then we would have the thing trapped; we could then rip this thing apart. Pete would be perfectly safe; it would be as if he was behind a brick wall."

254

"I still don't like it, Rich," Harry responded, "it's too dangerous; if he was to trip or stumble, it'll be over in seconds. No, I'm against it." I looked at Harry straight in the eyes.

"Look, I'm not exactly thrilled at the idea, but I'm the one it really wants, if I'm in there, it will come for me. How else do we get an entity to move into an enclosed space, it's the only way we have. I want a vote on it."

Harry then said, "You want to risk your life on a vote, do ya?"

"Yeah, I do," I replied without a moment's thought.

"Right, okay, well, take a vote on it, but if we vote against the idea, that's it, we forget the whole thing, agreed?" Harry was seriously adamant on this point.

"Agreed." Alan and Tony soon came over.

"What's all the noise about?" Alan asked. Harry then laid things on the line. "We're taking a vote, Alan."

Tony then responded with, "Oh goody, I like a vote, what's it about?" Harry then remarked, "This is serious, Tony, Pete here wants to use himself as human bait to entice the entity into a chamber; he will get himself into a safe zone, that we're gonna build and close it behind himself, but if he falters for even a second, he's dead, that's the vote, do we say yes, or no?"

Alan remarked, "Hang on a second, you want to do what?" Alan was really unsettled with the whole thing.

I tried to clear the air. "Look, this entity has been after me most of all, now this chamber could have three to four sections to it plus a safe zone, if I can get it to come after me, we can then seal each compartment behind it. I get to the safe zone, close it behind me, we have it trapped, we drop the canisters and kill it, that's the vote." The group paused for a few moments more.

Harry then said, "Right, okay, hands up for no." Harry raised his hand, so did Alan.

Harry then said, "In favour." Richard and Tony raised their hands as I slowly and reluctantly raised mine.

Harry then remarked, "Vote carried, you stupid idiot." Harry then immediately turned around and carried on working, you could see he wasn't happy with the whole thing.

Richard went to him and said, "Sorry, Dad."

Harry then said to his boy, "I suppose, you better start looking at designing something. I will come over after I've adjusted a few more components and help you with it."

"Right, okay," Richard replied.

Whilst Harry was busy doing some minor readjustments I moved across to where Richard was busy doing his technical drawing. "Well, I must say, Rich, your work's impressive, where did you get the geometry set?"

"Oh, that's me, Dad, he brought them for me once I started university. I always carry them on me, you never know when they will come in useful," he replied.

"So, this is going to be our chamber, is it?" I asked.

Richard responded by saying, "It's an anti-vacuum chamber, Pete, to be precise."

"Yeah, I knew that." I gave him a slight grin.

Richard then continued saying, "I'm thinking of a four-tier system. Now when I say tiers, I mean to say sections, but you get what I'm saying though." I nodded at him.

"Carry on."

"Well, we can use the field projection units instead of doors; the containers will go here on the third section's roof; now if we can get some liquid nitrogen, we could use that at the same time."

"I see, so what material are you thinking of for the actual chamber structure?" I asked enthusiastically.

"I was contemplating on using a relatively new material that the Chinese are working with."

"The Chinese, really, what's it called this Chinese thingy?" I asked.

"It's called graphene aerogel; it's a fantastic material; it can withstand heat as high as 1200 degrees Celsius, and it's also a thousand times stronger than its mass; it would be perfect for the job in hand, well, that's what I think anyway." Richard seemed pretty confident with all his suggestions.

Harry popped over and asked, "How's it going, Rich?"

Richard then responded to his dad, "Well, I believe I've got the general outlay sorted out now."

"Really, that's fast; let's have a gander then." Harry looked at his drawings whilst rubbing his chin. "I see, so you're thinking of that then, yeah, that's feasible. What do you think, Pete?"

"So, what's your opinion on his design and material?" Harry asked.

I in turn replied, "Well, it looks and sounds good, but it would take months for us to put this all together."

"Not really." Harry said. "We do have our own entity, don't we? We could get it to construct the chamber for us; all we need do is instruct the entity as to what we need. You're probably looking at two to three days' construction work, yeah. I think he's done a decent job designing his first anti-vacuum chamber, well, done, lad." Harry was elated, to say the least.

Alan and Tony came over and gazed at the technical designs; they then like Siamese twins both said in unison the same phrase, "Wow." Richard then explained to the pair of them as they hadn't receive an in-depth explanation.

"Well, it's just a first draft, that's all, but the design is spot on, you see, it's like what Pete said a little time back, so once Pete moves into the second chamber section, we activate the field projection unit, that should protect him.

"The entity will pursue him, well, that's what we hope it will do. As Pete moves to the third section, we drop the field unit and raise the third, this will entice the entity to go further inside. We then raise the units trapping the thing inside. Pete moves through and into the safe zone; we keep the entity in the third part and then all going well, we rip the thing to bits."

Alan commented, "Seems simple enough, Tony, what do you think?"

Tony responded with, "Yeah, I like it, when's it going to be ready then?"

Harry replied, "Jesus, you're keen, maybe a few days once we get the entity on board. Can you try and contact it, Pete?"

"I can give it a go," I replied. Concentrating, I passed the message on to what we needed; seconds later, the old boy appeared. I went across to it and spoke out of earshot. I explained the situation and what we needed from it; the old boy then evaporated. After the chat, I returned to the lads. "Sorted," I said.

"Oh wow." Richard was pleasantly surprised by the speed of this entity.

I then responded and said, "No one stands by that wall over there, that's where all the stuff's going to be placed, so distance yourselves; don't want anyone getting crushed." It was at that moment, I heard something once more coming from upstairs, another thud came pulsating through the floorboards directly above my head; this time we all heard it.

"What now!" Tony cried out. Richard reached for the disruptors.

"They're only a quarter charged, Pete."

"Well, we haven't much choice now, do we? Pass 'em out." He did just that; we then moved up the stairwell, there was nothing happening; we all looked around the area, there was nothing but silence. "Strange," I said. Now something had to have made that sound, but what was it? It was then we found the answer.

Rodents, there were multitudes of rats smashing out from the lath and plaster walls; timber splinters and plaster flew everywhere as they charged through the wall on our far side; these rodents were at least three times larger than standard-sized rats; they were massive in comparison.

They were snarling with a sort of white foam that drooled from their jaws; it was as if they were infected with the rabies virus. "What the fuck is this?" Tony cried out as panic streamed into his vocal chords.

I then shouted out, "Fire!" We were firing as fast as we possibly could; we were slaughtering them, but they still kept churning out; rats were breaking out of every wall around us, talk about clusters' last stand; it was like a flood, more and more rats poured into the area. Some of the entry holes that they were forming were more like cave entrances, at least double the initial size; we were seriously in danger of being overrun.

A few rats had managed to slip around and were trying to flank our position; it was as if they were being directed; it was then that a few of these pests managed to break into our circle; they pounced onto Richard's legs as they stuck their teeth deep into the flesh of his legs. Richard immediately fell to the floor as he started screaming for help. Harry and Tony rushed forward, and instead of firing their weapons, they began to use them as clubs, swinging back and forth in a great attempt to get the rats off his boy. After a few seconds, Harry grabbed his boy by his arms and dragged him backwards. Tony then started firing once more.

I moved ahead of him and carried on firing to give Harry enough time to get his boy away and down into the cellar. Grabbing Richard's disruptor as it lay on the floor and with both arms, I opened up firing sporadically. Once again, the rats must have seen an opening as they flanked us again. Within seconds, they were pouncing towards Alan; rats were flying through the air; it was like clay pigeon shooting; we were splattering them in mid-air as they flew towards us. Rat numbers were finally falling away as the attack slowly dwindled away.

Alan and Tony then moved forward as they were cutting down the distance between the rats and us; gradually, we had finally managed to get on top of the attack. I then joined them; the rats began to start their retreat back within the wall. The attack was over, all that was left was the massive wall damage.

We were all huffing and puffing. I then said to Tony, "Tony, get some field projection units, mate, we need to block these hole up and fast." Tony rushed downstairs and soon returned. Alan joined him as they moved off placing the units in strong defensive positions.

Shortly, the units became live, without hesitating, we then rushed down into the cellar. Harry had ripped Richard's trousers from the knees downward; his trousers looked like they had been through a shredding machine. Now by this time, he was dressing the wounds on his boy's legs. I asked, "How is he, mate?"

Harry looked at me and said, "Some are superficial, mate, but there's a few deep ones, he is going to need a hospital, Pete."

Alan then mentioned, "Sorry to say it but those rodents looked like they were full of rabies."

I went over and took Harry to one side and whispered to him, "Alan maybe is right, Harry, you know that, don't ya?" Harry replied.

"I don't need to hear it, Pete, let's just hope God's smiling down on us."

Alan then remarked, "What's it going to throw at us next, cockroaches?"

Tony responded with, "Guess, we will have to wait and see, mate." It wasn't long before the disruptors were once more on charge. As time went on, Harry kept a close vigil on Richard; every once and a while, he would take a look at his boy's legs; there were no signs of infection as yet, and that's exactly what we were all praying for.

Harry asked him, "How're you feeling, son?"

"I feel fine, Dad, but it's my right shin, it's really starting to give me some gip, guess, I was lucky."

"Guess, you were," Harry replied as he touched his boy's arm with relief. As Harry kept up his vigil over his boy, from out of the blue, a liquid nitrogen canister miraculously appeared over in the corner of the cellar, swiftly followed by a large piece of graphene aerogel sheeting; it made Richard nearly jumped off the chair he was sitting on.

He shouted, "Fucking hell, what was that!"

Harry said, "Looks like the entity's doing its bit for queen and country."

Tony and Alan moved across to the two items. Tony asked, "Where do you want to 'em put?"

Harry replied with, "Well, they're all right there at the moment, and will you two get the hell away from that area, we've got a lot more still to come; we can decide on what goes where later."

Tony remarked, "It's a big one, ain't it?" He referred to the sheeting.

I responded with, "Bigger the better, Tone, now move away, we need at least a ton of the stuff."

Tony then said, "Well, let's just hope we've enough nitrogen to do the job."

Richard then let out a yell. Harry immediately asked his boy with concern, "You okay, boy?" Richard then looked at him in a fair bit of discomfort.

"It's my bloody shin, Dad. I'm getting a sharp pain in it now; it's coming and going."

Harry then responded, "Okay, let's have a quick gander at it." Harry's facial expression said a thousand words; an infection had started to appear around several of the teeth bite marks; it was red in colour, as small amounts of some sort of pus began to seep out from the wounds.

Harry gently cleaned what he could and replaced the cloth that was laying over it. Harry then went to speak to me, whispering he said, "Pete, look, I know what our situation is, but I'm going to have to get Richard to a hospital, he has the start of an infection in his right shin."

I then stated the worst news I could give him, "You can't, Harry, you can't take him out of here."

Harry looked at me and said, "What, are you going to try and stop me? That's my boy, he could lose his leg if I don't get him medical assistance, you want that, do you?"

I grabbed his arm and said, "Harry, look, okay, there's an infection, but you're not thinking clearly here, you take him out of here and you're both dead.

"The curse will pounce on you like a ton of bricks; you won't stand a chance in hell; think about it."

"We can take a disruptor with us," Harry responded.

I then said, "Oh really, and how do you explain that when the hospital staff scream, nutter with a gun? Come on, Harry, use your logic."

Harry then glared at me and with a stern look he said, "Logic, fuck logic, that's my son."

I in turn glared back at him and said, "Look, tell you what, you stay here, I will go out with Alan and get a first aid kit, how's that?"

Harry then said, "He doesn't need a first aid kit, Pete, he needs drugs to fight this fucking infection, for god's sake." Harry was in danger of falling apart at this point; he was growing ever so fearful and agitated.

Richard at that point was in almost continual pain as he was moaning and groaning most of the time. I went back over to Richard with Harry; again, Harry lifted the covering from his boy's shin, the infection was moving fast; there was a hell of a lot more pus than before as it had changed its colour; the redness was virtually now gone, in its place lay the colours of green with a yellowing around the edge of the wounds; the veins were now turning to a deep black as they began to come out and settle just below a single layer of his skin. Harry said, "Jesus, Pete, what the fuck is this, please don't tell me that this is a standard infection."

Richard at that moment lost feeling in his leg, as he called out, "Dad, I can't feel anything down there, my leg's numb."

Harry turned back around to him. Richard's eyes started to drop away; within a few seconds, he was unconscious, his entire body became lose and limp. "Oh my god, Pete, help me!" Harry yelled. Seconds went by as we all rushed over to Richard's side; gently, we placed him on the floor. Harry looked at me helpless and asked, "What can I do?"

I stood up after I looked at Harry; it was then that I called for the old boy telepathically. As a micro-second takes to tick over and pass, our entity appeared. It carried with it the remainder of the graphene aerogel sheeting that we were in so desperate a need of; it stood their motionless as I went to it. "We need your help, Richard has been infected by the curse, we need you to save him. Please, please do something for him." The entity, now in the form of our old boy, just stood there motionless; it then eased its way over to where Richard was lying. Everyone moved away from the immediate area as to allow our old boy more freedom to move; the old boy looked at Richard's lifeless body, it then focussed upon his leg.

Chapter 20
The Visitor

As he scanned the wounded area, he placed his hands above and below the damage, a pulsating white line of pure energy followed its eye line in a horizontal pattern; again the old boy stood perfectly motionless, without any further hesitation, closing its eyes, pulses of multicoloured energy beams like those you would find in a rainbow transferred from the old boy's arms down through its fingertips and into Richard's leg.

An eternity passed, well, that's what it felt like. After a few moments, the old boy stood away from Harry's boy; it then spoke to Harry. "Will is strong, time to tell, infection is no more."

Harry just dropped to his knees. "Thank you, thank you for what you have done for him, just tell me, how long before he wakes up?"

The old boy stated, "Time will take, will is strong." With that, the old boy grinned and once more evaporated into thin air. Harry looked down at his boy's legs; the leg was now by a miracle back to normality, no more marks, pus or blood; it was as if nothing had happened to him whatsoever. Harry just couldn't hold back his joy; tears flooded down his face.

Richard at this point was still fast asleep. It was hours before Richard finally came back to reality. As his eyes slowly opened, Harry approached him, he gave him a fatherly hug. Richard once his senses had returned asked, "What's up, Dad?"

Harry was startled for a moment as he stated, "What do you remember, son?" Richard then looked about the place, he could see he was the centre of attention as he looked surprised.

He stated, "Well, nothing apart from seeing those rats coming out of the wall, what happened?"

Alan jumped in with, "We won by two submissions and a knockout, mate, you should've seen your dad move."

Harry then continued the charade, "Yeah, two falls and a knockout." Harry then smiled at Alan. "So you don't remember anything else after that then?"

Richard responded with, "Well, no." It really was a miracle as the old boy not only fixed his leg but removed any memory of how he sustained the injury.

Harry helped Richard to his feet. "How does that feel?" Harry asked.

"Dad, I'm fine; in fact, I've never felt better. I feel like, well, great; whatever happened I wouldn't mind having some more of it whatever it was." That was music to Harry's ears; his smile lit up the cellar.

The joyfulness passed through to everyone; the old boy had really come good once again. I then mentioned to Richard, "Oh, by the way, all the stuff we were asking for, chamber wise, well, it's all over there; all we need to do now is build the bloody thing."

"Oh yes," Richard replied enthusiastically, "what the hell are we waiting for then, let's get cracking; it ain't going to build itself now, is it." Richard was ready, willing and able to restart work.

Seconds passed by as he got into gear; he moved over to the graphene aerogel sheeting; we all one by one followed. We gathered around the sheets as Tony and Alan went either side of one of them; they tried to lift one of the sheets from the floor. They soon found out that it was impossible, they were miles too heavy.

Alan then said to me, "We're really going to need some strength on this, Pete, these sheets are far too heavy for us."

Tony then said, "He's right, Pete, we're going to need the old boy again, there's no way we can work with these sheets." Once again, I called for the old boy's presence. The old boy, yet again, within a micro-second, it was once more beside us.

Richard took it upon himself and approached the entity. "Excuse me, sir, but we're going to need your assistance in the construct of this chamber, those sheets you have brought us are far too heavy for us human beings." Richard then showed the old boy what he wanted from the drawings and diagrams from his work station, this included all the ducts for where the two containers were to be placed within the ceiling area of the third compartment, as well as the duct for where the liquid nitrogen was to be placed.

The old boy looked at the diagrams and the drawings; it then said to everyone in the area, "Evacuation needed, heat too great for humans."

Harry then said, "Well, what about all my equipment, the heat will melt everything."

The old boy simply said, "Safe will be, trust is vital to the understand." With that, we all left the cellar leaving the old boy to do its thing. Once upstairs, Harry then stopped suddenly and slapped his forehead.

Richard looked at him and asked, "Dad, what's up, you okay?"

With that, Harry faced him, and with a grimace, he stated, "We've messed up, boy." Richard's facial expression said it all.

"What! How?"

Harry then tried to explain, "The field projection unit."

"What about them?" Richard replied.

Harry stated, "They're no good for the job we want them to do."

"Dad, look, they're fine, we've already witnessed what they can do, what's the issue?" Harry made his concerns perfectly clear.

"Look, the units are designed to prevent anything from passing their position, yeah?"

Richard responded with, "Well, yeah?"

Harry then followed up with, "Yeah, but once we use them in the chambers, they're not only going to do what they're designed for but they will also start to wipe out anything we pump into those areas. We're using chemicals and gases remember that.

"Gas floats through the air, hence we're going to lose a hell of a lot when the units start vaporising." Richard's face then suddenly dropped as his understanding to what his dad had just explained became clear.

"Oh shit, you're right, why didn't we see that?"

"Maybe it was a simple case of not wanting to," Harry replied.

Overhearing the conversation, I stepped in between as I remarked, "Well, we're going to need extra-fast automatic door seals then."

"Shit, sorry, Pete—"

I interrupted him with, "You have nothing to say sorry for, Rich, you've been magnificent. We can blame it on the old git, what do you say?"

Richard let out a laugh as his dad stated, "Not so much of the git, I thank you."

The old boy must've been moving at tremendous speed as from the doorway leading down to the cellar, beams of light and heat flooded the area we were standing in; the heat was starting to get uncomfortable.

It wasn't long before we all began sweating like pigs, the salts were pouring out of us; at this rate, we would all collapse within the hour of dehydration.

Tony moaned, "Can't we open a window or something? Jesus, Pete, I'm melting here." Alan then joined in with the moaning.

"Yeah, just a little one, it's getting hard to breathe in here."

I looked and stated, "There's nothing I can do about the heat, hopefully, it won't be long before he's finished."

Harry approached; as he was wiping his brow, he said, "Hate to say this, Pete, but they have a point, it's bloody boiling in here. We're not going to be able to take much more of this heat."

I looked at Harry and said, "I do know that Harry, but we need this chamber built, and if heat is the only way the old boy can build it, then what can I do?"

Richard responded with, "Can't it be built in stages?" Richard then suddenly hit the floor as the heat became too much for him to bear; he was out cold. Harry grabbed him and gently lowered him to the floor.

"Jesus, Pete, how much more of this do we have to take, we're all going to collapse at this rate." It was at that exact moment that the heat started to dissipate and ease off; the temperature dropped to normal.

Moving off, I walked towards the cellar with terrific impatience. Alan and Tony followed whilst Harry spent the next few minutes reviving his boy. Within minutes, Harry and a wobbly Richard joined us.

Richard looked at what he had designed; his facial expression was as if he had just won a billion pounds on the lottery. Harry was gobsmacked as he gave a good impression of a fish gasping for oxygen. Tony and Alan just said nothing as they were mesmerised by what they were witnessing.

I just stood there, engulfed with delight. Harry and Richard then took point and walked inside the first compartment. Richard then noticed a pressure pad which lay on the floor in front of the first door; the flooring inside the second compartment also had a pressure pad; he pressed his weight on it, within micro-seconds, the entrance sealed itself with a sheet of this graphene aerogel sliding from within the wall. "The entity must have heard what we had been saying, Dad." Richard continually began to play footsie with the pad, opening and closing the door.

Harry then grabbed on to his hand. "Okay, boy, that's enough, don't break 'em before we've had a chance to use them."

Harry then noticed that the release and opening pressure pads were on both sides of each section; as they moved deeper within the chamber, the rest of us followed.

Shortly, they reached the safety zone. Harry ran his eye around the area and gave a smile of acceptance; the old boy had once more come good.

The chamber was a work of genius.

Harry immediately then said to Richard, "We better get this liquid nitrogen and the containers set up."

Richard responded, "We're going to need some sort of remote control system on these, especially these pads, Dad, we can't have this entity using 'em as it feels like."

It was like watching a Batman and Robin movie as they turned and rushed out of the chamber. I faced the old boy and said, "Thank you."

The old boy then said with a sort of happiness in its voice for the very first time, "Peace, soon peace, when time right, entity will be." It then once again altered its form into a mist vapour, then dissipated and vanished.

This was incredible to witness; we had finally arrived at the point of no return; it wouldn't be long before the final battle would take place; we now knew where it would be fought; all do we need to wait for the right time and place. The dampening fields were still activated; all we wanted was for Harry and Richard to sort out there last few bits on the third compartment ceiling and the remote for the pressure pads, we would then be ready for action; every point of the chambers design had been examined.

Tony asked me, "What exactly did the old boy mean when it said, 'entity will be'?"

I replied by saying, "Well, we're going to find out soon enough now, won't we?" Tony shrugged his shoulders in an understanding manner; it was then that I felt a cold shiver run down my spine.

A feeling of dread fell upon me. I shortly realised why; it was the automatic pressure pads by the door panels to each of the chambered section. I walked over to Richard and Harry as they were deeply immersed in their work. "Harry, Rich, look, we're gonna have to disconnect those pressure pads."

Richard looked at me and stated, "Everything's under control, Pete, we're working at a remote-controlled system."

I replied, "And what if the curse overrides the system, it's quite intelligent, you know?"

Harry suddenly had a mental realisation as he said, "God, I've been dumb. Jesus, I've been so pathetically stupid, the answer's been there all the time, it's your bloody voice."

"My what! my voice?" I cried out.

Harry proceeded, "Yeah, it's voice activation, that's the way ahead, bloody hell, yeah, voice activation, look, look at it like this, you've already said and as we all know, you're the one going in that's going in there, so we just take a recording of your voice pattern, all we need is to record two words! Open, close, we can leave the last mechanism alone, that's a one-way section, yeah, that's definitely the way forward. Now relax and leave the rest to Rich and me, we can deal with it; there's no real problems here, just a few minor circuit alterations."

"Now you're perfectly sure about this then?" I asked.

Harry then responded with, "Yeah, we're a hundred percent. Look, it's pointless you standing around here, why don't you try and make yourself busy, why don't you pop over and chat to Tony and Alan? I'm sure they want to talk to you about something."

"Yeah, okay, if you want me to," I answered.

Richard then said, "It's fine, Pete, we'll know where to find ya, chill man." I walked across to Alan and Tony and sat down with them.

"So, what's up?" I asked.

Tony said, "Not a lot, mate, we're just killing time, talking over the past, what our plans were for the future, that sort of crap."

Alan then said, "I tell you something though, Pete, once we drop those two containers and that liquid nitrogen on this bloody thing and what with Harry's vortex, Jesus, the curse won't know what's hit."

I looked at him and immediately interrupted, "Excuse me, what? What are you going on about, what vortex?" Alan and Tony glared at each other for a moment. "Well, what vortex?" I repeated myself.

Tony gazed at me and said, "But I, we thought you had been told about Harry coming through the timeline again?" I sat there in puzzlement.

"When did this happen?" I asked.

Alan responded with, "It was when you and Jim went off with the old boy. Oh, Pete, I'm sorry, we honestly thought Harry would've told you."

"No, he didn't." I twisted around in my chair and angrily gazed over and across towards Harry. I stood quickly and started my walk over towards him.

Alan said to Tony, "Thought he told him."

Tony responded, "So did I."

I was soon back over there and I wasn't particularly impressed. I then asked, "So how are things progressing, Harry?" At this point, my voice was a little more blunt and rude.

Harry looked at me with an unsettled look as he said hesitantly, "Yeah, not too bad, Pete, you okay?"

"I'm fine."

"Right, well, we've managed to sort the problem out with the pressure pad issues and the release devices on the two canisters; you sure you're okay, you seem tense? It now only leaves us to sort out your voice recording and the liquid nitrogen container, look, sorry, Pete, but something's not right here, what's up?"

I then continued with, "Well, that's excellent news then, ain't it? Shame about the vortex, ain't it?" It was like Harry had received a brick to his face, he was virtually in shock.

"Oh fuck, Pete, I'm, oh shit, Jesus, it went completely out of my head, what with Richard suddenly showing up.

"Then what with everything else, oh, Pete, I'm so sorry, mate, it wasn't deliberate."

"Well, maybe if you can find the time, you can talk to me now," I replied. Harry then started to talk.

"Well, our Timeline-Harry stayed here for roughly three to four minutes if I remember correctly, he has managed to increase the time duration that he can spend within another timeline, that's terrific in itself, but now, and this is the fun part, Harry's given us more designs and instructions so we can build our own vortex; we've got everything here we need in which to do it, Pete."

Harry then stated, "He also gave me this." He produced a small box, it was the size of a matchbox; it had a small black flat button on the top of it with a little lightbulb that sat just above that, a miniature little thing it was.

"What the hell do we do with that?" I asked.

Harry responded with, "Well, it's for the vortex communications device. You see, once we activate the vortex from this control panel switch here in front of me, all I need do is wait a little for the vortex to come through and into our time continuum. Once it's stable, then all I would then need to do is just press it; the signal then flows through the vortex into Harry's timeline. Harry in turn will then use whatever technology he has at his disposal; he's going to fire directly into his vortex; the power stream will then be directed straight into this chamber. We will have the power from both timelines. With this and what we have in store for this bloody thing, it doesn't stand a chance. Timeline-Harry doesn't even need to step one foot through the vortex." I looked at him once more.

"And all this you forgot to tell me?"

"Pete, what do you want me to say, I'm sorry." Harry felt as though he had let me down big time.

I gently punched his arm and responded with, "So where are we going to arrange for our vortex to be located then?" Harry then grinned and moved away, as he held my arm, we moved over to where he had in mind.

"I thought about here, you see what I mean? There's a clear line of fire straight down the chamber, if we can keep the second chamber compartment sealed with this entity inside the third, we can then bombard it with everything that we've got from that ceiling, then I can open all sections from here, press the vortex button" – Harry does his bit – "we then release hell from his side, well, what do you think?"

I looked at him, I was beaming with joy and eagerness. "You better get on doing whatever you were doing, mate. I wouldn't miss this execution if you paid me a billion pounds, you're a bloody genius."

Harry and I then went our separate ways. Harry moved back to where Richard was working and I proceeded back to Tony and Alan. Tony enquired, "How are you feeling, mate, you okay?"

"Yeah, I'm okay; actually to be honest with ya, I'm buzzing, mate, guess I was a bit of a dick. Harry's just under a lot of pressure at the moment, so I'm just gonna drop the whole thing. I can't really expect him to remember everything that goes on, now can I?"

Tony just sat there and responded with, "I guess not." Alan then produced from out of his trouser pocket a tiny, well, miniature pack of playing cards. I asked him with a very surprised look on my face, "Where the hell did those come from?"

Alan replied, "I had forgotten they were there, fancy a game while we're waiting for the two geniuses to finish their magic?"

I smiled as he shuffled the little things. Roughly twenty minutes had passed, when we heard Harry's voice call out, "Any chance of a bunk up?"

Tony immediately said, "You what, sorry, mate, love to oblige but I'm playing cards."

Harry responded with, "Oh, shut the fuck up, numb balls, Rich needs a hand with getting on the ceiling. Pete, can you bring over a chair please, going to need it inside."

Without delay, I grabbed the chair I was sitting on and took it inside the chamber. Alan and Tony then assisted Richard in getting him plus the liquid nitrogen and the two containers onto the ceiling.

Harry said whilst we were in the third section, "Just place it underneath the three holes please, Peter." We waited whilst Richard got himself into position.

Alan and Richard then turned the liquid nitrogen upside down and inserted it into its opening; as they secured it, Harry then got on to the chair and began to sort out the release mechanism that was needed.

Tony by this time also entered the chamber as we both were steadying the chair Harry was standing on; it took Harry just five minutes to complete what he needed to do. Giving the thumbs up sign, Harry then got off the chair and repositioned himself under the other two holes.

Alan and Richard then moved over and inserted the last two containers for Harry to finish off; it didn't take long before the job had been completed. Once everything was in place, the lads got off the ceiling as we came out of the chamber. I then moved over to Harry's little lab with Harry alongside. Harry mentioned, "Right, we now need to record your voice."

I said, "Hang on, before we do that" – I then turned to Tony and Alan – "Alan, can you go out to the car, take Tony with ya and a couple of disruptors, get that other disruptor out of the boot and bring it back in here, use those field projection units as well, we're going to need every single thing we've got."

Alan then remarked, "No problem."

Richard responded, "I'm coming too." Harry then went nuts.

"You're staying here, Richard, you're not going out there. What do you think this is, a game? You're staying put, here with me."

The place went quiet as Richard then said, "Dad, we've been over this before, now drop it, I'm going."

Harry's face had both symptoms of fear and pride if that was at all possible. Richard collected the field units whilst Tony and Alan collected three disruptors from the charging panel. As they moved off, I looked at Harry and said, "Don't worry, mate, Tony and Alan will look after him, just relax they're going to be fine."

Harry replied, "Can't help it, Pete, he's all I've got, when you become a dad, you'll understand what I mean."

"Maybe, well, what do you say, shall we get this recording done?"

Harry was still showing signs of worry as he said, "Yeah, let's do it." He then started to operate his recording unit.

Chapter 21
Battle Stations

Tony, Alan and Richard went from the cellar towards the car. As they proceeded, they were placing the field projection units around them in a circle formation every fifteen to twenty paces or so, disruptors at the ready for any attack the curse would try to attempt; the task was slow and methodical.

There weren't alarms ringing as the street was calm; they approached the car and opened the boot; there in wait was the last of our disruptors, still fully charged as it was still awaiting its first use.

Tony grabbed it. Alan closed the boot. As they started their retreat back to the house and safety, there was an eerie feel to the atmosphere around and in the street. Richard then said to Alan, "Should it be this quiet around here?"

Alan replied with, "How the hell should I know, I don't live here." The three of them continued to place the field units at around the same distance from themselves.

It was around this time that the skinheads once more appeared as if by magic; there were about forty of them. Within seconds, they had been totally surrounded, and within moments, the skinheads attacked.

The field units were doing a terrific job, but the problem with them was their range, great within a closed area but limited when faced with protecting a greater one; gaps started to appear as the skinheads poured through.

Tony and the other two opened fire, taking out a skinhead or two with each trigger function; the skinheads' numbers were dwindling fast, as before reinforcements arrived; they were pouring in thick and fast; it was like rush hour at Victoria train station. The threesome continued their firing as each one of them started to show panic. Richard shouted out, "Where are they all coming from!"

Tony without hesitating screamed back, "How the fuck should I know, keep firing." The battle had been raging for a good four to five solid minutes.

At this time, the skinheads who had suffered a good hundred of their number being obliterated gradually fell back; their attack then from out of the blue just instantly stopped; as quickly as it had begun, it was over.

The lads were safe and surprisingly with no injuries, collecting and placing the field units as they moved ever closer towards the house; it took them a short while before they managed to get back into the cellar. As they came down the stairs whilst activating the last field unit on top of the stairwell, Harry asked, "You three okay?"

Tony responded with, "Not really, we got into a little skirmish with a few skinheads, nice, lads."

Alan replied to that with, "Yeah, they certainly know how to die."

It took Richard the same time to say, "A few skinheads, Jesus, Tony, fuck me, more like a hundred; they were coming from all sides, left, right, bloody carnage, you ask me."

I then repeated myself, "So no real problems then."

Richard looked at me and replied, "Har, har, very funny."

Tony and Alan put the four disruptors on charge once again. Tony asked, "How are things going on here then?"

Harry replied, "We're done. Pete's voice has been recorded and installed, as our great once Admiral Nelson once said, 'England expects Everyman to do his duty'."

Richard looked at his dad, and with an expression of total bewilderment, he said, "What!"

Harry replied, "You should've learnt some history at school, young man, it's a quote from probably England's greatest naval commander, well, that's in my opinion anyway; it was on the eve of the Battle of Trafalgar back in 1805 when we defeated Napoleons at sea, and as a result, it was also the last major naval engagement for close to a hundred years.

"It was also the battle he died in, so to put it bluntly, my historical little doughnut, were able, willing and ready for battle." The group of us fell into a deadly silence; the cellar went an eerie dead calm, as we in turn looked at each other.

Anxiety began to creep its way on to our faces as the time drew nearer; this was the moment we had all been waiting for; we were also dreading at the same time; it was the thunder before the storm.

I then said to break the ice, "Shall we sit down then, we've a few things to discuss."

Harry looked stunned and said, "Have I forgot something then?"

I gave him a grin and asked, "So when the battle commences, Harry, what exactly are you going to do, what's your plan?" Harry felt stupid at that point.

"Har, right, yeah, you've made your point, loud and clear, guess we better sit down and have that little battle plan meeting." We all moved around the table as we formed a circle.

Naturally, there was nowhere for us to sit as the others greedily took their seats around the table before I had any chance of grabbing one. I then started, "So without further ado, this is how I see it, any one got a pen and paper?" Richard responded by producing a small pencil and scrap of paper from his pocket.

"Will this do?" he asked, taking it.

I glared at its small size, then uttered, "Guess, it will have to do, right, what I'm thinking of is this.

"Harry stays over by your equipment consul with Richard, now you should have enough cover over there if you've situated yourselves well. Tony, if you can get yourself over in that corner over there.

"Alan, if you go to that corner opposite Tony, we will have a decent chance of catching the bastard in a crossfire.

"I will place myself inside the first compartment of the chamber, anyone got any questions?"

As everyone looked at each other, Richard said, "So what if the entity decides that it wants to come at you directly?"

Harry looked at him and said, "That's a lot of what ifs."

I then just stated, "Well, Rich, this is just an idea, we don't know what action this thing's going to take; we don't know what direction it's coming from; we don't know anything; all I'm saying is that we need to have some sort of a plan going forward. At the end of the day, it's going to be a case of thinking on your feet. We must be able to cover each other's backs."

Richard replied with, "Yeah, sorry."

I then stated, "Don't be, you're right in your thinking, when this entity shows up, just be alert and watch every movement the thing makes. Harry, you know what to do with the canisters?"

"Yeah," Harry replied, "yeah, sure, as soon as we've got it inside the third compartment and you're safely behind the fourth, I operate the release mechanisms. I then open the vortex to our bloody good-looking Timeline-Harry." Harry gave a quick cheeky grin as the rest of us just gawped at him.

Tony then mentioned one small fact that none of us had thought about, "Where's our sixth member then, Pete, for as long as I can remember, you've been going on about this sixth person, so where is he?"

The guys then turned their attentions onto me. I gasped at each one in turn and simply stated, "Who is not here then?"

Alan remarked, "What're you on about, we're all here; you gone blind or something?"

I responded with, "I can't believe I have to explain this fact to you lot. Our sixth team member is our old boy, you know, who I'm talking about, do you also remember what it said? It'll be here when the time is right, well, that was what it meant."

Richard replied, "If that's the case, then we can't lose then."

Harry then responded with extreme bluntness, "Haven't I taught you a bloody thing, Richard, the first fuck up is when given any confrontation situation when facing an enemy is that you never, ever, underestimate your opponent, ever, as Pete just said to you a minute ago." Harry then increased his seriousness as he came out with, "You stay alert and I mean alert, Rich, you watch every poxy step that entity's going to make, you understand me, boy?"

"Yes, Dad, I got it, yeah, sorry."

Harry leaned slightly forward and clutched his boy's forearm, it was then that Alan suggested, "I suppose we could always try to lure it by using a funnelling technic." I immediately turned my attention to him.

"Do you know something, Alan, I was under the sole impression that we only had two geniuses in our company, I forgot we had a third. That's the greatest idea you have ever come up with, absolutely brilliant, mate, so what have you in mind then?"

"I don't bloody know, do I?" Alan responded.

I then stated, "Right, okay, forget the genius bit." We all had a little laugh to kill the tension that was clearly brewing within each of us.

Harry then suggested, "Why not place the field projector units in a straight line from the far edge of the anti-vacuum chamber, to just behind Alan's position, that would really cut down the entity's access into the cellar, we know it can't enter from the cellar from the stairwell as we've already cut that area off."

I then said, "Well, it's sorted then, great ideas, outstanding. Harry, the field units are all yours, mate, deploy them as you want, activate them as soon as you're ready." Richard then walked across to Harry as he mentioned something that Harry hadn't managed to sort out.

"Dad, I mean Harry, have you sorted those extra powerpacks for the disruptors yet?"

Harry replied, "I've got four at the ready, they're just over there, you want to rig them up. Shouldn't take too long to sort out the other two." Richard moved off and started to work on them. I shortly crossed over to Harry's position.

"Hiya, what we working on now then? I thought everything was sorted out."

Harry responded with, "Hi, Pete, yeah, everything's fine just completing a small bit of work I hadn't managed to finish."

"Really, what's that then?" I asked keenly.

"Oh, I'm just sorting extra powerpacks for the disruptors. Richard is installing them as we speak. All you need to do is flick the red switch; look, I will show you." Harry took me over to the disruptors' charger unit, he then lifted one of them that Richard had already fitted.

Harry then remarked, "You just flick this switch, simple, child's play really."

I looked over the new work and asked, "How much extra play time will we get out of them?"

Harry answered with, "I would say a good twenty minutes' worth."

"Oh, excellent, Harry, really bloody excellent."

I felt really confident in what we had accomplished so far, but it was something I couldn't tell the others for I knew it would be a very close run thing as to who would win and who would lose; our main problem was the not knowing in which direction the curse was going to come from, not even our friend knew that, yeah, okay, we had laid out our rough battle plans, used the field projection units, but nevertheless, the fear was extreme.

It was now two thirty in the early hours of the morning; the lads were trying to keep as relaxed as humanly possible; everyone had been brought up to speed regarding the extra powerpacks that were now put in place; it was around this time that the old boy began to seep out from the flooring in its form of a vapour, gradually the old boy came into view.

I moved across to it and said, "Well, this is it." The old boy's English was finally improving as it said, "Won't be long before end, thanking you for what have done for me." I was stunned by its gratitude; it hadn't ever said that to me before. I almost felt regret as I knew that no matter which way this battle was to end, our friend wouldn't be around afterwards.

I turned and faced the lads. "Okay, lads, it's zero hour, grab your disruptors, it's party time. Now you all know what the plan is, good luck." I looked at the old boy and asked it, "Will you deactivate the dampening fields?" The old boy did as instructed. Now I was expecting all of hell to come rushing into this cellar.

To our utter surprise and dismay, there was nothing; it was dead calm; the carbon dioxide from our breath was visible as the morning air had a chill to it. I looked at the old boy, the old boy then looked at me, within that moment, there was a loud crash from upstairs; something was trying to smash through the field projection units, this is it I thought.

Slowly, I moved forward the beginning of the stairs as to try and get a better look; the old boy stopped me by placing its arm out in front as if it was a barrier. It said, "I, not you, the Peter." The old boy walked up the stairs; again, there was terrific silence as our friend disappeared from our sight.

It was like a crescendo of noise as the sounds from above gradually increased in ferocity; the energy blasts were probably heard back in Scotland as they were that thunderous. As the old boy fought on, milliseconds passed, the rat infestation that we had fought off once before had re-emerged.

These rats were evening bigger than before; they poured through in there hundreds; the five of us opened fire at the rodent army as they charged; the field projection units were once again doing a great job as they were obliterating tons of these vicious rodents; the rat numbers by now were impossible to count, they just churned out multitudes through the broken laths and plaster.

The devastation was in our view going extremely well, but if anyone thought we would get a little rest bite, they were sadly mistaken for our dreaded mortal enemy from ages back came stumbling down the stairs, it was those formidable skeleton soldiers, four of them, as if one wasn't enough to deal with.

It dawned on me as I thought of two things, my first thought was, how did they get past the field projection unit from upstairs, my second thought was even worse, had our old friend finally fallen to its arch-enemy?

Harry and Richard focussed on the four skeleton soldiers that were by now getting too close for comfort; the boys were aiming excellently, blasting pieces of the soldiers into next week, but as before, they immediately regenerated that missing limb.

Meanwhile, Tony and Alan were kept busy as they continued firing in to the rodent population.

I for the time being held back my firing to conserve power. I glanced and looked at the lads whilst the fight for their very lives was raging fast and furious; it was then that time for some unexplainable reason just slowed down; it was like watching a film at the cinema in slow motion.

I started to ponder over thoughts, when and where was our next problem going to raise its ugly head. I then started to pray as hard as I possibly could, wishing with all my being that our old boy hadn't been destroyed. Can you imagine the sheer joy and relief I felt as I then witnessed the old boy coming down the stairs? I immediately knew that something wasn't right; I couldn't put my finger on it, but I knew there was something amiss; a strange feeling was twisting my gut as this dread rose up into my chest.

Something was drastically wrong, the old boy always seemed to float and hover, it had never walked before, was it injured, damaged in some way or had the fight just simply drained its power source? All I could was hope. Harry and Richard were on the verge of being overrun as the skeleton soldiers were managing to get bloody close by this time. I shouted out, "Tony, get over here. Alan, stand your ground where you are, here catch." I threw my disruptor over to him. Alan caught it magnificently and immediately opened fire with both weapons. Tony came rushing over to Harry's position for as he did so he wasted no time in pressurising his trigger finger; the three of us were pouring so much into the enemy that the skeletons were clearly having a difficult time replacing their bones that were being ripped away from their structure; slowly they had secured the area by holding their ground; the old boy for the first time showed emotion as he screamed out with an almighty rage, "Enough!!!!"

With that gutsy outburst, the giant rodents and all of the skeleton soldiers just disappeared; within the blink of an eye, the cellar was at peace once more; we had survived the first attack by the skin of our teeth.

Tony then let out an unwarranted remark as he looked across at me and stated, "Well, I must say, Pete, that battle plan really went well."

I glared at him with total disapproval, and with a great deal of sarcasm, I responded with, "Well, I certainly do beg for your forgiveness, Your Royal

Highness, shame I don't have in my up to date portfolio, extra sensory perception."

Richard turned to his dad and asked, "What's this extra thing he's talking about, Harry?"

Harry replied, "ESP, mate."

Richard then muttered, "Har, right, so that's what it stands for, always wondered about that one."

The atmosphere was intense as it was on the verge of growing out of control bloody quickly, to say it was getting a little heated would've been an understatement, for at this point, the sarcasm was on top of the agenda. Harry stepped forward and without prejudice said, "Right, that's enough, Pete, Tony, the fight's out there, not in here, we're not going to give this poxy entity any chance of reducing our numbers by doing it ourselves.

"Now for god's sake, drop it." Tony and I paused for a few moments whilst everyone else stood on tenterhooks as to which way this situation would blow, after a few more seconds had elapsed, we looked at each other and just nodded with agreement.

Some of us took to a chair and relaxed as they were unaware as to when they would ever get another chance to rest their bodies.

Harry and Richard kept themselves occupied by fiddling about with their electrical toys; the old boy and I were together; it said to me as its English was really by now getting decent, "Our next attack is going to be far more aggressive than the last one, Peter, this may cause some real damage to your numbers; it will also be my end; it is soon to be, Peter." I looked straight at it whilst feeling pretty gutted as I had really grown to like this old boy.

I asked, "Well, surely, there has to be a way for us to kill the curse but save you, you're not evil, come on, think about it, the greatness you could achieve by being on this planet, it would be immense." The old boy smiled but insisted.

"You want to exist, don't you, to stay with all you know, I don't." The old boy then twisted around as its senses were picking up signals from the curse; it then pushed me behind itself, as it then stated, "The entity comes, Peter, it comes."

I called out to the lads, "Sorry, boys, but the bastard's coming again." Tired but up for the fight, the lads got ready for the oncoming onslaught; we waited patiently, then we waited some more; there wasn't anything happening; this was now the worst time for us, the expectation was worse than the fighting.

As we started to feel as though nothing was to happen, it was at this point from above the stairwell the redness of the curse began to shine; it took on the human form once again; its entire shell shone brightly in a deep red glow; eerie screeching then began to increase as it moved down the steps, its eyes never left the old boy.

Starting its descent down the steps, the old boy stood strong and steadfast as it decided to move more closer to it; as it did so, our old boy kept one eye on me and the other was fixed upon its arch-enemy.

Harry and Richard then aimed there disruptors. As they did, the pair of them froze in time. They soon found themselves spinning and twisting around whilst doing cartwheels and flips; they were caught up in some type of vortex. Strangely enough, they could still breathe and talk. Richard shouted, "What's happening, Dad!"

Harry responded with, "Stay calm, son, stay calm, we're in a vortex. I think it's leading us to the other Harry."

"How do you know that!" shouted Richard.

Harry then shouted back, "A vortex is like a vacuum, we shouldn't be able to breathe let alone talk."

Richard then said, "Dad, what's that?"

Richard was pointing to something that was moving as it entered into their eye line. Harry was squinting as he tried to focus on this strange apparition that was drawing ever closer.

As it drew nearer, it gained the appearance of some type of creature from another world; it was one hundred percent certain that it wasn't from earth, not even a trillion years ago, for it had the structure of a crocodile but the head of a bird, a weird-looking thing, its teeth were razor sharp and elongated; its eyes were a blinding deep red. As it got to within six feet of our position, it began trying to snap its long jaws in the attempt that it would capture one of us.

Harry grabbed Richard by his arm and forced his boy to move behind himself; it was a futile attempt from trying to keep his son safe, Harry didn't see another one of these things moving up and behind the pair of them; both creatures were now ready to attack, as they moved in against Harry.

Harry managed to catch a glimpse of the second one of them; spinning as fast as he could, he began to kick out as hard as any human had ever done before. The creatures then snapped their jaws shut. Harry had been snared; with great force, the pair of these things had clamped on to his waist, their dinosaur-like jaws were penetrating the skin around Harry's body. Harry let out an almighty scream as the pain must have been tremendous.

Richard for who had witnessed the assault swam towards his dad; as Harry was thrashing about to try and free himself, Richard began to kick out in his attempt to free his dad.

Chapter 22
Mind Games

Using his fingers, Richard was trying desperately to poke the eyes out of these monsters in the hope of them releasing their grip on his dad. Harry was in a real dilemma as he struggled to break free. Another four of these monsters then came seeping out of the darkness way off in the distance. Harry could see these monstrosities approaching as he shouted out to Richard, "Go! Try and get away Rich, in god's name, run!"

Richard screamed back as his struggle continued, "No bloody way, Dad." The creatures then increased their ferocity as the two began performing the death roll that crocodiles do to kill their prey.

Harry let out a horrendous scream; he was in a seriously bad way by this time; as if by magic, our old boy came charging towards them, dressed in a cowboy outfit, lasso twirling above his head whilst riding hard on the Greek mythological Pegasus.

Harry looked on in astonishment; the pain he was under had gone.

Richard then once he had too witnessed the Pegasus galloping in their direction, he also stopped. It was then plainly obvious to them that they were suffering the effects of a ginormous nightmare.

Within seconds, the old boy lassoed the pair of them! Instantly, the pair were now unfrozen from time and back in the cellar; their position was the exact location as before they were taken into their dream state; it was over. "What's up, you two okay?" I asked, Harry looked at me, his disruptor still focussed on the red curse as it was still floating whilst descending the stairs.

"Thank god, for the old boy, Pete, I thought about it and it came for us. I really thought for a time I was dead."

I looked bewildered and stated, "What're you on about, Harry, you two just went dizzy for a moment, thought you were about to collapse at one point."

Richard then shouted, "It was a nightmare, a vortex, Pete, we were spinning out of control."

I cut Richard short and replied, "Rich, you haven't gone anywhere, you were dreaming, mate, that's all."

Harry faced me and said, "I'd like to see your reactions in the same situation, Pete, scary stuff."

The old boy then raised its voice. "The entity is trying to attack in your subconscious mind, mind games, focus, focus your thoughts upon me, just remember a simple fact, if you are killed in your dream state, there is no return, death is final; death is there waiting for all, focus, that goes for everyone."

Harry then looked at Richard and whispered in his boy's ear, "Don't mention the Pegasus, or the cowboy outfit, Richard, they'll have us sectioned." The red curse was still hovering over the stairs as we held fire awaiting its next surge. From out of the corner of my eye, I then witnessed Alan fumble as he held out his hand to stop himself from falling over.

Alan found himself on a cliff's face, his toes and fingertips were the only things holding him on to this massive rock; there were no rock climbing tools or equipment at his disposal; he shook with fear as he looked around; the wind was rustling past him as his hair swept out of control. He then looked down, that was one big mistake; his facial expressions told the story as he trembled the realisation of his situation suddenly became clear. "What the fuck." He was thousands of feet up in the air; his only thoughts were now based on how to stay alive.

Slowly, he began to find more grip holes as he slowly started his assent; from out of a deep hole in the rock, a single bat suddenly emerged and flew across his nose; the sudden shock made him lose his hand grip as he slipped. Within moments, he had recovered; the bat began to circle above and around his head; a second bat then suddenly appeared. As if the bats were on some sort of a mission, one of the flying creatures had managed to smash into his leg, he once more slipped but steadied himself just in time; his body and mind were in turmoil; fear was all around him; whilst not thinking at all clearly he carried on with his climbing.

All he was thinking of at the time was getting off that bloody rock face. Another wave of bats came hurtling down from above.

Alan was becoming very unsettled as he began swiping at a couple of them as they were now getting too close for comfort. Another slip from his foot made him grip the rock face even tighter than before. His body was visibly shaking with fear as he was in serious danger of losing control.

Alan knew that if he did lose it on this rock, he wouldn't survive, so with this in mind he refocussed.

Daylight hours were fading fast as he was still hundreds of feet short from safety. An eagle from high above began to dive bomb his position; its descent was bloody fast as it swooped close to his head. As Alan looked up above, there was clear movement from there; he realised why the eagle was dive bombing him, for the bird was on protection duties, Alan was approaching its nest that was wedged within a crevasse. Whilst Alan started to look at another route another eagle started to attack.

Talons open and wide, it began to swoop down. Within seconds, he was struck on his forearm as he screamed out in agony; a massive lump of flesh had been torn away. Alan was now in serious trouble of falling to his death.

He started to pray for help, wishing god would transport him to a place of safety; it was at that point he heard a voice from out of the blue, the wind whilst whistling around his ears was communicating with him. Listening intensively as he grimaced from the pain, it was his own consciousness talking to him, the voice called out to him, "Focus on me, focus on me."

Alan then realised what was going on as he cried out, "Is that you, if it's, for god's sake help me, for pity's sake."

Alan was now back in the cellar; his entire body was shaking with utter terror. Tony rushed over to him and said, "Al, relax, mate. Jesus, Pete, he's in a right state here, he can't stop shaking."

"Okay, I'm coming over," I answered.

Alan looked up at Tony and said, "I was on a rock face, Tony. Jesus, what a fucking nightmare that was, bats, eagles swirling around me, oh Jesus."

I got to them, as fast as I could, we attempted to calm Alan down by saying, "It was a dream, mate, you had a nightmare, that's all it was, a stinking poxy dream, you're okay, now, yeah." His shaking was starting to slow down as he became more relaxed as the fear was slowly passing by.

Tony then said to him, "That must have been a pure nightmare for you, mate."

Alan looked at him and said, "Tony, it was so real, it was so real, that bastard's gonna pay for this." As he looked towards the curse, the old boy then beckoned and called me back to its position.

There was no thinking on my part as I graciously accepted his invitation.

The red curse began to wander in the air ever so slowly. As Tony turned to go back to his original position, he found himself back on the grounds of Dover Castle. Tony immediately realised that something was within his grip of his left hand, for as he looked down, he witnessed with pure surprise that he was holding a javelin within his grasp.

He turned as he heard what sounded like someone clearing his throat; as he looked, there was his brother walking towards him. Once James had sighted him, he shouted, "Where the hell have you been, Mum's cooking dinner, we're gonna be late, come on."

Tony shouted back, "Oh chill, Mum's cooking's shirt anyway." The two of them had a good laugh over it.

James then said, "What's with the javelin for, Tone, you going to use that on me?"

Tony replied, "Don't be a dick, I want to see if I can catch some fish with it."

James then stated, "What the fuck do you want to catch fish for, you enjoy running them through then, do ya, all that pain?" James then grabbed the javelin from his brother's hand in a violent way; he looked at Tony and said, "Watch this." He then immediately started to thrust it into his own stomach; there was no pain just an empty look across his face; he was really forcing the javelin deeper and deeper into his stomach; the blood was gushing from the now gaping wound.

Tony was desperately trying to stop his brother from continually stabbing himself as they tussled for control of the javelin, but for each time Tony managed to withdraw it from his brother's stomach, James would then get the upper hand and would thrust it back in to his body. Whilst James was viciously ripping at his own stomach he started to say, "Tony, why do you want to stab fish, why do you want to stab fish?" It was as if his voice was on a scratched CD.

Tony was beside himself; the scene was horrific; tears were strolling down his cheeks at this point. The grief of seeing his brother's injuries increased with every thrust of this six foot javelin; the wound grew and grew; it was at that point that Tony screamed at the top of his lungs, "No more, please no more, I can't take it." Falling to his knees, he just wept uncontrollably like a baby.

James then joined him as he too dropped to his knees; they looked at each other for the last time. James was still without any kind of pain; he wiped the tears away from his brother's face and said, "Come over, Tony, join me, it's lovely here, want us to be together once more. Join me, Tony, it will be like old times." With that phrase, James slumped backwards.

The javelin was permanently fixed within his lifeless body by this time. Within that micro-second, Tony was back in the cellar; it soon became blatantly apparent that there was a problem with him. Tony instantly hit the floor and slumped forward over his knees.

Alan rushed over to him and raised him back to a seated position. Tony's eyes were fixed wide open, fresh tears were still visible on his cheeks whilst streaming down from his eyes; he had stopped breathing.

Tony was no more. Alan screamed out, "He's dead, Pete. Tony's dead."

As Alan dropped back in horror, the old boy then grasped the situation and stated, "Grieve later, curse to fight, focus everyone."

The loss of Tony was particularly hard for me to take as we had already lost his brother some time ago; the guilt of that loss was something I never got over. As I waited for my nightmare to arrive, it suddenly dawned on me that there wasn't to be any dream state for me.

Due to this telepathic link with the old boy, I was fully immune from any kind of subconscious attack; the entity changed its form by this time back to a vapour; it was having a really fun time as it engulfed the ceiling area of the entire cellar, laughing with its evil demented voice; its noise was getting extreme. I had now taken enough of this shit, holding my disruptor firmly in my grasp, I yelled out at the top of my lungs, "Fire!" The four of us opened up with a tremendous thunder as the curse took the full barrage against it.

This now lead to another situation for us to deal with, the problem that we now faced was that the shots we were firing just simply went straight through and into thin air; it was like shooting into a partially dissipated cloud. Alan shouted over at me and said, "This is bloody hopeless, Pete, we're missing more than hitting the bloody thing!"

Then Harry stated, "We need to start getting you into that chamber, Pete!"

I looked at the old boy and said, "They're right, I need to start getting over there." The old boy then moved ahead of me and entered the middle of the cellar floor; the curse then dropped lower, carefully missing the field projection units. Slowly, the curse's structure began to alter again as it returned to its humanlike form.

It wasn't long before the two entities stood in the middle of the cellar face to face; they were now inches from each other.

I moved away and stood near the entry of the anti-vacuum chamber; it was then that the old boy did something strange, it raised its hands as if it was going to surrender or something like it, when from out of nowhere, bolts of extreme energy that none of us had ever seen before flowed out and engulfed the curse. The flow of this power was gradually reducing the mass of the curse as it pulsated.

The old boy then started to retreat towards the chamber whilst keeping its full focus on its arch-enemy.

Alan moved ahead and joined Harry and Richard; they by now had all the disruptors apart from mine. Within seconds, the old boy was standing by my side; the curse without breaking a sweat broke free of its entrapment as it produced its own power blast. Keeping low, it moved towards my position, as by now it was clear as to its direction, the old boy and myself started our trek deeper into the chamber; it was working, the entity was on its way. Within moments, the entity had entered the first section of the chamber. By this time, I had reached the third section; the old boy stood firm by its entry point.

Alan screamed at Harry, "Now, mate, now, what're you waiting for?"

Harry responded, "No, not yet, we wait, we have to make sure Pete is secure." Harry was holding the remote by this time whilst Alan and Richard could only look on; the curse by this time had already passed the first section and it was now virtually on top of where the old boy stood. As they approached each other one last time, the structure of the curse started to alter in appearance once more; this time, it's structure began to illuminate itself; it was as if it could be building up into something that resembled an explosion of some sort.

The old boy then moved backwards; standing between me and the curse, the two of them once more faced off.

The curse then simply looked into our old boy's eyes. "Why?"

The old boy then responded by saying, "They have come to mean something." I positioned myself within the safe zone; the curse by this time was on the verge of erupting; it was only seconds before it actually did. Now my door was now firmly and secure as I found myself enclosed but safe; the entities fought like wild rabid dogs; it was as vicious as it could ever have become.

Alan shouted to Harry once more, "Now, Harry, now!" At that second, the chamber sections were sealed as Harry played the voice recording; the entities were now trapped inside.

The curse was literally unaware that the seals had been activated. Harry immediately through the switch that would release the deadly toxins from each of the containers, a gigantic cloud of white smoke filled the chamber, nothing could be seen by man or beast; seconds later, there was a tremendous explosion, the whole of the chamber shook but stayed firm and rigid.

Harry released the liquid nitrogen; now anything that had an atomic structure couldn't survive in that atmosphere, not even an entity, well, that was the thinking anyway. Richard then shouted as his dad became mesmerised, "The vortex, Dad, the vortex! We need to open it now!" Harry pressed the vortex connector switch, it immediately began to materialise; seconds ticked by as its spiralling shape seemed to twist and stir as it built itself into a solid stable structure. Inside of the chamber rumblings were being heard as the chamber began to shake violently.

It was at that moment that Harry opened the first and second sections to the chamber.

Timeline-Harry sent forth his magic weapon, blistering rays of energy that were blasting into the liquid nitrogen; the effects of the blasts smothered every single molecule within the chamber; it was like we were watching a Gatling gun display, swirls of rotating laser fire. Harry stood up, followed by Richard and Alan; the Gatling gun was still erupting its deadly cargo as they watched the fireworks. Ten seconds later, the blistering rays from the vortex stopped firing; the vortex closed and vaporised into nothing; the cellar was like a morgue, not a pin could be heard; dead silence filled the air. Alan and the others moved forward to see if one of them could see inside, but no one could at that moment.

All that could have been done, was done; it was now a clear case of waiting and praying for the right outcome; the waiting was intense, would the red curse reveal itself, then take its revenge out on us or would the old boy miraculously survive the torment of devastation.

It was at this point in time that cracking sounds could be heard from the thing in the chamber. As the lads watched, the chamber itself began to show cracks, the graphene aerogel had been breached.

Alan, Richard and Harry raised their disruptors, as fear and trepidation once more loomed their ugly heads.

It was then that I found myself once again being phase shifted from this safe zone to a police station, where I found myself sitting in a room with a copper as he was leaning across the table, arms stretched out in front of himself as a resting place, repeatedly asking, "Why can't you just admit you killed 'em?"

I reacted, "How many more times do I have to go over the same shit with you lot?"

The officer stepped back off the table. "Right, you just relax there for a minute." Taking his folder with him, he left the room, and as he did so, I had flashes of long white coats pound inside my head, were they visions of some sort, shaking my head in an attempt to clear my mind? The door closed.

This officer's clothing altered, his appearance was no longer that of a police officer but of a doctor in a long white coat; he approached another doctor at a desk, slammed his folder down onto it and said, "I don't get this guy, look, you're in charge of this case, so tell me what's the history of this guy, how long has this Mr Tate bloke been with us?"

Doctor Fred stated, "Three months next Thursday; we've come to refer this case as pure break down; we've tried everything we know, from electric shock treatment to hallucinogenic drugs, it's as if he has undergone some type of mental experimentation. We've a meeting next Monday to see what our next treatment will be; in my opinion, we've only one avenue left open to us."

"Really, and that is what?"

Doctor Fred responded with, "Lobotomy."

Waiting for the copper to return to my room, I quietly sat, astonishment hit me as a mirror appeared directly in front of me.

I stood and approached it. As I looked, an image began to form, it was that of the red curse's human face looming straight at me; it was smiling.

The End